Characters In Conflict

Second Edition

Pupil's Edition

HOLT, RINEHART AND WINSTON

Harcourt Brace & Company

Austin • New York • Orlando • Atlanta •
San Francisco • Boston • Dallas • Toronto • London

Printed in the United States of America

ISBN 0-03-008463-6

19   1083   12
4500370057

Acknowledgments

We wish to thank the following teachers who reviewed materials for *Short Stories: Characters in Conflict*.

Lisa M. Tittle
Bel Air Middle School
Bel Air, Maryland

Donna F. Turner
Miller Grove School
Miller Grove, Texas

Executive Editor: Mescal Evler
Managing Editor: Robert R. Hoyt
Project Editor: Charlene Rodgers
Editorial Staff: Laura Britton, Sigman Byrd, Christie Hillsmith-Jent, Guy Wesley Holland, Christy McBride, Michael Neibergall, Darleen Ramos, Robert Reynolds, Barbara Sutherland
Editorial Support Staff: Carla Beer, Stella Galvan, Don Goerner, Margaret Guerrero, Ruth Hooker, Pat Stover
Editorial Permissions: Amy Minor, Lee Noble
Design and Photo Research: Pun Nio, *Senior Art Director*; Richard Metzger, *Graphic Services Supervisor*; Stephen Sharpe, *Design Staff*; Tim Taylor, *Photo Researcher*; Cover Design: Kanokwalee Lee
Production: Beth Prevelige, *Senior Production Manager*; George Prevelige, *Production Manager*; Simira Davis, Rose Degollado, *Production Assistants*; Carol Martin, *Electronic Publishing Manager*; Kristy Sprott, *Electronic Publishing Supervisor*; Barbara Hudgens, Maria Veres Homic, *Electronic Publishing Staff*

Contents

To the Student

In the poem "There Is No Frigate Like a Book," Emily Dickinson compares a ship to a book. Short stories are also like ships because they, too, are vessels for transporting us to exotic locales, to different climates, to wondrous cultures, or simply to the next port over. Without ever leaving the comfort of our homes, we can experience any one of the varied adventures in the imaginary world of the short story.

Short stories also allow us to empathize with other people. As we immerse ourselves in the imaginary world of a story, we become acquainted with its inhabitants. We care about them and identify with their troubles and joys. Sometimes it is as though we temporarily become another person and experience that person's life and feelings.

Yet not only do we learn about other people; we also learn about ourselves. Sometimes we can see ourselves in the characters, even if their lives appear outwardly different from our own. How we react to the people, places, and events in a story reveals to us a great deal about our own lives and who we are.

No matter the setting or who the characters are, short stories very often give us some insight into life. They help us see and understand some part of life that we may never have considered or may have taken for granted.

As you read the stories in this book, you will see how short story writers make us laugh or cry, scare us silly or inspire us to act, help us to see the goodness in people or to realize their shortcomings, all by weaving tales about characters that never existed and events that never took place.

Enjoy the voyage.

THE MOST DANGEROUS GAME

Richard Connell

What kind of game did you think of when you read the title of this story? Was it a sport, a game of chance, a race? Or did you think of something else altogether? This popular adventure story will hold you in suspense from its intriguing title to its last word.

"Off there to the right—somewhere—is a large island," said Whitney. "It's rather a mystery—"

"What island is it?" Rainsford asked.

"The old charts call it 'Ship-Trap Island,'" Whitney replied. "A suggestive name, isn't it? Sailors have a curious dread of the place. I don't know why. Some superstition—"

"Can't see it," remarked Rainsford, trying to peer through the dank tropical night that was palpable as it pressed its thick, warm blackness in upon the yacht.

"You've good eyes," said Whitney, with a laugh, "and I've seen you pick off a moose moving in the brown fall bush at four hundred yards, but even you can't see four miles or so through a moonless Caribbean night."

"Nor four yards," admitted Rainsford. "Ugh! It's like moist black velvet."

"It will be light in Rio," promised Whitney. "We should make it in a few days. I hope the jaguar guns have come from Purdey's.[1] We should have some good hunting up the Amazon. Great sport, hunting."

"The best sport in the world," agreed Rainsford.

"For the hunter," amended Whitney. "Not for the jaguar."

"Don't talk rot, Whitney," said Rainsford. "You're a big-game hunter, not a philosopher. Who cares how a jaguar feels?"

"Perhaps the jaguar does," observed Whitney.

"Bah! They've no understanding."

---

1. **Purdey's:** a famous English manufacturer of hunting rifles and shotguns.

"Even so, I rather think they understand one thing—fear. The fear of pain and the fear of death."

"Nonsense," laughed Rainsford. "This hot weather is making you soft, Whitney. Be a realist. The world is made up of two classes—the hunters and the huntees. Luckily, you and I are hunters. Do you think we've passed that island yet?"

"I can't tell in the dark. I hope so."

"Why?" asked Rainsford.

"The place has a reputation—a bad one."

"Cannibals?" suggested Rainsford.

"Hardly. Even cannibals wouldn't live in such a Godforsaken place. But it's gotten into sailor lore, somehow. Didn't you notice that the crew's nerves seemed a bit jumpy today?"

"They were a bit strange, now you mention it. Even Captain Nielsen—"

"Yes, even that tough-minded old Swede, who'd go up to the devil himself and ask him for a light. Those fishy blue eyes held a look I never saw there before. All I could get out of him was: 'This place has an evil name among seafaring men, sir.' Then he said to me, very gravely: 'Don't you feel anything?'—as if the air about us was actually poisonous. Now, you mustn't laugh when I tell you this—I did feel something like a sudden chill.

"There was no breeze. The sea was as flat as a plate-glass window. We were drawing near the island then. What I felt was a—a mental chill; a sort of sudden dread."

"Pure imagination," said Rainsford. "One superstitious sailor can taint the whole ship's company with his fear."

"Maybe. But sometimes I think sailors have an extra sense that tells them when they are in danger. Sometimes I think evil is a tangible thing—with wavelengths, just as sound and light have. An evil place can, so to speak, broadcast vibrations of evil. Anyhow, I'm glad we're getting out of this zone. Well, think I'll turn in now, Rainsford."

"I'm not sleepy," said Rainsford. "I'm going to smoke another pipe up on the afterdeck."

"Good night, then, Rainsford. See you at breakfast."

"Right. Good night, Whitney."

There was no sound in the night as Rainsford sat there, but the muffled throb of the engine that drove the yacht swiftly through the darkness, and the swish and ripple of the wash of the propeller.

Rainsford, reclining in a steamer chair, indolently puffed on his favorite brier. The sensuous drowsiness of the night was on him. "It's so dark," he thought, "that I could sleep without closing my eyes; the night would be my eyelids—"

An abrupt sound startled him. Off to the right he heard it, and his ears, expert in such matters, could not be mistaken. Again he heard the sound, and again. Somewhere, off in the blackness, someone had fired a gun three times.

Rainsford sprang up and moved quickly to the rail, mystified. He strained his eyes in the direction from which the reports had come, but it was like trying to see through a blanket. He leaped upon the rail and balanced himself there, to get greater elevation; his pipe, striking a rope, was knocked from his mouth. He lunged for it; a short, hoarse cry came from his lips as he realized he had reached too far and had lost his balance. The cry was pinched off short as the blood-warm waters of the Caribbean Sea closed over his head.

He struggled up to the surface and tried to cry out, but the wash from the speeding yacht slapped him in the face and the salt water in his open mouth made him gag and strangle. Desperately he struck out with strong strokes after the receding lights of the yacht, but he stopped before he had swum fifty feet. A certain cool-headedness had come to him; it was not the first time he had been in a tight place. There was a chance that his cries could be heard by someone aboard the yacht, but that chance was slender, and grew more slender as the yacht raced on. He wrestled himself out of his clothes, and shouted with all his power. The lights of the yacht became faint and ever-vanishing fireflies; then they were blotted out entirely by the night.

Rainsford remembered the shots. They had come from the right, and doggedly he swam in that direction, swimming with slow, deliberate strokes, conserving his strength. For a seemingly endless time he fought the sea. He began to count his strokes; he could do possibly a hundred more and then—

Rainsford heard a sound. It came out of the darkness, a high screaming sound, the sound of an animal in an extremity of anguish and terror.

He did not recognize the animal that made the sound; he did not try to; with fresh vitality he swam toward the sound. He heard it again; then it was cut short by another noise, crisp, staccato.

"Pistol shot," muttered Rainsford, swimming on.

Ten minutes of determined effort brought another sound to his ears—the most welcome he had ever heard—the muttering and growling of the sea breaking on a rocky shore. He was almost on the rocks before he saw them; on a night less calm he would have been shattered against them. With his remaining strength he dragged himself from the swirling waters. Jagged crags appeared to jut into the opaqueness; he forced himself upward, hand over hand. Gasping, his hands raw, he reached a flat place at the top. Dense jungle came down to the very edge of the cliffs. What perils that tangle of trees and underbrush might hold for him did not concern Rainsford just then. All he knew was that he was safe from his enemy, the sea, and that utter weariness was on him. He flung himself down at the jungle edge and tumbled headlong into the deepest sleep of his life.

When he opened his eyes, he knew from the position of the sun that it was late in the afternoon. Sleep had given him new vigor; a sharp hunger was picking at him. He looked about him, almost cheerfully.

"Where there are pistol shots, there are men. Where there are men, there is food," he thought. But what kind of men, he wondered, in so forbidding a place? An unbroken front of snarled and ragged jungle fringed the shore.

He saw no sign of a trail through the closely knit web of weeds and trees; it was easier to go along the shore, and Rainsford floundered along by the water. Not far from where he had landed, he stopped.

Some wounded thing, by the evidence a large animal, had thrashed about in the underbrush; the jungle weeds were crushed down and the moss was lacerated; one patch of weeds was stained crimson. A small, glittering object not far away caught Rainsford's eye and he picked it up. It was an empty cartridge.

"A twenty-two," he remarked. "That's odd. It must have been a fairly large animal too. The hunter had his nerve to tackle it with a light gun. It's clear that the brute put up a fight. I suppose the first three shots I heard was when the hunter flushed his quarry[2] and wounded it. The last shot was when he trailed it here and finished it."

He examined the ground closely and found what he had hoped to find—the print of hunting boots. They pointed along the cliff in the direction he had been going. Eagerly he hurried along, now slipping on

---

2. Flushed his quarry: forced the game that was being hunted into the open.

a rotten log or a loose stone, but making headway; night was beginning to settle down on the island.

Bleak darkness was blacking out the sea and jungle when Rainsford
sighted the lights. He came upon them as he turned a crook in the
coastline, and his first thought was that he had come upon a village, *Thought*
for there were many lights. But as he forged along he saw, to his great
astonishment, that all the lights were in one enormous building—a
lofty structure with pointed towers plunging upward into the gloom.
His eyes made out the shadowy outlines of a palatial château;[3] it was set
on a high bluff, and on three sides of it cliffs dived down to where the
sea licked greedy lips in the shadows.

"Mirage," thought Rainsford. But it was no mirage, he found, when
he opened the tall spiked iron gate. The stone steps were real enough;
the massive door with a leering gargoyle[4] for a knocker was real
enough; yet about it all hung an air of unreality.

He lifted the knocker, and it creaked up stiffly, as if it had never
before been used. He let it fall, and it startled him with its booming
loudness. He thought he heard steps within; the door remained closed.
Again Rainsford lifted the heavy knocker, and let it fall. The door
opened then, opened as suddenly as if it were on a spring, and
Rainsford stood blinking in the river of glaring gold light that poured
out. The first thing Rainsford's eyes discerned was the largest man
Rainsford had ever seen—a gigantic creature, solidly made and black-
bearded to the waist. In his hand the man held a long-barreled revolver,
and he was pointing it straight at Rainsford's heart.

The man

Out of the snarl of beard two small eyes regarded Rainsford.

"Don't be alarmed," said Rainsford, with a smile which he hoped
was disarming. "I'm no robber. I fell off a yacht. My name is Sanger
Rainsford of New York City."

The menacing look in his eyes did not change. The revolver pointed
as rigidly as if the giant were a stature. He gave no sign that he understood Rainsford's words, or that he had even heard them. He was
dressed in uniform, a black uniform trimmed with gray astrakhan.[5]

"I'm Sanger Rainsford of New York," Rainsford began again. "I fell
off a yacht. I am hungry."

---

3. **château** (sha tō′): a castle or a large country house.
4. **gargoyle** (gär′goil′): a grotesque carved figure, usually of an animal or mythical creature.
5. **astrakhan** (as′trə kən): the curled fur of young lambs.

The man's only answer was to raise with his thumb the hammer of his revolver. Then Rainsford saw the man's free hand go to his forehead in a military salute, and he saw him click his heels together and stand at attention. Another man was coming down the broad marble steps, an erect, slender man in evening clothes. He advanced to Rainsford and held out his hand.

In a cultivated voice marked by a slight accent that gave it added precision and deliberateness, he said: "It is a very great pleasure and honor to welcome Mr. Sanger Rainsford, the celebrated hunter, to my home."

Automatically Rainsford shook the man's hand.

"I've read your book about hunting snow leopards in Tibet, you see," explained the man. "I am General Zaroff." *general*

Rainsford's first impression was that the man was singularly handsome; his second was that there was an original, almost bizarre quality about the general's face. He was a tall man past middle age, for his hair was a vivid white; but his thick eyebrows and pointed military mustache were as black as the night from which Rainsford had come. His eyes, too, were black and very bright. He had high cheekbones, a sharp-cut nose, a spare, dark face—the face of a man used to giving orders, the face of an aristocrat. Turning to the giant in uniform, the general made a sign. The giant put away his pistol, saluted, withdrew.

"Ivan is an incredibly strong fellow," remarked the general, "but he has the misfortune to be deaf and dumb. A simple fellow, but, I'm afraid, like all his race, a bit of a savage."

"Is he Russian?" *Cossack*

"He is a Cossack,"[6] said the general, and his smile showed red lips and pointed teeth. "So am I."

"Come," he said, "we shouldn't be chatting here. We can talk later. Now you want clothes, food, rest. You shall have them. This is a most restful spot."

Ivan had reappeared, and the general spoke to him with the lips that moved but gave forth no sound.

"Follow Ivan, if you please, Mr. Rainsford," said the general. "I was about to have my dinner when you came. I'll wait for you. You'll find that my clothes will fit you, I think."

---

6. **Cossack:** a people of the southern Soviet Union noted for their horsemanship and their courage and fierceness in battle.

Met people on Island

General Zaroff

It was to a huge, beam-ceilinged bedroom with a canopied bed big enough for six men that Rainsford followed the silent giant. Ivan laid out an evening suit, and Rainsford, as he put it on, noticed that it came from a London tailor who ordinarily cut and sewed for none below the rank of duke. *High in monarchy*

The dining room to which Ivan conducted him was, in many ways, remarkable. There was a medieval magnificence about it; it suggested a baronial hall of feudal times with its oaken panels, its high ceiling, its vast refectory table where twoscore men could sit down to eat. About the hall were the mounted heads of many animals—lions, tigers, elephants, moose, bears; larger or more perfect specimens Rainsford had never seen. At the great table the general was sitting, alone.

"You'll have a cocktail, Mr. Rainsford," he suggested. The cocktail was surpassingly good; and, Rainsford noted, the table appointments were of the finest—the linen, the crystal, the silver, the china. *Rich*

They were eating *borsch*, the rich, red soup with sour cream so dear to Russian palates. Half apologetically General Zaroff said: "We do our best to preserve the amenities of civilization here. Please forgive any lapses. We are well off the beaten track, you know. Do you think the champagne has suffered from its long ocean trip?"

"Not in the least," declared Rainsford. He was finding the general a most thoughtful and affable host, a true cosmopolite.[7] But there was one small trait of the general's that made Rainsford uncomfortable. Whenever he looked up from his plate he found the general studying him, appraising him narrowly. *very strange*

"Perhaps," said General Zaroff, "you were surprised that I recognized your name. You see, I read all books on hunting published in English, French, and Russian. I have but one passion in my life, Mr. Rainsford, and it is the hunt."

"You have some wonderful heads here," said Rainsford as he ate a particularly well cooked filet mignon. "That Cape buffalo is the largest I ever saw."

"Oh, that fellow. Yes, he was a monster."

"Did he charge you?"

"Hurled me against a tree," said the general. "Fractured my skull. But I got the brute."

---

7. **cosmopolite:** a person who is at home in all or many places and/or is representative of all or many countries.

strange but nice

"I've always thought," said Rainsford, "that the Cape buffalo is the most dangerous of all big game."

For a moment the general did not reply; he was smiling his curious red-lipped smile. Then he said slowly: "No. You are wrong, sir. The Cape buffalo is not the most dangerous big game." He sipped his wine. "Here in my preserve on this island," he said in the same slow tone, "I hunt more dangerous game." Bragging

Rainsford expressed his surprise. "Is there big game on this island?"

The general nodded, "The biggest."

"Really?"

"Oh, it isn't here naturally, of course. I have to stock the island."

"What have you imported, general?" Rainsford asked. "Tigers?"

The general smiled. "No." he said. "Hunting tigers ceased to interest me some years ago. I exhausted their possibilities, you see. No thrill left in tigers, no real danger. I live for danger, Mr. Rainsford."

The general took from his pocket a gold cigarette case and offered his guest a long black cigarette with a silver tip; it was perfumed and gave off a smell like incense.

"We will have some capital hunting, you and I," said the general. "I shall be most glad to have your society."

"But what game—" began Rainsford.

"I'll tell you," said the general. "You will be amused, I know. I think I may say, in all modesty, that I have done a rare thing. I have invented a new sensation. May I pour you another glass of port, Mr. Rainsford?"

"Thank you, General."

The general filled both glasses, and said: "God makes some men poets. Some He makes kings, some beggars. Me He made a hunter. My hand was made for the trigger, my father said. He was a very rich man with a quarter of a million acres in the Crimea, and he was an ardent sportsman. When I was only five years old he gave me a little gun, specially made in Moscow for me, to shoot sparrows with. When I shot some of his prize turkeys with it, he did not punish me; he complimented me on my marksmanship. I killed my first bear in the Caucasus when I was ten. My whole life has been one prolonged hunt. I went into the army—it was expected of noblemen's sons—and for a time commanded a division of Cossack cavalry, but my real interest was always the hunt. I have hunted every kind of game in every land. It would be impossible for me to tell you how many animals I have killed."

Dad was his mentor

Hunting story (kid)

The general puffed at his cigarette.

"After the debacle[8] in Russia I left the country, for it was imprudent for an officer of the Czar to stay there. Many noble Russians lost everything. I, luckily, had invested heavily in American securities, so I shall never have to open a tearoom in Monte Carlo or drive a taxi in Paris. Naturally, I continued to hunt—grizzlies in your Rockies, crocodiles in the Ganges, rhinoceroses in East Africa. It was in Africa that the Cape buffalo hit me and laid me up for six months. As soon as I recovered I started for the Amazon to hunt jaguars, for I had heard they were unusually cunning. They weren't." The Cossack sighed. "They were no match at all for a hunter with his wits about him, and a high-powered rifle. I was bitterly disappointed. I was lying in my tent with a splitting headache one night when a terrible thought pushed its way into my mind. Hunting was beginning to bore me! And hunting, remember, had been my life. I have heard that in America businessmen often go to pieces when they give up the business that has been their life."

"Yes, that's so," said Rainsford.

The general smiled. "I had no wish to go to pieces," he said. "I must do something. Now, mine is an analytical mind, Mr. Rainsford. Doubtless that is why I enjoy the problems of the chase."

"No doubt, General Zaroff."

"So," continued the general, "I asked myself why the hunt no longer fascinated me. You are much younger than I am, Mr. Rainsford, and have not hunted as much, but you perhaps can guess the answer."

"What was it?"

"Simply this: hunting had ceased to be what you call 'a sporting proposition.' It had become too easy. I always got my quarry. Always. There is no greater bore than perfection."

The general lit a fresh cigarette.

"No animal had a chance with me any more. That is no boast; it is a mathematical certainty. The animal had nothing but his legs and his instinct. Instinct is no match for reason. When I thought of this, it was a tragic moment for me, I can tell you."

Rainsford leaned across the table, absorbed in what his host was saying.

"It came to me as an inspiration what I must do," the general went on.

"And that was?"

---

8. **debacle** (di bä′kəl): a collapse; here, referring to the overthrow of the empire of the czars in 1917.

General traveled extensively

The general smiled the quiet smile of one who has faced an obstacle and surmounted it with success. "I had to invent a new animal to hunt," he said.

"A new animal? You're joking."

"Not at all," said the general. "I never joke about hunting. I needed a new animal. I found one. So I bought this island, built this house, and here I do my hunting. The island is perfect for my purposes—there are jungles with a maze of trails in them, hills, swamps—"

"But the animal, General Zaroff?"

"Oh," said the general, "it supplies me with the most exciting hunting in the world. No other hunting compares with it for an instant. Every day I hunt, and I never grow bored now, for I have a quarry with which I can match my wits."

Rainsford's bewilderment showed in his face.

"I wanted the ideal animal to hunt," explained the general. "So, I said: 'What are the attributes of an ideal quarry?' And the answer was, of course: 'It must have courage, cunning, and, above all, it must be able to reason.'"

"But no animal can reason," objected Rainsford.

"My dear fellow," said the general, "there is one that can."

"But you can't mean—" gasped Rainsford.

"And why not?"

"I can't believe you are serious, General Zaroff. This is a grisly joke."

"Why should I not be serious? I am speaking of hunting."

"Hunting? General Zaroff, what you speak of is murder."

The general laughed with entire good nature. He regarded Rainsford quizzically. "I refuse to believe that so modern and civilized a young man as you seem to be harbors romantic ideas about the value of human life. Surely your experiences in the war—"

"Did not make me condone coldblooded murder," finished Rainsford stiffly.

Laughter shook the general. "How extraordinarily droll[9] you are!" he said. "One does not expect nowadays to find a young man of the educated class, even in America, with such a naive, and, if I may say so, mid-Victorian point of view. It's like finding a snuffbox in a limousine. Ah, well, doubtless you had Puritan ancestors. So many

---

9. **droll:** funny; amusing in an odd way.

Americans appear to have had. I'll wager you'll forget your notions when you go hunting with me. You've a genuine new thrill in store for you, Mr. Rainsford."

"Thank you, I'm a hunter, not a murderer."

"Dear me," said the general, quite unruffled, "again that unpleasant word. But I think I can show you that your scruples are quite ill-founded."

"Yes?"

"Life is for the strong, to be lived by the strong, and, if need be, taken by the strong. The weak of the world were put here to give the strong pleasure. I am strong. Why should I not use my gift? If I wish to hunt, why should I not? I hunt the scum of the earth—sailors from tramp ships—lascars, blacks, Chinese, whites, mongrels—a thoroughbred horse or hound is worth more than a score of them."

"But they are men," said Rainsford hotly.

"Precisely," said the general. "That is why I use them. It gives me pleasure. They can reason, after a fashion. So they are dangerous."

"But where do you get them?"

The general's left eyelid fluttered down in a wink. "This island is called Ship-Trap," he answered. "Sometimes an angry god of the high seas sends them to me. Sometimes, when Providence is not so kind, I help Providence a bit. Come to the window with me."

Rainsford went to the window and looked out toward the sea.

"Watch! Out there!" exclaimed the general, pointing into the night. Rainsford's eyes saw only blackness, and then, as the general pressed a button, far out to sea Rainsford saw the flash of lights.

The general chuckled. "They indicate a channel," he said, "where there's none: giant rocks with razor edges crouch like a sea monster with wide-open jaws. They can crush a ship as easily as I crush this nut." He dropped a walnut on the hardwood floor and brought his heel grinding down on it. "Oh, yes," he said, casually, as if in answer to a question, "I have electricity. We try to be civilized here."

"Civilized? And you shoot down men?"

A trace of anger was in the general's black eyes, but it was there for but a second, and he said, in his most pleasant manner: "Dear me, what a righteous young man you are! I assure you I do not do the thing you suggest. That would be barbarous. I treat these visitors with every consideration. They get plenty of good food and exercise. They get into splendid physical condition. You shall see for yourself tomorrow."

"What do you mean?"

[handwritten: training school]

"We'll visit my training school," smiled the general. "It's in the cellar. I have about a dozen pupils down there now. They're from the Spanish bark *San Lucar* that had the bad luck to go on the rocks out there. A very inferior lot, I regret to say. Poor specimens and more accustomed to the deck than to the jungle." *[handwritten: Better on deck]*

He raised his hand, and Ivan, who served as waiter, brought thick Turkish coffee. Rainsford, with an effort, held his tongue in check.

[handwritten margin: The GAME]

"It's a game, you see," pursued the general blandly. "I suggest to one of them that we go hunting. I give him a supply of food and an excellent hunting knife. I give him three hours' start. I am to follow, armed only with a pistol of the smallest caliber and range. If my quarry eludes me for three whole days, he wins the game. If I find him"—the general smiled—"he loses."

"Suppose he refused to be hunted?"

[handwritten: kills them]

"Oh," said the general, "I give him his option, of course. He need not play that game if he doesn't wish to. If he does not wish to hunt, I turn him over to Ivan. Ivan once had the honor of serving as official knouter[10] to the Great White Czar, and he has his own ideas of sport. Invariably, Mr. Rainsford, invariably they choose the hunt."

"And if they win?"

The smile on the general's face widened. "To date I have not lost," he said.

Then he added, hastily: "I don't wish you to think me a braggart, Mr. Rainsford. Many of them afford only the most elementary sort of problem. Occasionally I strike a tartar. One almost did win. I eventually had to use the dogs."

"The dogs?" *[handwritten: If he can't find him then he used dogs]*

"This way, please. I'll show you."

The general steered Rainsford to a window. The lights from the windows sent a flickering illumination that made grotesque patterns on the courtyard below, and Rainsford could see moving about there a dozen or so huge black shapes; as they turned toward him, their eyes glittered greenly.

"A rather good lot, I think," observed the general. "They are let out at seven every night. If anyone should try to get into my house— or out of it—something extremely regrettable would occur to him." He hummed a snatch of song from the Folies Bergère.

---

10. **knouter** (nout' ər): a flogger (a knout is a leather whip).

[handwritten: He plays Acruel game]

collection just for heads

"And now," said the general, "I want to show you my new collection of heads. Will you come with me to the library?"

"I hope," said Rainsford, "that you will excuse me tonight, General Zaroff. I'm really not feeling at all well."

"Ah, indeed?" the general inquired solicitously. "Well, I suppose that's only natural, after your long swim. You need a good, restful night's sleep. Tomorrow you'll feel like a new man, I'll wager. Then we'll hunt, eh? I've one rather promising prospect——"

Rainsford was hurrying from the room.

"Sorry you can't go with me tonight," called the general. "I expect rather fair sport—a big, strong fellow. He looks resourceful—Well, good night, Mr. Rainsford; I hope you have a good night's rest."

The bed was good, and the pajamas of the softest silk, and he was tired in every fiber of his being, but nevertheless Rainsford could not quiet his brain with the opiate of sleep. He lay, eyes wide open. Once, he thought he heard stealthy steps in the corridor outside his room. He sought to throw open the door; it would not open. He went to the window and looked out. His room was high up in one of the towers. The lights of the château were out now, and it was dark and silent, but there was a fragment of sallow moon, and by its wan light he could see, dimly, the courtyard; there, weaving in and out in the pattern of shadow, were black, noiseless forms; the hounds heard him at the window and looked up, expectantly, with their green eyes. Rainsford went back to the bed and lay down. By many methods he tried to put himself to sleep. He had achieved a doze when, just as morning began to come, he heard, far off in the jungle, the faint report of a pistol.

General Zaroff did not appear until luncheon. He was dressed faultlessly in the tweeds of a country squire. He was solicitous about the state of Rainsford's health.

"As for me," sighed the general, "I do not feel so well. I am worried, Mr. Rainsford. Last night I detected traces of my old complaint."

To Rainsford's questioning glance the general said: "Ennui. Boredom."

Then, taking a second helping of crepes suzette, the general explained: "The hunting was not good last night. The fellow lost his head. He made a straight trail that offered no problems at all. That's the trouble with these sailors; they have dull brains to begin with, and they do not know how to get about in the woods. They do excessively stupid and obvious things. It's most annoying. Will you have another glass of Chablis, Mr. Rainsford?"

DID NOT feel comfortable

wants to leave

"General," said Rainsford firmly, "I wish to leave this island at once."

The general raised his thickets of eyebrows; he seemed hurt. "But, my dear fellow," the general protested, "you've only just come. You've had no hunting—"

"I wish to go today," said Rainsford. He saw the dead black eyes of the general on him, studying him. General Zaroff's face suddenly brightened.

He filled Rainsford's glass with venerable Chablis from a dusty bottle.

"Tonight," said the general, "we will hunt—you and I."

Rainsford shook his head. "No, general," he said, "I will not hunt."

The general shrugged his shoulders and delicately ate a hothouse grape. "As you wish, my friend," he said. "The choice rests entirely with you. But may I not venture to suggest that you will find my idea of sport more diverting than Ivan's?"

He nodded toward the corner to where the giant stood, scowling, his thick arms crossed on his hogshead of chest.

"You don't mean—" cried Rainsford.

"My dear fellow," said the general, "have I not told you I always mean what I say about hunting? This is really an inspiration. I drink to a foeman worthy of my steel—at last."

The general raised his glass, but Rainsford sat staring at him.

"You'll find this game worth playing," the general said enthusiastically. "Your brain against mine. Your woodcraft against mine. Your strength and stamina against mine. Outdoor chess! And the stake is not without value, eh?"

Playing the game

"And if I win—" began Rainsford huskily.

"I'll cheerfully acknowledge myself defeated if I do not find you by midnight of the third day," said General Zaroff. "My sloop will place you on the mainland near a town."

The general read what Rainsford was thinking.

"Oh, you can trust me," said the Cossack. "I will give you my word as a gentleman and a sportsman. Of course you, in turn, must agree to say nothing of your visit here."

"I'll agree to nothing of the kind," said Rainsford.

"Oh," said the general, "in that case—But why discuss that now? Three days hence we can discuss it over a bottle of Veuve Cliquot, unless—"

The general sipped his wine.

Then a businesslike air animated him. "Ivan," he said to Rainsford,

Small leather Shoes

"will supply you with hunting clothes, food, a knife. I suggest you wear moccasins; they leave a poorer trail. I suggest too that you avoid a big swamp in the southeast corner of the island. We call it Death Swamp. There's quicksand there. One foolish fellow tried it. The deplorable part of it was that Lazarus followed him. You can imagine my feelings, Mr. Rainsford. I loved Lazarus; he was the finest hound in my pack. Well, I must beg you to excuse me now. I always take a siesta after lunch. You'll hardly have time for a nap, I fear. You'll want to start, no doubt. I shall not follow till dusk. Hunting at night is so much more exciting than by day, don't you think? Au revoir,[11] Mr. Rainsford, au revoir."

General Zaroff, with a deep, courtly bow, strolled from the room.

From another door came Ivan. Under one arm he carried khaki hunting clothes, a haversack of food, a leather sheath containing a long-bladed hunting knife; his right hand rested on a cocked revolver thrust in the crimson sash about his waist. . . .

Rainsford had fought his way through the bush for two hours. "I must keep my nerve. I must keep my nerve," he said through tight teeth.

He had not been entirely clearheaded when the château gates snapped shut behind him. His whole idea at first was to put distance between himself and General Zaroff, and, to this end, he had plunged along, spurred on by the sharp rowels of something very like panic. Now he had got a grip on himself, had stopped, and was taking stock of himself and the situation.

He saw that straight flight was futile; inevitably it would bring him face to face with the sea. He was in a picture with a frame of water, and his operations, clearly, must take place within that frame.

"I'll give him a trail to follow," muttered Rainsford, and he struck off from the rude paths he had been following into the trackless wilderness. He executed a series of intricate loops; he doubled on his trail again and again, recalling all the lore of the fox hunt, and all the dodges of the fox. Night found him leg-weary, with hands and face lashed by the branches, on a thickly wooded ridge. He knew it would be insane to blunder on through the dark, even if he had the strength. His need for rest was imperative and he thought: "I have played the fox, now I must play the cat of the fable." A big tree with a thick trunk and

---

11. **au revoir** (ō'rə vwär'): French for "until we meet again."

The GAME

Part of tree

outspread branches was nearby, and, taking care to leave not the slightest mark, he climbed up into the crotch, and stretching out on one of the broad limbs, after a fashion, rested. Rest brought him new confidence and almost a feeling of security. Even so zealous a hunter as General Zaroff could not trace him there, he told himself; only the devil himself could follow that complicated trail through the jungle after dark. But, perhaps, the general was a devil—

An apprehensive night crawled slowly by like a wounded snake, and sleep did not visit Rainsford, although the silence of a dead world was on the jungle. Toward morning when a dingy gray was varnishing the sky, the cry of some startled bird focused Rainsford's attention in that direction. Something was coming through the bush, coming slowly, carefully, coming by the same winding way Rainsford had come. He flattened himself down on the limb, and through a screen of leaves almost as thick as tapestry, he watched. The thing that was approaching was a man. *the general was coming*

It was General Zaroff. He made his way along with his eyes fixed in utmost concentration on the ground before him. He paused, almost beneath the tree, dropped to his knees and studied the ground. Rainsford's impulse was to hurl himself down like a panther, but he saw that the general's right hand held something metallic—a small automatic pistol.

The hunter shook his head several times, as if he were puzzled. Then he straightened up and took from his case one of his black cigarettes; its pungent incense-like smoke floated up to Rainsford's nostrils.

Rainsford held his breath. The general's eyes had left the ground and were traveling inch by inch up the tree. Rainsford froze there, every muscle tensed for a spring. But the sharp eyes of the hunter stopped before they reached the limb where Rainsford lay; a smile spread over his brown face. Very deliberately he blew a smoke ring into the air; then he turned his back on the tree and walked carelessly away, back along the trail he had come. The swish of the underbrush against his hunting boots grew fainter and fainter.

The pent-up air burst hotly from Rainsford's lungs. His first thought made him feel sick and numb. The general could follow a trail through the woods at night; he could follow an extremely difficult trail; he must have uncanny powers; only by the merest chance had the Cossack failed to see his quarry.

Played with him

Does the general see him?

Rainsford's second thought was even more terrible. It sent a shudder of cold horror through his whole being. Why had the general smiled? Why had he turned back?

Rainsford did not want to believe what his reason told him was true, but the truth was as evident as the sun that had by now pushed through the morning mists. The general was playing with him! The general was saving him for another day's sport! The Cossack was the cat; he was the mouse. Then it was that Rainsford knew the full meaning of terror.

"I will not lose my nerve. I will not."

He slid down from the tree, and struck off again into the woods. His face was set and he forced the machinery of his mind to function. Three hundred yards from his hiding place, he stopped where a huge, dead tree leaned precariously on a smaller, living one. Throwing off his sack of food, Rainsford took his knife from its sheath and began to work with all his energy.

The job was finished at last, and he threw himself down behind a fallen log a hundred feet away. He did not have to wait long. The cat was coming again to play with the mouse.

Following the trail with the sureness of a bloodhound came General Zaroff. Nothing escaped those searching black eyes, no crushed blade of grass, no bent twig, no mark, no matter how faint, in the moss. So intent was the Cossack on his stalking that he was upon the thing Rainsford had made before he saw it. His foot touched the protruding bough that was the trigger. Even as he touched it, the general sensed his danger and leaped back with the agility of an ape. But he was not quite quick enough: the dead tree, delicately adjusted to rest on the cut living one, crashed down and struck the general a glancing blow on the shoulder as it fell; but for his alertness, he must have been smashed beneath it. He staggered, but he did not fall; nor did he drop his revolver. He stood there, rubbing his injured shoulder, and Rainsford, with fear again gripping his heart, heard the general's mocking laugh ring through the jungle.

"Rainsford," called the general, "if you are within sound of my voice, as I suppose you are, let me congratulate you. Not many men know how to make a Malay man-catcher. Luckily, for me, I too have hunted in Malacca. You are proving interesting, Mr. Rainsford. I am going now to have my wound dressed; it's only a slight one. But I shall be back. I shall be back."

When the general, nursing his bruised shoulder, had gone,

(margin note, left side: SWAMP MADE TRAP WITH DEATH)

Rainsford took up his flight again. It was flight now, a desperate, hopeless flight, that carried him on for some hours. Dusk came, then darkness, and still he pressed on. The ground grew softer under his moccasins; the vegetation grew ranker, denser; insects bit him savagely. Then, as he stepped forward, his foot sank into the ooze. He tried to wrench it back, but the muck sucked viciously at his foot as if it were a giant leech. With a violent effort, he tore his foot loose. He knew where he was now. Death Swamp and its quicksand.

His hands were tight closed as if his nerve were something tangible that someone in the darkness was trying to tear form his grip. The softness of the earth had given him an idea. He stepped back from the quicksand a dozen feet or so and, like some huge prehistoric beaver, he began to dig.

Rainsford had dug himself in in France when a second's delay meant death. That had been a placid pastime compared to his digging now. The pit grew deeper; when it was above his shoulder, he climbed out and from some hard saplings cut stakes and sharpened them to a fine point. These stakes he planted in the bottom of the pit with the points sticking up. With flying fingers he wove a rough carpet of weeds and branches and with it he covered the mouth of the pit. Then, wet with sweat and aching with tiredness, he crouched behind the stump of a lightning-charred tree. *(margin note: PLAN)*

He knew his pursuer was coming; he heard the padding sound of feet on the soft earth, and the night breeze brought him the perfume of the general's cigarette. It seemed to Rainsford that the general was coming with unusual swiftness; he was not feeling his way along, foot by foot. Rainsford, crouching there, could not see the general, nor could he see the pit. He lived a year in a minute. Then he felt an impulse to cry aloud with joy, for he heard the sharp crackle of the breaking branches as the cover of the pit gave way; he heard the sharp scream of pain as the pointed stakes found their mark. He leaped up from his place of concealment. Then he cowered back. Three feet from the pit a man was standing, with an electric torch in his hand.

(margin note, left side: The dog dies)

"You've done well, Rainsford," the voice of the general called. "Your Burmese tiger pit has claimed one of my best dogs. Again you score. I think, Mr. Rainsford, I'll see what you can do against my whole pack. I'm going home for a rest now. Thank you for a most amusing evening."

At daybreak Rainsford, lying near the swamp, was awakened by a [handwritten: location] sound that made him know that he had new things to learn about fear. It was a distant sound, faint and wavering, but he knew it. It was the baying of a pack of hounds.

Rainsford knew he could do one of two things. He could stay where he was and wait. That was suicide. He could flee. That was postponing the inevitable. For a moment he stood there, thinking. An idea that held a wild chance came to him, and tightening his belt, he headed away from the swamp.

[handwritten: Hounds were coming] The baying of the hounds drew nearer, then still nearer, nearer, ever nearer. On a ridge Rainsford climbed a tree. Down a watercourse, not a quarter of a mile away, he could see the bush moving. Straining his eyes, he saw the lean figure of General Zaroff; just ahead of him Rainsford made out another figure whose wide shoulders surged through the tall jungle weeds; it was the giant Ivan, and he seemed pulled forward by some unseen force; Rainsford knew that Ivan must be holding the pack in leash.

[handwritten left margin: TRICK he heard in Uganda]

[handwritten: GIANT IVAN HAD COME] They would be on him any minute now. His mind worked frantically. He though of a native trick he had learned in Uganda. He slid down the tree. He caught hold of a springy young sapling and to it he fastened his hunting knife, with the blade pointing down the trail; with a bit of wild grapevine he tied back the sapling. Then he ran for his life. The hounds raised their voices as they hit the fresh scent. Rainsford knew now how an animal at bay feels.

He had to stop to get his breath. The baying of the hounds stopped abruptly, and Rainsford's heart stopped too. They must have reached the knife.

He shinnied excitedly up a tree and looked back. His pursuers had stopped. But the hope that was in Rainsford's brain when he climbed died, for he saw in the shallow valley that general Zaroff was still on his feet. But Ivan was not. The knife, driven by the recoil of the springing tree, had not wholly failed. [handwritten: IVAN DIED]

Rainsford had hardly tumbled to the ground when the pack took up the cry again.

"Nerve, nerve, nerve!" he panted, as he dashed along. A blue gap showed between the trees dead ahead. Ever nearer drew the hounds. Rainsford forced himself on toward that gap. He reached it. It was the shore of the sea. Across a cove he could see the gloomy gray stone of the château. Twenty feet below him the sea rumbled and hissed. Rainsford hesitated. He heard the hounds. Then he leaped far out into the sea . . .

When the general and his pack reached the place by the sea, the Cossack stopped. For some minutes he stood regarding the blue-green expanse of water. He shrugged his shoulders. Then he sat down, took a drink of brandy from a silver flask, lit a perfumed cigarette, and hummed a bit from *Madame Butterfly.*[12]

General Zaroff had an exceedingly good dinner in his great paneled dining hall that evening. With it he had a bottle of Pol Roger and half a bottle of Chambertin. Two slight annoyances kept him from perfect enjoyment. One was the thought that it would be difficult to replace Ivan; the other was that his quarry had escaped him; of course the American hadn't played the game—so thought the general as he tasted his after-dinner liqueur. In his library he read, to soothe himself, from the works of Marcus Aurelius.[13] At ten he went up to his bedroom. He was deliciously tired, he said to himself, as he locked himself in. There was a little moonlight, so before turning on his light, he went to the window and looked down at the courtyard. He could see the great hounds, and he called: "Better luck another time," to them. Then he switched on the light. HOUNDS

A man, who had been hiding in the curtains of the bed, was standing there.

"Rainsford!" screamed the general. "How did you get here?"

"Swam," said Rainsford. "I found it quicker than walking through the jungle."

The general sucked in his breath and smiled. "I congratulate you," he said. "You have won the game."

Rainsford did not smile. "I am still a beast at bay," he said, in a low, hoarse voice. "Get ready, General Zaroff."

The general made one of his deepest bows. "I see," he said. "Splendid! One of us is to furnish a repast for the hounds. The other will sleep in this very excellent bed. On guard, Rainsford. . . ."

The General got defeated

He had never slept in a better bed, Rainsford decided.

12. *Madame Butterfly:* an opera by Giacomo Puccini in which Madame Butterfly takes her own life.
13. **Marcus Aurelius:** a Roman emperor (161–180), whose book, *Meditations,* is considered a classic of philosophy.

THE IMPACT OF THE STORY

From the time it was first published in 1924, this story has been extremely popular. Did you enjoy it? Why? In what ways is this story like today's popular movies, television shows, or novels?

What conclusions can you draw about what kinds of stories people enjoy?

THE FACTS OF THE STORY

Write short answers to the following items. Answers may be one word, a phrase, or several sentences.

1. The game that General Zaroff hunts is _____.

2. What is Zaroff's island called?

3. Zaroff gives Rainsford two choices: He can be hunted, or _____.

4. To win the game, how many days must Rainsford survive the hunt?

5. As a result of Rainsford's skill in setting traps on the trail, Zaroff loses a _____ and _____.

THE IDEAS OF THE STORY

Prepare to discuss the following questions in class.

1. At the beginning of the story, the author lets us know Rainsford's ideas about hunting and Whitney's reactions to these ideas. How do Whitney's and Rainsford's ideas differ? Why would the author want us to know about these ideas at the start of the story?

2. What are your reactions to the following ideas stated by two characters in the story?

   Rainsford: "The world is made up of two classes—the hunters and the huntees."

   Zaroff: "Life is for the strong, to be lived by the strong, and, if need be, taken by the strong. The weak of the

world were put here to give the strong pleasure. I am
strong. Why should I not use my gift?"

3. At first, Rainsford's ideas about hunting are similar to
Zaroff's. Do you think Rainsford's ideas are changed by
his experience with Zaroff? Why or why not?

THE ART OF THE STORYTELLER

Plot
Plot is a series of connected events which are brought to some kind
of conclusion—sometimes a happy one, sometimes an unhappy
one, sometimes an indefinite one. Three major elements of plot are
a conflict or conflicts to be resolved, suspense, and a climax.

Conflict, or Struggle
The first requirement for a plot is a **conflict** or struggle the main
character faces. A character can be in conflict with another person,
or with some natural force (such as a shark or an earthquake), or
with society as a whole, or even with ideas, emotions, or desires
within himself or herself. From the time he falls from the yacht,
Rainsford's conflicts are with forces that threaten his life. The first
obstacle he faces is the sea. He wins his struggle against the sea
only to be faced with other obstacles in the life-or-death struggle
with General Zaroff. Where does Rainsford also struggle against
his own mounting terror?

Characters: Protagonist and Antagonist
In many stories, the conflict is between two characters. The character who faces the struggle and must overcome obstacles in order
to win is called the **protagonist.** The character or the force that
opposes the protagonist is called the **antagonist.** The antagonist
stands in the way of the protagonist's victory. This does not mean
that the protagonist is always a "good guy" and the antagonist
always a "bad guy," though that's often the case. A bank robber
trying to solve the problem of how not to get caught could be the
protagonist, and a detective trying to catch the robber could be the
antagonist. Protagonist and antagonist are simply handy terms to
use in identifying the principal characters or forces involved in a

story's conflict. How does this writer make Zaroff seem like a totally evil antagonist?

Suspense

Many good stories, especially action stories, hold us in suspense. **Suspense** is our feeling that we have to keep on reading to find out what happens next. It is a feeling composed of a number of emotions—curiosity, fear, anxiety. When the suspense is great, we say we "can't put the book down" or, if the story is on television, we "can't turn off the set." "The Most Dangerous Game" creates suspense in the opening lines. Two of the first things that Whitney says about the island is that "the old charts call it 'Ship-Trap Island'" and "Sailors have a curious dread of the place." What other details about the island are supposed to arouse our curiosity and keep us reading?

The author builds suspense again in the dinner scene when Zaroff begins to talk about his new "game." At what point in the scene did you realize what "game" Zaroff hunts on his island?

Suspense again mounts during "the chase." You are probably familiar with "the chase" from the "cops-and-robbers" kind of story so common on television: cars racing through city streets; squealing tires; near collisions; the sudden stop; the slamming of car doors; the attempted escape, perhaps over rooftops; the blazing guns. In "The Most Dangerous Game," the manhunt is a form of "the chase," an almost sure-fire method of creating suspense. Were there any moments during the chase when you thought Rainsford had lost the game?

Climax

Usually an author makes us sympathize with one character in the story. We want this character to succeed, but we are afraid he or she may fail. The point at which our suspense and interest are the highest and we learn whether this character succeeds or fails is the climax of the story. It is the moment toward which all the action in the story has led us. In "The Most Dangerous Game," we do not reach the climax until we come to the very last line: "He had never slept in a better bed, Rainsford decided." In fact, Connell has been so skillful in plotting his story that we are not sure of the outcome until the last two words, "Rainsford decided." What were your feelings when you came to these last two words?

THE VOCABULARY IN THE STORY

Sometimes you can figure out the meaning of a new word (or a familiar word used in a new way) by using context clues. These are clues you get from other words in the sentence or paragraph:

> . . . Rainsford noted, the table appointments were of the finest—the linen, the crystal, the silver, the china.

The meaning of the word *appointments,* "equipment" or "furnishings," is made clear by the context.

Use context clues to determine the meaning of the italicized words in these sentences from the story. Check your answers in a dictionary.

1. Rainsford, reclining in a steamer chair, *indolently* puffed his favorite brier. The sensuous drowsiness of the night was on him.

2. His hands were tight closed as if his nerve were something *tangible* that someone in the darkness was trying to tear from his grip.

3. "I am worried, Mr. Rainsford. Last night I detected traces of my old complaint."
   To Rainsford's questioning glance the general said: "*Ennui.* Boredom."

COMPOSITION: Narrating an Imagined Action

In telling stories, writers usually choose not to give a detailed account of everything that happens. They decide which events to describe in detail and which not to describe. The descriptions of two important events are omitted from "The Most Dangerous Game." One is Rainsford's second swim, after which he hides in Zaroff's bedroom. The other is the final fight between the two men, which determines who is "to furnish a repast for the hounds."

Assuming the role of author, write a brief account (about 200 words) of one of these events. Either describe Rainsford's swim and how he got into Zaroff's bedroom, or describe the final fight.

Prewriting

Take time to imagine in detail exactly what happens. Then jot down a list of the obstacles Rainsford must overcome to reach the bedroom or to kill Zaroff. Beside each obstacle, write a word or two that vividly describes it, and make a note about how Rainsford overcomes the obstacle.

Writing

Write your first draft quickly. Don't worry about forgetting something or making a mistake. Write as though you are the author telling the story, not as though you are answering a question. How not to begin: "I think Rainsford would have . . ."; "One thing that might have happened is . . ." Begin by describing the action: "For the second time in three days, Rainsford felt the warm waters of the Caribbean close over him."

To create suspense, describe each obstacle or opponent's power or strength in detail. Let Rainsford almost lose, then win each struggle. To feel suspense, the reader must believe that Rainsford could lose.

Evaluating and Revising

Read your draft. Add, cut, reorder, or replace words, phrases, or sections as needed. Compare your prewriting list to your draft. Did you forget something you want to add?

ABOUT THE AUTHOR

Richard Connell (1893–1949), as a boy in Poughkeepsie, New York, learned something about writing when he tried his hand as a sportswriter for the newspaper his father edited. He continued his writing at Harvard, where he was the editor of the *Lampoon*. After his discharge from the Army following World War I, he worked for a newspaper and later for an advertising firm. In addition to hundreds of short stories, Connell wrote novels and screenplays. He is best known today as the author of "The Most Dangerous Game."

■ TO BUILD A FIRE

Jack London

In the 1890s, part of the Yukon Territory, a vast area in
northwest Canada, was the scene of a gold rush. That far
north, the sun does not rise above the horizon in the dead of
winter, and the temperature may drop as low as seventy-five
degrees below zero. In such a harsh climate, nature becomes
a force not to be treated lightly.

As you read, consider the relationship between the man
and nature. How do the man's actions affect the story's
outcome? Why do you think London put the dog in the story?

Day had broken cold and gray, exceedingly cold and gray, when
the man turned aside from the main Yukon trail[1] and climbed
the high earth bank, where a dim and little-traveled trail led
eastward through the fat spruce timberland. It was a steep bank, and
he paused for breath at the top, excusing the act to himself by looking
at his watch. It was nine o'clock. There was no sun or hint of sun,
though there was not a cloud in the sky. It was a clear day, and yet there
seemed an intangible pall over the face of things, a subtle gloom that
made the day dark, and that was due to the absence of sun. This fact
did not worry the man. He was used to the lack of sun. It had been
days since he had seen the sun, and he knew that a few more days must
pass before that cheerful orb, due south, would just peep above the
skyline and dip immediately from view.

The man flung a look back along the way he had come. The Yukon
lay a mile wide and hidden under three feet of ice. On top of this ice
were as many feet of snow. It was all pure white, rolling in gentle
undulations where the ice jams of the freeze-up had formed. North and
south, as far as his eye could see, it was unbroken white, save for a
dark hairline that curved and twisted from around the spruce-covered
island to the south, and that curved and twisted away into the north,
where it disappeared behind another spruce-covered island. This dark
hairline was the trail—the main trail—that led south five hundred

---

1. **Yukon trail:** refers to the Yukon River, which is frozen solid during the winter.

miles to the Chilkoot Pass, Dyea, and salt water; and that led north seventy miles to Dawson, and still on to the north a thousand miles to Nulato, and finally to St. Michael on the Bering Sea, a thousand miles and half a thousand more.

But all this—the mysterious, far-reaching hairline trail, the absence of sun from the sky, the tremendous cold, and the strangeness and weirdness of it all—made no impression on the man. It was not because he was long used to it. He was a newcomer in the land, a cheechako, and this was his first winter. The trouble with him was that he was without imagination. He was quick and alert in the things of life, but only in the things, and not in the significances. Fifty degrees below zero meant eighty-odd degrees of frost. Such fact impressed him as being cold and uncomfortable, and that was all. It did not lead him to meditate upon his frailty as a creature of temperature, and upon man's frailty in general, able only to live within certain narrow limits of heat and cold, and from there on it did not lead him to the conjectural field of immortality and man's place in the universe. Fifty degrees below zero stood for a bite of frost that hurt and that must be guarded against by the use of mittens, earflaps, warm moccasins, and thick socks. Fifty degrees below zero was to him just precisely fifty degrees below zero. That there should be anything more to it than that was a thought that never entered his head.

As he turned to go on, he spat speculatively. There was a sharp, explosive crackle that startled him. He spat again. And again, in the air, before it could fall to the snow, the spittle crackled. He knew that at fifty below, spittle crackled on the snow, but this spittle had crackled in the air. Undoubtedly it was colder than fifty below—how much colder he did not know. But the temperature did not matter. He was bound for the old claim on the left fork of Henderson Creek, where the boys were already. They had come over across the divide from the Indian Creek country, while he had come the roundabout way to take a look at the possibilities of getting out logs in the spring from the islands in the Yukon. He would be into camp by six o'clock; a bit after dark, it was true, but the boys would be there, a fire would be going, and a hot supper would be ready. As for lunch, he pressed his hand against the protruding bundle under his jacket. It was also under his shirt, wrapped up in a handkerchief and lying against the naked skin. It was the only way to keep the biscuits from freezing. He smiled agreeably to himself as he thought of those biscuits, each cut open and sopped in bacon grease, and each enclosing a generous slice of fried bacon.

He plunged in among the big spruce trees. The trail was faint. A foot of snow had fallen since the last sled had passed over, and he was glad he was without a sled, traveling light. In fact, he carried nothing but the lunch wrapped in the handkerchief. He was surprised, however, at the cold. It certainly was cold, he concluded, as he rubbed his numb nose and cheekbones with his mittened hand. He was a warm-whiskered man, but the hair on his face did not protect the high cheekbones and the eager nose that thrust itself aggressively into the frosty air.

At the man's heels trotted a dog, a big native husky, the proper wolf dog, gray-coated and without any visible or temperamental difference from its brother, the wild wolf. The animal was depressed by the tremendous cold. It knew that it was no time for traveling. Its instinct told it a truer tale than was told to the man by the man's judgment. In reality, it was not merely colder than fifty below zero; it was colder than sixty below, than seventy below. It was seventy-five below zero. Since the freezing point is thirty-two above zero, it meant that one hundred and seven degrees of frost obtained. The dog did not know anything about thermometers. Possibly in its brain there was no sharp consciousness of a condition of very cold such as was in the man's brain. But the brute had its instinct. It experienced a vague but menacing apprehension that subdued it and made it slink along at the man's heels, and that made it question eagerly every unwonted[2] movement of the man, as if expecting him to go into camp or to seek shelter somewhere and build a fire. The dog had learned fire, and it wanted fire, or else to burrow under the snow and cuddle its warmth away from the air.

The frozen moisture of its breathing had settled on its fur in a fine powder of frost, and especially were its jowls, muzzle, and eyelashes whitened by its crystaled breath. The man's red beard and mustache were likewise frosted, but more solidly, the deposit taking the form of ice and increasing with every warm, moist breath he exhaled. Also, the man was chewing tobacco, and the muzzle of ice held his lips so rigidly that he was unable to clear his chin when he expelled the juice. The result was that a crystal beard of the color and solidity of amber was

---

2. **unwonted:** unusual.

increasing its length on his chin. If he fell down it would shatter itself, like glass, into brittle fragments. But he did not mind the appendage. It was the penalty all tobacco-chewers paid in that country, and he had been out before in two cold snaps. They had not been so cold as this, he knew, but by the spirit thermometer[3] at Sixty Mile he knew they had been registered at fifty below and at fifty-five.

He held on through the level stretch of woods for several miles, crossed a wide flat, and dropped down a bank to the frozen bed of a small stream. This was Henderson Creek, and he knew he was ten miles from the forks. He looked at his watch. It was ten o'clock. He was making four miles an hour, and he calculated that he would arrive at the forks at half past twelve. He decided to celebrate that event by eating his lunch there.

The dog dropped in again at his heels, with a tail drooping discouragement, as the man swung along the creek bed. The furrow of the old sled trail was plainly visible, but a dozen inches of snow covered the marks of the last runners. In a month no man had come up or down that silent creek. The man held steadily on. He was not much given to thinking, and just then particularly, he had nothing to think about save that he would eat lunch at the forks and that at six o'clock he would be in camp with the boys. There was nobody to talk to; and, had there been, speech would have been impossible because of the ice muzzle on his mouth. So he continued monotonously to chew tobacco and to increase the length of his amber beard.

Once in a while the thought reiterated itself that it was very cold and that he had never experienced such cold. As he walked along he rubbed his cheekbones and nose with the back of his mittened hand. He did this automatically, now and again changing hands. But rub as he would, the instant he stopped his cheekbones went numb, and the following instant the end of his nose went numb. He was sure to frost his cheeks; he knew that, and experienced a pang of regret that he had not devised a nose strap of the sort Bud wore in the cold snaps. Such a strap passed across the cheeks, as well, and saved them. But it didn't matter much, after all. What were frosted cheeks? A bit painful, that was all; they were never serious.

Empty as the man's mind was of thought, he was keenly observant,

---

3. **spirit thermometer:** an alcohol thermometer, used in extreme cold.

and he noticed the changes in the creek, the curves and bends and timber jams, and always he sharply noted where he placed his feet. Once, coming around a bend, he shied abruptly, like a startled horse, curved away from the place where he had been walking, and retreated several paces back along the trail. The creek, he knew, was frozen clear to the bottom—no creek could contain water in that arctic winter—but he knew also that there were springs that bubbled out from the hillsides and ran along under the snow and on top of the ice of the creek. He knew that the coldest snaps never froze these springs, and he knew likewise their danger. They were traps. They hid pools of water under the snow that might be three inches deep, or three feet. Sometimes a skin of ice half an inch thick covered them, and in turn was covered by the snow. Sometimes there were alternate layers of water and ice skin, so that when one broke through he kept on breaking through for a while, sometimes wetting himself to the waist.

That was why he had shied in such panic. He had felt the give under his feet and heard the crackle of a snow-hidden ice skin. And to get his feet wet in such a temperature meant trouble and danger. At the very least it meant delay, for he would be forced to stop and build a fire, and under its protection to bare his feet while he dried his socks and moccasins. He stood and studied the creek bed and its banks, and decided that the flow of water came from the right. He reflected awhile, rubbing his nose and cheeks, then skirted to the left, stepping gingerly and testing the footing for each step. Once clear of the danger, he took a fresh chew of tobacco and swung along at his four-mile gait.

In the course of the next two hours he came upon several similar traps. Usually the snow above the hidden pools had a sunken, candied appearance that advertised the danger. Once again, however, he had a close call; and once, suspecting danger, he compelled the dog to go on in front. The dog did not want to go. It hung back until the man shoved it forward, and then it went quickly across the white, unbroken surface. Suddenly it broke through, floundered to one side, and got away to firmer footing. It had wet its forefeet and legs, and almost immediately the water that clung to it turned to ice. It made quick efforts to lick the ice off its legs, then dropped down in the snow and began to bite out the ice that had formed between the toes. This was a matter of instinct. To permit the ice to remain would mean sore feet. It did not know this. It merely obeyed the mysterious prompting that arose from the deep crypts[4] of its being. But the man knew, having achieved a judgment on the subject, and he removed the mitten from his right hand and helped tear out the ice particles. He did not expose his fingers more than a minute, and was astonished at the swift numbness that smote them. It certainly was cold. He pulled on the mitten hastily, and beat the hand savagely across his chest.

At twelve o'clock the day was at its brightest. Yet the sun was too far south on its winter journey to clear the horizon. The bulge of the earth intervened between it and Henderson Creek, where the man walked under a clear sky at noon and cast no shadow. At half past twelve, to the minute, he arrived at the forks of the creek. He was pleased at the speed he had made. If he kept it up, he would certainly be with the boys by six. He unbuttoned his jacket and shirt and drew forth his lunch. The action consumed no more than a quarter of a minute, yet in that brief moment the numbness laid hold of the exposed fingers. He did not put the mitten on, but instead struck the fingers a dozen sharp smashes against his leg. Then he sat down on a snow-covered log to eat. The sting that followed upon the striking of his fingers against his leg ceased so quickly that he was startled. He had had no chance to take a bite of biscuit. He struck the fingers repeatedly and returned them to the mitten, baring the other hand for the purpose of eating. He tried to take a mouthful, but the ice muzzle prevented. He had forgotten to build a fire and thaw out. He chuckled at his foolishness, and as he chuckled he noted the numbness creeping into the exposed fingers. Also, he noted that the stinging which had first come to his toes when he sat down was already passing away. He wondered whether the toes were warm or numb. He moved them inside the moccasins and decided that they were numb.

He pulled the mitten on hurriedly and stood up. He was a bit frightened. He stamped up and down until the stinging returned into the feet. It certainly was cold, was his thought. That man from Sulfur Creek had spoken the truth when telling how cold it sometimes got in the country. And he had laughed at him at the time! That showed one must not be too sure of things. There was no mistake about it, it *was* cold. He strode up and down, stamping his feet and threshing his arms, until reassured by the returning warmth. Then he got out matches and proceeded to make a fire. From the undergrowth, where high water of

---

4. **crypts** (kripts): underground chambers or vaults.

the previous spring had lodged a supply of seasoned twigs, he got his firewood. Working carefully from a small beginning, he soon had a roaring fire, over which he thawed the ice from his face and in the protection of which he ate his biscuits. For the moment the cold of space was outwitted. The dog took satisfaction in the fire, stretching out close enough for warmth and far enough away to escape being singed.

When the man had finished, he filled his pipe and took his comfortable time over a smoke. Then he pulled on his mittens, settled the earflaps of his cap firmly about his ears, and took the creek trail up the left fork. The dog was disappointed and yearned back toward the fire. This man did not know cold. Possibly all the generations of his ancestry had been ignorant of cold, of real cold, of cold one hundred and seven degrees below freezing point. But the dog knew; all its ancestry knew, and it had inherited the knowledge. And it knew that it was not good to walk abroad in such fearful cold. It was the time to lie snug in a hole in the snow and wait for a curtain of cloud to be drawn across the face of outer space whence this cold came. On the other hand, there was no keen intimacy between the dog and the man. The one was the toil slave of the other, and the only caresses it had ever received were the caresses of the whiplash and of harsh and menacing throat sounds that threatened the whiplash. So the dog made no effort to communicate its apprehension to the man. It was not concerned in the welfare of the man; it was for its own sake that it yearned back toward the fire. But the man whistled, and spoke to it with the sound of whiplashes, and the dog swung in at the man's heels and followed after.

The man took a chew of tobacco and proceeded to start a new amber beard. Also, his moist breath quickly powdered with white his mustache, eyebrows, and lashes. There did not seem to be so many springs on the left fork of the Henderson, and for half an hour the man saw no signs of any. And then it happened. At a place where there were no signs, where the soft, unbroken snow seemed to advertise solidity beneath, the man broke through. It was not deep. He wet himself halfway to the knees before he floundered out to the firm crust.

He was angry, and cursed his luck aloud. He had hoped to get into camp with the boys at six o'clock, and this would delay him an hour, for he would have to build a fire and dry out his footgear. This was imperative at that low temperature—he knew that much; and he turned aside to the bank, which he climbed. On top, tangled in the underbrush about the trunks of several small spruce trees, was a high-water deposit of dry firewood—sticks and twigs, principally, but also larger portions of seasoned branches and fine, dry, last year's grasses. He threw down several large pieces on top of the snow. This served for a foundation and prevented the young flame from drowning itself in the snow it otherwise would melt. The flame he got by touching a match to a small shred of birch bark that he took from his pocket. This burned even more readily than paper. Placing it on the foundation, he fed the young flame with wisps of dry grass and with the tiniest dry twigs.

He worked slowly and carefully, keenly aware of his danger. Gradually, as the flame grew stronger, he increased the size of the twigs with which he fed it. He squatted in the snow, pulling the twigs out from their entanglement in the brush and feeding directly to the flame. He knew there must be no failure. When it is seventy-five below zero, a man must not fail in his first attempt to build a fire—that is, if his feet are wet. If his feet are dry, and he fails, he can run along the trail for a half a mile and restore his circulation. But the circulation of wet and freezing feet cannot be restored by running when it is seventy-five below. No matter how fast he runs, the wet feet will freeze the harder.

All this the man knew. The old-timer on Sulfur Creek had told him about it the previous fall, and now he was appreciating the advice. Already all sensation had gone out of his feet. To build the fire, he had been forced to remove his mittens, and the fingers had quickly gone numb. His pace of four miles an hour had kept his heart pumping blood to the surface of his body and to all the extremities. But the instant he stopped, the action of the pump eased down. The cold of space smote the unprotected tip of the planet, and he, being on that unprotected tip, received the full force of the blow. The blood of his body recoiled before it. The blood was alive, like the dog, and like the dog it wanted to hide away and cover itself up from the fearful cold. So long as he walked four miles an hour, he pumped that blood, willy-nilly, to the surface; but now it ebbed away and sank down into the recesses of his body. The extremities were the first to feel its absence. His wet feet froze the faster, and his exposed fingers numbed the faster, though they had not yet begun to freeze. Nose and cheeks were already freezing, while the skin of all his body chilled as it lost its blood.

But he was safe. Toes and nose and cheeks would be only touched by the frost, for the fire was beginning to burn with strength. He was feeding it with twigs the size of his finger. In another minute he would be able to feed it with branches the size of his wrist, and then he could remove his wet footgear, and, while it dried, he could keep his naked feet warm by the fire, rubbing them at first, of course, with snow. The fire was a success. He was safe. He remembered the advice of the old-timer on Sulfur Creek, and smiled. The old-timer had been very serious in laying down the law that no man must travel alone in the Klondike after fifty below. Well, here he was; he had had the accident; he was alone; and he had saved himself. Those old-timers were rather womanish, some of them, he thought. All a man had to do was to keep his head and he was all right. Any man who was a man could travel alone. But it was surprising, the rapidity with which his cheeks and nose were freezing. And he had not thought his fingers could go life-less in so short a time. Lifeless they were, for he could scarcely make them move together to grip a twig, and they seemed remote from his body and from him. When he touched a twig, he had to look and see whether or not he had hold of it. The wires were pretty well down between him and his finger ends.

All of which counted for little. There was the fire, snapping and crackling and promising life with every dancing flame. He started to untie his moccasins. They were coated with ice; the thick German socks were like sheaths of iron halfway to the knees; and the moccasin strings were like rods of steel all twisted and knotted as by some conflagration. For a moment he tugged with his numb fingers, then, realizing the folly of it, he drew his sheath knife.

But before he could cut the strings it happened. It was his own fault, or, rather, his mistake. He should not have built the fire under the spruce tree. He should have built it in the open. But it had been easier to pull the twigs from the bush and drop them directly on the fire. Now the tree under which he had done this carried a weight of snow on its boughs. No wind had blown for weeks, and each bough was fully freighted. Each time he pulled a twig he had communicated a slight agitation to the tree—an imperceptible agitation, so far as he was concerned, but an agitation sufficient to bring about the disaster. High up in the tree one bough capsized its load of snow. This fell on the boughs beneath, capsizing them. This process continued, spread-ing out and involving the whole tree. It grew like an avalanche, and it descended without warning upon the man and the fire, and the fire was blotted out! Where it had burned was a mantle of fresh and disordered snow.

The man was shocked. It was as though he had just heard his own sentence of death. For a moment he sat and stared at the spot where the fire had been. Then he grew very calm. Perhaps the old-timer on Sulfur Creek was right. If he had only had a trail mate, he would have been in no danger now. The trail mate could have built the fire. Well, it was up to him to build the fire over again, and this second time there must be no failure. Even if he succeeded, he would most likely lose some toes. His feet must be badly frozen by now, and there would be some time before the second fire was ready.

Such were his thoughts, but he did not sit and think them. He was busy all the time they were passing through his mind. He made a new foundation for a fire, this time in the open, where no treacherous tree could blot it out. Next he gathered dry grasses and tiny twigs from the high-water flotsam. He could not bring his fingers together to pull them out, but he was able to gather them by the handful. In this way he got many rotten twigs and bits of green moss that were undesirable, but it was the best he could do. He worked methodically, even collecting an armful of the larger branches to be used later when the fire gathered strength. And all the while the dog sat and watched him, a certain yearning wistfulness in its eyes, for it looked upon him as the fire provider, and the fire was slow in coming.

When all was ready, the man reached in his pocket for a second piece of birch bark. He knew the bark was there, and, though he could not feel it with his fingers, he could hear its crisp rustling as he fumbled for it. Try as he would, he could not clutch hold of it. And all the time, in his consciousness, was the knowledge that each instant his feet were freezing. This thought tended to put him in a panic, but he fought against it and kept calm. He pulled on his mittens with his teeth, and threshed his arms back and forth, beating his hands with all his might against his sides. He did this sitting down, and he stood up to do it; and all the while the dog sat in the snow, its wolf brush of a tail curled around warmly over its forefeet, its sharp wolf ears pricked forward intently as it watched the man. And the man, as he beat and threshed with his arms and hands, felt a great surge of envy as he regarded the creature that was warm and secure in its natural covering.

After a time he was aware of the first faraway signals of sensation in his beaten fingers. The faint tingling grew stronger till it evolved into a stinging ache that was excruciating, but which the man hailed with satisfaction. He stripped the mitten from his right hand and fetched forth the birch bark. The exposed fingers were quickly going numb again. Next he brought out his bunch of sulfur matches. But the tremendous cold had already driven the life out of his fingers. In his effort to separate one match from the others, the whole bunch fell in the snow. He tried to pick it out of the snow, but failed. The dead fingers could neither touch nor clutch. He was very careful. He drove the thought of his freezing feet, and nose, and cheeks, out of his mind, devoting his whole soul to the matches. He watched, using the sense of vision in place of that of touch, and when he saw his fingers on each side of the bunch, he closed them—that is, he willed to close them, for the wires were down, and the fingers did not obey. He pulled the mitten on the right hand, and beat it fiercely against his knee. Then, with both mittened hands, he scooped the bunch of matches, along with much snow, into his lap. Yet he was no better off.

After some manipulation he managed to get the bunch between the heels of his mittened hands. In this fashion he carried it to his mouth. The ice crackled and snapped when by a violent effort he opened his mouth. He drew the lower jaw in, curled the upper lip out of the way, and scraped the bunch with his upper teeth in order to separate a match. He succeeded in getting one, which he dropped on his lap. He was no better off. He could not pick it up. Then he devised a way. He picked it up in his teeth and scratched it on his leg. Twenty times he scratched before he succeeded in lighting it. As it flamed he held it with his teeth to the birch bark. But the burning brimstone went up his nostrils and into his lungs, causing him to cough spasmodically. The match fell into the snow and went out.

The old-timer on Sulfur Creek was right, he thought in the moment of controlled despair that ensued: after fifty below, a man should travel with a partner. He beat his hands, but failed in exciting any sensation. Suddenly he bared both hands, removing the mittens with his teeth. He caught the whole bunch between the heels of his hands. His arm muscles, not being frozen, enabled him to press the hand heels tightly against the matches. Then he scratched the bunch along his leg. It flared into flame, seventy sulfur matches at once! There was no wind to blow them out. He kept his head to one side to escape the strangling fumes, and held the blazing bunch to the birch bark. As he so held it, he became aware of sensation in his hand. His flesh was burning. He could smell it. Deep down below the surface he could feel it. The sensation developed into pain that grew acute. And still he endured it, holding the flame of the matches clumsily to the bark that would not light readily because his own burning hands were in the way, absorbing most of the flame.

At last, when he could endure no more, he jerked his hands apart. The blazing matches fell sizzling into the snow, but the birch bark was alight. He began laying dry grass and the tiniest twigs on the flame. He could not pick and choose, for he had to lift the fuel between the heels of his hands. Small pieces of rotten wood and green moss clung to the twigs, and he bit them off as well as he could with his teeth. He cherished the flame carefully and awkwardly. It meant life, and it must not perish. The withdrawal of blood from the surface of his body now made him begin to shiver, and he grew more awkward. A large piece of green moss fell squarely on the little fire. He tried to poke it out with his fingers, but his shivering frame made him poke too far, and he disrupted the nucleus of the little fire, the burning grasses and tiny twigs separating and scattering. He tried to poke them together again, but in spite of the tenseness of the effort, his shivering got away with him, and the twigs were hopelessly scattered. Each twig gushed a puff of smoke and went out. The fire provider had failed. As he looked apathetically about him, his eyes chanced on the dog, sitting across the ruins of the fire from him, in the snow, making restless, hunching movements, slightly lifting one forefoot and then the other, shifting its weight back and forth on them with wistful eagerness.

The sight of the dog put a wild idea into his head. He remembered the tale of the man, caught in a blizzard, who killed a steer and crawled inside the carcass, and so was saved. He would kill the dog and bury his hands in the warm body until the numbness went out of them. Then he could build another fire. He spoke to the dog, calling it to him; but in his voice was a strange note of fear that frightened the animal, who had never known the man to speak in such a way before. Something was the matter, and its suspicious nature sensed danger— it knew not what danger, but somewhere, somehow, in its brain arose an apprehension of the man. It flattened its ears down at the sound of the man's voice, and its restless, hunching movements and the liftings and shiftings of its forefeet became more pronounced; but it would not come to the man. He got on his hands and knees and crawled toward the dog. This unusual posture again excited suspicion, and the animal sidled mincingly away.

The man sat up in the snow for a moment and struggled for calmness.

Then he pulled on his mittens, by means of his teeth, and got up on his feet. He glanced down at first in order to assure himself that he was really standing up, for the absence of sensation in his feet left him unrelated to the earth. His erect position in itself started to drive the webs of suspicion from the dog's mind; and when he spoke peremptorily, with the sound of whiplashes in his voice, the dog rendered its customary allegiance and came to him. As it came within reaching distance, the man lost his control. His arms flashed out to the dog, and he experienced genuine surprise when he discovered that his hands could not clutch, that there was neither bend nor feeling in the fingers. He had forgotten for the moment that they were frozen and that they were freezing more and more. All this happened quickly, and before the animal could get away, he encircled its body with his arms. He sat down in the snow, and in this fashion held the dog, while it snarled and whined and struggled.

But it was all he could do, hold its body encircled in his arms and sit there. He realized that he could not kill the dog. There was no way to do it. With his helpless hands he could neither draw nor hold his sheath knife nor throttle the animal. He released it, and it plunged wildly away, its tail between its legs and still snarling. It halted forty feet away and surveyed him curiously, with ears sharply pricked forward. The man looked down at his hands in order to locate them, and found them hanging on the ends of his arms. It struck him as curious that one should have to use his eyes in order to find out where his hands were. He began threshing his arms back and forth, beating the mittened hands against his sides. He did this for five minutes, violently, and his heart pumped enough blood up to the surface to put a stop to his shivering. But no sensation was aroused in his hands. He had an impression that they hung like weights on the ends of his arms, but when he tried to run the impression down, he could not find it.

A certain fear of death, dull and oppressive, came to him. This fear quickly became poignant as he realized that it was no longer a mere matter of freezing his fingers and toes, or of losing his hands and feet, but that it was a matter of life and death, with the chances against him. This threw him into a panic, and he turned and ran up the creek bed along the old, dim trail. The dog joined in behind and kept up with him. He ran blindly, without intention, in fear such as he had never known in his life. Slowly, as he plowed and floundered through the snow, he began to see things again—the banks of the creek, the old timber jams, the leafless aspens, and the sky. The running made him feel better. He did not shiver. Maybe, if he ran on, his feet would thaw out; and, anyway, if he ran far enough, he would reach the camp and the boys. Without doubt he would lose some fingers and toes and some of his face; but the boys would take care of him, and save the rest of him when he got there. And, at the same time, there was another thought in his mind that said he would never get to the camp and the boys; that it was too many miles away, that the freezing had too great a start on him, and that he would soon be stiff and dead. This thought he kept in the background and refused to consider. Sometimes it pushed itself forward and demanded to be heard, but he thrust it back and strove to think of other things.

It struck him as curious that he could run at all on feet so frozen that he could not feel them when they struck the earth and took the weight of his body. He seemed to himself to skim along above the surface, and to have no connection with the earth. Somewhere he had once seen a winged Mercury,[5] and he wondered if Mercury felt as he felt when skimming over the earth.

His theory of running until he reached camp and the boys had one flaw in it: he lacked the endurance. Several times he stumbled, and finally he tottered, crumpled up, and fell. When he tried to rise, he failed. He must sit and rest, he decided, and next time he would merely walk and keep on going. As he sat and regained his breath, he noted that he was feeling quite warm and comfortable. He was not shivering, and it even seemed that a warm glow had come to his chest and trunk. And yet, when he touched his nose or cheeks, there was no sensation. Running would not thaw them out. Nor would it thaw out his hands and feet. Then the thought came to him that the frozen portions of his body must be extending. He tried to keep this thought down, to forget it, to think of something else; he was aware of the panicky feeling that it caused, and he was afraid of the panic. But the thought asserted itself, and persisted, until it produced a vision of his body totally frozen.

This was too much, and he made another wild run along the trail. Once he slowed down to a walk, but the thought of the freezing extending itself made him run again.

And all the time the dog ran with him, at his heels. When he fell

---

5. **Mercury:** the messenger of the gods in Roman mythology.

down a second time, it curled its tail over its forefeet and sat in front of him, facing him, curiously eager and intent. The warmth and security of the animal angered him, and he cursed it till it flattened down its ears appeasingly. This time the shivering came more quickly upon the man. He was losing in his battle with the frost. It was creeping into his body from all sides. The thought of it drove him on, but he ran no more than a hundred feet when he staggered and pitched headlong. It was his last panic. When he had recovered his breath and control, he sat up and entertained in his mind the conception of meeting death with dignity. However, the conception did not come to him in such terms. His idea of it was that he had been making a fool of himself, running around like a chicken with its head cut off—such was the simile that occurred to him. Well, he was bound to freeze anyway, and he might as well take it decently. With this new-found peace of mind came the first glimmerings of drowsiness. A good idea, he thought, to sleep off to death. It was like taking an anesthetic. Freezing was not so bad as people thought. There were lots worse ways to die.

He pictured the boys finding his body next day. Suddenly he found himself with them, coming along the trail and looking for himself. And, still with them, he came around a turn in the trail and found himself lying in the snow. He did not belong with himself any more, for even then he was out of himself, standing with the boys and looking at himself in the snow. It certainly was cold, was his thought. When he got back to the States, he could tell the folks what real cold was. He drifted on from this to a vision of the old-timer on Sulfur Creek. He could see him quite clearly, warm and comfortable, and smoking a pipe.

"You were right, old hoss; you were right," the man mumbled to the old-timer of Sulfur Creek.

Then the man drowsed off into what seemed to him the most comfortable and satisfying sleep he had ever known. The dog sat facing him and waiting. The brief day drew to a close in a long, slow twilight. There were no signs of a fire to be made, and, besides, never in the dog's experience had it known a man to sit like that in the snow and make no fire. As the twilight drew on, its eager yearning for the fire mastered it, and with a great lifting and shifting of forefeet, it whined softly, then flattened its ears down in anticipation of being chidden[6]

---

6. **chidden:** scolded.

by the man. But the man remained silent. Later, the dog whined loudly. And still later it crept close to the man and caught the scent of death. This made the animal bristle and back away. A little longer it delayed, howling under the stars that leaped and danced and shone brightly in the cold sky. Then it turned and trotted up the trail in the direction of the camp it knew, where were the other food providers and fire providers. ■

THE IMPACT OF THE STORY

Jack London believed that life was a struggle for survival, whether against nature or against other people. Based on your own experience, do you agree or disagree? Why or why not?

THE FACTS OF THE STORY

On your own paper, write answers to the following items. Answers may be one word, a phrase, or several sentences.

1. Why is the man making this journey?

2. At first, why doesn't the cold make an impression on the man?

3. What advice had the old-timer on Sulfur Creek given the man?

4. What serious accident does the man suffer?

5. Why is the story called "To Build a Fire"?

THE IDEAS IN THE STORY

Prepare to discuss the following ideas in class.

1. In "The Most Dangerous Game," General Zaroff explains why he has become bored with hunting animals. He says, "'No animal had a chance with me any more. . . . The animal had nothing but his legs and his instinct. Instinct is no match for reason.'" Early in "To Build a Fire," London says about the dog, "The animal was depressed by the tremendous cold. It knew that it was no time for traveling. Its instinct told it a truer tale than was told to the man by the man's judgment." London's story seems to suggest that the lack of animal instinct is a human frailty. In fact, London probably included the dog in the story so that he could make this observation about instinct and reason. Referring to specific passages in the story, tell how instinct becomes a more important quality than reason, or judgment. What do you think of this idea?

2. In this story, the man's weaknesses are chiefly physical. By referring to events in the story, explain how London shows that people are physically frail, or weak. Where does he show that the dog is equipped to survive where humans cannot?

3. London says that the man lacked imagination. He did not meditate upon ". . . his frailty as a creature of temperature, and upon man's frailty in general. . . ." Name some other nonphysical weaknesses that human beings may suffer from, and explain how they also can cause problems.

THE ART OF THE STORYTELLER

Plot

The plot of "To Build a Fire" is simple, yet it clearly illustrates the elements of plot explained in the discussion of "The Most Dangerous Game." Here the protagonist is the man. What is the antagonist—the force that opposes the protagonist? What problems does the protagonist have to overcome to get what he wants, in this case, to reach the camp on Henderson Creek?

You probably will agree that the story is full of suspense and that the suspense builds steadily to the **climax**—the moment of greatest emotional intensity, when we know how the conflict will turn out. In "The Most Dangerous Game," the climax comes with the last sentence, where we learn that Rainsford wins his struggle against Zaroff. The climax in "To Build a Fire" occurs earlier in the story. At what point do you strongly suspect that the man will not survive? At what moment do you know for certain that he does not survive?

The story moves on from the climax to the conclusion. What does the storyteller say after you know for certain that the man is dead? What were your feelings as you read the conclusion of the story?

Foreshadowing

Suspense is often increased when the writer hints at what will happen later in the story. This use of hints is called **foreshadowing**. For example, the final sentences in the third paragraph hint that we are going to find out something about survival in extreme cold, something this man does not understand: "Fifty degrees below zero was to him just precisely fifty degrees below zero. That there should be anything more to it than that was a thought that never entered his head." Indeed, as you know, later events in the story show how dangerous such extreme cold really is.

How does each of the following statements foreshadow events that occur later in the story?

1. ". . . there seemed an intangible pall over the face of things, a subtle gloom. . . ."

2. "And to get his feet wet in such a temperature meant trouble and danger."

3. "But the dog knew . . . that it was not good to walk abroad in such fearful cold."

Look over the opening pages of "The Most Dangerous Game." Find an example of foreshadowing there.

Characters and Characterization

One of a writer's jobs is to make the personalities of the characters clear and believable to the reader. The process by which a writer does this is called **characterization**. The writer may describe a character's actions or physical appearance, reveal the character's thoughts, reveal what others think about the character, or comment directly on the character.

While one important element of "To Build a Fire" is the plot, or what happens to the man, consider how the story would be different if the character of the man were not as London develops him.

Find instances in the story that contribute to your understanding of the man's personality. (You may not be able to find all of the methods of characterization mentioned above. For example, London never tells us what the man looks like beyond the fact that he has a beard.) What kind of person do you think he is? Do you think London wants readers to sympathize with the man's plight?

THE VOCABULARY IN THE STORY

The kinds of words a writer chooses determine a story's descriptive power. While the dominant impression in "To Build a Fire" is of a bleak, cold landscape, London uses lively verbs to depict the story's action, for example, *crackled, thrust, gushed, plunged, plowed,* and *floundered.*

In the following paragraph, fill in the blanks with appropriate, vivid action verbs. Compare your answers with your classmates'.

A light rain (1) _____ against the windows to the house while a cold wind (2) _____ through the nearby tree branches. The dog (3) _____ anxiously on the narrow porch, just barely protected by the overhanging eave. Every now and then the wind (4) _____ and (5) _____ the rain onto the shivering animal. Soon, the people would return, and he would (6) _____ peacefully before the fire.

COMPOSITION: Developing a Paragraph

A well-constructed paragraph often (but not always) begins with a **topic sentence**—that is, a main idea about the topic to be discussed. The writer develops the paragraph by giving information to support the idea in the topic sentence. Sometimes, the paragraph, especially if it is a long one, ends with a concluding statement called a **clincher sentence**. This concluding statement may either restate the idea in the topic sentence in different words or present a new idea about the topic based on the supporting information in the paragraph.

Using details from "To Build a Fire," write a paragraph (about 100 words) developing one of the following topic sentences.

1. In "To Build a Fire," Jack London uses details that make us almost *feel* the effects of the severe cold.

2. If the man in "To Build a Fire" had had more imagination, he would not have frozen to death.

3. A wolf dog is better equipped than a human being is to survive at seventy-five degrees below zero.

Prewriting
Search through the story for as many details (sensory details, facts, or examples) as you can find that support the topic sentence you

chose. Compile them into a list, and arrange them in a logical order—by time or by order of importance (from least important to most important, or vice versa).

Writing

Using the details from your list that will most strongly support your topic sentence, develop a first draft of your paragraph. If you decide to include a clincher sentence, let it flow naturally from the ideas you have assembled in the paragraph.

Evaluating and Revising

Read your draft, making sure each of your details from the story directly relates to the main idea in your topic sentence. Review your prewriting list to see whether you have left out any details that might better support your topic sentence. Then rearrange, replace, or add words, phrases, or examples as needed.

ABOUT THE AUTHOR

 Jack London (1876–1916) was born in poverty in San Francisco and grew up having more experience with the rough life of the waterfront than with the inside of a classroom. However, his great love of reading made up for his lack of schooling. Adventurer, vagabond, sailor, and prospector for gold in the Klondike area of the Yukon Territory, London acquired fame and fortune as a writer of fiction. Although his participation in the Klondike gold rush yielded him no gold, it did give him something very valuable—material for the stories that made him, at one time, America's best-paid and most popular writer. Two of his novels, *The Call of the Wild* and *White Fang,* are among the greatest dog stories ever written.

■ THE BIRDS

Daphne du Maurier

Suppose all the birds in the world decided without warning
to attack human beings, with the apparent intention of
destroying the human race. How would you protect yourself?
Which birds would you fear most? Do you think the birds
could succeed?

On December the third the wind changed overnight and it
was winter. Until then the autumn had been mellow, soft.
The leaves had lingered on the trees, golden-red, and the
hedgerows were still green. The earth was rich where the plow had
turned it.

Nat Hocken, because of a wartime disability, had a pension and did
not work full time at the farm. He worked three days a week, and they
gave him the lighter jobs: hedging, thatching, repairs to the farm
buildings.

Although he was married, with children, his was a solitary disposition; he liked best to work alone. It pleased him when he was given a
bank to build up, or a gate to mend at the far end of the peninsula,
where the sea surrounded the farmland on either side. Then, at midday,
he would pause and eat the pasty[1] that his wife had baked for him,
and, sitting on the cliff's edge, would watch the birds. Autumn was best
for this, better than spring. In spring the birds flew inland, purpose-
ful, intent; they knew where they were bound; the rhythm and ritual
of their life brooked no delay. In autumn those that had not migrated
overseas but remained to pass the winter were caught up in the same
driving urge, but because migration was denied them, followed a
pattern of their own. Great flocks of them came to the peninsula, restless, uneasy, spending themselves in motion; now wheeling, circling in
the sky, now settling to feed on the rich, new-turned soil; but even
when they fed, it was as though they did so without hunger, without
desire. Restlessness drove them to the skies again.

Black and white, jackdaw and gull, mingled in strange partnership,
seeking some sort of liberation, never satisfied, never still. Flocks of

---

1. **pasty:** a small meat pie.

starlings, rustling like silk, flew to fresh pasture, driven by the same necessity of movement, and the smaller birds, the finches and the larks, scattered from tree to hedge as if compelled.

Nat watched them, and he watched the sea birds too. Down in the bay they waited for the tide. They had more patience. Oyster catchers, redshank, sanderling, and curlew watched by the water's edge; as the slow sea sucked at the shore and then withdrew, leaving the strip of seaweed bare and the shingle[2] churned, the sea birds raced and ran upon the beaches. Then that same impulse to flight seized upon them too. Crying, whistling, calling, they skimmed the placid sea and left the shore. Make haste, make speed, hurry and begone; yet where, and to what purpose? The restless urge of autumn, unsatisfying, sad, had put a spell upon them and they must flock, and wheel, and cry; they must spill themselves of motion before winter came.

"Perhaps," thought Nat, munching his pasty by the cliff's edge, "a message comes to the birds in autumn, like a warning. Winter is coming. Many of them perish. And like people who, apprehensive of death before their time, drive themselves to work or folly, the birds do likewise."

The birds had been more restless than ever this fall of the year, the agitation more marked because the days were still. As the tractor traced its path up and down the western hills, the figure of the farmer silhouetted on the driving seat, the whole machine and the man upon it, would be lost momentarily in the great cloud of wheeling, crying birds. There were many more than usual; Nat was sure of this. Always, in autumn, they followed the plow, but not in great flocks like these, nor with such clamor.

Nat remarked upon it when hedging was finished for the day. "Yes," said the farmer, "there are more birds about than usual; I've noticed it too. And daring, some of them, taking no notice of the tractor. One or two gulls came so close to my head this afternoon I thought they'd knock my cap off! As it was, I could scarcely see what I was doing, when they were overhead and I had the sun in my eyes. I have a notion the weather will change. It will be a hard winter. That's why the birds are restless."

Nat, tramping home across the fields and down the lane to his cottage, saw the birds still flocking over the western hills, in the last

---

2. **shingle:** a pebbly beach.

glow of the sun. No wind, and the gray sea calm and full. Campion in bloom yet in the hedges, and the air mild. The farmer was right, though, and it was that night the weather turned. Nat's bedroom faced east. He woke just after two and heard the wind in the chimney. Not the storm and bluster of a sou'westerly gale, bringing the rain, but east wind, cold and dry. It sounded hollow in the chimney, and a loose slate rattled on the roof. Nat listened, and he could hear the sea roaring in the bay. Even the air in the small bedroom had turned chill: a draft came under the skirting of the door, blowing upon the bed. Nat drew the blanket round him, leant closer to the back of his sleeping wife, and stayed wakeful, watchful, aware of misgiving without cause.

Then he heard the tapping on the window. There was no creeper on the cottage walls to break loose and scratch upon the pane. He listened, and the tapping continued until, irritated by the sound, Nat got out of bed and went to the window. He opened it, and as he did so something brushed his hand, jabbing at his knuckles, grazing the skin. Then he saw the flutter of the wings and it was gone, over the roof, behind the cottage.

It was a bird; what kind of bird he could not tell. The wind must have driven it to shelter on the sill.

He shut the window and went back to bed, but, feeling his knuckles wet, put his mouth to the scratch. The bird had drawn blood. Frightened, he supposed, and bewildered, the bird, seeking shelter, had stabbed at him in the darkness. Once more he settled himself to sleep.

Presently the tapping came again, this time more forceful, more insistent, and now his wife woke at the sound and, turning in the bed, said to him, "See to the window, Nat, it's rattling."

"I've already seen to it," he told her; "there's some bird there trying to get in. Can't you hear the wind? It's blowing from the east, driving the birds to shelter."

"Send them away," she said, "I can't sleep with that noise."

He went to the window for the second time, and now when he opened it, there was not one bird upon the sill but half a dozen; they flew straight into his face, attacking him.

He shouted, striking out at them with his arms, scattering them; like the first one, they flew over the roof and disappeared. Quickly he let the window fall and latched it.

"Did you hear that?" he said. "They went for me. Tried to peck my eyes." He stood by the window, peering into the darkness, and could see nothing. His wife, heavy with sleep, murmured from the bed.

"I'm not making it up," he said, angry at her suggestion. "I tell you the birds were on the sill, trying to get into the room."

Suddenly a frightened cry came from the room across the passage where the children slept.

"It's Jill," said his wife, roused at the sound, sitting up in bed. "Go to her, see what's the matter."

Nat lit the candle, but when he opened the bedroom door to cross the passage the draft blew out the flame.

There came a second cry of terror, this time from both children, and stumbling into their room, he felt the beating of wings about him in the darkness. The window was wide open. Through it came the birds, hitting first the ceiling and the walls, then swerving in midflight, turning to the children in their beds.

"It's all right, I'm here," shouted Nat, and the children flung themselves, screaming, upon him, while in the darkness the birds rose and dived and came for him again.

"What is it, Nat, what's happened?" his wife called from the further bedroom, and swiftly he pushed the children through the door to the passage and shut it upon them, so that he was alone now in their bedroom with the birds.

He seized a blanket from the nearest bed and, using it as a weapon, flung it to right and left about him in the air. He felt the thud of bodies, heard the fluttering of wings, but they were not yet defeated, for again and again they returned to the assault, jabbing his hands, his head, the little stabbing beaks sharp as pointed forks. The blanket became a weapon of defense; he wound it about his head, and then in greater darkness beat at the birds with his bare hands. He dared not stumble to the door and open it, lest in doing so the birds should follow him.

How long he fought with them in the darkness he could not tell, but at last the beating of the wings about him lessened and then withdrew, and through the density of the blanket he was aware of light. He waited, listened; there was no sound except the fretful crying of one of the children from the bedroom beyond. The fluttering, the whirring of the wings had ceased.

He took the blanket from his head and stared about him. The cold gray morning light exposed the room. Dawn and the open window had called the living birds; the dead lay on the floor. Nat gazed at the little corpses, shocked and horrified. They were all small birds, none of any size; there must have been fifty of them lying there upon the floor. There were robins, finches, sparrows, blue tits, larks, and bramblings, birds that by nature's law kept to their own flock and their own territory, and now, joining one with another in their urge for battle, had destroyed themselves against the bedroom walls, or in the strife had been destroyed by him. Some had lost feathers in the fight; others had blood, his blood, upon their beaks.

Sickened, Nat went to the window and stared out across his patch of garden to the fields.

It was bitter cold, and the ground had all the hard, black look of frost. Not white frost, to shine in the morning sun, but the black frost that the east wind brings. The sea, fiercer now with the turning tide, white-capped and steep, broke harshly in the bay. Of the birds there was no sign. Not a sparrow chattered in the hedge beyond the gate, no early missel thrush or blackbird pecked on the grass for worms. There was no sound at all but the east wind and the sea.

Nat shut the window and the door of the small bedroom, and went back across the passage to his own. His wife sat up in bed, one child asleep beside her, the smaller in her arms, his face bandaged. The curtains were tightly drawn across the window, the candles lit. Her face looked garish in the yellow light. She shook her head for silence.

"He's sleeping now," she whispered, "but only just. Something must have cut him, there was blood at the corner of his eyes. Jill said it was the birds. She said she woke up, and the birds were in the room."

His wife looked up at Nat, searching his face for confirmation. She looked terrified, bewildered, and he did not want her to know that he was also shaken, dazed almost, by the events of the past few hours.

"There are birds in there," he said, "dead birds, nearly fifty of them. Robins, wrens, all the little birds from hereabouts. It's as though a madness seized them, with the east wind." He sat down on the bed beside his wife, and held her hand. "It's the weather," he said, "it must be that, it's the hard weather. They aren't the birds, maybe, from here around. They've been driven down from upcountry."

"But, Nat," whispered his wife, "It's only this night that the weather turned. There's been no snow to drive them. And they can't be hungry yet. There's food for them out there in the fields."

"It's the weather," repeated Nat. "I tell you, it's the weather."

His face, too, was drawn and tired, like hers. They stared at one another for a while without speaking.

"I'll go downstairs and make a cup of tea," he said.

The sight of the kitchen reassured him. The cups and saucers, neatly stacked upon the dresser, the table and chairs, his wife's roll of knitting on her basket chair, the children's toys in a corner cupboard.

He knelt down, raked out the old embers, and relit the fire. The glowing sticks brought normality, the steaming kettle and the brown teapot comfort and security. He drank his tea, carried a cup up to his wife. Then he washed in the scullery, and, putting on his boots, opened the back door.

The sky was hard and leaden, and the brown hills that had gleamed in the sun the day before looked dark and bare. The east wind, like a razor, stripped the trees, and the leaves, crackling and dry, shivered and scattered with the wind's blast. Nat stubbed the earth with his boot. It was frozen hard. He had never known a change so swift and sudden. Black winter had descended in a single night.

The children were awake now. Jill was chattering upstairs and young Johnny crying once again. Nat heard his wife's voice, soothing, comforting. Presently they came down. He had breakfast ready for them, and the routine of the day began.

"Did you drive away the birds?" asked Jill, restored to calm because of the kitchen fire, because of day, because of breakfast.

"Yes, they've all gone now," said Nat. "It was the east wind brought them in. They were frightened and lost, they wanted shelter."

"They tried to peck us," said Jill. "They went for Johnny's eyes."

"Fright made them do that," said Nat. "They didn't know where they were in the dark bedroom."

"I hope they won't come again," said Jill. "Perhaps if we put bread for them outside the window they will eat that and fly away."

She finished her breakfast and then went for her coat and hood, her schoolbooks and her satchel. Nat said nothing, but his wife looked at him across the table. A silent message passed between them.

"I'll walk with her to the bus," he said. "I don't go to the farm today."

And while the child was washing in the scullery he said to his wife, "Keep all the windows closed, and the doors too. Just to be on the safe side. I'll go to the farm. Find out if they heard anything in the night." Then he walked with his small daughter up the lane. She seemed to have forgotten her experience of the night before. She danced ahead of him, chasing the leaves, her face whipped with the cold and rosy under the pixie hood.

"Is it going to snow, Dad?" she said. "It's cold enough."

He glanced up at the bleak sky, felt the wind tear at his shoulders.

"No," he said, "it's not going to snow. This is a black winter, not a white one."

All the while he searched the hedgerows for the birds, glanced over the top of them to the fields beyond, looked to the small wood above the farm where the rooks and jackdaws gathered. He saw none.

The other children waited by the bus stop, muffled, hooded, like Jill, the faces white and pinched with cold.

Jill ran to them, waving. "My dad says it won't snow," she called, "it's going to be a black winter."

She said nothing of the birds. She began to push and struggle with another little girl. The bus came ambling up the hill. Nat saw her onto it, then turned and walked back towards the farm. It was not his day for work, but he wanted to satisfy himself that all was well. Jim, the cowman, was clattering in the yard.

"Boss around?" asked Nat.

"Gone to market," said Jim. "It's Tuesday, isn't it?"

He clumped off round the corner of a shed. He had no time for Nat. Nat was said to be superior. Read books, and the like. Nat had forgotten it was Tuesday. This showed how the events of the preceding night had shaken him. He went to the back door of the farmhouse and heard Mrs. Trigg singing in the kitchen, the wireless[3] making a background to her song.

"Are you there, missus?" called out Nat.

She came to the door, beaming, broad, a good-tempered woman.

"Hullo, Mr. Hocken," she said. "Can you tell me where this cold is coming from? Is it Russia? I've never seen such a change. And it's going on, the wireless says. Something to do with the Arctic Circle."

"We didn't turn on the wireless this morning," said Nat. "Fact is, we had trouble in the night."

"Kiddies poorly?"

"No . . ." He hardly knew how to explain it. Now, in daylight, the battle of the birds would sound absurd.

---

3. **wireless:** a radio.

He tried to tell Mrs. Trigg what had happened, but he could see from her eyes that she thought his story was the result of a nightmare.

"Sure they were real birds," she said, smiling, "with proper feathers and all? Not the funny-shaped kind that the men see after closing hours on a Saturday night?"

"Mrs. Trigg," he said, "there are fifty dead birds, robins, wrens, and such, lying low on the floor of the children's bedroom. They went for me; they tried to go for young Johnny's eyes."

Mrs. Trigg stared at him doubtfully.

"Well there, now," she answered, "I suppose the weather brought them. Once in the bedroom, they wouldn't know where they were to. Foreign birds maybe, from that Arctic Circle."

"No," said Nat, "they were the birds you see about here every day."

"Funny thing," said Mrs. Trigg, "no explaining it, really. You ought to write up and ask the *Guardian*. They'd have some answer for it. Well, I must be getting on."

She nodded, smiled, and went back into the kitchen.

Nat, dissatisfied, turned to the farm gate. Had it not been for those corpses on the bedroom floor, which he must now collect and bury somewhere, he would have considered the tale exaggeration too.

Jim was standing by the gate.

"Had any trouble with the birds?" asked Nat.

"Birds? What birds?"

"We got them up our place last night. Scores of them, came in the children's bedroom. Quite savage they were."

"Oh?" It took time for anything to penetrate Jim's head. "Never heard of birds acting savage," he said at length. "They get tame, like, sometimes. I've seen them come to the windows for crumbs."

"These birds last night weren't tame."

"No? Cold, maybe. Hungry. You put out some crumbs."

Jim was no more interested than Mrs. Trigg had been. It was, Nat thought, like air raids in the war.[4] No one down this end of the country knew what the Plymouth folk had seen and suffered. You had to endure something yourself before it touched you. He walked back along the lane and crossed the stile to his cottage. He found his wife in the kitchen with young Johnny.

"See anyone?" she asked.

---

4. **the war:** World War II.

"Mrs. Trigg and Jim," he answered. "I don't think they believed me. Anyway, nothing wrong up there."

"You might take the birds away," she said. "I daren't go into the room to make the beds until you do. I'm scared."

"Nothing to scare you now," said Nat. "They're dead, aren't they?"

He went up with a sack and dropped the stiff bodies into it, one by one. Yes, there were fifty of them, all told. Just the ordinary, common birds of the hedgerow, nothing as large even as a thrush. It must have been fright that made them act the way they did. Blue tits, wrens— it was incredible to think of the power of their small beaks jabbing at his face and hands the night before. He took the sack out into the garden and was faced now with a fresh problem. The ground was too hard to dig. It was frozen solid, yet no snow had fallen, nothing had happened in the past hours but the coming of the east wind. It was unnatural, queer. The weather prophets must be right. The change was something connected with the Arctic Circle.

The wind seemed to cut him to the bone as he stood there uncertainly, holding the sack. He could see the white-capped seas breaking down under the bay. He decided to take the birds to the shore and bury them.

When he reached the beach below the headland he could scarcely stand, the force of the east wind was so strong. It hurt to draw breath, and his bare hands were blue. Never had he known such cold, not in all the bad winters he could remember. It was low tide. He crunched his way over the shingle to the softer sand and then, his back to the wind, ground a pit in the sand with his heel. He meant to drop the birds into it, but as he opened up the sack the force of the wind carried them, lifted them, as though in flight again, and they were blown away from him along the beach, tossed like feathers, spread and scattered, the bodies of the fifty frozen birds. There was something ugly in the sight. He did not like it. The dead birds were swept away from him by the wind.

"The tide will take them when it turns," he said to himself.

He looked out to sea and watched the crested breakers, combing green. They rose stiffly, curled, and broke again, and because it was ebb tide the roar was distant, more remote, lacking the sound and thunder of the flood.

Then he saw them. The gulls. Out there, riding the seas.

What he had thought at first to be the white caps of the waves were

gulls. Hundreds, thousands, tens of thousands . . . They rose and fell
in the trough of the seas, heads to the wind, like a mighty fleet at
anchor, waiting on the tide. To eastward, and to the west, the gulls were
there. They stretched as far as his eye could reach, in close formation,
line upon line. Had the sea been still, they would have covered the bay
like a white cloud, head to head, body packed to body. Only the east
wind, whipping the sea to breakers, hid them from the shore.

Nat turned and, leaving the beach, climbed the steep path home.
Someone should know of this. Someone should be told. Something
was happening, because of the east wind and the weather, that he did
not understand. He wondered if he should go to the call box by the
bus stop and ring up the police. Yet what could they do? What could
anyone do? Tens of thousands of gulls riding the sea there in the bay
because of storm, because of hunger. The police would think him mad,
or drunk, or take the statement from him with great calm. "Thank you.
Yes, the matter has already been reported. The hard weather is driving
the birds inland in great numbers." Nat looked about him. Still no sign
of any other bird. Perhaps the cold had sent them all from upcountry?
As he drew near to the cottage his wife came to meet him at the door.
She called to him, excited. "Nat," she said, "it's on the wireless. They've
just read out a special news bulletin. I've written it down."

"What's on the wireless?" he said.

"About the birds," she said. "It's not only here, it's everywhere. In
London, all over the country. Something has happened to the birds."

Together they went into the kitchen. He read the piece of paper lying
on the table.

"Statement from the Home Office at 11 A.M. today. Reports from all
over the country are coming in hourly about the vast quantity of birds
flocking above towns, villages, and outlying districts, causing obstruc-
tion and damage and even attacking individuals. It is thought that the
Arctic air stream, at present covering the British Isles, is causing birds
to migrate south in immense numbers, and that intense hunger may
drive these birds to attack human beings. Householders are warned to
see to their windows, doors, and chimneys, and to take reasonable precautions for the safety of their children. A further statement will be
issued later."

A kind of excitement seized Nat; he looked at his wife in triumph.

"There you are," he said. "Let's hope they'll hear that at the farm.
Mrs. Trigg will know it wasn't any story. It's true. All over the country.

I've been telling myself all morning there's something wrong. And just now, down on the beach, I looked out to sea and there are gulls, thousands of them, tens of thousands—you couldn't put a pin between their heads—and they're all out there, riding on the sea, waiting."

"What are they waiting for, Nat?" she asked.

He stared at her, then looked down again at the piece of paper.

"I don't know," he said slowly. "It says here the birds are hungry."

He went over to the drawer where he kept his hammer and tools.

"What are you going to do, Nat?"

"See to the windows and the chimneys too, like they tell you."

"You think they would break in, with the windows shut? Those sparrows and robins and such? Why, how could they?"

He did not answer. He was not thinking of the robins and the sparrows. He was thinking of the gulls. . . .

He went upstairs and worked there the rest of the morning, boarding the windows of the bedrooms, filling up the chimney bases. Good job it was his free day and he was not working at the farm. It reminded him of the old days, at the beginning of the war. He was not married then, and he had made all the blackout boards for his mother's house in Plymouth. Made the shelter too. Not that it had been of any use when the moment came. He wondered if they would take these precautions up at the farm. He doubted it. Too easy going, Harry Trigg and his missus. Maybe they'd laugh at the whole thing. Go off to a dance or a whist drive.[5]

"Dinner's ready." She called him, from the kitchen.

"All right. Coming down."

He was pleased with his handiwork. The frames fitted nicely over the little panes and at the bases of the chimneys.

When dinner was over and his wife was washing up, Nat switched on the one o'clock news. The same announcement was repeated, the one which she had taken down during the morning, but the news bulletin enlarged upon it. "The flocks of birds have caused dislocation in all areas," read the announcer, "and in London the sky was so dense at ten o'clock this morning that it seemed as if the city was covered by a vast black cloud.

"The birds settled on rooftops, on window ledges, and on chimneys. The species included blackbird, thrush, the common house sparrow,

---

5. **whist drive:** a marathon card game.

and, as might be expected in the metropolis, a vast quantity of pigeons and starlings, and that frequenter of the London river, the black-headed gull. The sight has been so unusual that traffic came to a standstill in many thoroughfares, work was abandoned in shops and offices, and the streets and pavements were crowded with people standing about to watch the birds."

Various incidents were recounted, the suspected reason of cold and hunger stated again, and warnings to householders repeated. The announcer's voice was smooth and suave. Nat had the impression that this man, in particular, treated the whole business as he would an elaborate joke. There would be others like him, hundreds of them, who did not know what it was to struggle in darkness with a flock of birds. There would be parties tonight in London, like the ones they gave on election nights. People standing about, shouting and laughing, getting drunk. "Come and watch the birds!"

Nat switched off the wireless. He got up and started work on the kitchen windows. His wife watched him, young Johnny at her heels.

"What, boards for down here too?" she said. "Why, I'll have to light up before three o'clock. I see no call for boards down here."

"Better be sure than sorry," answered Nat. "I'm not going to take any chances."

"What they ought to do," she said, "is to call the Army out and shoot the birds. That would soon scare them off."

"Let them try," said Nat. "How'd they set about it?"

"They have the Army to the docks," she answered, "when the dockers strike. The soldiers go down and unload the ships."

"Yes," said Nat, "and the population of London is eight million or more. Think of all the buildings, all the flats and houses. Do you think they've enough soldiers to go round shooting birds from every roof?"

"I don't know. But something should be done. They ought to do something."

Nat thought to himself that "they" were no doubt considering the problem at that very moment, but whatever "they" decided to do in London and the big cities would not help the people here, three hundred miles away. Each householder must look after his own.

"How are we off for food?" he said.

"Now, Nat, whatever next?"

"Never mind. What have you got in the larder?"

"It's shopping day tomorrow, you know that. I don't keep uncooked food hanging about, it goes off. Butcher doesn't call till the day after. But I can bring back something when I go in tomorrow."

Nat did not want to scare her. He thought it possible that she might not go to town tomorrow. He looked in the larder for himself, and in the cupboard where she kept her tins. They would do for a couple of days. Bread was low.

"What about the baker?"

"He comes tomorrow too."

He saw she had flour. If the baker did not call she had enough to bake one loaf.

"We'd be better off in old days," he said, "when the women baked twice a week, and had pilchards[6] salted, and there was food for a family to last a siege, if need be."

"I've tried the children with tinned fish, they don't like it," she said.

Nat went on hammering the boards across the kitchen windows. Candles. They were low in candles too. That must be another thing she meant to buy tomorrow. Well, it could not be helped. They must go early to bed tonight. That was, if . . .

He got up and went out of the back door and stood in the garden, looking down towards the sea. There had been no sun all day, and now, at barely three o'clock, a kind of darkness had already come, the sky sullen, heavy, colorless like salt. He could hear the vicious sea drumming on the rocks. He walked down the path, halfway to the beach. And then he stopped. He could see the tide had turned. The rock that had shown in midmorning was now covered, but it was not the sea that held his eyes. The gulls had risen. They were circling, hundreds of them, thousands of them, lifting their wings against the wind. It was the gulls that made the darkening of the sky. And they were silent. They made not a sound. They just went on soaring and circling, rising, falling, trying their strength against the wind.

Nat turned. He ran up the path, back to the cottage.

"I'm going for Jill," he said. "I'll wait for her at the bus stop."

"What's the matter?" asked his wife. "You've gone quite white."

"Keep Johnny inside," he said. "Keep the door shut. Light up now, and draw the curtains."

---

6. **pilchards:** a kind of fish.

"It's only just gone three," she said.

"Never mind. Do what I tell you."

He looked inside the toolshed outside the back door. Nothing there of much use. A spade was too heavy, and a fork no good. He took the hoe. It was the only possible tool, and light enough to carry.

He started walking up the lane to the bus stop, and now and again glanced back over his shoulder.

The gulls had risen higher now; their circles were broader, wider; they were spreading out in huge formation across the sky.

He hurried on; although he knew the bus would not come to the top of the hill before four o'clock, he had to hurry. He passed no one on the way. He was glad of this. No time to stop and chatter.

At the top of the hill he waited. He was much too soon. There was half an hour still to go. The east wind came whipping across the fields from the higher ground. He stamped his feet and blew upon his hands. In the distance he could see the clay hills, white and clean, against the heavy pallor of the sky. Something black rose from behind them, like a smudge at first, then widening, becoming deeper, and the smudge became a cloud, and the cloud divided again into five other clouds, spreading north, east, south, and west, and they were not clouds at all; they were birds. He watched them travel across the sky, and as one section passed overhead, within two or three hundred feet of him, he knew, from their speed, they were bound inland, upcountry; they had no business with the people here on the peninsula. They were rooks, crows, jackdaws, magpies, jays, all birds that usually preyed upon the smaller species; but this afternoon they were bound on some other mission.

"They've been given the towns," thought Nat; "they know what they have to do. We don't matter so much here. The gulls will serve for us. The others go to the towns."

He went to the call box, stepped inside, and lifted the receiver. The exchange would do. They would pass the message on.

"I'm speaking from Highway," he said, "by the bus stop. I want to report large formations of birds traveling upcountry. The gulls are also forming in the bay."

"All right," answered the voice, laconic, weary.

"You'll be sure and pass this message on to the proper quarter?"

"Yes . . . yes . . ." Impatient now, fed-up. The buzzing note resumed.

"She's another," thought Nat, "she doesn't care. Maybe she's had to answer calls all day. She hopes to go to the pictures tonight. She'll squeeze some fellow's hand, and point up at the sky, and say 'Look at all them birds!' She doesn't care."

The bus came lumbering up the hill. Jill climbed out, and three or four other children. The bus went on towards the town.

"What's the hoe for, Dad?"

They crowded around him, laughing, pointing.

"I just brought it along," he said. "Come on now, let's get home. It's cold, no hanging about. Here, you. I'll watch you across the fields, see how fast you can run."

He was speaking to Jill's companions, who came from different families, living in the council houses.[7] A shortcut would take them to the cottages.

"We want to play a bit in the lane," said one of them.

"No, you don't. You go off home or I'll tell your mammy."

They whispered to one another, round-eyed, then scuttled off across the fields. Jill stared at her father, her mouth sullen.

"We always play in the lane," she said.

"Not tonight, you don't," he said. "Come on now, no dawdling."

He could see the gulls now, circling the fields, coming in towards the land. Still silent. Still no sound.

"Look, Dad, look over there, look at all the gulls."

"Yes. Hurry, now."

"Where are they flying to? Where are they going?"

"Upcountry, I dare say. Where it's warmer."

He seized her hand and dragged her after him along the lane.

"Don't go so fast. I can't keep up."

The gulls were copying the rooks and crows. They were spreading out in formation across the sky. They headed, in bands of thousands, to the four compass points.

"Dad, what is it? What are the gulls doing?"

They were not intent upon their flight, as the crows, as the jackdaws had been. They still circled overhead. Nor did they fly so high. It was as though they waited upon some signal. As though some decision had yet to be given. The order was not clear.

"Do you want me to carry you, Jill? Here, come pick-a-back."

This way he might put on speed; but he was wrong. Jill was heavy.

---

7. **council houses:** public housing.

She kept slipping. And she was crying too. His sense of urgency, of fear, had communicated itself to the child.

"I wish the gulls would go away. I don't like them. They're coming closer to the lane."

He put her down again. He started running, swinging Jill after him. As they went past the farm turning, he saw the farmer backing his car out of the garage. Nat called to him.

"Can you give us a lift?" he said.

"What's that?"

Mr. Trigg turned in the driving seat and stared at them. Then a smile came to his cheerful, rubicund face.

"It looks as though we're in for some fun," he said. "Have you seen the gulls? Jim and I are going to take a crack at them. Everyone's gone bird-crazy, talking of nothing else. I hear you were troubled in the night. Want a gun?"

Nat shook his head.

The small car was packed. There was just room for Jill, if she crouched on top of petrol tins on the back seat.

"I don't want a gun," said Nat, "but I'd be obliged if you'd run Jill home. She's scared of the birds."

He spoke briefly. He did not want to talk in front of Jill.

"OK," said the farmer, "I'll take her home. Why don't you stop behind and join the shooting match? We'll make the feathers fly."

Jill climbed in, and, turning the car, the driver sped up the lane. Nat followed after. Trigg must be crazy. What use was a gun against a sky of birds?

Now Nat was not responsible for Jill, he had time to look about him. The birds were circling still above the fields. Mostly herring gull, but the black-backed gull amongst them. Usually they kept apart. Now they were united. Some bond had brought them together. It was the black-backed gull that attacked the smaller birds, and even newborn lambs, so he'd heard. He'd never seen it done. He remembered this now, though, looking above him in the sky. They were coming in toward the farm. They were circling lower in the sky, and the black-backed gulls were to the front, the black-backed gulls were leading. The farm, then, was their target. They were making for the farm.

Nat increased his pace towards his own cottage. He saw the farmer's car turn and come back along the lane. It drew up beside him with a jerk.

"The kid has run inside," said the farmer. "Your wife was watching for her. Well, what do you make of it? They're saying in town the Russians have done it. The Russians have poisoned the birds."

"How could they do that?" asked Nat.

"Don't ask me. You know how stories get around. Will you join my shooting match?"

"No, I'll get along home. The wife will be worried else."

"My missus says if you could eat gull there'd be some sense in it," said Trigg, "we'd have roast gull, baked gull, and pickle 'em into the bargain. You wait until I let off a few barrels into the brutes. That'll scare 'em."

"Have you boarded your windows?" asked Nat.

"No. Lot of nonsense. They like to scare you on the wireless. I've had more to do today than to go round boarding up my windows."

"I'd board them now, if I were you."

"Garn. You're windy.[8] Like to come to our place to sleep?"

"No, thanks all the same."

"All right. See you in the morning. Give you a gull breakfast."

The farmer grinned and turned his car to the farm entrance.

Nat hurried on. Past the little wood, past the old barn, and then across the stile to the remaining field.

As he jumped the stile he heard the whir of wings. A black-backed gull dived down at him from the sky, missed, swerved in flight, and rose to dive again. In a moment it was joined by others, six, seven, a dozen, black-backed and herring mixed. Nat dropped his hoe. The hoe was useless. Covering his head with his arms, he ran toward the cottage. They kept coming at him from the air, silent save for the beating wings. The terrible, fluttering wings. He could feel the blood on his hands, his wrists, his neck. Each stab of a swooping beak tore his flesh. If only he could keep them from his eyes. Nothing else mattered. He must keep them from his eyes. They had not learnt yet how to cling to a shoulder, how to rip clothing, how to dive in mass upon the head, upon the body. But with each dive, with each attack, they became bolder. And they had no thought for themselves. When they dived low and missed, they crashed bruised and broken, on the ground. As Nat ran he stumbled, kicking their spent bodies in front of him.

---

8. **windy:** skittish; jumpy.

He found the door; he hammered upon it with his bleeding hands.
Because of the boarded windows no light shone. Everything was
dark.

"Let me in," he shouted, "it's Nat. Let me in."

He shouted loud to make himself heard above the whir of the gulls'
wings.

Then he saw the gannet, poised for the dive, above him in the sky.
The gulls circled, retired, soared, one after another, against the wind.
Only the gannet remained. One single gannet above him in the sky.
The wings folded suddenly to its body. It dropped like a stone. Nat
screamed, and the door opened. He stumbled across the threshold,
and his wife threw her weight against the door.

They heard the thud of the gannet as it fell.

His wife dressed his wounds. They were not deep. The backs of his
hands had suffered most, and his wrists. Had he not worn a cap they
would have reached his head. As to the gannet . . . the gannet could
have split his skull.

The children were crying, of course. They had seen the blood on
their father's hands.

"It's all right now," he told them. "I'm not hurt. Just a few scratches.
You play with Johnny, Jill. Mammy will wash these cuts."

He half shut the door to the scullery so that they could not see. His
wife was ashen. She began running water from the sink.

"I saw them overhead," she whispered. "They began collecting just
as Jill ran in with Mr. Trigg. I shut the door fast, and it jammed. That's
why I couldn't open it at once when you came."

"Thank God they waited for me," he said. "Jill would have fallen at
once. One bird alone would have done it."

Furtively, so as not to alarm the children, they whispered together
as she bandaged his hands and the back of his neck.

"They're flying inland," he said, "thousands of them. Rooks, crows,
all the bigger birds. I saw them from the bus stop. They're making for
the towns."

"But what can they do, Nat?"

"They'll attack. Go for everyone out in the streets. Then they'll try
the windows, the chimneys."

"Why don't the authorities do something? Why don't they get the
Army, get machine guns, anything?"

"There's been no time. Nobody's prepared. We'll hear what they have to say on the six o'clock news."

Nat went back into the kitchen, followed by his wife. Johnny was playing quietly on the floor. Only Jill looked anxious.

"I can hear the birds," she said. "Listen, Dad."

Nat listened. Muffled sounds came from the windows, from the door. Wings brushing the surface, sliding, scraping, seeking a way of entry. The sound of many bodies, pressed together, shuffling on the sills. Now and again came a thud, a crash, as some bird dived and fell. "Some of them will kill themselves that way," he thought, "but not enough. Never enough."

"All right," he said aloud. "I've got boards over the windows, Jill. The birds can't get in."

He went and examined all the windows. His work had been thorough. Every gap was closed. He would make extra certain, however. He found wedges, pieces of old tin, strips of wood and metal, and fastened them at the sides to reinforce the boards. His hammering helped to deafen the sound of the birds, the shuffling, the tapping, and more ominous—he did not want his wife or the children to hear it—the splinter of cracked glass.

"Turn on the wireless," he said, "let's have the wireless."

This would drown the sound also. He went upstairs to the bedrooms and reinforced the windows there. Now he could hear the birds on the roof, the scraping of claws, a sliding, jostling sound.

He decided they must sleep in the kitchen, keep up the fire, bring down the mattresses, and lay them out on the floor. He was afraid of the bedroom chimneys. The boards he had placed at the chimney bases might give way. In the kitchen they would be safe because of the fire. He would have to make a joke of it. Pretend to the children they were playing at camp. If the worst happened, and the birds forced an entry down the bedroom chimneys, it would be hours, days perhaps, before they could break down the doors. The birds would be imprisoned in the bedrooms. They could do no harm there. Crowded together, they would stifle and die.

He began to bring the mattresses downstairs. At the sight of them his wife's eyes widened in apprehension. She thought the birds had already broken in upstairs.

"All right," he said cheerfully, "we'll all sleep together in the kitchen tonight. More cozy here by the fire. Then we shan't be worried by those silly old birds tapping at the windows."

He made the children help him rearrange the furniture, and he took the precaution of moving the dresser, with his wife's help, across the window. It fitted well. It was an added safeguard. The mattresses could now be lain, one beside the other, against the wall where the dresser had stood.

"We're safe enough now," he thought. "We're snug and tight, like an air-raid shelter. We can hold out. It's just the food that worries me. Food, and coal for the fire. We've enough for two or three days, not more. By that time . . ."

No use thinking ahead as far as that. And they'd be giving directions on the wireless. People would be told what to do. And now, in the midst of many problems, he realized that it was dance music only, coming over the air. Not Children's Hour, as it should have been. He glanced at the dial. Yes, they were on the Home Service all right. Dance records. He switched to the Light program. He knew the reason. The usual programs had been abandoned. This only happened at exceptional times. Elections and such. He tried to remember if it had happened in the war, during the heavy raids on London. But of course. The BBC[9] was not stationed in London during the war. The programs were broadcast from other, temporary quarters. "We're better off here," he thought; "we're better off here in the kitchen, with the windows and the doors boarded, than they are up in the towns. Thank God we're not in the towns."

At six o'clock the records ceased. The time signal was given. No matter if it scared the children, he must hear the news. There was a pause after the pips. Then the announcer spoke. His voice was solemn, grave. Quite different from midday.

"This is London," he said. "A national emergency was proclaimed at four o'clock this afternoon. Measures are being taken to safeguard the lives and property of the population, but it must be understood that these are not easy to effect immediately, owing to the unforeseen and unparalleled nature of the present crisis. Every householder must take precautions to his own building, and where several people live together, as in flats and apartments, they must unite to do the utmost they can to prevent entry. It is absolutely imperative that every individual stay indoors tonight and that no one at all remain on the streets, or roads, or anywhere withoutdoors. The birds, in vast

---

9. **BBC:** British Broadcasting Corporation.

numbers, are attacking anyone on sight, and have already begun an assault upon buildings; but these, with due care, should be impenetrable. The population is asked to remain calm and not to panic. Owing to the exceptional nature of the emergency, there will be no further transmission from any broadcasting station until 7 A.M. tomorrow."

They played the national anthem. Nothing more happened. Nat switched off the set. He looked at his wife. She stared back at him.

"What's it mean?" said Jill. "What did the news say?"

"There won't be any more programs tonight," said Nat. "There's been a breakdown at the BBC."

"Is it the birds?" asked Jill. "Have the birds done it?"

"No," said Nat, "It's just that everyone's very busy, and then of course they have to get rid of the birds, messing everything up, in the towns. Well, we can manage without the wireless for one evening."

"I wish we had a gramophone,"[10] said Jill, "that would be better than nothing."

She had her face turned to the dresser backed against the windows. Try as they did to ignore it, they were all aware of the shuffling, the stabbing, the persistent beating and sweeping of wings.

"We'll have supper early," suggested Nat, "something for a treat. Ask Mammy. Toasted cheese, eh? Something we all like?"

He winked and nodded at his wife. He wanted the look of dread, of apprehension, to go from Jill's face.

He helped with the supper, whistling, singing, making as much clatter as he could, and it seemed to him that the shuffling and the tapping were not so intense as they had been at first. Presently he went up to the bedrooms and listened, and he no longer heard the jostling for place upon the roof.

"They've got reasoning powers," he thought; "they know it's hard to break in here. They'll try elsewhere. They won't waste their time with us."

Supper passed without incident, and then, when they were clearing away, they heard a new sound, droning, familiar, a sound they all knew and understood.

His wife looked up at him, her face alight. "It's planes," she said; "they're sending out planes after the birds. That's what I said they ought to do all along. That will get them. Isn't that gunfire? Can't you hear guns?"

---

10. **gramaphone:** a phonograph; record player.

It might be gunfire out at sea. Nat could not tell. Big naval guns might have an effect upon the gulls out at sea, but the gulls were inland now. The guns couldn't shell the shore because of the population.

"It's good, isn't it," said his wife, "to hear the planes?" And Jill, catching her enthusiasm, jumped up and down with Johnny. "The planes will get the birds. The planes will shoot them."

Just then they heard a crash about two miles distant, followed by a second, then a third. The droning became more distant, passed away out to sea.

"What was that?" asked his wife. "Were they dropping bombs on the birds?"

"I don't know," answered Nat. "I don't think so."

He did not want to tell her that the sound they had heard was the crashing of aircraft. It was, he had no doubt, a venture on the part of the authorities to send out reconnaissance forces, but they might have known the venture was suicidal. What could aircraft do against birds that flung themselves to death against propeller and fuselage, but hurtle to the ground themselves? This was being tried now, he supposed, over the whole country. And at a cost. Someone high up had lost his head.

"Where have the planes gone, Dad?" asked Jill.

"Back to base," he said. "Come on, now, time to tuck down for bed."

It kept his wife occupied, undressing the children before the fire, seeing to the bedding, one thing and another, while he went round the cottage again, making sure that nothing had worked loose. There was no further drone of aircraft, and the naval guns had ceased. "Waste of life and effort," Nat said to himself. "We can't destroy enough of them that way. Cost too heavy. There's always gas. Maybe they'll try spraying with gas, mustard gas. We'll be warned first, of course, if they do. There's one thing, the best brains of the country will be onto it tonight."

Somehow the thought reassured him. He had a picture of scientists, naturalists, technicians, and all those chaps they called the back-room boys, summoned to a council; they'd be working on the problem now. This was not a job for the government, for the chiefs of staff—they would merely carry out the orders of the scientists.

"They'll have to be ruthless," he thought. "Where the trouble's worst they'll have to risk more lives, if they use gas. All the livestock, too, and the soil—all contaminated. As long as everyone doesn't panic.

That's the trouble. People panicking, losing their heads. The BBC was right to warn us of that."

Upstairs in the bedrooms all was quiet. No further scraping and stabbing at the windows. A lull in battle. Forces regrouping. Wasn't that what they called it in the old wartime bulletins? The wind hadn't dropped, though. He could still hear it roaring in the chimneys. And the sea breaking down on the shore. Then he remembered the tide. The tide would be on the turn. Maybe the lull in battle was because of the tide. There was some law the birds obeyed, and it was all to do with the east wind and the tide.

He glanced at his watch. Nearly eight o'clock. It must have gone high water an hour ago. That explained the lull: the birds attacked with the flood tide. It might not work that way inland, upcountry, but it seemed as if it was so this way on the coast. He reckoned the time limit in his head. They had six hours to go without attack. When the tide turned again, around one twenty in the morning, the birds would come back. . . .

There were two things he could do. The first to rest, with his wife and the children, and all of them snatch what sleep they could, until the small hours. The second to go out, see how they were faring at the farm, see if the telephone was still working there, so that they might get news from the exchange.

He called softly to his wife, who had just settled the children. She came halfway up the stairs and he whispered to her.

"You're not to go," she said at once, "you're not to go and leave me alone with the children. I can't stand it."

Her voice rose hysterically. He hushed her, calmed her.

"All right," he said, "all right. I'll wait till morning. And we'll get the wireless bulletin then too, at seven. But in the morning, when the tide ebbs again, I'll try for the farm, and they may let us have bread and potatoes, and milk too."

His mind was busy again, planning against emergency. They would not have milked, of course, this evening. The cows would be standing by the gate, waiting in the yard, with the household inside, battened behind boards, as they were here at the cottage. That is, if they had time to take precautions. He thought of the farmer, Trigg, smiling at him from the car. There would have been no shooting party, not tonight.

The children were asleep. His wife, still clothed, was sitting on her mattress. She watched him, her eyes nervous.

"What are you going to do?" she whispered.

He shook his head for silence. Softly, stealthily, he opened the back door and looked outside.

It was pitch dark. The wind was blowing harder than ever, coming in steady gusts, icy, from the sea. He kicked at the step outside the door. It was heaped with birds. There were dead birds everywhere. Under the windows, against the walls. These were the suicides, the divers, the ones with broken necks. Wherever he looked he saw dead birds. No trace of the living. The living had flown seaward with the turn of the tide. The gulls would be riding the seas now, as they had done in the forenoon.

In the far distance, on the hill where the tractor had been two days before, something was burning. One of the aircraft that had crashed; the fire, fanned by the wind, had set light to a stack.

He looked at the bodies of the birds, and he had a notion that if he heaped them, one upon the other, on the windowsills they would make added protection for the next attack. Not much, perhaps, but something. The bodies would have to be clawed at, pecked, and dragged aside before the living birds could gain purchase on the sills and attack the panes. He set to work in the darkness. It was queer; he hated touching them. The bodies were still warm and bloody. The blood matted their feathers. He felt his stomach turn, but he went on with his work. He noticed grimly that every windowpane was shattered. Only the boards had kept the birds from breaking in. He stuffed the cracked panes with the bleeding bodies of the birds.

When he had finished he went back into the cottage. He barricaded the kitchen door, made it doubly secure. He took off his bandages, sticky with the birds' blood, not with his own cuts, and put on fresh plaster.

His wife had made him cocoa and he drank it thirstily. He was very tired.

"All right," he said, smiling, "don't worry. We'll get through."

He lay down on his mattress and closed his eyes. He slept at once. He dreamt uneasily, because through his dreams there ran a thread of something forgotten. Some piece of work, neglected, that he should have done. Some precaution that he had known well but had not taken, and he could not put a name to it in his dreams. It was connected in some way with the burning aircraft and the stack upon the hill. He went on sleeping, though; he did not awake. It was his wife shaking his shoulder that awoke him finally.

"They've begun," she sobbed, "they've started this last hour. I can't listen to it any longer alone. There's something smelling bad too, something burning."

Then he remembered. He had forgotten to make up the fire. It was smoldering, nearly out. He got up swiftly and lit the lamp. The hammering had started at the windows and the doors, but it was not that he minded now. It was the smell of singed feathers. The smell filled the kitchen. He knew at once what it was. The birds were coming down the chimney, squeezing their way down to the kitchen range.

He got sticks and paper and put them on the embers, then reached for the can of paraffin.

"Stand back," he shouted to his wife. "We've got to risk this."

He threw the paraffin onto the fire. The flame roared up the pipe, and down upon the fire fell the scorched, blackened bodies of the birds.

The children woke, crying. "What is it?" said Jill. "What's happened?"

Nat had no time to answer. He was raking the bodies from the chimney, clawing them out onto the floor. The flames still roared, and the danger of the chimney catching fire was one he had to take. The flames would send away the living birds from the chimney top. The lower joint was the difficulty, though. This was choked with the smoldering, helpless bodies of the birds caught by fire. He scarcely heeded the attack on the windows and the door: let them beat their wings, break their beaks, lose their lives, in the attempt to force an entry into his home. They would not break in. He thanked God he had one of the old cottages, with small windows, stout walls. Not like the new council houses. Heaven help them up the lane in the new council houses.

"Stop crying," he called to the children. "There's nothing to be afraid of, stop crying."

He went on raking at the burning, smoldering bodies as they fell into the fire.

"This'll fetch them," he said to himself, "the draft and the flames together. We're all right, as long as the chimney doesn't catch. I ought to be shot for this. It's all my fault. Last thing, I should have made up the fire. I knew there was something."

Amid the scratching and tearing at the window boards came the sudden homely striking of the kitchen clock. Three A.M. A little more than four hours yet to go. He could not be sure of the exact time of high water. He reckoned it would not turn much before half past seven, twenty to eight.

"Light up the Primus,"[11] he said to his wife. "Make us some tea, and the kids some cocoa. No use sitting around doing nothing."

That was the line. Keep her busy, and the children too. Move about, eat, drink; always best to be on the go.

He waited by the range. The flames were dying. But no more blackened bodies fell from the chimney. He thrust his poker up as far as it could go and found nothing. It was clear. The chimney was clear. He wiped the sweat from his forehead.

"Come on now, Jill," he said, "bring me some more sticks. We'll have a good fire going directly." She wouldn't come near him, though. She was staring at the heaped singed bodies of the birds.

"Never mind them," he said, "we'll put those in the passage when I've got the fire steady."

The danger of the chimney was over. It could not happen again, not if the fire was kept burning day and night.

"I'll have to get more fuel from the farm tomorrow," he thought. "This will never last. I'll manage, though. I can do all that with the ebb tide. It can be worked, fetching what we need, when the tide's turned. We've just got to adapt ourselves, that's all."

They drank tea and cocoa and ate slices of bread and Bovril.[12] Only half a loaf left, Nat noticed. Never mind, though, they'd get by.

"Stop it," said young Johnny, pointing to the windows with his spoon, "stop it, you old birds."

"That's right," said Nat, smiling, "we don't want the old beggars, do we? Had enough of 'em."

They began to cheer when they heard the thud of the suicide birds.

"There's another, Dad," cried Jill, "he's done for."

"He's had it," said Nat. "There he goes, the blighter."

This was the way to face up to it. This was the spirit. If they could keep this up, hang on like this until seven, when the first news bulletin came through, they would not have done too badly.

"Give us a cigarette," he said to his wife. "A bit of a smoke will clear away the smell of the scorched feathers."

---

11. **Primus:** a small portable stove.
12. **Bovril:** a kind of instant beef broth.

"There's only two left in the packet," she said. "I was going to buy you some from the co-op."

"I'll have one," he said, "t'other will keep for a rainy day."

No sense trying to make the children rest. There was no rest to be got while the tapping and the scratching went on at the windows. He sat with one arm round his wife and the other round Jill, with Johnny on his mother's lap and the blankets heaped about them on the mattress.

"You can't help admiring the beggars," he said; "they've got persistence. You'd think they'd tire of the game, but not a bit of it."

Admiration was hard to sustain. The tapping went on and on and a new rasping note struck Nat's ear, as though a sharper beak than any hitherto had come to take over from its fellows. He tried to remember the names of birds; he tried to think which species would go for this particular job. It was not the tap of the woodpecker. That would be light and frequent. This was more serious, because if it continued long the wood would splinter, as the glass had done. Then he remembered the hawks. Could the hawks have taken over from the gulls? Were there buzzards now upon the sills, using talons as well as beaks? Hawks, buzzards, kestrels, falcons—he had forgotten the birds of prey. He had forgotten the gripping power of the birds of prey. Three hours to go, and while they waited, the sound of the splintering wood, the talons tearing at the wood.

Nat looked about him, seeing what furniture he could destroy to fortify the door. The windows were safe because of the dresser. He was not certain of the door. He went upstairs, but when he reached the landing he paused and listened. There was a soft patter on the floor of the children's bedroom. The birds had broken through. . . . He put his ear to the door. No mistake. He could hear the rustle of wings and the light patter as they searched the floor. The other bedroom was still clear. He went into it and began bringing out the furniture, to pile at the head of the stairs should the door of the children's bedroom go. It was a preparation. It might never be needed. He could not stack the furniture against the door, because it opened inward. The only possible thing was to have it at the top of the stairs.

"Come down, Nat, what are you doing?" called his wife.

"I won't be long," he shouted. "Just making everything shipshape up here."

He did not want her to come; he did not want her to hear the pattering of the feet in the children's bedroom, the brushing of those wings against the door.

At five thirty he suggested breakfast, bacon and fried bread, if only to stop the growing look of panic in his wife's eyes and to calm the fretful children. She did not know about the birds upstairs. The bedroom, luckily, was not over the kitchen. Had it been so, she could not have failed to hear the sound of them up there, tapping the boards. And the silly, senseless thud of the suicide birds, the death and glory boys, who flew into the bedroom, smashing their heads against the walls. He knew them of old, the herring gulls. They had no brains. The black-backs were different; they knew what they were doing. So did the buzzards, the hawks . . .

He found himself watching the clock, gazing at the hands that went so slowly round the dial. If his theory was not correct, if the attack did not cease with the turn of the tide, he knew they were beaten. They could not continue through the long day without air, without rest, without more fuel, without . . . His mind raced. He knew there were so many things they needed to withstand siege. They were not fully prepared. They were not ready. It might be that it would be safer in the towns, after all. If he could get a message through on the farm telephone to his cousin, only a short journey by train upcountry, they might be able to hire a car. That would be quicker—hire a car between tides . . .

His wife's voice, calling his name, drove away the sudden, desperate desire for sleep.

"What is it? What now?" he said sharply.

"The wireless," said his wife. "I've been watching the clock. It's nearly seven."

"Don't twist the knob," he said, impatient for the first time. "It's on the Home where it is. They'll speak from the Home."

They waited. The kitchen struck seven. There was no sound. No chimes, no music. They waited until a quarter past, switching to the Light. The result was the same. No news bulletin came through.

"We've heard wrong," he said. "They won't be broadcasting until eight o'clock."

They left it switched on, and Nat thought of the battery, wondered how much power was left in it. It was generally recharged when his wife went shopping in the town. If the battery failed they would not hear the instructions.

"It's getting light," whispered his wife. "I can't see it, but I can feel it. And the birds aren't hammering so loud."

She was right. The rasping, tearing sound grew fainter every moment. So did the shuffling, the jostling for place upon the step, upon the sills. The tide was on the turn. By eight there was no sound at all. Only the wind. The children, lulled at last by the stillness, fell asleep. At half past eight Nat switched the wireless off.

"What are you doing? We'll miss the news," said his wife.

"There isn't going to be any news," said Nat. "We've got to depend upon ourselves."

He went to the door and slowly pulled away the barricades. He drew the bolts and, kicking the bodies from the step outside the door, breathed the cold air. He had six working hours before him, and he knew he must reserve his strength for the right things, not waste it in any way. Food, and light, and fuel; these were the necessary things. If he could get them in sufficiency, they could endure another night.

He stepped into the garden, and as he did so he saw the living birds. The gulls had gone to ride the sea, as they had done before; they sought sea food, and the buoyancy of the tide, before they returned to the attack. Not so the land birds. They waited and watched. Nat saw them, on the hedgerows, on the soil, crowded in the trees, outside in the field, line upon line of birds, all still, doing nothing.

He went to the end of his small garden. The birds did not move. They went on watching him.

"I've got to get food," said Nat to himself. "I've got to go to the farm to find food."

He went back to the cottage. He saw to the windows and the doors. He went upstairs and opened the children's bedroom. It was empty, except for the dead birds on the floor. The living were out there, in the garden, in the fields. He went downstairs.

"I'm going to the farm," he said.

His wife clung to him. She had seen the living birds from the open door.

"Take us with you," she begged. "We can't stay here alone. I'd rather die than stay here alone."

He considered the matter. He nodded.

"Come on, then," he said. "Bring baskets, and Johnny's pram. We can load up the pram."

They dressed against the biting wind, wore gloves and scarves. His wife put Johnny in the pram. Nat took Jill's hand.

"The birds," she whimpered, "they're all out there in the fields."

"They won't hurt us," he said, "not in the light."

They started walking across the field towards the stile, and the birds did not move. They waited, their heads turned to the wind.

When they reached the turning to the farm, Nat stopped and told his wife to wait in the shelter of the hedge with the two children.

"But I want to see Mrs. Trigg," she protested. "There are lots of things we can borrow if they went to market yesterday; not only bread, and . . ."

"Wait here," Nat interrupted. "I'll be back in a moment."

The cows were lowing, moving restlessly in the yard, and he could see a gap in the fence where the sheep had knocked their way through, to roam unchecked in the front garden before the farmhouse. No smoke came from the chimneys. He was filled with misgiving. He did not want his wife or the children to go down to the farm.

"Don't gib[13] now," said Nat, harshly, "do what I say."

She withdrew with the pram into the hedge, screening herself and the children from the wind.

He went down alone to the farm. He pushed his way through the herd of bellowing cows, which turned this way and that, distressed, their udders full. He saw the car standing by the gate, not put away in the garage. The windows of the farmhouse were smashed. There were many dead gulls lying in the yard and around the house. The living birds perched on the group of trees behind the farm and on the roof of the house. They were quite still. They watched him.

Jim's body lay in the yard . . . what was left of it. When the birds had finished, the cows had trampled him. His gun was beside him. The door of the house was shut and bolted, but as the windows were smashed, it was easy to lift them and climb through. Triggs' body was close to the telephone. He must have been trying to get through to the exchange when the birds came for him. The receiver was hanging loose, the instrument torn from the wall. No sign of Mrs. Trigg. She would be upstairs. Was it any use going up? Sickened, Nat knew what he would find.

"Thank God," he said to himself, "there were no children."

He forced himself to climb the stairs, but halfway he turned and descended again. He could see her legs protruding from the open

---

13. **gib:** balk; hesitate.

bedroom door. Beside her were the bodies of black-backed gulls, and an umbrella, broken.

"It's no use," thought Nat, "doing anything. I've only got five hours, less than that. The Triggs would understand. I must load up with what I can find."

He tramped back to his wife and children.

"I'm going to fill up the car with stuff," he said. "I'll put coal in it, and paraffin for the Primus. We'll take it home and return for a fresh load."

"What about the Triggs?" asked his wife.

"They must have gone to friends," he said.

"Shall I come and help you, then?"

"No; there's a mess down there. Cows and sheep all over the place. Wait, I'll get the car. You can sit in it."

Clumsily he backed the car out of the yard and into the lane. His wife and the children could not see Jim's body from there.

"Stay here," he said, "never mind the pram. The pram can be fetched later. I'm going to load the car."

Her eyes watched his all the time. He believed she understood; otherwise she would have suggested helping him to find the bread and groceries.

They made three journeys altogether, backwards and forwards between their cottage and the farm, before he was satisfied they had everything they needed. It was surprising, once he started thinking, how many things were necessary. Almost the most important of all was planking for the windows. He had to go round searching for timber. He wanted to renew the boards on all the windows at the cottage. Candles, paraffin, nails, tinned stuff; the list was endless. Besides all that, he milked three of the cows. The rest, poor brutes, would have to go on bellowing.

On the final journey he drove the car to the bus stop, got out, and went to the telephone box. He wanted a few minutes, jangling the receiver. No good, though. The line was dead. He climbed onto a bank and looked over the countryside, but there was no sign of life at all, nothing in the fields but the waiting, watching birds. Some of them slept—he could see the beaks tucked into the feathers.

"You'd think they'd be feeding," he said to himself, "not just standing in that way."

Then he remembered. They were gorged with food. They had eaten their fill during the night. That was why they did not move this morning. . . .

No smoke came from the chimneys of the council houses. He thought of the children who had run across the fields the night before.

"I should have known," he thought; "I ought to have taken them home with me."

He lifted his face to the sky. It was colorless and gray. The bare trees on the landscape looked bent and blackened by the east wind. The cold did not affect the living birds waiting out there in the fields.

"This is the time they ought to get them," said Nat; "they're a sitting target now. They must be doing this all over the country. Why don't our aircraft take off now and spray them with mustard gas? What are all our chaps doing? They must know, they must see for themselves."

He went back to the car and got into the driver's seat.

"Go quickly past that second gate," whispered his wife. "The postman's lying there. I don't want Jill to see."

He accelerated. The little Morris bumped and rattled along the lane. The children shrieked with laughter.

"Up-a-down, up-a-down," shouted young Johnny.

It was a quarter to one by the time they reached the cottage. Only an hour to go.

"Better have cold dinner," said Nat. "Hot up something for yourself and the children, some of that soup. I've no time to eat now. I've got to unload all this stuff."

He got everything inside the cottage. It could be sorted later. Give them all something to do during the long hours ahead. First he must see to the windows and the doors.

He went round the cottage methodically, testing every window, every door. He climbed onto the roof also, and fixed boards across every chimney, except the kitchen. The cold was so intense he could hardly bear it, but the job had to be done. Now and again he would look up, searching the sky for aircraft. None came. As he worked he cursed the inefficiency of the authorities.

"It's always the same," he muttered, "they always let us down. Muddle, muddle, from the start. No plan, no real organization. And we don't matter down here. That's what it is. The people upcountry have priority. They're using gas up there, no doubt, and all the aircraft. We've got to wait and take what comes."

He paused, his work on the bedroom chimney finished, and looked out to sea. Something was moving out there. Something gray and white amongst the breakers.

"Good old Navy," he said, "they never let us down. They're coming down-channel, they're turning in the bay."

He waited, straining his eyes, watering in the wind, towards the sea. He was wrong, though. It was not ships. The Navy was not there. The gulls were rising from the sea. The massed flocks in the fields, with ruffled feathers, rose in formation from the ground and, wing to wing, soared upwards to the sky.

The tide had turned again.

Nat climbed down the ladder and went inside the kitchen. The family were at dinner. It was a little after two. He bolted the door, put up the barricade, and lit the lamp.

"It's nighttime," said young Johnny.

His wife had switched on the wireless once again, but no sound came from it.

"I've been all round the dial," she said, "foreign stations, and that lot. I can't get anything."

"Maybe they have the same trouble," he said, "maybe it's the same right through Europe."

She poured out a plateful of the Triggs' soup, cut him a large slice of the Triggs' bread, and spread their dripping upon it.

They ate in silence. A piece of the dripping ran down young Johnny's chin and fell onto the table.

"Manners, Johnny," said Jill, "you should learn to wipe your mouth."

The tapping began at the windows, at the door. The rustling, the jostling, the pushing for position on the sills. The first thud of the suicide gulls upon the step.

"Won't America do something?" said his wife. "They've always been our allies, haven't they? Surely America will do something?"

Nat did not answer. The boards were strong against the windows, and on the chimneys too. The cottage was filled with stores, with fuel, with all they needed for the next few days. When he had finished dinner he would put the stuff away, stack it neatly, get everything ship-shape, handy like. His wife could help him, and the children too. They'd tire themselves out, between now and a quarter to nine, when the tide would ebb; then he'd tuck them down on their mattresses, see that they slept good and sound until three in the morning.

He had a new scheme for the windows, which was to fix barbed wire in front of the boards. He had brought a great roll of it from the farm. The nuisance was, he'd have to work at this in the dark, when the lull came between nine and three. Pity he had not thought of it before. Still, as long as the wife slept, and the kids, that was the main thing.

The smaller birds were at the window now. He recognized the light tap-tapping of their beaks and the soft brush of their wings. The hawks ignored the windows. They concentrated their attack upon the door. Nat listened to the tearing sound of splintering wood, and wondered how many million years of memory were stored in those little brains, behind the stabbing beaks, the piercing eyes, now giving them this instinct to destroy mankind with all the deft precision of machines.

"I'll smoke that last cigarette," he said to his wife. "Stupid of me, it was the one thing I forgot to bring back from the farm."

He reached for it, switched on the silent wireless. He threw the empty packet on the fire, and watched it burn. ■

THE IMPACT OF THE STORY

This nightmarish story is set in rural England shortly after the second World War. The movie version of "The Birds," directed by Alfred Hitchcock, takes place in California. Do you think it matters where the events described by Daphne du Maurier occur? Why or why not?

THE FACTS OF THE STORY

On your own paper, write answers to the following items. Answers may be one word, a phrase, or several sentences.

1. At first, how does Nat account for the vast numbers of birds?

2. Why does Nat especially fear attacks by the gulls and, later, by the hawks?

3. What regular occurrence in nature seems to determine when the birds attack and when they rest?

4. What important thing does Nat forget to do before going to sleep the second night?

5. What does the final failure of the wireless suggest?

THE IDEAS IN THE STORY

Prepare to discuss the following questions in class.

1. In "To Build a Fire," Jack London refers to human frailty. The man in his story is too frail to cope with the severe cold. In its ability to survive the cold, the dog is stronger than the man. In her story, Daphne du Maurier also seems to be saying something about human frailty. Her story reminds us of how fragile we really are, of how thin the barrier is that protects us from other creatures. What powers of the birds make it possible for them to win? Can you think of ways that the people might defeat the birds?

2. Is there any hint in the story as to what is *causing* the birds to behave abnormally?

3. The distinction between reason and instinct is essential to the **theme** (the main idea about life) of both "The Most Dangerous Game" and "To Build a Fire." In the first story, Richard Connell seems to say that the ability to reason is more important than instinct. In "To Build a Fire," London seems to emphasize the superiority of instinct over reason or judgment. What significance do reason and instinct have in "The Birds"?

THE ART OF THE STORYTELLER

Plot
Like the plot of "To Build a Fire," the plot of "The Birds" is simple. The conflict is between Nat, the protagonist, and the birds, the antagonist; the plot is composed of Nat's struggle to survive the birds' attacks. Much of Nat's struggle must be devoted to making the house safe. He also must try to get help, as well as food and light and fuel to withstand a siege. Du Maurier plants two questions in the mind of the reader: *Will the struggle be a losing one? Is there any way that Nat can win?* What do you think?

Climax
The outcome of this horror story is not stated, but it is forcefully suggested. Explain how each of the following passages suggests the same outcome. Which of these passages suggests most clearly to you that the birds will succeed in destroying the human race? That passage marks the climax.

1. No smoke came from the chimneys of the council houses. (Page 78)

2. He paused, his work on the bedroom chimney finished, and looked out to sea. Something was moving out there. Something gray and white amongst the breakers.
   "Good old Navy," he said, "they never let us down. They're coming down-channel, they're turning in the bay."
   He waited, straining his eyes, watering in the wind, towards the sea. He was wrong, though. It was not ships. The Navy was not there. The gulls were rising from the sea. The

massed flocks in the fields, with ruffled feathers, rose in formation from the ground and, wing to wing, soared upwards to the sky.

The tide had turned again. (Pages 78–79)

3. His wife had switched on the wireless once again, but no sound came from it.

   "I've been all round the dial," she said, "foreign stations, and that lot. I can't get anything." (Page 79)

4. The hawks ignored the windows. They concentrated their attack upon the door. (Page 80)

Foreshadowing

In the first few pages of the story, the author gives us clues that hint at the horrible events to come. What are some of these instances of foreshadowing, and how do they help to establish a mood of uneasiness and foreboding?

Another instance of foreshadowing not only states the problem of the protagonist but also suggests the outcome of the conflict. Nat has just seen tens of thousands of gulls riding the waves. His reaction foreshadows what is to come:

> Something was happening, because of the east wind and the weather, that he did not understand. He wondered if he should go to the call box by the bus stop and ring up the police. Yet what could they do? What could anyone do?

The answer to this final question is suggested by everything that happens in the story. What is that answer?

Fantasy

While you were reading "The Birds," you probably had a feeling that these events could never happen. Birds would never behave this way. The whole story is so contrary to experience that it simply is not to be believed. This kind of story is called **fantasy.** All of us have read and enjoyed fantasies—such as fables, fairy tales, and children's stories in which animals talk and behave like people. Although a fantasy is not factually true, a skillful writer makes us *believe* the story while we are reading it. By concentrating on the experience of one family in rural England, Daphne du Maurier shows, in convincing detail, what might happen if all the birds in the world set out to destroy the human race.

While the situation du Maurier describes is clearly fictional, she is careful to make the characters believable. Our knowledge of human nature tells us that, should such a horrible event occur, people probably would react exactly as her characters do. What reactions of the Triggs, for example, seem true to life? Are the explanations for the birds' unnatural behavior offered by Nat and by the government over the wireless believable? Explain Nat's refusal to give up, even when he knows that the odds against him are overwhelming. Would you expect human beings to act this way?

THE VOCABULARY IN THE STORY

You might have noticed that du Maurier often uses in her story familiar words and phrases but in a way that may sound strange to you.

"Have you boarded your windows?" asked Nat.

"No. Lot of nonsense. . . ."

"I'd board them now, if I were you."

"Garn. You're windy. Like to come to our place to sleep?"

Here *windy* obviously does not refer to the wind blowing. Its British meaning, "frightened" or "skittish," is different from the meaning it has in American usage. Quite a few English language words are used differently in England and America. This is a characteristic of **dialect**, that is the variations in a language found in a particular geographic region, including differences in pronunciation and vocabulary.

Replace the italicized words below with appropriate words that you would use in everyday American speech.

Good job it was his free day and he was not working at the farm.

He looked . . . in the cupboard where she kept her *tins*.

"Don't *gib* now," said Nat, harshly, "do what I say."

"He's had it," said Nat. "There he goes, the *blighter.*"

"You can't help admiring the *beggars,*" he said; "they've got persistence. . . ."

COMPOSITION: Writing a "What If" Story

One reason that "The Birds" is so effective is that du Maurier has imagined the events in great detail. We might call a fantasy like this a "what if" story. *What if* all the birds in the world suddenly decided to destroy us? *What if* some other kind of seemingly innocent force suddenly acted aggressively toward human beings? Many possibilities have already been suggested in short stories, novels, movies, and television shows, such as destruction by insects, by rodents, and by bees. Or *what if* some other kind of disaster, such as heavy rainfall, disease, or planetary disruption, threatened the entire human race? What would the results be?

Following the pattern of "The Birds," write your own "what if" fantasy, imagining the events in detail. In three or four pages, describe what you think it would be like to experience such a disaster.

Prewriting
Jot down as many different kinds of scenarios as come to mind. Beside each one, briefly write the kinds of weapons the adversary might use or the specific ways that human beings would be threatened. Then choose the most appealing and most vivid scenario from your list.

Writing
Without worrying overly about structure or sense, write your first draft quickly, letting your imagination run freely. Try to make the events you are describing as believable as possible by using graphic details in your narrative.

Evaluating and Revising
Read your draft several times, looking for ways to improve the content, organization, and style. Pay special attention to the sequence of the plot. Do you give the reader any clues as to what will happen

in your story? Remember to check for errors in punctuation, spelling, and grammar, too.

Publishing
Consider submitting your story to the school newspaper or creative writing magazine for publication.

ABOUT THE AUTHOR

 Daphne du Maurier (1907–1989) was born into the London world of artists and writers. She was the daughter of a famous English actor, Sir Gerald du Maurier, and granddaughter of George du Maurier, an artist and a novelist. Although she wrote several books of short stories, she is best known for her novels, in particular for the Gothic romance *Rebecca,* which was made into an Academy Award–winning movie under the direction of Alfred Hitchcock. "The Birds," typical of du Maurier's fiction in its fast-moving action, its use of suspense, and its inescapable tragedy, was also made into a famous horror movie under Hitchcock's direction.

■ THE CASK OF AMONTILLADO

Edgar Allan Poe

Revenge is an emotion that sometimes leads to cruelty, even to murder. This dark tale of revenge takes you beneath the streets of an Italian city in search of a cask of wine—"The Cask of Amontillado."

The thousand injuries of Fortunato I had borne as I best could; but when he ventured upon insult, I vowed revenge. You, who so well know the nature of my soul, will not suppose, however, that I gave utterance to a threat. *At length* I would be avenged; this was a point definitively settled—but the very definitiveness with which it was resolved, precluded the idea of risk. I must not only punish, but punish with impunity. A wrong is unredressed when retribution overtakes its redresser. It is equally unredressed when the avenger fails to make himself felt as such to him who has done the wrong.

It must be understood that neither by word nor deed had I given Fortunato cause to doubt my good will. I continued, as was my wont,[1] to smile in his face, and he did not perceive that my smile *now* was at the thought of his immolation.

He had a weak point—this Fortunato—although in other regards he was a man to be respected and even feared. He prided himself on his connoisseurship in wine. Few Italians have the true virtuoso spirit. For the most part their enthusiasm is adopted to suit the time and opportunity—to practice imposture upon the British and Austrian millionaires. In painting and gemmary[2] Fortunato, like his countrymen, was a quack—but in the matter of old wines he was sincere. In this respect I did not differ from him materially: I was skillful in the Italian vintages myself, and bought largely whenever I could.

It was about dusk, one evening during the supreme madness of the carnival season, that I encountered my friend. He accosted me with excessive warmth, for he had been drinking much. The man

---

1. **wont:** custom; habit.
2. **gemmary:** jewelry.

wore motley.[3] He had on a tight-fitting parti-striped dress, and his head was surmounted by the conical cap and bells. I was so pleased to see him that I thought I should never have done wringing his hand.

I said to him: "My dear Fortunato, you are luckily met. How remarkably well you are looking today! But I have received a pipe[4] of what passes for Amontillado, and I have my doubts."

"How?" said he. "Amontillado? A pipe? Impossible! And in the middle of the carnival!"

"I have my doubts," I replied; "and I was silly enough to pay the full Amontillado price without consulting you in the matter. You were not to be found, and I was fearful of losing a bargain."

"Amontillado!"

"I have my doubts."

"Amontillado!"

"And I must satisfy them."

"Amontillado!"

"As you are engaged, I am on my way to Luchesi. If anyone has a critical turn, it is he. He will tell me—"

"Luchesi cannot tell Amontillado from sherry."

"And yet some fools will have it that his taste is a match for your own."

"Come, let us go."

"Whither?"

"To your vaults."

"My friend, no; I will not impose upon your good nature. I perceive you have an engagement. Luchesi—"

"I have no engagement—come."

"My friend, no. It is not the engagement, but the severe cold with which I perceive you are afflicted. The vaults are insufferably damp. They are encrusted with niter."[5]

"Let us go, nevertheless. The cold is merely nothing. Amontillado! You have been imposed upon. And as for Luchesi, he cannot distinguish sherry from Amontillado."

Thus speaking, Fortunato possessed himself of my arm. Putting on

---

3. **motley:** a multi-colored costume worn by court jesters or clowns.
4. **pipe:** a large cask, or barrel.
5. **niter:** a nitrate mineral deposit.

a mask of black silk, and drawing a *roquelaure*[6] closely about my person, I suffered him to hurry me to my palazzo.[7]

There were no attendants at home; they had absconded to make merry in honor of the time. I had told them that I should not return until the morning, and had given them explicit orders not to stir from the house. These orders were sufficient, I well knew, to insure their immediate disappearance, one and all, as soon as my back was turned.

I took from their sconces two flambeaux,[8] and giving one to Fortunato, bowed him through several suites of rooms to the archway that led into the vaults. I passed down a long and winding staircase, requesting him to be cautious as he followed. We came at length to the foot of the descent, and stood together on the damp ground of the catacombs of the Montresors.

The gait of my friend was unsteady, and the bells upon his cap jingled as he strode.

"The pipe?" said he.

"It is farther on," said I; "but observe the white webwork which gleams from these cavern walls."

He turned toward me, and looked into my eyes with two filmy orbs that distilled the rheum of intoxication.

"Niter?" he asked, at length.

"Niter," I replied. "How long have you had that cough?"

"Ugh! ugh! ugh!—ugh! ugh! ugh!—ugh! ugh! ugh!—ugh! ugh! ugh!—ugh! ugh! ugh!"

My poor friend found it impossible to reply for many minutes.

"It is nothing," he said, at last.

"Come," I said with decision, "we will go back; your health is precious. You are rich, respected, admired, beloved; you are happy, as once I was. You are a man to be missed. For me it is no matter. We will go back; you will be ill, and I cannot be responsible. Besides, there is Luchesi—"

"Enough," he said; "the cough is a mere nothing; it will not kill me. I shall not die of a cough."

"True—true," I replied; "and, indeed, I had no intention of alarming you unnecessarily; but you should use all proper caution. A draft of this Medoc will defend us from the damps."

---

6. *roquelaure* (răk′ə lōr′): a cloak or short robe.
7. **palazzo**: a palace or a large, elegant house.
8. **flambeaux**: torches or large candles.

Here I knocked off the neck of a bottle which I drew from a long row of its fellows that lay upon the mold.

"Drink," I said, presenting him the wine.

He raised it to his lips with a leer. He paused and nodded to me familiarly, while his bells jingled.

"I drink," he said, "to the buried that repose around us."

"And I to your long life."

He again took my arm, and we proceeded.

"These vaults," he said, "are extensive."

The Montresors," I replied, "were a great and numerous family."

"I forget your arms."

"A huge human foot d'or,[9] in a field azure; the foot crushes a serpent rampant whose fangs are imbedded in the heel."

"And the motto?

"*Nemo me impune lacessit.*"[10]

"Good!" he said.

The wine sparkled in his eyes and the bells jingled. My own fancy grew warm with the Medoc. We had passed through walls of piled bones, with casks and puncheons[11] intermingling, into the inmost recesses of the catacombs. I paused again, and this time I made bold to seize Fortunato by an arm above the elbow.

"The niter!" I said; "see, it increases. It hangs like moss upon the vaults. We are below the river's bed. The drops of moisture trickle among the bones. Come, we will go back ere it is too late. Your cough—"

"It is nothing," he said; "let us go on. But first, another draft of the Medoc."

I broke and reached him a flagon of De Grâve. He emptied it at a breath. His eyes flashed with a fierce light. He laughed and threw the bottle upward with a gesticulation I did not understand.

I looked at him in surprise. He repeated the movement—a grotesque one.

"You do not comprehend?" he said.

"Not I," I replied.

"Then you are not of the brotherhood."

---

9. **d'or:** French for "of gold."
10. *Nemo me impune lacessit:* Latin for "No one injures me without punishment."
11. **puncheons:** large casks.

"How?"

"You are not of the masons."[12]

"Yes, yes," I said; "yes, yes."

"You? Impossible! A mason?"

"A mason," I replied.

"A sign," he said.

"It is this," I answered, producing a trowel from beneath the folds of my *roquelaure*.

"You jest," he exclaimed, recoiling a few paces. "But let us proceed to the Amontillado."

"Be it so," I said, replacing the tool beneath the cloak, and again offering him my arm. He leaned upon it heavily. We continued our route in search of the Amontillado. We passed through a range of low arches, descended, passed on, and descending again, arrived at a deep crypt, in which the foulness of the air caused our flambeaux rather to glow than flame.

At the most remote end of the crypt there appeared another less spacious. Its walls had been lined with human remains, piled to the vault overhead, in the fashion of the great catacombs of Paris. Three sides of this interior crypt were still ornamented in this manner. From the fourth the bones had been thrown down, and lay promiscuously upon the earth, forming at one point a mound of some size. Within the wall thus exposed by the displacing of the bones, we perceived a still interior recess, in depth about four feet, in width three, in height six or seven. It seemed to have been constructed for no especial use within itself, but formed merely the interval between two of the colossal supports of the roof of the catacombs, and was backed by one of their circumscribing walls of solid granite.

It was in vain that Fortunato, uplifting his dull torch, endeavored to pry into the depth of the recess. Its termination the feeble light did not enable us to see.

"Proceed," I said; "herein is the Amontillado. As for Luchesi—"

"He is an ignoramus," interrupted my friend, as he stepped unsteadily forward, while I followed immediately at his heels. In an instant he had reached the extremity of the niche, and finding his progress arrested by the rock, stood stupidly bewildered. A moment

---

12. **masons:** Freemasons; members of a worldwide secret fraternal order that originated among masons or stoneworkers during the Middle Ages.

more and I had fettered[13] him to the granite. In its surface were two iron staples, distant from each other about two feet, horizontally. From one of these depended a short chain, from the other a padlock. Throwing the links about his waist, it was but the work of a few seconds to secure it. He was too much astounded to resist. Withdrawing the key I stepped back from the recess.

"Pass your hand," I said, "over the wall; you cannot help feeling the niter. Indeed it is *very* damp. Once more let me *implore* you to return. No? Then I must positively leave you. But I must first render you all the little attentions in my power."

"The Amontillado!" ejaculated my friend, not yet recovered from his astonishment.

"True," I replied; "the Amontillado."

As I said these words I busied myself among the pile of bones of which I have before spoken. Throwing them aside, I soon uncovered a quantity of building stone and mortar. With these materials and with the aid of my trowel, I began vigorously to wall up the entrance of the niche.

I had scarcely laid the first tier of the masonry when I discovered that the intoxication of Fortunato had in a great measure worn off. The earliest indication I had of this was a low moaning cry from the depth of the recess. It was *not* the cry of a drunken man. There was then a long and obstinate silence. I laid the second tier, and the third, and the fourth; and then I heard the furious vibrations of the chain. The noise lasted for several minutes, during which, that I might hearken to it with the more satisfaction, I ceased my labors and sat down upon the bones. When at last the clanking subsided, I resumed the trowel, and finished without interruption the fifth, the sixth, and the seventh tier. The wall was now nearly upon a level with my breast. I again paused, and holding the flambeaux over the masonwork, threw a few feeble rays upon the figure within.

A succession of loud and shrill screams, bursting suddenly from the throat of the chained form, seemed to thrust me violently back. For a brief moment I hesitated—I trembled. Unsheathing my rapier,[14] I began to grope with it about the recess; but the thought of an instant reassured me. I placed my hand upon the solid fabric of the catacombs,

---

13. **fettered:** chained.
14. **rapier:** a long sword.

and felt satisfied. I reapproached the wall. I replied to the yells of him who clamored. I re-echoed—I aided—I surpassed them in volume and in strength. I did this, and the clamorer grew still.

It was now midnight, and my task was drawing to a close. I had completed the eighth, the ninth, and the tenth tier. I had finished a portion of the last and the eleventh; there remained but a single stone to be fitted and plastered in. I struggled with its weight; I placed it partially in its destined position. But now there came from out the niche a low laugh that erected the hairs upon my head. It was succeeded by a sad voice, which I had difficulty in recognizing as that of the noble Fortunato. The voice said: "Ha! ha! ha!—he! he!—a very good joke indeed—an excellent jest. We will have many a rich laugh about it at the palazzo—he! he! he!—over our wine—he! he! he!"

"The Amontillado!" I said.

"He! he! he!—he! he! he!—yes, the Amontillado. But is it not getting late? Will not they be awaiting us at the palazzo, the Lady Fortunato and the rest? Let us be gone."

"Yes," I said, "let us be gone."

"For the love of God, Montresor!"

"Yes," I said, "for the love of God!"

But to these words I hearkened in vain for a reply. I grew impatient. I called aloud: "Fortunato!"

No answer. I called again: "Fortunato!"

No answer still. I thrust a torch through the remaining aperture and let it fall within. There came forth in return only a jingling of the bells. My heart grew sick—on account of the dampness of the catacombs. I hastened to make an end of my labor. I forced the last stone into its position; I plastered it up. Against the new masonry I re-erected the old rampart of bones. For half of a century no mortal has disturbed them. *In pace requiescat!* [15] ■

---

15. *In pace requiescat:* Latin for "May he rest in peace."

THE IMPACT OF THE STORY

Like "The Birds," "The Cask of Amontillado" is a horror story: The author intentionally sets out to scare the reader. However, this story is *not* a fantasy; the event that Edgar Allan Poe describes could possibly occur. Which story did you find more frightening? Why?

Think about some popular movies or television shows whose purpose also is to frighten. How are they like Poe's short story?

THE FACTS OF THE STORY

On your own paper, write answers to the following items. Answers may be one word, a phrase, or several sentences.

1. Why does Montresor want to kill Fortunato?

2. At the beginning of the story, Montresor says there are two requirements for an effective act of revenge. What are these requirements?

3. In Montresor's opinion, what is Fortunato's weak point?

4. How is Montresor able to persuade Fortunato to accompany him into the catacombs?

5. What specific details describing the setting (the catacombs) help to create a sense of horror and disgust?

THE IDEAS IN THE STORY

Prepare to discuss the following questions in class.

1. Montresor himself narrates the story of his grisly deed. Everything we see is filtered through his eyes. How do we know what his victim is feeling? What behavior or attitudes of Fortunato might Montresor find insulting or "injurious"? When do you think Fortunato first suspects that something is very wrong with this trip to the catacombs?

2. Do you have any reason to believe that Montresor might be mentally ill?

3. The desire "to get even," or seek revenge upon another person, is not one of the best of our human emotions. However, while many people may think about getting revenge, few people actually do so. Think about other stories, movies, or television shows in which revenge plays a large role, or consider instances in your own life when you might have felt wronged by another and possibly entertained the idea of revenge. Do you think revenge can ever be justified? Do you think Montresor is justified in his actions?

THE ART OF THE STORYTELLER

Plot

Plot, you will recall, is the series of related events that make up a story. In general, the main ingredient of a plot is a problem that must be solved by the protagonist. The protagonist's attempts to overcome obstacles involve him or her in a **conflict,** or a struggle. As we read a story, our feeling of suspense intensifies steadily as the action moves toward a **climax,** the point at which we know whether the protagonist succeeds or fails.

In "The Cask of Amontillado," Montresor, who is the protagonist, sets out to get revenge on Fortunato by murdering him without being caught or even suspected. The conflict lies in Montresor's struggle to solve four problems:

1. He must make sure that he and Fortunato are not seen together.

2. He must devise a way to get Fortunato into the vaults without arousing his suspicions.

3. He must be sure he can control Fortunato once he gets him into the vault.

4. He must be certain the body is never found.

How does Montresor solve each of his problems?

A Single Effect

Poe believed that a good short story should produce a single effect. Most readers agree that the effect produced in "The Cask of Amontillado" is a feeling of horror. Everything Poe includes in the story makes us feel the horror. Montresor states his grisly goal in the first sentence. Then he proceeds, without letup, to tell us how he achieved his goal. Our horror grows as we see Fortunato, drunk and sick, led to his death without offering any opposition because he does not understand what is happening until it is too late. Our horror reaches its peak in the next-to-last sentence. What final, shocking fact do we learn there?

Irony

When you mean the opposite of what you say, you are using **irony;** you are being ironic. For example, if you were to meet a friend while sloshing miserably through a heavy rain, and say, "Hi, nice day for a picnic, isn't it?" your remark would be ironic. You would mean the opposite of what you were saying. This kind of verbal irony is common. It appears in Poe's story when Montresor (as he encounters Fortunato) remarks, "My dear Fortunato, you are luckily met." Luckily for whom?

When events turn out contrary to the way we normally expect, we say the situation is ironic. It is ironic, for example, that Fortunato, who is obviously out for a good time at the carnival, should have such a very bad time.

Sometimes when we are reading a story, we know something that a person in the story does not know. Such a situation frequently produces irony. Explaining that he is not worried about his cough, Fortunato says, "I shall not die of a cough." Montresor replies, "True—true." This conversation is ironic, since we know that Montresor plans to kill Fortunato.

Fortunato exclaims "Good!" when he learns that the motto on the Montresors' coat of arms is "No one injures me without punishment." What is ironic about Fortunato's remark?

What is ironic about Montresor saying to his victim: ". . . your health is precious"? What is ironic about the victim's name—Fortunato?

THE VOCABULARY IN THE STORY

By changing or adding a suffix or prefix, or even one or two letters, to a root word, you can change the word to a different part of speech. Sometimes, by doing so, you change the meaning of the word.

A wrong is unredressed when retribution overtakes its redresser.

The word *unredressed* is an adjective which means in this story "not revenged"; the noun *redresser* is "a person who gets revenge."

Change each word in the list below to the part of speech indicated beside it. Not all of the words will need suffixes or prefixes added, although you will need to change the words in some way. Check your answers in a dictionary.

definitiveness	adverb
clamored	noun
avenger	verb
descent	verb

COMPOSITION: Creating a Single Effect

Suppose you decide to describe your room to a friend who has never visited your home. What kind of impression do you want to convey? Do you want to create an image of messiness, peacefulness, tidiness, or perhaps coziness? Everything that you include in your description must help to create the single, overall effect that you want to communicate.

Write a descriptive paragraph or paragraphs (100–200 words) that will give your reader a single strong impression. You may describe your room, or you may try one of these scenes:

Scene	Single Effect
a peaceful outdoor setting	happiness
a severe storm	discomfort or misery
a crowd	confusion
an attack	fear
an accident	horror
a stage performance	nervousness
a close game	excitement

Prewriting
Because your success will depend on how many details you can use to build up the single effect, brainstorm to generate as many

sensory details—details of sight, sound, taste, touch, and smell—as you can. Review your list, omitting details, no matter how interesting you may find them, that do not contribute to the single impression that you want to convey. Then organize the details of your description. If there is action in the scene, think of your draft as a brief narrative told in chronological order—that is, in the order in which the events occur. If the scene is static, or without action, like the description of a bedroom, use spatial order (left to right, top to bottom, and so on) to make clear where each element in the scene is located.

Writing
When writing your first draft, follow your prewriting organization from memory if possible so that you can write quickly.

Evaluating and Revising
Read your draft. Check especially to see that you have used appropriate chronological or spatial transitional expressions such as *first, later, then* or *on the floor, on the bed, on the right wall, under the desk*. Rearrange, replace, or add words and phrases as needed.

ABOUT THE AUTHOR

Edgar Allan Poe (1809–1849) was born in Boston, the son of traveling actors. His father deserted the family, and his mother died in Richmond, Virginia, when Edgar was three years old. The child was brought up by John Allan, a wealthy Richmond merchant. Poe was given a superior education, but he broke with his guardian because the older man disapproved of his literary ambitions. During his adult life, Poe lived in the big cities of the East Coast—Richmond, Baltimore, Philadelphia, New York, and Boston—where he struggled to support himself as a magazine writer and editor. Although Poe suffered from poverty and poor health, he achieved in his short life a position of the highest rank among American writers. He succeeded in realizing his early ambition to become a poet, but he is best known for his short stories, which reflect his intense, nightmarish imagination. "The Cask of Amontillado" is one of his horror stories, which have been popular with generations of readers. Other famous tales of horror are "The Tell-Tale Heart," "The Black Cat," and "The Pit and the Pendulum." Poe is often said to have originated the modern detective story. His detective, Dupin, is seen at work in "The Purloined Letter" and "The Murders in the Rue Morgue."

■ ANTAEUS

Borden Deal

T. J. is a boy from the rural South who, with his family, moves
to a Northern city. You can imagine the difficulties such a boy
would experience in adjusting to life in a poor and crowded
section of a big industrial city. When he meets the boys in the
neighborhood , T. J. asks in disbelief: "Don't you-all have no
woods around here? . . . You mean you ain't got no fields to
raise nothing in?"

This was during the wartime,[1] when lots of people were coming
North for jobs in factories and war industries, when people
moved around a lot more than they do now and sometimes kids
were thrown into new groups and new lives that were completely
different from anything they had ever known before. I remember this
one kid; T. J. his name was, from somewhere down South, whose
family moved into our building during that time. They'd come North
with everything they owned piled into the back seat of an old-model
sedan that you wouldn't expect could make the trip, with T. J. and his
three younger sisters riding shakily atop the load of junk.

Our building was just like all the others there, with families crowded
into a few rooms, and I guess there were twenty-five or thirty kids
about my age in that one building. Of course, there were a few of us
who formed a gang and ran together all the time after school, and I
was the one who brought T. J. in and started the whole thing.

The building right next door to us was a factory where they made
walking dolls. It was a low building with a flat, tarred roof that had a
parapet[2] all around it about head-high and we'd found out a long time
before that no one, not even the watchman, paid any attention to the
roof because it was higher than any of the other buildings around. So
my gang used the roof as a headquarters. We could get up there by
crossing over to the fire escape from our own roof on a plank and then
going on up. It was a secret place for us, where nobody else could go
without our permission.

---

1. **wartime:** the war being referred to here is World War II.
2. **parapet:** a low wall or railing enclosing a terrace or roof.

I remember the day I first took T. J. up there to meet the gang. He was a stocky, robust kid with a shock of white hair, nothing sissy about him except his voice—he talked different from any of us and you noticed it right away. But I liked him anyway, so I told him to come on up.

We climbed up over the parapet and dropped down on the roof. The rest of the gang were already there.

"Hi," I said. I jerked my thumb at T. J. "He just moved into the building yesterday."

He just stood there, not scared or anything, just looking, like the first time you see somebody you're not sure you're going to like.

"Hi," Blackie said. "Where you from?"

"Marion County," T. J. said.

We laughed. "Marion County?" I said. "Where's that?"

He looked at me like I was a stranger, too. "It's in Alabama," he said, like I ought to know where it was.

"What's your name?" Charley said.

"T. J.," he said, looking back at him. He had pale blue eyes that looked washed-out but he looked directly at Charley, waiting for his reaction. He'll be all right, I thought. No sissy in him . . . except that voice. Who ever talked like that?

"T. J.," Blackie said. "That's just initials. What's your real name? Nobody in the world has just initials."

"I do," he said. "And they're T. J. That's all the name I got."

His voice was resolute with the knowledge of his rightness and for a moment no one had anything to say. T. J. looked around at the rooftop and down at the black tar under his feet. "Down yonder where I come from," he said, "we played out in the woods. Don't you-all have no woods around here?"

"Naw," Blackie said. "There's the park a few blocks over, but it's full of kids and cops and old women. You can't do a thing."

T. J. kept looking at the tar under his feet. "You mean you ain't got no fields to raise nothing in? No watermelons or nothing?"

"Naw," I said scornfully. "What do you want to grow something for? The folks can buy everything they need at the store."

He looked at me again with that strange, unknowing look. "In Marion County," he said, "I had my own acre of cotton and my own acre of corn. It was mine to plant ever' year."

He sounded like it was something to be proud of, and in some obscure way it made the rest of us angry. "Heck!" Blackie said. "Who'd want to have their own acre of cotton and corn? That's just work. What can you do with an acre of cotton and corn?"

T. J. looked at him. "Well, you get part of the bale offen your acre," he said seriously. "And I fed my acre of corn to my calf."

We didn't really know what he was talking about, so we were more puzzled than angry; otherwise, I guess, we'd have chased him off the roof and wouldn't let him be part of our gang. But he was strange and different and we were all attracted by his stolid sense of rightness and belonging, maybe by the strange softness of his voice contrasting our own tones of speech into harshness.

He moved his foot against the black tar. "We could make our own field right here," he said softly, thoughtfully. "Come spring we could raise us what we want to . . . watermelons and garden truck³ and no telling what all."

"You'd have to be a good farmer to make these tar roofs grow any watermelons," I said. We all laughed.

But T. J. looked serious. "We could haul us some dirt up here," he said. "And spread it out even and water it and before you know it we'd have us a crop in here." He looked at us intently. "Wouldn't that be fun?"

"They wouldn't let us," Blackie said quickly.

"I thought you said this was you-all's roof," T. J. said to me. "That you-all could do anything you wanted up here."

"They've never bothered us," I said. I felt the idea beginning to catch fire in me. It was a big idea and it took a while for it to sink in, but the more I thought about it the better I liked it. "Say," I said to the gang, "he might have something there. Just make us a regular roof garden, with flowers and grass and trees and everything. And all ours, too," I said. "We wouldn't let anybody up here except the ones we wanted to."

"It'd take a while to grow trees," T. J. said quickly, but we weren't paying any attention to him. They were all talking about it suddenly, all excited with the idea after I'd put it in a way they could catch hold of it. Only rich people had roof gardens, we knew, and the idea of our own private domain excited them.

"We could bring it up in sacks and boxes," Blackie said. "We'd have to do it while the folks weren't paying any attention to us. We'd have

---

3. **garden truck:** fruits and vegetables grown for sale at a farmers' market.

to come up to the roof of our building and then cross over with it."

"Where could we get the dirt?" somebody said worriedly.

"Out of those vacant lots over close to school," Blackie said. "Nobody'd notice if we scraped it up."

I slapped T. J. on the shoulder. "Man, you had a wonderful idea," I said, and everybody grinned at him, remembering he had started it. "Our own private roof garden."

He grinned back. "It'll be ourn," he said. "All ourn." Then he looked thoughtful again. "Maybe I can lay my hands on some cotton seed, too. You think we could raise us some cotton?"

We'd started big projects before at one time or another, like any gang of kids, but they'd always petered out for lack of organization and direction. But this one didn't . . . somehow or other T. J. kept it going all through the winter months. He kept talking about the watermelons and the cotton we'd raise, come spring, and when even that wouldn't work he'd switch around to my idea of flowers and grass and trees, though he was always honest enough to add that it'd take a while to get any trees started. He always had it on his mind and he'd mention it in school, getting them lined up to carry dirt that afternoon, saying, in a casual way, that he reckoned a few more weeks ought to see the job through.

Our little area of private earth grew slowly. T. J. was smart enough to start in one corner of the building, heaping up the carried earth two or three feet thick, so that we had an immediate result to look at, to contemplate with awe. Some of the evenings T. J. alone was carrying earth up to the building, the rest of the gang distracted by other enterprises or interests, but T. J. kept plugging along on his own and eventually we'd all come back to him again, and then our own little acre would grow more rapidly.

He was careful about the kind of dirt he'd let us carry up there and more than once he dumped a sandy load over the parapet into the areaway below because it wasn't good enough. He found out the kinds of earth in all the vacant lots for blocks around. He'd pick it up and feel it and smell it, frozen though it was sometimes, and then he'd say it was good growing soil or it wasn't worth anything and we'd have to go on somewhere else.

Thinking about it now, I don't see how he kept us at it. It was hard work, lugging paper sacks and boxes of dirt all the way up the stairs of our own building, keeping out of the way of the grown-ups so they wouldn't catch on to what we were doing. They probably wouldn't have cared, for they didn't pay much attention to us, but we wanted to keep it secret anyway. Then we had to go through the trapdoor to our roof, teeter over a plank to the fire escape, then climb two or three stories to the parapet and drop down onto the roof. All that for a small pile of earth that sometimes didn't seem worth the effort. But T. J. kept the vision bright within us, his words shrewd and calculated toward the fulfillment of his dream; and he worked harder than any of us. He seemed driven toward a goal that we couldn't see, a particular point in time that would be definitely marked by signs and wonders that only he could see.

The laborious earth just lay there during the cold months, inert and lifeless, the clods lumpy and cold under our feet when we walked over it. But one day it rained, and afterward there was a softness in the air and the earth was alive and giving again with moisture and warmth. That evening T. J. smelled the air, his nostrils dilating with the odor of the earth under his feet.

"It's spring," he said, and there was a gladness rising in his voice that filled us all with the same feeling. "It's mighty late for it, but it's spring. I'd just about decided it wasn't never gonna get here at all."

We were all sniffing at the air, too, trying to smell it the way that T. J. did, and I can still remember the sweet odor of the earth under our feet. It was the first time in my life that spring and spring earth had meant anything to me. I looked at T. J. then, knowing in a faint way the hunger within him through the toilsome winter months, knowing the dream that lay behind his plan. He was a new Antaeus,[4] preparing his own bed of strength.

"Planting time," he said, "We'll have to find us some seed."

"What do we do?" Blackie said. "How do we do it?"

"First we'll have to break up the clods," T. J. said. "That won't be hard to do. Then we plant the seed, and after a while they come up. Then you got you a crop." He frowned. "But you ain't got it raised yet. You got to tend it and hoe it and take care of it and all the time it's growing and growing while you're awake and while you're asleep. Then you lay it by when it's growed and let it ripen and then you got you a crop."

---

4. **Antaeus** (an tē′əs): in Greek mythology, a giant whose strength came from his contact with the earth.

"There's those wholesale seed houses over on Sixth," I said. "We could probably swipe some grass seed over there."

T. J. looked at the earth. "You-all seem mighty set on raising some grass," he said. "I ain't never put no effort into that. I spent all my life trying not to raise grass."

"But it's pretty," Blackie said. "We could play on it and take sunbaths on it. Like having our own lawn. Lots of people got lawns."

"Well," T. J. said. He looked at the rest of us, hesitant for the first time. He kept on looking at us for a moment. "I did have it in mind to raise some corn and vegetables. But we'll plant grass."

He was smart. He knew where to give in. And I don't suppose it made any difference to him, really. He just wanted to grow something, even if it was grass.

"Of course," he said, "I do think we ought to plant a row of watermelons. They'd be mighty nice to eat while we was a-laying on that grass."

We all laughed. "All right," I said. "We'll plant us a row of watermelons."

Things went very quickly then. Perhaps half the roof was covered with the earth, the half that wasn't broken by ventilators, and we swiped pocketfuls of grass seed from the open bins in the wholesale seed house, mingling among the buyers on Saturdays and during the school lunch hour. T. J. showed us how to prepare the earth, breaking up the clods and smoothing it and sowing the grass seed. It looked rich and black now with moisture, receiving of the seed, and it seemed that the grass sprang up overnight, pale green in the early spring.

We couldn't keep from looking at it, unable to believe that we had created this delicate growth. We looked at T. J. with understanding now, knowing the fulfillment of the plan he had carried alone within his mind. We had worked without full understanding of the task, but he had known all the time.

We found that we couldn't walk or play on the delicate blades, as we had expected to, but we didn't mind. It was enough just to look at it, to realize that it was the work of our own hands, and each evening the whole gang was there, trying to measure the growth that had been achieved that day.

One time a foot was placed on the plot of ground . . . one time only, Blackie stepping onto it with sudden bravado. Then he looked at the crushed blades and there was shame in his face. He did not do it again. This was his grass, too, and not to be desecrated. No one said anything, for it was not necessary.

T. J. had reserved a small section for watermelons and he was still trying to find some seed for it. The wholesale house didn't have any watermelon seed and we didn't know where we could lay our hands on them. T. J. shaped the earth into mounds, ready to receive them, three mounds lying in a straight line along the edge of the grass plot.

We had just about decided that we'd have to buy the seed if we were to get them. It was a violation of our principles, but we were anxious to get the watermelons started. Somewhere or other, T. J. got his hands on a seed catalog and brought it one evening to our roof garden.

"We can order them now," he said, showing us the catalog. "Look!"

We all crowded around, looking at the fat, green watermelons pictured in full color on the pages. Some of them were split open, showing the red tempting meat, making our mouths water.

"Now we got to scrape up some seed money," T. J. said, looking at us. "I got a quarter. How much you-all got?"

We made up a couple of dollars between us and T. J. nodded his head. "That'll be more than enough. Now we got to decide what kind to get. I think them Kleckley Sweets. What do you-all think?"

He was going into esoteric matters, beyond our reach. We hadn't even known there were different kinds of melons. So we just nodded our heads and agreed that yes, we thought the Kleckley Sweets, too.

"I'll order them tonight," T. J. said. "We ought to have them in a few days."

Then an adult voice said behind us: "What are you boys doing up here?"

It startled us, for no one had ever come up here before, in all the time we had been using the roof of the factory. We jerked around and saw three men standing near the trapdoor at the other end of the roof. They weren't policemen, or night watchmen, but three men in plump business suits, looking at us. They walked toward us.

"What are you boys doing up here?" the one in the middle said again.

We stood still, guilt heavy among us, levied by the tone of voice, and looked at the three strangers.

The men stared at the grass flourishing behind us. "What's this?" the man said. "How did this get up here?"

"Sure is growing good, ain't it?" T. J. said conversationally. "We planted it."

The men kept looking at the grass as if they didn't believe it. It was a thick carpet over the earth now, a patch of deep greenness startling in the sterile industrial surroundings.

"Yes, sir," T. J. said proudly. "We toted that earth up here and planted that grass." He fluttered the seed catalog. "And we're just fixing to plant us some watermelon."

The man looked at him then, his eyes strange and faraway. "What do you mean, putting this on the roof of my building?" he said. "Do you want to go to jail?"

T. J. looked shaken. The rest of us were silent, frightened by the authority of his voice. We had grown up aware of adult authority, of policemen and night watchmen and teachers, and this man sounded like all the others. But it was a new thing to T. J.

"Well, you wan't using the roof," T. J. said. He paused a moment and added shrewdly, "So we just thought to pretty it up a little bit."

"And sag it so I'd have to rebuild it," the man said sharply. He turned away, saying to a man beside him, "See that all that junk is shoveled off by tomorrow."

"Yes, sir," the man said.

T. J. started forward. "You can't do that," he said. "We toted it up here and it's our earth. We planted it and raised it and toted it up here."

The man stared at him coldly. "But it's my building," he said. "It's to be shoveled off tomorrow."

"It's our earth," T. J. said desperately. "You ain't got no right!"

The men walked on without listening and descended clumsily through the trapdoor. T. J. stood looking after them, his body tense with anger, until they had disappeared. They wouldn't even argue with him, wouldn't let him defend his earth-rights.

He turned to us. "We won't let 'em do it," he said fiercely. "We'll stay up here all day tomorrow and the day after that and we won't let 'em do it."

We just looked at him. We knew that there was no stopping it. He saw it in our faces and his face wavered for a moment before he gripped it into determination.

"They ain't got no right," he said. "It's our earth. It's our land. Can't nobody touch a man's own land."

We kept on looking at him, listening to the words but knowing that it was no use. The adult world had descended on us even in our richest dream, and we knew there was no calculating the adult world, no fighting it, no winning against it.

We started moving slowly toward the parapet and the fire escape, avoiding a last look at the green beauty of the earth that T. J. had planted for us . . . had planted deeply in our minds as well as in our experience. We filed slowly over the edge and down the steps to the plank, T. J. coming last, and all of us could feel the weight of his grief behind us.

"Wait a minute," he said suddenly, his voice harsh with the effort of calling. We stopped and turned, held by the tone of his voice, and looked up at him standing above us on the fire escape.

"We can't stop them?" he said, looking down at us, his face strange in the dusky light. "There ain't no way to stop 'em?"

"No," Blackie said with finality. "They own the building."

We stood still for a moment, looking up at T. J., caught into inaction by the decision working in his face. He stared back at us and his face was pale and mean in the poor light, with a bald nakedness in his skin like cripples have sometimes.

"They ain't gonna touch my earth," he said fiercely. "They ain't gonna lay a hand on it! Come on."

He turned around and started up the fire escape again, almost running against the effort of climbing. We followed more slowly, not knowing what he intended. By the time we reached him, he had seized a board and thrust it into the soil, scooping it up and flinging it over the parapet into the areaway below. He straightened and looked us squarely in the face.

"They can't touch it," he said. "I won't let 'em lay a dirty hand on it!"

We saw it then. He stooped to his labor again and we followed it, the gusts of his anger moving in frenzied labor among us as we scattered along the edge of earth, scooping it and throwing it over the parapet, destroying with anger the growth we had nurtured with such tender care. The soil carried so laboriously upward to the light and the sun cascaded swiftly into the dark areaway, the green blades of grass crumpled and twisted in the falling.

It took less time than you would think . . . the task of destruction is infinitely easier than that of creation. We stopped at the end, leaving only a scattering of loose soil, and when it was finally over, a stillness stood among the group and over the factory building. We looked down at the bare sterility of black tar, felt the harsh texture of it under the soles of our shoes, and the anger had gone out of us, leaving only a sore aching in our minds like overstretched muscles.

T. J. stooped for a moment, his breathing slowing from anger and effort, caught into the same contemplation of destruction as all of us. He stooped slowly, finally, and picked up a lonely blade of grass left trampled under our feet, and put it between his teeth, tasting it, sucking the greenness out of it into his mouth. Then he started walking toward the fire escape, moving before any of us were ready to move, and disappeared over the edge while we stared after him.

We followed him but he was already halfway down to the ground, going on past the board where we crossed over, climbing down into the areaway. We saw the last section swing down with his weight and then he stood on the concrete below us, looking at the small pile of anonymous earth scattered by our throwing. Then he walked across the place where we could see him and disappeared toward the street without glancing back, without looking up to see us watching him.

They did not find him for two weeks. Then the Nashville police caught him just outside the Nashville freight yards. He was walking along the railroad track; still heading south, still heading home.

As for us, who had no remembered home to call us . . . none of us ever again climbed the escapeway to the roof. ∎

THE IMPACT OF THE STORY

Like "The Cask of Amontillado," "Antaeus" is told from the point of view of a person many years after the events happened. You may be familiar with this kind of personal recollection from reading Harper Lee's novel *To Kill a Mockingbird* or from watching movies such as *Fried Green Tomatoes.*

Take some time to think of other movies, stories, or television shows that are structured in this way. How does this apparent interval between the time of the story and the time of the narration contribute to a story's overall effect?

THE FACTS OF THE STORY

On your own paper, write answers to the following items. Answers may be one word, a phrase, or several sentences.

1. The plot of this story is based on the attempts of the boys to _____.

2. What obstacles must they overcome in their struggle?

3. Why do they fail?

4. The climax of the story occurs when _____.

5. There are two settings in this story—the garden and the city surrounding it. How do the two settings contrast?

THE IDEAS IN THE STORY

Prepare to discuss the following questions in class.

1. In the final sentence of the story, the narrator says that he and the other boys "had no remembered home to call us." What do you think he means by this? Do you think people need "green worlds" such as the one created on the rooftop? What does the narrator mean when he says that T. J. had planted "the green beauty of the earth . . . deeply in our minds"?

2. In "The Birds," you saw that people like the Triggs often cannot understand what they themselves have not experienced.

Explain how and where this same kind of human characteristic appears in "Antaeus."

3. A major problem faced by all young people is how to adjust to the demands of the adult world. What in their experience makes the other boys react differently than T. J. does to the orders of the factory owner?

THE ART OF THE STORYTELLER

Characterization
Characterization is more important in some stories than in others. Plot is the main element in both "The Most Dangerous Game" and "To Build a Fire." However, to a certain extent, characterization is also important in both of these stories. General Zaroff's peculiarities must be made clear to the reader because the whole story hinges on his "different" taste in games. Although the principal character in "To Build a Fire" is not even given a name in the story, it is his lack of understanding that fuels the plot.

In "Antaeus" the characters are more interesting and memorable than the plot. While you are not likely to forget what happens in the story, the chances are that you will remember even more vividly T. J. himself. It is his ideas and his personality that determine the action. Through what actions does T. J. demonstrate the following qualities of a natural leader?

1. imagination

2. ability to persuade

3. ability to organize and plan

4. willingness to compromise, to give in, on occasion

5. willingness to set an example for others

Allusion
The title of this story, "Antaeus," refers to a character in Greek mythology. Antaeus was a powerful giant who forced any stranger who entered his land to wrestle with him. One of the sons of Gaea, or Mother Earth, he could not die as long as he touched

the ground. Antaeus finally met his match in battle with the famed Heracles (Hercules in Roman mythology). As they fought, Antaeus grew stronger every time he fell to the ground. Realizing what was happening, Heracles lifted the giant into the air so that he could not get strength from the ground. Then Heracles strangled him.

This kind of reference to something not in the story is called an **allusion.** An author uses allusions to help readers deepen their understanding of something in the story by linking it to something else. How does the allusion to the mythological Antaeus help us to better understand the boy T. J. in the story "Antaeus"?

This particular allusion is a *literary allusion*, that is, a reference to a character, place, or event in literature. A *historical allusion* refers to an event, person, or place in history.

Without realizing it, we use many allusions in everyday language. "Playing Cupid" refers to the mythological character Cupid. The expression "We reap what we sow" comes from the Bible. During the administration of President Kennedy, the White House was called "Camelot," an allusion to the legend of King Arthur. Can you think of other common allusions?

THE VOCABULARY IN THE STORY

When talking about literature, we often refer to **voice,** the language style used by the author to create the effect of a particular speaker. The style of language used by the narrator is his voice. As readers, we infer much about the narrator's background, feelings, and attitudes from the words he uses and how he uses them.

In "Antaeus," the narrator is an adult looking back at an incident from childhood. Thus, he uses some formal language with complex constructions as well as some more relaxed vocabulary and usages, including colloquialisms and contractions.

> Thinking about it now, I don't see how he kept us at it. It was hard work, lugging paper sacks and boxes of dirt all the way up the stairs of our own building, keeping out of the way of the grown-ups so they wouldn't catch on to what we were doing.

Notice how the use of the words *lugging, grown-ups,* and *catch on* creates an informal tone here.

Look closely at the following excerpts from the story. Where does the language sound more like an adult and where does it sound like a young boy's way of speaking?

1. They were all talking about it suddenly, all excited with the idea after I'd put it in a way they could catch hold of it. Only rich people had roof gardens, we knew, and the idea of our own private domain excited them.

2. His voice was resolute with the knowledge of his rightness and for a moment no one had anything to say.

3. Perhaps half the roof was covered with the earth, the half that wasn't broken by ventilators, and we swiped pocketfuls of grass seed from the open bins in the wholesale seed house, mingling among the buyers on Saturdays and during the school lunch hour.

COMPOSITION: Writing a Character Sketch

A writer may portray a fictional person by writing a short story about him or her, as Borden Deal did when he wrote about T. J. Or a writer may portray a real person in an article of the kind found in newspapers or popular magazines about important people in the news or people prominent in theater, television, movies, music, or sports. Such an article is called a *character sketch.*

Write a character sketch (about 200 words) of someone you know or once knew. You might choose to write about someone you admire or about someone you dislike.

Prewriting

Before you begin, jot down the main character traits of the person you have chosen. Then select the traits you want to emphasize, especially those that reflect your attitude toward that person.

Also, think of at least one interesting anecdote, a very brief story, telling about something that the person did. Remember that it is through their *actions* that we learn most about what people are like.

Writing
Open the character sketch with a topic sentence introducing your subject. You might want to describe the person physically, but don't spend a lot of time doing it. Your sketch should concentrate on your subject's personality and actions, not appearance.

Evaluating and Revising.
Read your draft. Make sure your character sketch clearly reveals your attitude toward the person. Add, cut, rearrange, or replace words or phrases as needed. Do you think a reader who is unfamiliar with your subject would be able to describe briefly the person on the basis of your sketch?

ABOUT THE AUTHOR

 Borden Deal (1922–   ) was born into a farm family in Pontotoc, Mississippi. He knows well what life was like in Southern farming communities during the hard years of the 1930s Depression and during World War II. Many of his stories and novels are about similar communities. Deal witnessed the migration of families from farms in the South to cities in the North, where jobs were available in war industries. Note that his story "Antaeus" begins, "This was during the wartime . . . "

■ THE CHALLENGE

Gary Soto

The new girl in school is cute and can eat a lunch that puts
a weightlifter to shame, but try as he might, José can't get
her attention. He even starts studying in order to make
good grades to impress her. Now he's found a way to make
contact, but it may turn out to be the toughest challenge of
his young life.

For three weeks José tried to get the attention of Estela, the
new girl at his middle school. She's cute, he said to himself
when he first saw her in the cafeteria, unloading her lunch of
two sandwiches, potato chips, a piece of cake wrapped in waxed
paper, and boxed juice from a brown paper bag. "Man, can she
grub!"

On the way home from school he walked through the alleys of his
town, Fresno, kicking cans. He was lost in a dream, trying to figure
out a way to make Estela notice him. He thought of tripping in front
of her while she was leaving her math class, but he had already tried
that with a girl in sixth grade. All he did was rip his pants and bruise
his knee, which kept him from playing in the championship soccer
game. And that girl had just stepped over him as he lay on the ground,
the shame of rejection reddening his face.

He thought of going up to Estela and saying, in his best James
Bond voice, "Camacho. José Camacho, at your service." He imagined
she would say, "Right-o," and together they would go off and talk
in code.

He even tried doing his homework. Estela was in his history class,
and so he knew she was as bright as a cop's flashlight shining in your
face. While they were studying Egypt, José amazed the teacher, Mrs.
Flores, when he scored twenty out of twenty on a quiz—and then eighteen out of twenty when she retested him the same day because she
thought that he had cheated.

"Mrs. Flores, I studied hard—*¡de veras!*[1] You can call my mom," he

---

1. *¡de veras!*: Spanish for "really," "seriously."

argued, his feelings hurt. And he *had* studied, so much that his mother had asked, "*¿Qué pasó?*[2] What's wrong?"

"I'm going to start studying," he'd answered.

His mother bought him a lamp because she didn't want him to strain his eyes. She even fixed him hot chocolate and watched her son learn about the Egyptian god Osiris, about papyrus and mummification. The mummies had scared her so much that she had heated up a second cup of chocolate to soothe herself.

But when the quizzes had been returned and José bragged, "Another A-plus," Estela didn't turn her head and ask, "Who's that brilliant boy?" She just stuffed her quiz into her backpack and left the classroom, leaving José behind to retake the test.

One weekend he had wiped out while riding his bike, popping up over curbs with his eyes closed. He somersaulted over his handlebars and saw a flash of shooting stars as he felt the slap of his skin against the asphalt. Blood rushed from his nostrils like twin rivers. He bicycled home, his blood-darkened shirt pressed to his nose. When he examined his face in the mirror, he saw that he had a scrape on his chin, and he liked that. He thought Estela might pity him. In history class she would cry, "Oh, what happened?" and then he would talk nonsense about a fight with three *vatos*.[3]

But Estela had been absent the Monday and Tuesday after his mishap. By the time she returned on Wednesday his chin had nearly healed.

José figured out another way to get to know her. He had noticed the grimy, sweat-blackened handle of a racket poking out of her backpack. He snapped his fingers and said to himself, "Racquetball. I'll challenge her to a game."

He approached her during lunch. She was reading from her science book and biting into her second sandwich, which was thick with slabs of meat, cheese, and a blood-red tomato. "Hi," José said, sitting across the table from her. "How do you like our school?"

Estela swallowed, cleared her throat, drank from her milk carton until it collapsed, and said, "It's OK. But the hot water doesn't work in the girls' showers."

---

2. *¿Qué pasó?*: Spanish for "What's going on?"
3. *vatos*: Spanish slang for "guys" or "dudes."

"It doesn't work in ours either," he remarked. Trying to push the conversation along, he continued, "Where are you from?"

"San Diego," she said. She took another monstrous bite of her sandwich, which amazed José and made him think of his father, a carpenter, who could eat more than anyone José knew.

José, eager to connect, took a deep breath and said, "I see that you play racquetball. You wanna play a game?"

"Are you good?" Estela asked flatly. She picked up a slice of tomato that had slid out of her sandwich.

"Pretty good," he said without thinking as he slipped into a lie. "I won a couple of tournaments."

He watched as the tomato slice slithered down Estela's throat. She wiped her mouth and said, "Sure. How about after school on Friday."

"That's tomorrow," José said.

"That's right. Today's Thursday and tomorrow's Friday." She flattened the empty milk carton with her fist, slapped her science book closed, and hurled the carton and her balled-up lunch at the plastic-lined garbage can. "What's your name?"

"Camacho. José Camacho."

"I'm Estela. My friends call me Stinger."

"Stinger?"

"Yeah, Stinger. I'll meet you at the courts at 3:45." She got up and headed toward the library.

After school José pedaled his bike over to his uncle Freddie's house. His uncle was sixteen, only three years older than José. It made José feel awkward when someone, usually a girl, asked, "Who's that hunk?" and he would have to answer, "My uncle."

"Freddie," José yelled, skidding to a stop in the driveway.

Freddie was in the garage lifting weights. He was dressed in sweats and a Raiders sweatshirt, the hem of his T-shirt sticking out in a fringe. He bench-pressed 180 pounds, then put the weights down and said, "Hey, dude."

"Freddie, I need to borrow your racquetball racket," José said.

Freddie rubbed his sweaty face on the sleeve of his sweatshirt. "I didn't know you played."

"I don't. I got a game tomorrow."

"But you don't know how to play."

José had been worrying about this on his bike ride over. He had told Estela that he had won tournaments.

"I'll learn," José said.

"In one day? Get serious."

"It's against a girl."

"So. She'll probably whip you twenty-one to *nada*."[4]

"No way."

But José's mind twisted with worry. What if she did, he asked himself. What if she whipped him through and through. He recalled her crushing the milk carton with one blow of her fist. He recalled the sandwiches she downed at lunch. Still, he had never encountered a girl who was better than he was at sports, except for Dolores Ramirez, who could hit homers with the best of them.

Uncle Freddie pulled his racket from the garage wall. Then he explained to José how to grip the racket. He told him that the game was like handball, that the play was off the front, the ceiling, and the side walls. "Whatever you do, don't look behind you. The ball comes back—fast. You can get your *ojos*[5] knocked out."

"Yeah, I got it," José said vaguely, feeling the weight of the racket in his hand. He liked how it felt when he pounded the sweet spot of the strings against his palm.

Freddie resumed lifting weights, and José biked home, swinging the racket as he rode.

That night after dinner José went outside and asked his father, "Dad, has a girl ever beaten you at anything?"

His father was watering the grass, his shirt off and a stub of cigarette dangling from his mouth. His pale belly hung over his belt, just slightly, like a deflated ball.

"Only talking," he said. "They can outtalk a man any day of the week."

"No, in sports."

His father thought for a while and then said, "No, I don't think so."

His father's tone of voice didn't encourage José. So he took the racket and a tennis ball and began to practice against the side of the garage. The ball raced away like a rat. He retrieved it and tried again. Every time, he hit it either too softly or too hard, and he couldn't get the rhythm of a rally going.

---

4. **nada**: Spanish, for "nothing."
5. **ojos**: Spanish for "eyes."

"It's hard," he said to himself. But then he remembered that he was playing with a tennis ball, not a racquetball. He assumed that he would play better with a real ball.

The next day school was as dull as usual. He took a test in history and returned to his regular score of twelve out of twenty. Mrs. Flores was satisfied.

"I'll see you later," Estela said, hoisting her backpack onto one shoulder, the history quiz crumpled in her fist.

"OK, Estela," he said.

"Stinger," she corrected.

"Yeah, Stinger. 3:45."

José was beginning to wonder whether he really liked her. Now she seemed abrupt, not cute. She was starting to look like Dolores "Hit 'n' Spit" Ramirez—tough.

After school José walked slowly to the outdoor three-walled courts. They were empty, except for a gang of sparrows pecking at an old hamburger wrapper.

José practiced hitting the tennis ball against the wall. It was too confusing. The ball would hit the front wall, then ricochet off the side wall. He spent most of his time running after the ball or cursing himself for bragging that he had won tournaments.

Estela arrived, greeting José with a jerk of her chin and a "Hey, dude." She was dressed in white sweats. A pair of protective goggles dangled around her neck like a necklace, and she wore sweatbands on both wrists. She opened a can of balls and rolled one out into her palm, squeezing it so tightly that her forearm rippled with muscle. When she smacked the ball against the wall so hard that the echo hurt his ears, José realized that he was in trouble. He felt limp as a dead fish.

Estela hit the ball repeatedly. When she noticed that José was just standing there, his racket in one hand and a dog-slobbered tennis ball in the other, she asked, "Aren't you going to practice?"

"I forgot my balls at home," he said.

"Help yourself." She pointed with the racket toward the can.

José took a ball, squeezed it, and bounced it once. He was determined to give Estela a show. He bounced it again, swung with all his might, and hit it out of the court.

"Oops," he said. "I'll go get it, Stinger."

He found the ball in the gutter, splotched with mud that he wiped off on his pants. When he returned to the court Estela had peeled off her sweats and was working a pair of knee pads up her legs. José noticed that her legs were bigger than his, and they quivered like the flanks of a thoroughbred horse.

"You ready?" she asked, adjusting her goggles over her eyes. "I have to leave at five."

"Almost," he said. He took off his shirt, then put it back on when he realized how skinny his chest was. "Yeah, I'm ready. You go first."

Estela, sizing him up, said, "No, you go first."

José decided to accept the offer. He figured he needed all the help he could get. He bounced the ball and served into the ground twice.

"You're out," she said, scooping the ball up onto her racket and walking briskly to the service box. José wanted to ask why, but he kept quiet. After all, he thought, I am the winner of several tournaments.

"Zero-zero," Estela said, then served the ball, which ricocheted off the front and side walls. José swung wildly and missed by at least a foot. Then he ran after the ball, which had rolled out of the court onto the grass. He returned it to Estela and said, "Nice, Estela."

"Stinger."

"Yeah, Stinger."

Estela called out, "One-nothing." She wound up again and sizzled the ball right at José's feet. He swung and hit his kneecap with the racket. The pain jolted him like a shock of electricity as he went down, holding his knee and grimacing. Estela chased the ball for him.

"Can you play?" she asked.

He nodded as he rose to his feet.

"Two-nothing," she said, again bouncing the ball off the front wall, this time slower so that José swung before the ball reached his racket. He swung again, the racket spinning like a whirlwind. The ball sailed slowly past him, and he had to chase it down again.

"I guess that's three to nothing, right?" José said lamely.

"Right." Estela lobbed the ball. As it came down, José swung hard. His racket slipped from his fingers and flew out of the court.

"Oops," he said. The racket was caught on the top of the chain-link fence surrounding the courts. For a moment José thought of pulling the racket down and running home. But he had to stick it out. Anyway, he thought, my backpack is at the court.

"Four-nothing," Estela called when she saw José running back to the court, his chest heaving. She served again, and José, closing his eyes, connected. The ball hit the wall, and for three seconds they had a rally going. But then Estela moved in and killed the ball with a low corner shot.

"Five-nothing," she said. "It's getting cold. Let me get my sweats back on."

She slipped into her sweats and threw off her sweatbands. José thought about asking to borrow the sweatbands because he had worked up a lather of sweat. But his pride kept him quiet.

Estela served again and again until the score was seventeen to nothing and José was ragged from running. He wished the game would end. He wished he would score just one point. He took off his shirt and said, "Hey, you're pretty good."

Estela served again, gently this time, and José managed to return the ball to the front wall. Estela didn't go after it, even though she was just a couple of feet from the ball. "Nice corner shot," she lied. "Your serve."

José served the ball and, hunching over with his racket poised, took crab steps to the left, waiting for the ball to bounce off the front wall. Instead he heard a thunderous smack and felt himself leap like a trout. The ball had hit him in the back, and it stung viciously. He ran off the court and threw himself on the grass, grimacing from the pain. It took him two minutes to recover, time enough for Estela to take a healthy swig from the bottle of Gatorade in her sport bag. Finally, through his teeth, he muttered, "Good shot, Stinger."

"Sorry," Estela said. "You moved into my lane. Serve again."

José served and then cowered out of the way, his racket held to his face for protection. She fired the ball back, clean and low, and once again she was standing at the service line calling, "Service."

Uncle Freddie was right. He had lost twenty-one to *nada*. After a bone-jarring handshake and a pat on his aching back from Estela, he hobbled to his uncle's house, feeling miserable. Only three weeks ago he'd been hoping that Estela—Stinger—might like him. Now he hoped she would stay away from him.

Uncle Freddie was in the garage lifting weights. Without greeting him, José hung the racket back on the wall. Uncle Freddie lowered the weights, sat up, and asked, "So how did it go?"

José didn't feel like lying. He lifted his T-shirt and showed his uncle the big red mark the ball had raised on his back. "She's bad."

"It could have been your face," Freddie said as he wiped away sweat and lay back down on his bench. "Too bad."

José sat on a pile of bundled newspapers, hands in his lap. When his uncle finished his "reps,"[6] José got up slowly and peeled the weights down to sixty pounds. It was his turn to lift. He needed strength to mend his broken heart and for the slight chance that Stinger might come back, looking for another victory. ■

---

6. **"reps"**: repetitions.

THE IMPACT OF THE STORY

Getting to know someone you would like to date or befriend can be a tricky matter because it involves some risk—risk that you will be rejected or that you will not like the other person once you get acquainted. If you were approached by someone who found you interesting, how might you want that person to start the conversation? How might you respond?

THE FACTS OF THE STORY

On your own paper, write answers to the following items. Answers may be one word, a phrase, or several sentences.

1. Why does José decide to begin studying for school? Are his efforts successful?

2. What are some of the clues that Estela may be more than José's match at racquetball?

3. José's father says a woman can beat him at _____.

4. In what way is Estela kind to José during the racquetball game?

5. What is the final score of José and Estela's racquetball game?

THE IDEAS IN THE STORY

Prepare to discuss the following questions in class.

1. José assumes that because he is male he will automatically be as good as or better at sports than a female. In light of the story's events, do you think this is a valid assumption? Do you think boys are better at sports than girls? Explain.

2. This story's title refers to José's main challenge to play a game of racquetball against Estela. What other challenges does José face?

3. Like José, most people have probably at one time or another changed their behavior or told a white lie to impress another

person or to avoid appearing foolish or inferior. What are the consequences of José's pretending that he is a good racquetball player? Do you think José learns anything from his experiences? If so, what?

THE ART OF THE STORYTELLER

The Character Story

"The Challenge" is a story in which characterization is the most important element. The author concentrates on José. The story has a plot, of course, but the events are important only because of what they show us about José and Estela.

Gary Soto uses three methods of characterization: He describes what José *does;* he tells us what José *thinks* and *says;* and he shows us how *others react* to José. In the following excerpts from the story, identify these three types of characterization.

1. On the way home from school he walked through the alleys of his town, Fresno, kicking cans. He was lost in a dream, trying to figure out a way to make Estela notice him. He thought of tripping in front of her while she was leaving her math class, but he had already tried that with a girl in sixth grade. All he did was rip his pants and bruise his knee, which kept him from playing in the championship soccer game. And that girl had just stepped over him as he lay on the ground, the shame of rejection reddening his face.

2. He even tried doing his homework. Estela was in his history class, and so he knew she was as bright as a cop's flashlight shining in your face. While they were studying Egypt, José amazed the teacher, Mrs. Flores, when he scored twenty out of twenty on a quiz—and then eighteen out of twenty when she retested him the same day because she thought that he had cheated.

   "Mrs. Flores, I studied hard—¡de veras! You can

call my mom," he argued, his feelings hurt. And he *had* studied, so much that his mother had asked, "*¿Qué pasó?* What's wrong?"

3. Estela served again and again until the score was seventeen to nothing and José was ragged from running. He wished the game would end. He wished he would score just one point. He took off his shirt and said, "Hey, you're pretty good."

   Estela served again, gently this time, and José managed to return the ball to the front wall. Estela didn't go after it, even though she was just a couple of feet from the ball. "Nice corner shot," she lied. "Your serve."

Theme

The theme is rarely stated directly in literature. Most often, you have to infer the theme of a story after considerable thought. Theme is different from subject. For example, a story's subject might be stated as "growing up," "love," "heroism," or "fear." The theme of a story is the statement about that subject: "For most young people, growing up is a process that involves the pain of achieving self-knowledge." A theme must be stated in at least one sentence; most themes are complex enough to require several sentences, or even an essay.

The subjects of "The Challenge" are preconceptions, prejudice, pride, honesty, and growing up. José Camacho spends a great deal of time thinking about and trying to impress girls, particularly Estela, by pretending he is something or someone he isn't. He imagines scenes in which he is the object of Estela's admiration or pity and in which Estela's role is reduced to little more than a stereotype. However, José's fantasy of Estela as a female differs greatly from the real-life Estela. How does José's perception of Estela change during the story? In what ways does José grow up? What do you think is the theme of the story?

Humor

Much of what occurs in this story is memorable because of the humorous way in which the author characterizes José. Consider how the following humorous passage tells us something about José's character and personality:

He thought of going up to Estela and saying, in his best James Bond voice, "Camacho. José Camacho, at your service." He imagined she would say, "Right-o," and together they would go off and talk in code.

What is humorous about José's performance and manner during the racquetball game? Find other examples of humor in the story.

THE VOCABULARY IN THE STORY

Gary Soto's vivid descriptions of the characters in "The Challenge" and his lively action verbs help us to visualize the characters and the action. For instance, José didn't simply ride his bike; he "pedaled" it. The word *pedaled* reminds us that a bike has pedals and that it requires a specific kind of action to make it work. Estela didn't just hit the ball; she "fired" it. The word *fired* tells the reader how Estela hit the ball—hard, fast, and competitively. After José served the ball, he didn't just get out of the way; he "cowered out of the way." The word *cowered* suggests cowardice, fear, and a hunched up or crouching position.

Below is a list of some vivid verbs that Soto uses in "The Challenge." On your own paper, replace the italicized verb in each sentence with one from this list.

sizzled	jolted	flattened	slithered
skidded	hurled	stuffed	fired

1. Early Saturday morning, the jarring sound of the telephone *brought* me out of a sound sleep.

2. Later that morning, each of the twins *threw* an entire bowlful of hot oatmeal against the wall.

3. The boys laughed as the soft gray lumps slowly *fell* to the floor.

4. I was halfway to the garage to fetch a mop, when a bright red spoon *came* to a stop at my feet.

5. The next thing I knew, a blue spoon *came* by, missing my nose by an inch.

COMPOSITION: Writing an Explanation of How to Play a Game

Write a detailed explanation (about 300 words) of how to play a game. The game may be a sport such as racquetball, a computer game, a card or board game, or any other kind of game. You will need to explain such aspects as terminology, scorekeeping, strategy, and anything else that is necessary for a person to know in order to play this particular game.

Prewriting

Choose a game that you enjoy and that you know well. Begin by jotting down a statement that explains the object or purpose of the game. For example, the object of football is to score the most points by getting the ball across the goal line. Spend a few minutes reviewing the elements of the game you have selected and make a basic outline that follows the game's order. Begin with the opening move or play and end with the game's conclusion.

Writing

Using your outline as necessary, write your draft. Focus on writing quickly. You can correct spelling and grammar after your draft is completed.

Evaluating and Revising

Read your draft. Define any technical or unfamiliar terms. Your explanation should be clear, and it should follow the order of your outline. However, remember that you can still change or reorganize your outline. Finally, cut, reorder, or add words, phrases, or sections as needed.

ABOUT THE AUTHOR

Gary Soto (1952–) was born in Fresno, California. He grew up in the San Joaquin Valley where, as a child, he and his family were migrant laborers. Today he is an associate professor in the Department of English-Chicano Studies at the University of California, Berkeley. Soto is both a poet and prose writer who draws on his Mexican-American background.

His works have appeared in numerous collections such as *The Elements of San Joaquin* (poems); *Living up the Street: Narrative Recollections* (prose memoirs), for which he won the American Book Award from the Before Columbus Foundation in 1985; and *Lesser Evils: Ten Quartets* (essays).

RED DRESS

Alice Munro

This story is about a girl whose mother makes her a red dress
to wear to a Christmas dance at her school. The girl is thirteen
and in the ninth grade. Through her experiences at the dance,
she learns something about her mother, about herself, about
other people, and about happiness and unhappiness.

My mother was making me a dress. All through the month of
November I would come from school and find her in the
kitchen, surrounded by cut-up red velvet and scraps of
tissue-paper pattern. She worked at an old treadle machine pushed up
against the window to get the light, and also to let her look out, past
the stubble fields and bare vegetable garden, to see who went by on
the road. There was seldom anybody to see.

The red velvet material was hard to work with, it pulled, and the
style my mother had chosen was not easy either. She was not really a
good sewer. She liked to make things; that is different. Whenever she
could she tried to skip basting and pressing, and she took no pride in
the fine points of tailoring, the finishing of buttonholes and the
overcasting of seams, as, for instance, my aunt and my grandmother
did. Unlike them she started off with an inspiration, a brave and dazzling idea; from that moment on, her pleasure ran downhill. In the first
place she could never find a pattern to suit her. It was no wonder; there
were no patterns made to match the ideas that blossomed in her head.
She had made me, at various times when I was younger, a flowered
organdy dress with a high Victorian neckline edged in scratchy lace,
with a poke bonnet to match; a Scottish plaid outfit with a velvet jacket
and tam; an embroidered peasant blouse worn with a full, red skirt
and black-laced bodice. I had worn these clothes with docility, even
pleasure, in the days when I was unaware of the world's opinion. Now,
grown wiser, I wished for dresses like those my friend Lonnie had,
bought at Beale's store.

I had to try it on. Sometimes Lonnie came home from school with
me and she would sit on the couch watching. I was embarrassed by
the way my mother crept around me, her knees creaking, her breath

129

coming heavily. She muttered to herself. Around the house she wore no corset or stockings, she wore wedge-heeled shoes and ankle socks; her legs were marked with lumps of blue-green veins. I thought her squatting position shameless, even obscene; I tried to keep talking to Lonnie so that her attention would be taken away from my mother as much as possible. Lonnie wore the composed, polite, appreciative expression that was her disguise in the presence of grown-ups. She laughed at them and was a ferocious mimic, and they never knew.

My mother pulled me about, and pricked me with pins. She made me turn around, she made me walk away, she made me stand still. "What do you think of it, Lonnie?" she said around the pins in her mouth.

"It's beautiful," said Lonnie, in her mild, sincere way. Lonnie's own mother was dead. She lived with her father, who never noticed her, and this, in my eyes, made her seem both vulnerable and privileged.

"It *will* be, if I can ever manage the fit," my mother said. "Ah, well," she said theatrically, getting to her feet with a woeful creaking and sighing, "I doubt if she appreciates it." She enraged me, talking like this to Lonnie, as if Lonnie were grown up and I were still a child. "Stand still," she said, hauling the pinned and basted dress over my head. My head was muffled in velvet, my body exposed, in an old cotton school slip. I felt like a great raw lump, clumsy and goose-pimpled. I wished I was like Lonnie, light-boned, pale and thin; she had been a Blue Baby.[1]

"Well, nobody ever made me a dress when I was going to high school," my mother said, "I made my own, or I did without." I was afraid she was going to start again on the story of her walking seven miles to town and finding a job waiting on tables in a boarding house, so that she could go to high school. All the stories of my mother's life which had once interested me had begun to seem melodramatic, irrelevant, and tiresome.

"One time I had a dress given to me," she said. "It was a cream-colored cashmere wool with royal blue piping down the front and lovely mother-of-pearl buttons, I wonder whatever became of it?"

When we got free Lonnie and I went upstairs to my room. It was cold, but we stayed there. We talked about the boys in our class, going up and down the rows and saying, "Do you like him? Well, do you half

---

1. **Blue Baby:** a baby born with bluish skin caused by a lung or heart problem.

like him? Do you *hate* him? Would you go out with him if he asked you?" Nobody had asked us. We were thirteen, and we had been going to high school for two months. We did questionnaires in magazines, to find out whether we had personality and whether we would be popular. We read articles on how to make up our faces to accentuate our good points and how to carry on a conversation on the first date. We had made a pact to tell each other everything. But one thing I did not tell was about this dance, the high school Christmas Dance for which my mother was making me a dress. It was that I did not want to go.

At high school I was never comfortable for a minute. I did not know about Lonnie. Before an exam, she got icy hands and palpitations, but I was close to despair at all times. When I was asked a question in class, any simple little question at all, my voice was apt to come out squeaky, or else hoarse and trembling. My hands became slippery with sweat when they were required to work the blackboard compass. I could not hit the ball in volleyball; being called upon to perform an action in front of others made all my reflexes come undone. I hated Business Practice because you had to rule pages for an account book, using a straight pen, and when the teacher looked over my shoulder all the delicate lines wobbled and ran together. I hated Science; we perched on stools under harsh lights behind tables of unfamiliar, fragile equipment, and were taught by the principal of the school, a man with a cold, self-relishing voice—he read the Scriptures every morning—and a great talent for inflicting humiliation. I hated English because the boys played bingo at the back of the room while the teacher, a stout, gentle girl, slightly cross-eyed, read Wordsworth at the front. She threatened them, she begged them, her face red and her voice as unreliable as mine. They offered burlesqued apologies and when she started to read again they took up rapt postures, made swooning faces, crossed their eyes, flung their hands over their hearts. Sometimes she would burst into tears, there was no help for it, she had to run out into the hall. Then the boys made loud mooing noises; our hungry laughter—oh, mine too—pursued her. There was a carnival atmosphere of brutality in the room at such times, scaring weak and suspect people like me.

But what was really going on in the school was not Business Practice and Science and English; there was something else that gave life its urgency and brightness. That old building, with its rock-walled clammy basements and black cloakrooms and pictures of dead royalties and lost explorers, was full of the tension and excitement of sexual competition, and in this, in spite of daydreams of vast successes, I had premonitions of total defeat. Something had to happen, to keep me from that dance.

With December came snow, and I had an idea. Formerly I had considered falling off my bicycle and spraining my ankle and I had tried to manage this, as I rode home along the hard-frozen, deeply rutted country roads. But it was too difficult. However, my throat and bronchial tubes were supposed to be weak; why not expose them? I started getting out of bed at night and opening my window a little. I knelt down and let the wind, sometimes stinging with snow, rush in around my bared throat. I took off my pajama top. I said to myself the words "blue with cold" and as I knelt there, my eyes shut, I pictured my chest and throat turning blue, the cold, grayed blue of veins under the skin. I stayed until I could not stand it any more, and then I took a handful of snow from the windowsill and smeared it all over my chest, before I buttoned my pajamas. It would melt against the flannelette and I would be sleeping in wet clothes, which was supposed to be the worst thing of all. In the morning, the moment I woke up, I cleared my throat, testing for soreness, coughed experimentally, hopefully, touched my forehead to see if I had fever. It was no good. Every morning, including the day of the dance, I rose defeated, and in perfect health.

The day of the dance I did my hair up in steel curlers. I had never done this before, because my hair was naturally curly, but today I wanted the protection of all possible female rituals. I lay on the couch in the kitchen, reading *The Last Days of Pompeii*[2] and wishing I was there. My mother, never satisfied, was sewing a white lace collar on the dress; she had decided it was too grown-up-looking. I watched the hours. It was one of the shortest days of the year. Above the couch, on the wallpaper, were old games of X's and O's, old drawings and scribblings my brother and I had done when we were sick with bronchitis. I looked at them and longed to be back safe behind the boundaries of childhood.

When I took out the curlers my hair, both naturally and artificially stimulated, sprang out in an exuberant glossy bush. I wet it, I combed

---

2. **Pompeii:** an ancient city in Italy which was destroyed in A.D. 79 by the eruption of the volcano Mount Vesuvius.

it, beat it with the brush and tugged it down along my cheeks. I applied face powder, which stood out chalkily on my hot face. My mother got out her Ashes of Roses cologne, which she never used, and let me splash it over my arms. Then she zipped up the dress and turned me around to the mirror. The dress was princess-style, very tight in the midriff.

"Well, I wish I could take a picture," my mother said. "I am really, genuinely proud of that fit. And you might say thank you for it."

"Thank you," I said.

The first thing Lonnie said when I opened the door to her was, "What did you do to your hair?"

"I did it up."

"You look like a Zulu. Oh, don't worry. Get me a comb and I'll do the front in a roll. It'll look all right. It'll even make you look older."

I sat in front of the mirror and Lonnie stood behind me, fixing my hair. My mother seemed unable to leave us. I wished she would. She watched the roll take shape and said, "You're a wonder, Lonnie. You should take up hairdressing."

"That's a thought," Lonnie said. She had on a pale blue crepe dress, with a peplum and bow; it was much more grown-up than mine even without the collar. Her hair had come out as sleek as the girl's on the bobby-pin card. I had always thought secretly that Lonnie could not be pretty because she had crooked teeth, but now I saw that crooked teeth or not, her stylish dress and smooth hair made me look a little like a golliwog, stuffed into red velvet, wide-eyed, wild-haired, with a suggestion of delirium.

My mother followed us to the door and called out into the dark, "Au reservoir!"[3] This was a traditional farewell of Lonnie's and mine; it sounded foolish and desolate coming from her, and I was so angry with her for using it that I did not reply. It was only Lonnie who called back cheerfully, encouragingly, "Good night!"

The gymnasium smelled of pine and cedar. Red and green bells of fluted paper hung from the basketball hoops; the high, barred windows were hidden by green boughs. Everybody in the upper grades seemed to have come in couples. Some of the Grade Twelve and Thirteen girls had brought boy friends who had already graduated,

---

3. **Au reservoir!** (ō rez′ ər vwär): a silly play on the French expression *au revoir* (ō′ rə vwär′), meaning "until we meet again."

who were young businessmen around the town. These young men smoked in the gymnasium, nobody could stop them, they were free. The girls stood beside them, resting their hands casually on male sleeves, their faces bored, aloof and beautiful. I longed to be like that. They behaved as if only they—the older ones—were really at the dance, as if the rest of us, whom they moved among and peered around, were, if not invisible, inanimate; when the first dance was announced—a Paul Jones—they moved out languidly, smiling at each other as if they had been asked to take part in some half-forgotten childish game. Holding hands and shivering, crowding up together, Lonnie and I and the other Grade Nine girls followed.

I didn't dare look at the outer circle as it passed me, for fear I should see some unmannerly hurrying-up. When the music stopped I stayed where I was, and half raising my eyes I saw a boy named Mason Williams coming reluctantly towards me. Barely touching my waist and my fingers, he began to dance with me. My legs were hollow, my arms trembled from the shoulder, I could not have spoken. This Mason Williams was one of the heroes of the school; he played basketball and hockey and walked the halls with an air of royal sullenness and barbaric contempt. To have to dance with a nonentity like me was as offensive to him as having to memorize Shakespeare. I felt this as keenly as he did, and imagined that he was exchanging looks of dismay with his friends. He steered me, stumbling, to the edge of the floor. He took his hand from my waist and dropped my arm.

"See you," he said. He walked away.

It took me a minute or two to realize what had happened and that he was not coming back. I went and stood by the wall alone. The Physical Education teacher, dancing past energetically in the arms of a Grade Ten boy, gave me an inquisitive look. She was the only teacher in the school who made use of the words "social adjustment," and I was afraid that if she had seen, or if she found out, she might make some horribly public attempt to make Mason finish out the dance with me. I myself was not angry or surprised at Mason; I accepted his position, and mine, in the world of school and I saw that what he had done was the realistic thing to do. He was a Natural Hero, not a Student Council type of hero bound for success beyond the school; one of those would have danced with me courteously and patronizingly and left me feeling no better off. Still, I hoped not many people had seen. I hated people seeing. I began to bite the skin on my thumb.

When the music stopped I joined the surge of girls to the end of the gymnasium. Pretend it didn't happen, I said to myself. Pretend this is the beginning, now.

The band began to play again. There was movement in the dense crowd at our end of the floor; it thinned rapidly. Boys came over, girls went out to dance. Lonnie went. The girl on the other side of me went. Nobody asked me. I remembered a magazine article Lonnie and I had read, which said *Be gay! Let the boys see your eyes sparkle, let them hear laughter in your voice! Simple, obvious, but how many girls forget!* It was true, I had forgotten. My eyebrows were drawn together with tension; I must look scared and ugly. I took a deep breath and tried to loosen my face. I smiled. But I felt absurd, smiling at no one. And I observed that girls on the dance floor, popular girls, were not smiling; many of them had sleepy, sulky faces and never smiled at all.

Girls were still going out to the floor. Some, despairing, went with each other. But most went with boys. Fat girls, girls with pimples, a poor girl who didn't own a good dress and had to wear a skirt and sweater to the dance; they were claimed, they danced away. Why take them and not me? Why everybody else and not me? I have a red velvet dress, I did my hair in curlers, I used a deodorant and put on cologne. *Pray,* I thought. I couldn't close my eyes but I said over and over again in my mind, *Please, me, please,* and I locked my fingers behind my back in a sign more potent than crossing, the same secret sign Lonnie and I used not to be sent to the blackboard in Math.

It did not work. What I had been afraid of was true. I was going to be left. There was something mysterious the matter with me, something that could not be put right like bad breath or overlooked like pimples, and everybody knew it, and I knew it; I had known it all along. But I had not known it for sure, I had hoped to be mistaken. Certainty rose inside me like sickness. I hurried past one or two girls who were also left and went into the girls' washroom. I hid myself in a cubicle.

There was where I stayed. Between dances girls came in and went out quickly. There were plenty of cubicles; nobody noticed that I was not a temporary occupant. During the dances, I listened to the music which I liked but had no part of any more. For I was not going to try any more. I only wanted to hide in here, get out without seeing anybody, get home.

One time after the music started somebody stayed behind. She was taking a long time running the water, washing her hands, combing her hair. She was going to think it funny that I stayed in so long. I had better go out and wash my hands, and maybe while I was washing them she would leave.

It was Mary Fortune. I knew her by name, because she was an officer of the Girls' Athletic Society and she was on the Honor Roll and she was always organizing things. She had something to do with organizing this dance; she had been around to all the classrooms asking for volunteers to do the decorations. She was in Grade Eleven or Twelve.

"Nice and cool in here," she said. "I came in to get cooled off. I get so hot."

She was still combing her hair when I finished my hands. "Do you like the band?" she asked.

"It's all right." I didn't really know what to say. I was surprised at her, an older girl, taking this time to talk to me.

"I don't. I can't stand it. I hate dancing when I don't like the band. Listen. They're so choppy. I'd just as soon not dance as dance to that."

I combed my hair. She leaned against a basin, watching me.

"I don't want to dance and don't particularly want to stay in here. Let's go and have a cigarette."

"Where?"

"Come on, I'll show you."

At the end of the washroom there was a door. It was unlocked and led into a dark closet full of mops and pails. She had me hold the door open, to get the washroom light until she found the knob of another door. This door opened into darkness.

"I can't turn on the light or somebody might see," she said. "It's the janitor's room." I reflected that athletes always seemed to know more than the rest of us about the school as a building; they knew where things were kept and they were always coming out of unauthorized doors with a bold, preoccupied air. "Watch out where you're going," she said. "Over at the far end there's some stairs. They go up to a closet on the second floor. The door's locked at the top, but there's like a partition between the stairs and the room. So if we sit on the steps, even if by chance someone did come in here, they wouldn't see us."

"Wouldn't they smell smoke?" I said.

"Oh, well. Live dangerously."

There was a high window over the stairs which gave us a little light.

Mary Fortune had cigarettes and matches in her purse. I had not smoked before except the cigarettes Lonnie and I made ourselves, using papers and tobacco stolen from her father; they came apart in the middle. These were much better.

"The only reason I even came tonight," Mary Fortune said, "is because I am responsible for the decorations and I wanted to see, you know, how it looked once people got in there and everything. Otherwise, why bother? I'm not boy-crazy."

In the light from the high window I could see her narrow, scornful face, her dark skin pitted with acne, her teeth pushed together at the front, making her look adult and commanding.

"Most girls are. Haven't you noticed that? The greatest collection of boy-crazy girls you could imagine is right here in this school."

I was grateful for her attention, her company and her cigarette. I said I thought so too.

"Like this afternoon. This afternoon I was trying to get them to hang the bells and junk. They just get up on the ladders and fool around with boys. They don't care if it ever gets decorated. It's just an excuse. That's the only aim they have in life, fooling around with boys. As far as I'm concerned, they're idiots."

We talked about teachers, and things at school. She said she wanted to be a physical education teacher and she would have to go to college for that, but her parents did not have enough money. She said she planned to work her own way through, she wanted to be independent anyway, she would work in the cafeteria and in the summer she would do farm work, like picking tobacco. Listening to her, I felt the acute phase of my unhappiness passing. Here was someone who had suffered the same defeat as I had—I saw that—but she was full of energy and self-respect. She had thought of other things to do. She would pick tobacco.

We stayed there talking and smoking during the long pause in the music, when, outside, they were having doughnuts and coffee. When the music started again Mary said, "Look, do we have to hang around here any longer? Let's get our coats and go. We can go down to Lee's and have a hot chocolate and talk in comfort, why not?"

We felt our way across the janitor's room, carrying ashes and cigarette butts in our hands. In the closet, we stopped and listened to make sure there was nobody in the washroom. We came back into the light and threw the ashes into the toilet. We had to go out and cut across the dance floor to the cloakroom, which was beside the outside door.

A dance was just beginning. "Go around the edge of the floor," Mary said. "Nobody'll notice us."

I followed her. I didn't look at anybody. I didn't look for Lonnie. Lonnie was probably not going to be my friend any more, not as much as before anyway. She was what Mary would call boy-crazy.

I found that I was not so frightened, now that I had made up my mind to leave the dance behind. I was not waiting for anybody to choose me. I had my own plans. I did not have to smile or make signs for luck. It did not matter to me. I was on my way to have a hot chocolate, with my friend.

A boy said something to me. He was in my way. I thought he must be telling me that I had dropped something or that I couldn't go that way or that the cloakroom was locked. I didn't understand that he was asking me to dance until he said it over again. It was Raymond Bolting from our class, whom I had never talked to in my life. He thought I meant yes. He put his hand on my waist and almost without meaning to, I began to dance.

We moved to the middle of the floor. I was dancing. My legs had forgotten to tremble and my hands to sweat. I was dancing with a boy who had asked me. Nobody told him to, he didn't have to, he just asked me. Was it possible, could I believe it, was there nothing the matter with me after all?

I thought that I ought to tell him there was a mistake, that I was just leaving, I was going to have a hot chocolate with my girl friend. But I did not say anything. My face was making certain delicate adjustments, achieving with no effort at all the grave, absent-minded look of those who were chosen, those who danced. This was the face that Mary Fortune saw, when she looked out of the cloakroom door, her scarf already around her head. I made a weak waving motion with the hand that lay on the boy's shoulder, indicating that I apologized, that I didn't know what had happened and also that it was no use waiting for me. Then I turned my head away, and when I looked again she was gone.

Raymond Bolting took me home and Harold Simons took Lonnie home. We all walked together as far as Lonnie's corner. The boys were having an argument about a hockey game, which Lonnie and I could not follow. Then we separated into couples and Raymond continued with me the conversation he had been having with Harold. He did not seem to notice that he was now talking to me instead. Once or twice I said, "Well, I don't know, I didn't see that game," but after a while I decided just to say "H'm hmm," and that seemed to be all that was necessary.

One other thing he said was, "I didn't realize you lived such a long ways out." And he sniffled. The cold was making my nose run a little too, and I worked my fingers through the candy wrappers in my coat pocket until I found a shabby Kleenex. I didn't know whether I ought to offer it to him or not, but he sniffled so loudly that I finally said, "I just have this one Kleenex, it probably isn't even clean, it probably has ink on it. But if I was to tear it in half we'd each have something."

"Thanks," he said. "I sure could use it."

It was a good thing, I thought, that I had done that, for at my gate, when I said, "Well, good night," and after he said, "Oh, yeah. Good night," he leaned towards me and kissed me, briefly, with the air of one who knew his job when he saw it, on the corner of my mouth. Then he turned back to town, never knowing he had been my rescuer, that he had brought me from Mary Fortune's territory into the ordinary world.

I went around the house to the back door, thinking, I have been to a dance and a boy has walked me home and kissed me. It was all true. My life was possible. I went past the kitchen window and I saw my mother. She was sitting with her feet on the open oven door, drinking tea out of a cup without a saucer. She was just sitting and waiting for me to come home and tell her everything that had happened. And I would not do it, I never would. But when I saw the waiting kitchen, and my mother in her faded, fuzzy paisley kimono, with her sleepy but doggedly expectant face, I understood what a mysterious and oppressive obligation I had, to be happy, and how I had almost failed it, and would be likely to fail it, every time, and she would not know. ■

THE IMPACT OF THE STORY

The narrator of this story expresses her insecurities in terms of her relationship with her mother, her view of high school, and the Christmas dance, all as they are seen and experienced by a thirteen-year-old girl. Her encounters with other people at the dance cause her to reevaluate her assumptions about what makes a person happy.

Think about a time when you were in a situation which caused you to reconsider some of your ideas and feelings.

THE FACTS OF THE STORY

On your own paper write answers to the following items. Answers may be one word, a phrase, or several sentences.

1. What fact about her attitude toward the dance does the narrator keep from her closest friend?

2. What personal characteristic accounts for the girl's unhappiness in school?

3. What two experiences at the dance increase her unhappiness?

4. How does she try to escape from her unhappy situation at the dance?

5. What happens that makes the narrator feel that her life is possible after all?

THE IDEAS IN THE STORY

Prepare to discuss the following questions in class.

1. The narrator of this story says she fears something is wrong with her because no one asks her to dance. Only when Raymond asks her to dance (after she has stopped caring) does she think it is possible that there might be nothing wrong with her at all. Why do you suppose a simple invitation to dance would have such an impact on the girl? If Raymond had not invited her to dance and had not walked her home

and kissed her, would you agree that something is wrong with her? Did you find her response to Raymond's invitation and to his rather businesslike kiss believable? Tell why or why not.

2. We learn that the girl narrating the story is afraid of leaving the "safe" boundaries of her childhood, and that she sees the dance as a big test which she would prefer to avoid. Two things happen to her as a result of her experiences at the dance. One has to do with her feelings about herself: She realizes that there is basically nothing wrong with her. The other has to do with her feelings about her mother. What is the girl's attitude toward her mother before the dance? What does she decide when she sees her mother sitting in the kitchen waiting for her after the dance? Her decision reflects a change in attitude on the part of the girl toward her mother. How would you characterize this new attitude? How is this change in attitude related to the girl's newly discovered sense of self?

3. Think about the girl's discovery of Mary Fortune in the washroom, her "rescue" by Raymond Bolting, and her relief at being released from Mary's "territory" and returned to the "ordinary world." Do you think the girl cares for Raymond, or is she just relieved to be like everyone else? Why do you think she finds it desirable to be ordinary in an "ordinary world"? Why does the girl fear Mary Fortune's "territory"? Do you think Mary means what she says so scornfully about the "boy-crazy girls"?

THE ART OF THE STORYTELLER

Characterization

In life you get to know people well by watching what they do, by hearing what they say, by noticing what they look like, and by hearing what others say about them. Writers bring characters to life in the same ways: (1) They show us characters in action. (2) They let us know what the characters say and think. (3) They tell us what the characters look like. (4) They tell us how other people react to the characters. (5) Often, writers will tell us directly something about their characters. In "The Scarlet Ibis" James Hurst tells us directly that Doodle is "a nice crazy, like someone you meet in your dreams." In "To Build a Fire", Jack London directly states that his main character is "without imagination."

Each of the following quotations from "Red Dress" characterizes the narrator's mother. Tell which of the five methods of characterization are being used and what traits of the mother are revealed.

We also learn about the narrator of the story from what she says about her mother. What do these comments about her mother reveal about the narrator?

1. She was not really a good sewer. She liked to make things; that is different. . . . she took no pride in the fine points of tailoring. . . . she started off with an inspiration, a brave and dazzling idea; from that moment on, her pleasure ran downhill. In the first place she could never find a pattern to suit her. It was no wonder; there were no patterns made to match the ideas that blossomed in her head.

2. Around the house she wore no corset or stockings, she wore wedge-heeled shoes and ankle socks; her legs were marked with lumps of blue-green veins. I thought her squatting position shameless, even obscene. . . .

3. "Ah, well," she said theatrically, getting to her feet with a woeful creaking and sighing, "I doubt if she appreciates it."

4. She enraged me, talking like this to Lonnie, as if Lonnie were grown up and I were still a child.

5. She was sitting with her feet on the open oven door, drinking tea out of a cup without a saucer. She was just sitting and waiting for me to come home and tell her everything that had happened.

Theme

As you may have realized already, short stories are not only entertaining to read, but they also provide insight and commentary about human life. The main idea, or insight, in a story is its **theme**.

Sometimes the theme is stated directly by the author. More often, however, the author tells the story and leaves it to the reader to grasp the theme.

A short story, because it is relatively brief, usually has only one theme. Sometimes, however, depending on how complex the subject is, it may address more than one important idea.

The theme of "Red Dress" has to do with the importance of appearances: Sometimes an emphasis on appearances is at the expense of honesty. Name some instances in the story that support this theme.

THE VOCABULARY IN THE STORY

Connotation is the emotion or association that a word or phrase may arouse. Connotation is distinct from *denotation,* which is the literal or "dictionary" meaning of a word or phrase. For instance, take the words *chow* and *cuisine.* Both words refer to food, but *cuisine* connotes elegance, gourmet tastes, expensive restaurants, and ease. However, most people would probably associate *chow* with ordinary surroundings, plain or unappealing food, mess halls, or even indigestion.

In "Red Dress," the words that describe clothing often have connotations that add meaning to the story. For example, in the last scene of the story, the mother is wearing a "faded, fuzzy paisley kimono." With this description, Munro surrounds the mother with associations of both the exotic and the everyday. Because a kimono is a Japanese robe and paisleys are designs of Scottish origin, feelings of excitement, romance, and far-off places arise. Yet, the looseness of a kimono connotes comfort and relaxation. And, just as the robe is "faded" and "fuzzy," so, too, have the mother's dreams become faded, old, worn, and no longer clearly focused.

Give your associations for the italicized words in each of the following items. If you don't know a word's denotation, look it up in the dictionary.

1. . . . . a high Victorian neckline edged in scratchy lace, with a *poke* bonnet to match. . . .

2. . . . a Scottish plaid outfit with a velvet jacket and *tam* . . . .

3. "One time I had a dress given to me," she said. "It was a cream-colored cashmere wool with royal blue piping down the front and lovely *mother-of-pearl* buttons. . . ."

4. She worked at an old *treadle* machine pushed up against the window to get light.

COMPOSITION: Expressing an Opinion About a Story

Everyone who reads a story has an opinion about it. It is important that you learn to express your opinions clearly and to explain why you hold them.

Write a short paper (about 200 words) in which you give your opinion of "Red Dress."

Prewriting

Think about the story for a few minutes before you begin writing. What kinds of emotional responses do you have to it? Jot these down. Beside each response, briefly note why you feel this particular way. Before beginning your first draft, decide which response or responses most honestly represent your opinion of the story.

Writing

Express your opinion in your opening sentence. Try to say more than "I liked the story" or "I didn't like the story." Say something more specific and interesting, such as "I felt as if I were reading about myself in this story" or "I don't believe this story gives a realistic picture of a thirteen-year-old girl." Support your opening statement with at least three reasons that explain why you hold this opinion about the story.

Evaluating and Revising

Read your draft. Have you expressed your opinion clearly and concisely? Have you supported your opening statement with at least three reasons that clarify your opinion? Revise your draft as many times as necessary—adding, cutting, or reordering words or phrases.

ABOUT THE AUTHOR

Alice Munro's (1931–) stories and novels are about the day-to-day lives of ordinary people who live in the small towns and farms of Ontario, Canada, where she grew up and attended college. "Red Dress" is part of a collection of stories called *Dance of the Happy Shades*. The book won the Governor General's Award for Fiction in Canada in 1968.

■RULES OF THE GAME

Amy Tan

Waverly Jong, or Meimei as she is called by her family,
becomes a national chess champion by practicing hard and
learning well the "rules of the game" of chess. However, as
the young, American-born daughter of Chinese immigrant
parents living in San Francisco's Chinatown, she learns there
are other rules to a different kind of game—a game in which
her most formidable opponent is her own mother.

I was six when my mother taught me the art of invisible strength. It
was a strategy for winning arguments, respect from others, and
eventually, though neither of us knew it at the time, chess games.

"Bite back your tongue," scolded my mother when I cried loudly,
yanking her hand toward the store that sold bags of salted plums. At
home, she said, "Wise guy, he not go against wind. In Chinese we
say, Come from South, blow with wind—poom!—North will follow.
Strongest wind cannot be seen."

The next week I bit back my tongue as we entered the store with
the forbidden candies. When my mother finished her shopping, she
quietly plucked a small bag of plums from the rack and put it on the
counter with the rest of the items.

My mother imparted her daily truths so she could help my older brothers and me rise above our circumstances. We lived in San Francisco's
Chinatown.[1] Like most of the other Chinese children who played in the
back alleys of restaurants and curio shops, I didn't think we were poor.
My bowl was always full, three five-course meals every day, beginning
with a soup full of mysterious things I didn't want to know the names of.

We lived on Waverly Place, in a warm, clean, two-bedroom flat that
sat above a small Chinese bakery specializing in steamed pastries and
dim sum. In the early morning, when the alley was still quiet, I could
smell fragrant red beans as they were cooked down to a pasty sweet-
ness. By daybreak, our flat was heavy with the odor of fried sesame
balls and sweet curried chicken crescents. From my bed, I would listen

---

1. Chinatown: the Chinese district of San Francisco comprised of twelve square city blocks.

as my father got ready for work, then locked the door behind him, one-two-three clicks.

At the end of our two-block alley was a small sandlot playground with swings and slides well-shined down the middle with use. The play area was bordered by wood-slat benches where old-country people sat cracking roasted watermelon seeds with their golden teeth and scattering the husks to an impatient gathering of gurgling pigeons. The best playground, however, was the dark alley itself. It was crammed with daily mysteries and adventures. My brothers and I would peer into the medicinal herb shop, watching old Li dole out onto a stiff sheet of white paper the right amount of insect shells, saffron-colored seeds, and pungent leaves for his ailing customers. It was said that he once cured a woman dying of an ancestral curse that had eluded the best of American doctors. Next to the pharmacy was a printer who specialized in gold-embossed wedding invitations and festive red banners.

Farther down the street was Ping Yuen Fish Market. The front window displayed a tank crowded with doomed fish and turtles struggling to gain footing on the slimy green-tiled sides. A hand-written sign informed tourists, "Within this store, is all for food, not for pet." Inside, the butchers with their bloodstained white smocks deftly gutted the fish while customers cried out their orders and shouted, "Give me your freshest," to which the butchers always protested, "All are freshest." On less crowded market days, we would inspect the crates of live frogs and crabs which we were warned not to poke, boxes of dried cuttlefish, and row upon row of iced prawns, squid, and slippery fish. The sanddabs made me shiver each time; their eyes lay on one flattened side and reminded me of my mother's story of a careless girl who ran into a crowded street and was crushed by a cab. "Was smash flat," reported my mother.

At the corner of the alley was Hong Sing's, a four-table café with a recessed stairwell in front that led to a door marked "Tradesmen." My brothers and I believed the bad people emerged from this door at night. Tourists never went to Hong Sing's, since the menu was printed only in Chinese. A Caucasian man with a big camera once posed me and my playmates in front of the restaurant. He had us move to the side of the picture window so the photo would capture the roasted duck with its head dangling from a juice-covered rope. After he took the picture, I told him he should go into Hong Sing's and eat dinner. When he smiled and asked me what they served, I shouted, "Guts and duck's feet and octopus gizzards!" Then I ran off with my friends, shrieking with laughter as we scampered across the alley and hid in the entryway grotto of the China Gem Company, my heart pounding with hope that he would chase us.

My mother named me after the street that we lived on: Waverly Place Jong, my official name for important American documents. But my family called me Meimei, "Little Sister." I was the youngest, the only daughter. Each morning before school, my mother would twist and yank on my thick black hair until she had formed two tightly wound pigtails. One day, as she struggled to weave a hard-toothed comb through my disobedient hair, I had a sly thought.

I asked her, "Ma, what is Chinese torture?" My mother shook her head. A bobby pin was wedged between her lips. She wetted her palm and smoothed the hair above my ear, then pushed the pin in so that it nicked sharply against my scalp.

"Who say this word?" she asked without a trace of knowing how wicked I was being. I shrugged my shoulders and said, "Some boy in my class said Chinese people do Chinese torture."

"Chinese people do many things," she said simply. "Chinese people do business, do medicine, do painting. Not lazy like American people. We do torture. Best torture."

My older brother Vincent was the one who actually got the chess set. We had gone to the annual Christmas party held at the First Chinese Baptist Church at the end of the alley. The missionary ladies had put together a Santa bag of gifts donated by members of another church. None of the gifts had names on them. There were separate sacks for boys and girls of different ages.

One of the Chinese parishioners had donned a Santa Claus costume and a stiff paper beard with cotton balls glued to it. I think the only children who thought he was the real thing were too young to know that Santa Claus was not Chinese. When my turn came up, the Santa man asked me how old I was. I thought it was a trick question; I was seven according to the American formula and eight by the Chinese calendar.[2] I said I was born on March 17, 1951. That seemed to satisfy him. He then solemnly asked if I had been a very, very good girl this year and did I believe in Jesus Christ and obey my parents. I knew the only answer to that. I nodded back with equal solemnity.

Having watched the other children opening their gifts, I already

---

2. **Chinese calendar:** the lunar calendar, as opposed to the Western (Gregorian) solar calendar.

knew that the big gifts were not necessarily the nicest ones. One girl my age got a large coloring book of biblical characters, while a less greedy girl who selected a smaller box received a glass vial of lavender toilet water. The sound of the box was also important. A ten-year-old boy had chosen a box that jangled when he shook it. It was a tin globe of the world with a slit for inserting money. He must have thought it was full of dimes and nickels, because when he saw that it had just ten pennies, his face fell with such undisguised disappointment that his mother slapped the side of his head and led him out of the church hall, apologizing to the crowd for her son who had such bad manners he couldn't appreciate such a fine gift.

As I peered into the sack, I quickly fingered the remaining presents, testing their weight, imagining what they contained. I chose a heavy, compact one that was wrapped in shiny silver foil and a red satin ribbon. It was a twelve-pack of Life Savers and I spent the rest of the party arranging and rearranging the candy tubes in the order of my favorites. My brother Winston chose wisely as well. His present turned out to be a box of intricate plastic parts; the instructions on the box proclaimed that when they were properly assembled he would have an authentic miniature replica of a World War II submarine.

Vincent got the chess set, which would have been a very decent present to get at a church Christmas party, except it was obviously used and, as we discovered later, it was missing a black pawn and a white knight. My mother graciously thanked the unknown benefactor, saying, "Too good. Cost too much." At which point, an old lady with fine white, wispy hair nodded toward our family and said with a whistling whisper, "Merry, merry Christmas."

When we got home, my mother told Vincent to throw the chess set away. "She not want it. We not want it," she said, tossing her head stiffly to the side with a tight, proud smile. My brothers had deaf ears. They were already lining up the chess pieces and reading from the dog-eared instruction book.

I watched Vincent and Winston play during Christmas week. The chessboard seemed to hold elaborate secrets waiting to be untangled. The chessmen were more powerful than Old Li's magic herbs that cured ancestral curses. And my brothers wore such serious faces that I was sure something was at stake that was greater than avoiding the tradesmen's door to Hong Sing's.

"Let me! Let me!" I begged between games when one brother or the other would sit back with a deep sigh of relief and victory, the other annoyed, unable to let go of the outcome. Vincent at first refused to let me play, but when I offered my Life Savers as replacements for the buttons that filled in for the missing pieces, he relented. He chose the flavors: wild cherry for the black pawn and peppermint for the white knight. Winner could eat both.

As our mother sprinkled flour and rolled out small doughy circles for the steamed dumplings that would be our dinner that night, Vincent explained the rules, pointing to each piece. "You have sixteen pieces and so do I. One king and queen, two bishops, two knights, two castles, and eight pawns. The pawns can only move forward one step, except on the first move. Then they can move two. But they can only take men by moving crossways like this, except in the beginning, when you can move ahead and take another pawn."

"Why?" I asked as I moved my pawn. "Why can't they move more steps?"

"Because they're pawns," he said.

"But why do they go crossways to take other men. Why aren't there any women and children?"

"Why is the sky blue? Why must you always ask stupid questions?" asked Vincent. "This is a game. These are the rules. I didn't make them up. See. Here. In the book." He jabbed a page with a pawn in his hand. "Pawn. P-A-W-N. Pawn. Read it yourself."

My mother patted the flour off her hands. "Let me see book," she said quietly. She scanned the pages quickly, not reading the foreign English symbols, seeming to search deliberately for nothing in particular.

"This American rules," she concluded at last. "Every time people come out from foreign country, must know rules. You not know, judge say, Too bad, go back. They not telling you why so you can use their way go forward. They say, Don't know why, you find out yourself. But they knowing all the time. Better you take it, find out why yourself." She tossed her head back with a satisfied smile.

I found out about all the whys later. I read the rules and looked up all the big words in a dictionary. I borrowed books from the Chinatown library. I studied each chess piece, trying to absorb the power each contained.

I learned about opening moves and why it's important to control the center early on; the shortest distance between two points is straight down the middle. I learned about the middle game and why tactics between two adversaries are like clashing ideas; the one who plays better has the clearest plans for both attacking and getting out of traps. I learned why it is essential in the endgame[3] to have foresight, a mathematical understanding of all possible moves, and patience; all weaknesses and advantages become evident to a strong adversary and are obscured to a tiring opponent. I discovered that for the whole game one must gather invisible strengths and see the endgame before the game begins.

I also found out why I should never reveal "why" to others. A little knowledge withheld is a great advantage one should store for future use. That is the power of chess. It is a game of secrets in which one must show and never tell.

I loved the secrets I found within the sixty-four black and white squares. I carefully drew a handmade chessboard and pinned it to the wall next to my bed, where at night I would stare for hours at imaginary battles. Soon I no longer lost any games or Life Savers, but I lost my adversaries. Winston and Vincent decided they were more interested in roaming the streets after school in their Hopalong Cassidy cowboy hats.

On a cold spring afternoon, while walking home from school, I detoured through the playground at the end of our alley. I saw a group of old men, two seated across a folding table playing a game of chess, others smoking pipes, eating peanuts, and watching. I ran home and grabbed Vincent's chess set, which was bound in a cardboard box with rubber bands. I also carefully selected two prized rolls of Life Savers. I came back to the park and approached a man who was observing the game.

"Want to play?" I asked him. His face widened with surprise and he grinned as he looked at the box under my arm.

"Little sister, been a long time since I play with dolls," he said, smiling benevolently. I quickly put the box down next to him on the bench and displayed my retort.

Lau Po, as he allowed me to call him, turned out to be a much better player than my brothers. I lost many games and many Life Savers. But over the weeks, with each diminishing roll of candies, I added new secrets. Lau Po gave me the names. The Double Attack from the East and West Shores. Throwing Stones on the Drowning Man. The Sudden Meeting of the Clan. The Surprise from the Sleeping Guard. The

---

3. endgame: the final stages of a chess game.

Humble Servant Who Kills the King. Sand in the Eyes of Advancing Forces. A Double Killing Without Blood.

There were also the fine points of chess etiquette. Keep captured men in neat rows, as well-tended prisoners. Never announce "Check"[4] with vanity, lest someone with an unseen sword slit your throat. Never hurl pieces into the sandbox after you have lost a game, because then you must find them again, by yourself, after apologizing to all around you. By the end of the summer, Lau Po had taught me all he knew, and I had become a better chess player.

A small weekend crowd of Chinese people and tourists would gather as I played and defeated my opponents one by one. My mother would join the crowds during these outdoor exhibition games. She sat proudly on the bench, telling my admirers with proper Chinese humility, "Is luck."

A man who watched me play in the park suggested that my mother allow me to play in local chess tournaments. My mother smiled graciously, an answer that meant nothing. I desperately wanted to go, but I bit back my tongue. I knew she would not let me play among strangers. So as we walked home I said in a small voice that I didn't want to play in the local tournament. They would have American rules. If I lost, I would bring shame on my family.

"Is shame you fall down nobody push you," said my mother.

During my first tournament, my mother sat with me in the front row as I waited for my turn. I frequently bounced my legs to unstick them from the cold metal seat of the folding chair. When my name was called, I leapt up. My mother unwrapped something in her lap. It was her *chang*, a small tablet of red jade which held the sun's fire. "Is luck," she whispered, and tucked it into my dress pocket. I turned to my opponent, a fifteen-year-old boy from Oakland. He looked at me, wrinkling his nose.

As I began to play, the boy disappeared, the color ran out of the room, and I saw only my white pieces and his black ones waiting on the other side. A light wind began blowing past my ears. It whispered secrets only I could hear.

"Blow from the South," it murmured. "The wind leaves no trail." I saw a clear path, the traps to avoid. The crowd rustled. "Shhh! Shhh!"

---

4. "Check": the word spoken by a chess player when threatening to capture the opponent's king.

said the corners of the room. The wind blew stronger. "Throw sand from the East to distract him." The knight came forward ready for the sacrifice. The wind hissed, louder and louder. "Blow, blow, blow. He cannot see. He is blind now. Make him lean away from the wind so he is easier to knock down."

"Check," I said, as the wind roared with laughter. The wind died down to little puffs, my own breath.

My mother placed my first trophy next to a new plastic chess set that the neighborhood Tao society had given to me. As she wiped each piece with a soft cloth, she said, "Next time win more, lose less."

"Ma, it's not how many pieces you lose," I said. "Sometimes you need to lose pieces to get ahead."

"Better to lose less, see if you really need."

At the next tournament, I won again, but it was my mother who wore the triumphant grin.

"Lost eight piece this time. Last time was eleven. What I tell you? Better off lose less!" I was annoyed, but I couldn't say anything.

I attended more tournaments, each one farther away from home. I won all games, in all divisions. The Chinese bakery downstairs from our flat displayed my growing collection of trophies in its window, amidst the dust-covered cakes that were never picked up. The day after I won an important regional tournament, the window encased a fresh sheet cake with whipped-cream frosting and red script saying, "Congratulations, Waverly Jong, Chinatown Chess Champion." Soon after that, a flower shop, headstone engraver, and funeral parlor offered to sponsor me in national tournaments. That's when my mother decided I no longer had to do the dishes. Winston and Vincent had to do my chores.

"Why does she get to play and we do all the work," complained Vincent.

"Is new American rules," said my mother. "Meimei play, squeeze all her brains out for win chess. You play, worth squeeze towel."

By my ninth birthday, I was a national chess champion. I was still some 429 points away from grand-master status,[5] but I was touted as the Great American Hope, a child prodigy and a girl to boot. They ran

---

5. **grand-master status:** refers to a *grand master,* the chess player who possesses the highest level of expertise.

a photo of me in *Life* magazine next to a quote in which Bobby Fischer[6] said, "There will never be a woman grand master." "Your move, Bobby," said the caption.

The day they took the magazine picture I wore neatly plaited braids clipped with plastic barrettes trimmed with rhinestones. I was playing in a large high school auditorium that echoed with phlegmy coughs and the squeaky rubber knobs of chair legs sliding across freshly waxed wooden floors. Seated across from me was an American man, about the same age as Lau Po, maybe fifty. I remember that his sweaty brow seemed to weep at my every move. He wore a dark, malodorous suit. One of his pockets was stuffed with a great white kerchief on which he wiped his palm before sweeping his hand over the chosen chess piece with great flourish.

In my crisp pink-and-white dress with scratchy lace at the neck, one of two my mother had sewn for these special occasions, I would clasp my hands under my chin, the delicate points of my elbows poised lightly on the table in the manner my mother had shown me for posing for the press. I would swing my patent leather shoes back and forth like an impatient child riding on a school bus. Then I would pause, suck in my lips, twirl my chosen piece in midair as if undecided, and then firmly plant it in its new threatening place, with a triumphant smile thrown back at my opponent for good measure.

I no longer played in the alley of Waverly Place. I never visited the playground where the pigeons and old men gathered. I went to school, then directly home to learn new chess secrets, cleverly concealed advantages, more escape routes.

But I found it difficult to concentrate at home. My mother had a habit of standing over me while I plotted out my games. I think she thought of herself as my protective ally. Her lips would be sealed tight, and after each move I made, a soft "Hmmmmph" would escape from her nose.

"Ma, I can't practice when you stand there like that," I said one day. She retreated to the kitchen and made loud noises with the pots and pans. When the crashing stopped, I could see out of the corner of my eye that she was standing in the doorway. "Hmmmph!" Only this one came out of her tight throat.

---

6. **Bobby Fischer (Robert James)** (1943–): a famous U.S. chess champion.

My parents made many concessions to allow me to practice. One time I complained that the bedroom I shared was so noisy that I couldn't think. Thereafter, my brothers slept in a bed in the living room facing the street. I said I couldn't finish my rice; my head didn't work right when my stomach was too full. I left the table with half-finished bowls and nobody complained. But there was one duty I couldn't avoid. I had to accompany my mother on Saturday market days when I had no tournament to play. My mother would proudly walk with me, visiting many shops, buying very little. "This my daughter Wave-ly Jong," she said to whoever looked her way.

One day, after we left a shop I said under my breath, "I wish you wouldn't do that, telling everybody I'm your daughter." My mother stopped walking. Crowds of people with heavy bags pushed past us on the sidewalk, bumping into first one shoulder, then another.

"Aiii-ya. So shame be with mother?" She grasped my hand even tighter as she glared at me.

I looked down. "It's not that, it's just so obvious. It's just so embarrassing."

"Embarrass you be my daughter?" Her voice was cracking with anger.

"That's not what I meant. That's not what I said."

"What you say?"

I knew it was a mistake to say anything more, but I heard my voice speaking. "Why do you have to use me to show off? If you want to show off, then why don't you learn to play chess?"

My mother's eyes turned into dangerous black slits. She had no words for me, just sharp silence.

I felt the wind rushing around my hot ears. I jerked my hand out of my mother's tight grasp and spun around, knocking into an old woman. Her bag of groceries spilled to the ground.

"Aii-ya! Stupid girl!" my mother and the woman cried. Oranges and tin cans careened down the sidewalk. As my mother stooped to help the old woman pick up the escaping food, I took off.

I raced down the street, dashing between people, not looking back as my mother screamed shrilly, "Meimei! Meimei!" I fled down an alley, past dark curtained shops and merchants washing the grime off their windows. I sped into the sunlight, into a large street crowded with tourists examining trinkets and souvenirs. I ducked into another dark alley, down another street, up another alley. I ran until it hurt and I realized I had nowhere to go, that I was not running from anything. The alleys contained no escape routes.

My breath came out like angry smoke. It was cold. I sat down on an upturned plastic pail next to a stack of empty boxes, cupping my chin with my hands, thinking hard. I imagined my mother, first walking briskly down one street or another looking for me, then giving up and returning home to await my arrival. After two hours, I stood up on creaking legs and slowly walked home.

The alley was quiet and I could see the yellow lights shining from our flat like two tiger's eyes in the night. I climbed the sixteen steps to the door, advancing quietly up each so as not to make any warning sounds. I turned the knob; the door was locked. I heard a chair moving, quick steps, the locks turning—click! click! click!—and then the door opened.

"About time you got home," said Vincent. "Boy, are you in trouble."

He slid back to the dinner table. On a platter were the remains of a large fish, its fleshy head still connected to bones swimming upstream in vain escape. Standing there waiting for my punishment, I heard my mother speak in a dry voice.

"We not concerning this girl. This girl not have concerning for us."

Nobody looked at me. Bone chopsticks clinked against the insides of bowls being emptied into hungry mouths.

I walked into my room, closed the door, and lay down on my bed. The room was dark, the ceiling filled with shadows from the dinnertime lights of neighboring flats.

In my head, I saw a chessboard with sixty-four black and white squares. Opposite me was my opponent, two angry black slits. She wore a triumphant smile. "Strongest wind cannot be seen," she said.

Her black men advanced across the plane, slowly marching to each successive level as a single unit. My white pieces screamed as they scurried and fell off the board one by one. As her men drew closer to my edge, I felt myself growing light. I rose up into the air and flew out the window. Higher and higher, above the alley, over the tops of tiled roofs, where I was gathered up by the wind and pushed up toward the night sky until everything below me disappeared and I was alone.

I closed my eyes and pondered my next move. ∎

THE IMPACT OF THE STORY

In "Rules of the Game," Waverly Jong works very hard to become a skillful chess player. Like Waverly, we all have activities we enjoy and special talents we may be proud of.

Take a few minutes to think about your own talents. Use these questions to help focus your thoughts. Are you as dedicated as Waverly to your particular pursuit—whether it be computer games, in-line skating, speaking another language, or even playing chess? Do you think Waverly's level of dedication is necessary for a person to enjoy a particular activity? Do you believe that a person enjoys an activity more if he or she is successful in that area?

THE FACTS OF THE STORY

On your own paper, write answers to the following items. Answers may be one word, a phrase, or several sentences.

1. Why does Waverly believe she is not poor?

2. Why does Waverly's mother tell her brother Vincent to throw away the chess set he receives for Christmas?

3. What does Waverly learn from playing chess with Lau Po?

4. How does Waverly's family life change as a result of her success in playing chess?

5. What is Waverly's punishment for criticizing her mother and running away outside the store?

THE IDEAS IN THE STORY

Prepare to discuss the following questions in class.

1. As a very young girl, Waverly learns how to "bite back her tongue" as part of the Chinese art of invisible strength. What is the Chinese art of invisible strength, and how does it work? Give at least one example from the story of how Waverly uses this technique successfully.

2. After examining the rule booklet accompanying the chess set, Waverly's mother changes her mind and decides to let her children keep the game. She explains

> "Every time people come out from foreign country, must know rules. You not know, judge say, Too bad, go back. They not telling you why so you can use their way go forward. They say, Don't know why, you find out yourself. But they knowing all the time. Better you take it, find out why yourself."

What do you think she means? Do you agree with her assessment of Americans' attitudes toward immigrants? Explain your answer.

3. The first sign of tension between Waverly and her mother occurs when her mother suggests that Waverly lose fewer chess pieces at her next game. Waverly tries to explain, "'Sometimes you need to lose pieces to get ahead.'" Yet her mother merely replies, "'Better to lose less, see if you really need.'" What might motivate her mother to want Waverly to lose fewer pieces? Why do you think Waverly would find this suggestion objectionable?

THE ART OF THE STORYTELLER

Conflict
As a chess player, Waverly faces many different opponents, including her brothers, Lau Po, and the players at the various tournaments in which she participates. However, a far more intense struggle takes place between Waverly and her mother, and it reaches a tense and ominous climax by the story's end. What do you think is the source of the conflict between the mother and daughter? What will Waverly lose if she does not win her struggle against her mother?

Waverly's struggle with her mother is an *external* conflict. What *internal* conflicts does Waverly experience in the story?

Characterization
The narrator of "Rules of the Game" gives us a vivid picture of her strong-willed mother. We see a woman who continues to hold on

to the culture and values of her native country while understanding the value that her children will derive from learning the ways of their adopted country. Describe some of the mother's actions and attitudes that reflect her native Chinese culture.

We also learn a great deal about the narrator from her description of her own actions and appearance, from what she thinks, from how she reacts to other people such as her mother, and from observing her relationship with the game of chess. What qualities must Waverly possess to be such a successful chess player? What do her behavior and appearance at chess tournaments say about her character?

During the summer that Waverly plays chess with Lau Po, he teaches her not only various strategies but also the fine points of chess etiquette. What do these particular points of chess etiquette indirectly tell us about Waverly?

Waverly's mother is characterized negatively at times in the story; however, she does make major concessions that enable Waverly to devote herself to chess. What do we learn about both mother and daughter from these concessions?

Symbols

As you may recall, a **symbol** is anything that possesses meaning in itself but that also stands for something else that is much broader than itself. By the end of the story, chess takes on another meaning for Waverly. What do you think it symbolizes? What might the words *rules* and *game* in the story's title refer to besides chess?

Waverly tells us that in chess

> A little knowledge withheld is a great advantage one
> should store for future use. That is the power of chess. It is
> a game of secrets in which one must show and never tell.

Of what else in the story do these insights remind you? How does Waverly fail to apply these insights to her own life?

THE VOCABULARY IN THE STORY

Synonyms are defined as "words that have the same or nearly the same meaning." In actuality, synonyms rarely have exactly the same meaning. For example, both the word *discuss* and the word *chat* mean to talk. However, *discuss* implies a serious subject and a slightly formal situation in which people talk. *Chat* suggests a relatively unimportant subject and an informal situation.

By choosing words carefully, a writer conveys not only the events of a story but also vivid mental pictures and the emotional impact of the story. Amy Tan's choice of words is as precise as a chess champion's choice of moves. Read each of the following passages. For each italicized word, give three synonyms. Then give your explanation of why you think Tan chose the italicized word. (You might want to reread the passage in the story.)

1. My mother *imparted* her daily truths so she could help my older brothers and me rise above our circumstances.

2. Never *hurl* pieces into the sandbox after you have lost a game . . .

3. He wore a dark, *malodorous* suit.

4. Oranges and tin cans *careened* down the sidewalk.

5. I closed my eyes and *pondered* my next move.

COMPOSITION: Writing about Your Family History

The protagonist of "Rules of the Game" is the product of two cultures—the Chinese world of her mother and the American world where she resides. However, American culture is actually the fusing of many different cultures and peoples. Some families, like Waverly Jong's, are quite new to this country while others may have lived here for decades, even centuries.

Write an essay (about 500 words) describing your family's history. If you like, you may write about the origins of your surname (your last, or family, name) instead.

Prewriting

Interview your parents, grandparents, aunts and uncles, or other family members who may be able to give you information about your ancestors and, if they were immigrants, when they came to this country and why. During your interviews make written notes to refer to later while writing your draft. A tape recorder may also be helpful. If you decide to research your surname, start by investigating your school library. Your local public library will probably have some helpful information, as well. Don't be shy about asking the librarians for help.

Take some time to organize your notes and ideas. You may want to arrange your explanation in chronological, or time-related, order, starting with your first known family members or those who first came to this country or with the first historical appearance of your surname.

Writing
Write the first draft of your essay as quickly as possible.

Evaluating and Revising
Read your draft. Add, cut, reorder, or replace words, phrases, or sections as needed. Compare your interview or library notes to your draft. Is it clear who your family is, where it is from, and when and why members of it first came to the United States? Have you clearly explained the origins of your family name?

ABOUT THE AUTHOR

Amy Tan (1952–) grew up in a Chinese American family, but as a teenager she wanted desperately to blend into mainstream America. However, she gradually grew to value her family's culture, and a trip to China when she was thirty-five helped her to rediscover her Chinese heritage.

Before Tan turned her attention to fiction writing, she was a freelance business writer. But in 1985, she submitted a story, which evolved into "Rules of the Game," to a writers' workshop; out of this story grew her first and highly praised book, *The Joy Luck Club,* which has since been made into a movie. This book examines the relationships between mothers and daughters in Chinese American families and looks closely at the difficulties faced by the younger women in their struggle to balance the two cultures.

■RAYMOND'S RUN

Toni Cade Bambara

"Raymond's Run" doesn't have very much to do with either
Raymond or his run. The story is about Raymond's ten-year-old
sister, Hazel Elizabeth Deborah Parker, nicknamed "Squeaky,"
who looks after Raymond because he is "not quite right." She
tells you about herself, her brother, her friends, and her ability
to run. Whether or not you like her, you will probably find
reasons to admire her.

I don't have much work to do around the house like some girls. My
mother does that. And I don't have to earn my pocket money;
George runs errands for the big boys and sells Christmas cards. And
anything else that's got to get done, my father does. All I have to do in
life is mind my brother Raymond, which is enough.

Sometimes I slip and say my little brother Raymond. But as any fool
can see he's much bigger and he's older too. But a lot of people call him
my little brother cause he needs looking after cause he's not quite right.
And a lot of smart mouths got lots to say about that too, especially
when George was minding him. But now, if anybody has anything to
say to Raymond, anything to say about his big head, they have to come
by me. And I don't play the dozens[1] or believe in standing around with
somebody in my face doing a lot of talking. I much rather just knock
you down and take my chances even if I am a little girl with skinny
arms and a squeaky voice, which is how I got the name Squeaky. And
if things get too rough, I run. And as anybody can tell you, I'm the
fastest thing on two feet.

There is no track meet that I don't win the first-place medal. I used
to win the twenty-yard dash when I was a little kid in kindergarten.
Nowadays, it's the fifty-yard dash. And tomorrow I'm subject to run
the quarter-meter relay all by myself and come in first, second, and
third. The big kids call me Mercury[2] cause I'm the swiftest thing in the

---

1. **the dozens:** a game in which the players trade insults: The first one to show anger loses
   the game.
2. **Mercury:** in Roman mythology, the messenger of the gods, who was known for his great
   speed.

neighborhood. Everybody knows that—except two people who know better, my father and me. He can beat me to Amsterdam Avenue with me having a two fire-hydrant head start and him running with his hands in his pockets and whistling. But that's private information. Cause can you imagine some thirty-five-year-old man stuffing himself into PAL[3] shorts to race little kids? So as far as everyone's concerned, I'm the fastest and that goes for Gretchen, too, who has put out the tale that she is going to win the first-place medal this year. Ridiculous. In the second place, she's got short legs. In the third place, she's got freckles. In the first place, no one can beat me and that's all there is to it.

I'm standing on the corner admiring the weather and about to take a stroll down Broadway so I can practice my breathing exercises, and I've got Raymond walking on the inside close to the buildings, cause he's subject to fits of fantasy and starts thinking he's a circus performer and that the curb is a tightrope strung high in the air. And sometimes after a rain he likes to step down off his tightrope right into the gutter and slosh around getting his shoes and cuffs wet. Then I get hit when I get home. Or sometimes if you don't watch him he'll dash across traffic to the island in the middle of Broadway and give the pigeons a fit. Then I have to go behind him apologizing to all the old people sitting around trying to get some sun and getting all upset with the pigeons fluttering around them, scattering their newspapers and upsetting the wax-paper lunches in their laps. So I keep Raymond on the inside of me, and he plays like he's driving a stagecoach which is OK by me so long as he doesn't run me over or interrupt my breathing exercises, which I have to do on account of I'm serious about my running, and I don't care who knows it.

Now some people like to act like things come easy to them, won't let on that they practice. Not me. I'll high-prance down 34th Street like a rodeo pony to keep my knees strong even if it does get my mother uptight so that she walks ahead like she's not with me, don't know me, is all by herself on a shopping trip, and I am somebody else's crazy child. Now you take Cynthia Procter for instance. She's just the opposite. If there's a test tomorrow, she'll say something like, "Oh, I guess I'll play handball this afternoon and watch television tonight," just to let you know she ain't thinking about the test. Or like

---

3. **PAL:** Police Athletic League.

last week when she won the spelling bee for the millionth time, "A good thing you got *receive*, Squeaky, cause I would have got it wrong. I completely forgot about the spelling bee." And she'll clutch the lace on her blouse like it was a narrow escape. Oh, brother. But of course when I pass her house on my early morning trots around the block, she is practicing the scales on the piano over and over and over and over. Then in music class she always lets herself get bumped around so she falls accidentally on purpose onto the piano stool and is so surprised to find herself sitting there that she decides just for fun to try out the ole keys. And what do you know—Chopin's waltzes just spring out of her fingertips and she's the most surprised thing in the world. A regular prodigy. I could kill people like that. I stay up all night studying the words for the spelling bee. And you can see me any time of day practicing running. I never walk if I can trot, and shame on Raymond if he can't keep up. But of course he does, cause if he hangs back someone's liable to walk up to him and get smart, or take his allowance from him, or ask him where he got that great big pumpkin head. People are so stupid sometimes.

So I'm strolling down Broadway breathing out and breathing in on counts of seven, which is my lucky number, and here comes Gretchen and her sidekicks: Mary Louise, who used to be a friend of mine when she first moved to Harlem from Baltimore and got beat up by everybody till I took up for her on account of her mother and my mother used to sing in the same choir when they were young girls, but people ain't grateful, so now she hangs out with the new girl Gretchen and talks about me like a dog; and Rosie, who is as fat as I am skinny and has a big mouth where Raymond is concerned and is too stupid to know that there is not a big deal of difference between herself and Raymond and that she can't afford to throw stones. So they are steady coming up Broadway and I see right away that it's going to be one of those Dodge City[4] scenes cause the street ain't that big and they're close to the buildings just as we are. First I think I'll step into the candy store and look over the new comics and let them pass. But that's chicken and I've got a reputation to consider. So then I think I'll just walk straight on through them or even over them if necessary. But as they get to me, they slow down. I'm ready to fight, cause like I said I don't

---

4. Dodge City: the setting of the television series *Gunsmoke,* which often featured a show-down between the marshal and a gunfighter.

feature a whole lot of chitchat, I much prefer to just knock you down right from the jump and save everybody a lotta precious time.

"You signing up for the May Day races?" smiles Mary Louise, only it's not a smile at all. A dumb question like that doesn't deserve an answer. Besides, there's just me and Gretchen standing there really, so no use wasting my breath talking to shadows.

"I don't think you're going to win this time," says Rosie, trying to signify with her hands on her hips all salty, completely forgetting that I have whupped her behind many times for less salt than that.

"I always win cause I'm the best," I say straight at Gretchen who is, as far as I'm concerned, the only one talking in this ventriloquist-dummy routine. Gretchen smiles, but it's not a smile, and I'm thinking that girls never really smile at each other because they don't know how and don't want to know how and there's probably no one to teach us how, cause grown-up girls don't know either. Then they all look at Raymond who has just brought his mule team to a standstill. And they're about to see what trouble they can get into through him.

"What grade you in now, Raymond?"

"You got anything to say to my brother, you say it to me, Mary Louise Williams of Raggedy Town, Baltimore."

"What are you, his mother?" sasses Rosie.

"That's right, Fatso. And the next word out of anybody and I'll be *their* mother too." So they just stand there and Gretchen shifts from one leg to the other and so do they. Then Gretchen puts her hands on her hips and is about to say something with her freckle-face self but doesn't. Then she walks around me looking me up and down but keeps walking up Broadway, and her sidekicks follow her. So me and Raymond smile at each other and he says, "Gidyap" to his team and I continue with my breathing exercises, strolling down Broadway toward the ice man on 145th with not a care in the world cause I am Miss Quicksilver herself.

I take my time getting to the park on May Day because the track meet is the last thing on the program. The biggest thing on the program is the May Pole dancing, which I can do without, thank you, even if my mother thinks it's a shame I don't take part and act like a girl for a change. You'd think my mother'd be grateful not to have to make me a white organdy dress with a big satin sash and buy me new white baby-doll shoes that can't be taken out of the box till the big day. You'd think she'd be glad her daughter ain't out there prancing around a May

Pole getting the new clothes all dirty and sweaty and trying to act like a fairy or a flower or whatever you're supposed to be when you should be trying to be yourself, whatever that is, which is, as far as I am concerned, a poor black girl who really can't afford to buy shoes and a new dress you only wear once a lifetime cause it won't fit next year.

I was once a strawberry in a Hansel and Gretel pageant when I was in nursery school and didn't have no better sense than to dance on tiptoe with my arms in a circle over my head doing umbrella steps and being a perfect fool just so my mother and father could come dressed up and clap. You'd think they'd know better than to encourage that kind of nonsense. I am not a strawberry. I do not dance on my toes. I run. That is what I am all about. So I always come late to the May Day program, just in time to get my number pinned on and lay in the grass till they announce the fifty-yard dash.

I put Raymond in the little swings, which is a tight squeeze this year and will be impossible next year. Then I look around for Mr. Pearson, who pins the numbers on. I'm really looking for Gretchen if you want to know the truth, but she's not around. The park is jam-packed. Parents in hats and corsages and breast-pocket handkerchiefs peeking up. Kids in white dresses and light-blue suits. The parkees unfolding chairs and chasing the rowdy kids from Lenox as if they had no right to be there. The big guys with their caps on backwards, leaning against the fence swirling the basketballs on the tips of their fingers, waiting for all these crazy people to clear out the park so they can play. Most of the kids in my class are carrying bass drums and glockenspiels and flutes. You'd think they'd put in a few bongos or something for real like that.

Then here comes Mr. Pearson with his clipboard and his cards and pencils and whistles and safety pins and fifty million other things he's always dropping all over the place with his clumsy self. He sticks out in a crowd because he's on stilts. We used to call him Jack and the Beanstalk to get him mad. But I'm the only one that can outrun him and get away, and I'm too grown for that silliness now.

"Well, Squeaky," he says, checking my name off the list and handing me number seven and two pins. And I'm thinking he's got no right to call me Squeaky, if I can't call him Beanstalk.

"Hazel Elizabeth Deborah Parker," I correct him and tell him to write it down on his board.

"Well, Hazel Elizabeth Deborah Parker, going to give someone else a break this year?" I squint at him real hard to see if he is seriously thinking I should lose the race on purpose just to give someone else a break. "Only six girls running this time," he continues, shaking his head sadly like it's my fault all of New York didn't turn out in sneakers. "That new girl should give you a run for your money." He looks around the park for Gretchen like a periscope in a submarine movie. "Wouldn't it be a nice gesture if you were . . . to ahhh . . ."

I gave him such a look he couldn't finish putting that idea into words. Grown-ups got a lot of nerve sometimes. I pin number seven to myself and stomp away, I'm so burnt. And I go straight for the track and stretch out on the grass while the band winds up with "Oh, the Monkey Wrapped His Tail Around the Flag Pole," which my teacher calls by some other name. The man on the loudspeaker is calling everyone over to the track and I'm on my back looking at the sky, trying to pretend I'm in the country, but I can't, because even grass in the city feels hard as sidewalk, and there's just no pretending you are anywhere but in a "concrete jungle" as my grandfather says.

The twenty-yard dash takes all of two minutes cause most of the little kids don't know no better than to run off the track or run the wrong way or run smack into the fence and fall down and cry. One little kid, though, has got the good sense to run straight for the white ribbon up ahead so he wins. Then second-graders line up for the thirty-yard dash and I don't even bother to turn my head to watch cause Raphael Perez always wins. He wins before he even begins by psyching the runners, telling them they're going to trip on their shoelaces and fall on their faces or lose their shorts or something, which he doesn't really have to do since he is very fast, almost as fast as I am. After that is the forty-yard dash which I use to run when I was in first grade. Raymond is hollering from the swings cause he knows I'm about to do my thing cause the man on the loudspeaker has just announced the fifty-yard dash, although he might just as well be giving a recipe for angel food cake cause you can hardly make out what he's sayin for the static. I get up and slip off my sweat pants and then I see Gretchen standing at the starting line, kicking her legs out like a pro. Then as I get into place I see that ole Raymond is on line on the other side of the fence, bending down with his fingers on the ground just like he knew what he was doing. I was going to yell at him but then I didn't. It burns up your energy to holler.

Every time, just before I take off in a race, I always feel like I'm in a dream, the kind of dream you have when you're sick with fever and feel all hot and weightless. I dream I'm flying over a sandy beach in the early morning sun, kissing the leaves of the trees as I fly by. And there's always the smell of apples, just like in the country when I was little and used to think I was a choo-choo train, running through the fields of corn and chugging up the hill to the orchard. And all the time I'm dreaming this, I get lighter and lighter until I'm flying over the beach again, getting blown through the sky like a feather that weighs nothing at all. But once I spread my fingers in the dirt and crouch over the Get on Your Mark, the dream goes and I am solid again and am telling myself, Squeaky you must win, you must win, you are the fastest thing in the world, you can even beat your father up Amsterdam if you really try. And then I feel my weight coming back just behind my knees then down to my feet then into the earth and the pistol shot explodes in my blood and I am off and weightless again, flying past the other runners, my arms pumping up and down and the whole world is quiet except for the crunch as I zoom over the gravel in the track. I glance to my left and there is no one. To the right, a blurred Gretchen, who's got her chin jutting out as if it would win the race all by itself. And on the other side of the fence is Raymond with his arms down to his side and the palms tucked up behind him, running in his very own style, and it's the first time I ever saw that and I almost stop to watch my brother Raymond on his first run. But the white ribbon is bouncing toward me and I tear past it, racing into the distance till my feet with a mind of their own start digging up footfuls of dirt and brake me short. Then all the kids standing on the side pile on me, banging me on the back and slapping my head with their May Day programs, for I have won again and everybody on 151st Street can walk tall for another year.

"In first place . . . " the man on the loudspeaker is clear as a bell now. But then he pauses and the loudspeaker starts to whine. Then static. And I lean down to catch my breath and here comes Gretchen walking back, for she's overshot the finish line too, huffing and puffing with her hands on her hips, taking it slow, breathing in steady time like a real pro, and I sort of like her a little for the first time. "In first place . . ." and then three or four voices get all mixed up on the loudspeaker and I dig my sneaker into the grass and stare at Gretchen who's staring back, we both wondering just who did win. I can hear old Beanstalk arguing with the man on the loudspeaker and then a few others running their mouths about what the stopwatches say. Then I hear

Raymond yanking at the fence to call me and I wave to shush him, but he keeps rattling the fence like a gorilla in a cage like in them gorilla movies, but then like a dancer or something he starts climbing up nice and easy but very fast. And it occurs to me, watching how smoothly he climbs hand over hand and remembering how he looked running with his arms down to his side and with the wind pulling his mouth back and his teeth showing and all, it occurred to me that Raymond would make a very fine runner. Doesn't he always keep up with me on my trots? And he surely knows how to breathe in counts of seven cause he's always doing it at the dinner table, which drives my brother George up the wall. And I'm smiling to beat the band cause if I've lost this race, or if me and Gretchen tied, or even if I've won, I can always retire as a runner and begin a whole new career as a coach with Raymond as my champion. After all, with a little more study I can beat Cynthia and her phony self at the spelling bee. And if I bugged my mother, I could get piano lessons and become a star. And I have a big rep as the baddest thing around. And I've got a roomful of ribbons and medals and awards. But what has Raymond got to call his own?

So I stand there with my new plans, laughing out loud by this time as Raymond jumps down from the fence and runs over with his teeth showing and his arms down to the side, which no one before him has quite mastered as a running style. And by the time he comes over I'm jumping up and down so glad to see him—my brother Raymond, a great runner in the family tradition. But of course everyone thinks I'm jumping up and down because the men on the loudspeaker have finally gotten themselves together and compared notes and are announcing "In first place—Miss Hazel Elizabeth Deborah Parker." (Dig that.) "In second place—Miss Gretchen P. Lewis." And I look over at Gretchen wondering what the "P" stands for. And I smile. Cause she's good, no doubt about it. Maybe she'd like to help me coach Raymond; she obviously is serious about running, as any fool can see. And she nods to congratulate me and then she smiles. And I smile. We stand there with this big smile of respect between us. It's about as real a smile as girls can do for each other, considering we don't practice real smiling every day, you know, cause maybe we too busy being flowers or fairies or strawberries instead of something honest and worthy of respect . . . you know . . . like being people. ■

THE IMPACT OF THE STORY

Some of you may identify with Squeaky's strong personality; others of you may find her self-confidence and frank honesty annoying.

Do you like to read about people who are similar to or different from yourself? Why or why not? If Squeaky's personality weren't so forceful, would you be interested in what happens to her?

THE FACTS OF THE STORY

On your own paper, write short answers to the following items. Answers may be one word, a phrase, or several sentences.

1. What is Squeaky's one responsibility?

2. What does Squeaky do on her walks with Raymond?

3. What is Squeaky "all about"?

4. What does Mr. Pearson try to suggest that Squeaky do?

5. Who wins the fifty-yard dash?

THE IDEAS IN THE STORY

Prepare to discuss the following questions in class.

1. Squeaky is a self-assured person who has a great deal of confidence in her own abilities. At times, it may be difficult to distinguish this blunt self-confidence from conceitedness. How do we know that Squeaky is not conceited? How does Raymond's run affect Squeaky? What else happens after the race that reveals the depth of Squeaky's character?

2. One of Squeaky's outstanding character traits is honesty. She is honest about herself and her abilities and in her appraisal of other people. What are some of the ways in which people act dishonestly in the story?

3. Squeaky believes that girls don't know how to smile genuinely because they are too busy being phony. Some of the

phoniness that she objects to are the May Day pageantry and the school plays in which girls are playing flowers, butterflies, or fairies. She also says that grown-up girls are not genuine with each other for the same reason. How does her mother's attitude toward Squeaky support her beliefs? Do you agree with Squeaky's complaint that girls are too busy being what they are not instead of simply being people? Do you think that boys might also be guilty of this?

THE ART OF THE STORYTELLER

Believable Characters

Writers use certain techniques to make the characters in a story believable, to make them seem true to life. For example, the language a character uses must be the kind that a person with the same background, living in the same environment, and of the same age would use in actual life. Because Squeaky tells this story, the author pays close attention to the language that Squeaky uses in order to make her believable. Squeaky should speak the way a ten-year-old African American girl living in Harlem would really speak. If you think that Squeaky's grammar, vocabulary, and use of slang are believable, find examples to prove it. If you think her speech is not true to life, find examples to support that opinion.

Not only must the characters' language be true, but also their actions. If their actions are not what we expect from a real person, we find it difficult to believe the story. Tell whether you find Squeaky's actions and opinions in this story believable. Do you find her feelings toward Gretchen at the end believable?

Point of View

The perspective, or vantage point, from which a writer tells a story is called the story's **point of view.** A writer can choose from several different points of view. When a story is told by a character in the story, using the first-person pronoun *I,* it is said to be told from the first-person point of view.

When writers choose to tell a story from the first-person point of view, they are limited in what they can tell us. Their whole story must be told from the narrator's point of view. In "Raymond's Run," Squeaky, the narrator, can tell only what she herself thinks, feels, and sees. She cannot look into the minds of other characters and tell their thoughts and feelings, although she may guess at them. Neither can she describe what is happening someplace else, unless her part as a character in the story takes her to the place and allows her to see the action.

The third-person point of view is narrated by someone not in the story, using the third-person pronoun (*he* or *she*). There are two types of this point of view that we are accustomed to reading. When the narrator has access to the minds of all the characters in a story and can show us events from different vantage points, the point of view is called third-person omniscient. *Omniscient* means "knowing all." It comes from two Latin words, *omnis,* which means "all," and *sciens,* which means "knowing." Jack London's "To Build a Fire" is an example of the third-person omniscient point of view.

Another variation of the third-person point of view is the limited third-person point of view. The narrator is not a character in the story, but the narrator uses the third-person pronoun (*he* or *she*) and lets us know only what is going on in one character's mind. "The Birds" aptly demonstrates this point of view.

Why do you think Toni Cade Bambara uses first-person point of view to tell "Raymond's Run"?

THE VOCABULARY IN THE STORY

Slang words are those that are forced, exaggerated, or sometimes humorous and are used in extremely informal writing or speech. The author has Squeaky use slang to make her sound believable.

> (*Dig* that.)

> And I have a big *rep* as the *baddest* thing around.

Dig is slang for "listen to" or "pay attention to." *Rep* is short for "reputation." The slang word *baddest* really means "best." Can you see the humor and intensity conveyed by the fact that this slang word means the exact opposite of the word's literal meaning?

Think of some popular slang words and translate them into more formal language.

COMPOSITION: Using a Different Point of View

Consider how this story would be different if it were told from someone else's point of view. Because Squeaky is the narrator of "Raymond's Run," we do not know what is in the other characters' minds. We only know what they say or what Squeaky observes about them.

Choose one of the other characters in the story and, using the first-person point of view, write a narrative (200–300 words) in which you talk about Squeaky. Use the events in the story as examples or reference points. Try to be as much like the characters as they are portrayed in the story. For example, if you were to choose Rosie's viewpoint, you might not see Squeaky in a very favorable light.

Prewriting

Before you begin writing, take time to imagine what it would feel like to be the character you have chosen. How would you react to Squeaky's assertions of her swiftness? Would you admire the way she protects Raymond? Would you think that she is *too* honest in her assessment of other people? Jot down these feelings along with specific examples from the story that may support them.

Writing

Write your first draft as quickly as possible so that you won't lose the "freshness" of your character. Remember to use the first-person pronoun *I* because your narrative is written from the first-person point of view.

Your narrative might begin something like this: "That Squeaky really burns me up because she thinks she's so fast."

Evaluating and Revising

Read your draft. Add, cut, rearrange, or replace words or phrases as needed. Check to make sure that you have stayed "in character"; it is important that you don't let your own feelings about Squeaky slip into the narrative.

ABOUT THE AUTHOR

 Toni Cade Bambara (1939–   ) knows well the people who live in the sections of New York City where she grew up—Harlem and Bedford-Stuyvesant. Two of her books are *Tales and Stories for Black Folks* and *Gorilla, My Love*, a collection of stories which contains "Raymond's Run." During the 1960s and 1970s, she was active in civil rights issues. In addition to being a writer, Bambara has been a social worker and a college professor.

■ THE SCARLET IBIS

James Hurst

This story is about Doodle, a physically disabled child. It is told by his older brother, who at times feels love and tenderness for the younger boy, but who also, at other times, feels angry with him. The story shows how these two emotional attitudes affect not only the brothers' relationship but also Doodle's life itself.

I t was in the clove of seasons, summer was dead but autumn had not yet been born, that the ibis lit in the bleeding tree. The flower garden was stained with rotting brown magnolia petals and ironweeds grew rank amid the purple phlox. The five o'clocks by the chimney still marked time, but the oriole nest in the elm was untenanted and rocked back and forth like an empty cradle. The last graveyard flowers were blooming, and their smell drifted across the cotton field and through every room of our house, speaking softly the names of our dead.

It's strange that all this is still so clear to me, now that that summer has long since fled and time has had its way. A grindstone stands where the bleeding tree stood, just outside the kitchen door, and now if an oriole sings in the elm, its song seems to die up in the leaves, a silvery dust. The flower garden is prim, the house a gleaming white, and the pale fence across the yard stands straight and spruce. But sometimes (like right now), as I sit in the cool, green-draped parlor, the grindstone begins to turn, and time with all its changes is ground away—and I remember Doodle.

Doodle was just about the craziest brother a boy ever had. Of course, he wasn't crazy crazy like old Miss Leedie, who was in love with President Wilson and wrote him a letter every day, but was a nice crazy, like someone you meet in your dreams. He was born when I was six and was, from the outset, a disappointment. He seemed all head, with a tiny body which was red and shriveled like an old man's. Everybody thought he was going to die—everybody except Aunt Nicey, who had delivered him. She said he would live because he was born with a caul[1]

---

1. **caul:** a membrane called the amniotic sac that sometimes covers the head of a newborn.

and cauls were made from Jesus' nightgown. Daddy had Mr. Heath, the carpenter, build a little mahogany coffin for him. But he didn't die, and when he was three months old Mama and Daddy decided they might as well name him. They named him William Armstrong, which was like tying a big tail on a small kite. Such a name sounds good only on a tombstone.

I thought myself pretty smart at many things, like holding my breath, running, jumping, or climbing the vines in Old Woman Swamp, and I wanted more than anything else someone to race to Horsehead Landing, someone to box with, and someone to perch with in the top fork of the great pine behind the barn, where across the fields and swamps you could see the sea. I wanted a brother. But Mama, crying, told me that even if William Armstong lived, he would never do these things with me. He might not, she sobbed, even be "all there." He might, as long as he lived, lie on the rubber sheet in the center of the bed in the front bedroom, where the white marquisette curtains billowed out in the afternoon sea breeze, rustling like palmetto fronds.

It was bad enough having an invalid brother, but having one who possibly was not all there was unbearable, so I began to make plans to kill him by smothering him with a pillow. However, one afternoon as I watched him, my head poked between the iron posts of the foot of the bed, he looked straight at me and grinned. I skipped through the rooms, down the echoing halls, shouting, "Mama, he smiled. He's all there! He's all there!" and he was.

When he was two, if you laid him on his stomach, he began to try to move himself, straining terribly. The doctor said that with his weak heart this strain would probably kill him, but it didn't. Trembling, he'd push himself up, turning first red, then a soft purple, and finally collapse back onto the bed like an old worn-out doll. I can still see Mama watching him, her hand pressed tight across her mouth, her eyes wide and unblinking. But he learned to crawl (it was his third winter), and we brought him out of the front bedroom, putting him on the rug before the fireplace. For the first time he became one of us.

As long as he lay all the time in bed, we called him William Armstrong, even though it was formal and sounded as if we were referring to one of our ancestors, but with his creeping around on the deerskin rug and beginning to talk, something had to be done about his name. It was I who renamed him. When he crawled, he crawled backward, as if he were in reverse and couldn't change gears. If you called him, he'd turn around as if he were going in the other direction, then he'd back right up to you to be picked up. Crawling backward made him look like a doodle-bug, so I began to call him Doodle, and in time even Mama and Daddy thought it was a better name than William Armstrong. Only Aunt Nicey disagreed. She said caul babies should be treated with special respect since they might turn out to be saints. Renaming my brother was perhaps the kindest thing I ever did for him, because nobody expects much from someone called Doodle.

Although Doodle learned to crawl, he showed no signs of walking, but he wasn't idle. He talked so much that we all quit listening to what he said. It was about this time that Daddy built him a go-cart and I had to pull him around. At first I just paraded him up and down the piazza, but then he started crying to be taken out into the yard and it ended up by my having to lug him wherever I went. If I so much as picked up my cap, he'd start crying to go with me and Mama would call from wherever she was, "Take Doodle with you."

He was a burden in many ways. The doctor had said that he mustn't get too excited, too hot, too cold, or too tired and that he must always be treated gently. A long list of don'ts went with him, all of which I ignored once we got out of the house. To discourage his coming with me, I'd run with him across the ends of the cotton rows and careen him around corners on two wheels. Sometimes I accidentally turned him over, but he never told Mama. His skin was very sensitive, and he had to wear a big straw hat whenever he went out. When the going got rough and he had to cling to the sides of the go-cart, the hat slipped all the way down over his ears. He was a sight. Finally, I could see I was licked. Doodle was my brother and he was going to cling to me forever, no matter what I did, so I dragged him across the burning cotton field to share with him the only beauty I knew, Old Woman Swamp. I pulled the go-cart through the sawtooth fern, down into the green dimness where the palmetto fronds whispered by the stream. I lifted him out and set him down in the soft rubber grass beside a tall pine. His eyes were round with wonder as he gazed about him, and his little hands began to stroke the rubber grass. Then he began to cry.

"For heaven's sake, what's the matter?" I asked, annoyed.

"It's so pretty," he said. "So pretty, pretty, pretty."

After that day Doodle and I often went down into Old Woman Swamp. I would gather wildflowers, wild violets, honeysuckle, yellow jasmine, snakeflowers, and water lilies, and with wire grass we'd weave them into necklaces and crowns. We'd bedeck ourselves with our handiwork and loll about thus beautified, beyond the touch of the everyday world. Then when the slanted rays of the sun burned orange in the tops of the pines, we'd drop our jewels into the stream and watch them float away toward the sea.

There is within me (and with sadness I have watched it in others) a knot of cruelty borne by the stream of love, much as our blood sometimes bears the seed of our destruction, and at times I was mean to Doodle. One day I took him up to the barn loft and showed him his casket, telling him how we all had believed he would die. It was covered with a film of Paris green[2] sprinkled to kill the rats, and screech owls had built a nest inside it.

Doodle studied the mahogany box for a long time, then said, "It's not mine."

"It is," I said. "And before I'll help you down from the loft, you're going to have to touch it.

"I won't touch it," he said sullenly.

"Then I'll leave you here by yourself," I threatened, and made as if I were going down.

Doodle was frightened of being left. "Don't go leave me, Brother," he cried, and he leaned toward the coffin. His hand, trembling, reached out, and when he touched the casket he screamed. A screech owl flapped out of the box into our faces, scaring us and covering us with Paris green. Doodle was paralyzed, so I put him on my shoulder and carried him down the ladder, and even when we were outside in the bright sunshine, he clung to me, crying, "Don't leave me. Don't leave me."

When Doodle was five years old, I was embarrassed at having a brother of that age who couldn't walk, so I set out to teach him. We were down in Old Woman Swamp and it was spring and the sick-sweet smell of bay flowers hung everywhere like a mournful song. "I'm going to teach you to walk, Doodle," I said.

He was sitting comfortably on the soft grass, leaning back against the pine. "Why?" he asked.

I hadn't expected such an answer. "So I won't have to haul you around all the time."

---

2. **Paris green:** a poisonous bright-green powder.

"I can't walk, Brother," he said.

"Who says so?" I demanded.

"Mama, the doctor—everybody."

"Oh, you can walk," I said, and I took him by the arms and stood him up. He collapsed onto the grass like a half-empty flour sack. It was as if he had no bones in his little legs.

"Don't hurt me, Brother," he warned.

"Shut up. I'm not going to hurt you. I'm going to teach you to walk." I heaved him up again, and again he collapsed.

This time he did not lift his face up out of the rubber grass. "I just can't do it. Let's make honeysuckle wreaths."

"Oh yes you can, Doodle," I said. "All you got to do is try. Now come on," and I hauled him up once more.

It seemed so hopeless from the beginning that it's a miracle I didn't give up. But all of us must have something or someone to be proud of, and Doodle had become mine. I did not know then that pride is a wonderful, terrible thing, a seed that bears two vines, life and death. Every day that summer we went to the pine beside the stream of Old Woman Swamp, and I put him on his feet at least a hundred times each afternoon. Occasionally I too became discouraged because it didn't seem as if he was trying, and I would say, "Doodle, don't you *want* to learn to walk?"

He'd nod his head, and I'd say, "Well, if you don't keep trying, you'll never learn." Then I'd paint for him a picture of us as old men, white-haired, him with a long white beard and me still pulling him around in the go-cart. This never failed to make him try again.

Finally one day, after many weeks of practicing, he stood alone for a few seconds. When he fell, I grabbed him in my arms and hugged him, our laughter pealing through the swamp like a ringing bell. Now we knew it could be done. Hope no longer hid in the dark palmetto thicket but perched like a cardinal in the lacy toothbrush tree, brilliantly visible. "Yes, yes," I cried, and he cried it too, and the grass beneath us was soft and the smell of the swamp was sweet.

With success so imminent, we decided not to tell anyone until he could actually walk. Each day, barring rain, we sneaked into Old Woman Swamp, and by cotton-picking time Doodle was ready to show what he could do. He still wasn't able to walk far, but we could wait no longer. Keeping a nice secret is very hard to do, like holding your breath. We chose to reveal all on October eighth, Doodle's sixth birthday, and

for weeks ahead we mooned around the house, promising everybody
a most spectacular surprise. Aunt Nicey said that, after so much talk,
if we produced anything less tremendous than the Resurrection, she
was going to be disappointed.

At breakfast on our chosen day, when Mama, Daddy, and Aunt
Nicey were in the dining room, I brought Doodle to the door in the
go-cart just as usual and had them turn their backs, making them cross
their hearts and hope to die if they peeked. I helped Doodle up, and
when he was standing alone I let them look. There wasn't a sound as
Doodle walked slowly across the room and sat down at his place at the
table. Then Mama began to cry and ran over to him, hugging him and
kissing him. Daddy hugged him too, so I went to Aunt Nicey, who was
thanks-praying in the doorway, and began to waltz her around. We
danced together quite well until she came down on my big toe with
her brogans, hurting me so badly I thought I was crippled for life.

Doodle told them it was I who had taught him to walk, so everyone
wanted to hug me, and I began to cry.

"What are you crying for?" asked Daddy, but I couldn't answer. They
did not know that I did it for myself; that pride, whose slave I was,
spoke to me louder than all their voices, and that Doodle walked only
because I was ashamed of having a crippled brother.

Within a few months Doodle had learned to walk well and his
go-cart was put up in the barn loft (it's still there) beside his little
mahogany coffin. Now, when we roamed off together, resting often, we
never turned back until our destination had been reached, and to help
pass the time, we took up lying. From the beginning Doodle was a
terrible liar and he got me in the habit. Had anyone stopped to listen
to us, we would have been sent off to Dix Hill.

My lies were scary, involved, and usually pointless, but Doodle's
were twice as crazy. People in his stories all had wings and flew
wherever they wanted to go. His favorite lie was about a boy named
Peter who had a pet peacock with a ten-foot tail. Peter wore a golden
robe that glittered so brightly that when he walked through the
sunflowers they turned away from the sun to face him. When Peter
was ready to go to sleep, the peacock spread his magnificent tail,
enfolding the boy gently like a closing go-to-sleep flower, burying him
in the gloriously iridescent, rustling vortex. Yes, I must admit it. Doodle
could beat me lying.

Doodle and I spent lots of time thinking about our future. We decided that when we were grown we'd live in Old Woman Swamp and pick dog-tongue for a living. Beside the stream, he planned, we'd build us a house of whispering leaves and the swamp birds would be our chickens. All day long (when we weren't gathering dog-tongue) we'd swing through the cypresses on the rope vines, and if it rained we'd huddle beneath an umbrella tree and play stickfrog. Mama and Daddy could come and live with us if they wanted to. He even came up with the idea that he could marry Mama and I could marry Daddy. Of course, I was old enough to know this wouldn't work out, but the picture he painted was so beautiful and serene that all I could do was whisper Yes, yes.

Once I had succeeded in teaching Doodle to walk, I began to believe in my own infallibility and I prepared a terrific development program for him, unknown to Mama and Daddy, of course. I would teach him to run, to swim, to climb trees, and to fight. He, too, now believed in my infallibility, so we set the deadline for these accomplishments less than a year away, when, it had been decided, Doodle could start to school.

That winter we didn't make much progress, for I was in school and Doodle suffered from one bad cold after another. But when spring came, rich and warm, we raised our sights again. Success lay at the end of summer like a pot of gold, and our campaign got off to a good start. On hot days, Doodle and I went down to Horsehead Landing and I gave him swimming lessons or showed him how to row a boat. Sometimes we descended into the cool greenness of Old Woman Swamp and climbed the rope vines or boxed scientifically beneath the pine where he had learned to walk. Promise hung about us like the leaves, and wherever we looked, ferns unfurled and birds broke into song.

That summer, the summer of 1918, was blighted. In May and June there was no rain and the crops withered, curled up, then died under the thirsty sun. One morning in July a hurricane came out of the east, tipping over the oaks in the yard and splitting the limbs of the elm trees. That afternoon it roared back out of the west, blew the fallen oaks around, snapping their roots and tearing them out of the earth like a hawk at the entrails of a chicken. Cotton bolls were wrenched from the stalks and lay like green walnuts in the valleys between the rows, while the cornfield leaned over uniformly so that the tassels touched the ground. Doodle and I followed Daddy out into the cotton field, where he stood, shoulders sagging, surveying the ruin. When his chin sank down onto his chest, we were frightened, and Doodle slipped his hand into mine. Suddenly Daddy straightened his shoulders, raised a giant knuckly fist, and with a voice that seemed to rumble out of the earth itself began cursing heaven, hell, the weather, and the Republican Party. Doodle and I, prodding each other and giggling, went back to the house, knowing that everything would be all right.

And during that summer, strange names were heard through the house: Château Thierry, Amiens, Soissons, and in her blessing at the supper table, Mama once said, "And bless the Pearsons, whose boy Joe was lost at Belleau Wood."[3]

So we came to that clove of seasons. School was only a few weeks away, and Doodle was far behind schedule. He could barely clear the ground when climbing up the rope vines and his swimming was certainly not passable. We decided to double our efforts, to make that last drive and reach our pot of gold. I made him swim until he turned blue and row until he couldn't lift an oar. Wherever we went, I purposely walked fast, and although he kept up, his face turned red and his eyes became glazed. Once, he could go no further, so he collapsed on the ground and began to cry.

"Aw, come on, Doodle," I urged. "You can do it. Do you want to be different from everybody else when you start school?"

"Does it make any difference?"

"It certainly does," I said. "Now, come on," and I helped him up.

As we slipped through dog days, Doodle began to look feverish, and Mama felt his forehead, asking him if he felt ill. At night he didn't sleep well, and sometimes he had nightmares, crying out until I touched him and said, "Wake up, Doodle. Wake up."

It was Saturday noon, just a few days before school was to start. I should have already admitted defeat, but my pride wouldn't let me. The excitement of our program had now been gone for weeks, but still we kept on with a tired doggedness. It was too late to turn back, for we had both wandered too far into a net of expectations and had left no crumbs behind.

Daddy, Mama, Doodle, and I were seated at the dining-room table

---

3. **Château Thierry** (sha′ tō′ tē er′ē), **Amiens** (à myan′), **Soissons** (swä sōn′), and **Belleau** (be lō′) **Wood:** World War I battle sites in France.

having lunch. It was a hot day, with all the windows and doors open in case a breeze should come. In the kitchen Aunt Nicey was humming softly. After a long silence, Daddy spoke. "It's so calm, I wouldn't be surprised if we had a storm this afternoon."

"I haven't heard a rain frog," said Mama, who believed in signs, as she served the bread around the table.

"I did," declared Doodle. "Down in the swamp."

"He didn't," I said contrarily.

"You did, eh?" said Daddy, ignoring my denial.

"I certainly did," Doodle reiterated, scowling at me over the top of his iced-tea glass, and we were quiet again.

Suddenly, from out in the yard, came a strange croaking noise. Doodle stopped eating, with a piece of bread poised ready for his mouth, his eyes popped round like two blue buttons. "What's that?" he whispered.

I jumped up, knocking over my chair, and had reached the door when Mama called, "Pick up the chair, sit down again, and say excuse me."

By the time I had done this, Doodle had excused himself and had slipped out into the yard. He was looking up into the bleeding tree. "It's a great big red bird!" he called.

The bird croaked loudly again, and Mama and Daddy came out into the yard. We shaded our eyes with our hands against the hazy glare of the sun and peered up through the still leaves. On the topmost branch a bird the size of a chicken, with scarlet feathers and long legs, was perched precariously. Its wings hung down loosely, and as we watched, a feather dropped away and floated slowly down through the green leaves.

"It's not even frightened of us," Mama said.

"It looks tired," Daddy added. "Or maybe sick."

Doodle's hands were clasped at his throat, and I had never seen him stand still so long. "What is it?" he asked.

Daddy shook his head. "I don't know, maybe it's—"

At that moment the bird began to flutter, but the wings were un-coordinated, and amid much flapping and a spray of flying feathers, it tumbled down, bumping through the limbs of the bleeding tree and landing at our feet with a thud. Its long, graceful neck jerked twice into an S, then straightened out, and the bird was still. A white veil came over the eyes and the long white beak unhinged. Its legs were crossed and its clawlike feet were delicately curved at rest. Even death did not mar its grace, for it lay on the earth like a broken vase of red flowers, and we stood around it, awed by its exotic beauty.

"It's dead," Mama said.

"What is it?" Doodle repeated.

"Go bring me the bird book," said Daddy.

I ran into the house and brought back the bird book. As we watched, Daddy thumbed through its pages. "It's a scarlet ibis," he said, pointing to a picture. "It lives in the tropics—South America to Florida. A storm must have brought it here."

Sadly, we all looked back at the bird. A scarlet ibis! How many miles it had traveled to die like this, in *our* yard, beneath the bleeding tree.

"Let's finish lunch," Mama said, nudging us back toward the dining room.

"I'm not hungry," said Doodle, and he knelt down beside the ibis.

"We've got peach cobbler for dessert," Mama tempted from the doorway.

Doodle remained kneeling. "I'm going to bury him."

"Don't you dare touch him," Mama warned. "There's no telling what disease he might have had."

"All right," said Doodle. "I won't."

Daddy, Mama, and I went back to the dining-room table, but we watched Doodle through the open door. He took out a piece of string from his pocket and, without touching the ibis, looped one end around its neck. Slowly, while singing softly "Shall We Gather at the River," he carried the bird around to the front yard and dug a hole in the flower garden, next to the petunia bed. Now we were watching him through the front window, but he didn't know it. His awkwardness at digging the hole with a shovel whose handle was twice as long as he was made us laugh, and we covered our mouths with our hands so he wouldn't hear.

When Doodle came into the dining room, he found us seriously eating our cobbler. He was pale and lingered just inside the screen door. "Did you get the scarlet ibis buried?" asked Daddy.

Doodle didn't speak but nodded his head.

"Go wash your hands, and then you can have some peach cobbler," said Mama.

"I'm not hungry," he said.

"Dead birds is bad luck," said Aunt Nicey, poking her head from the kitchen door. "Specially *red* dead birds!"

As soon as I had finished eating, Doodle and I hurried off to Horsehead Landing. Time was short, and Doodle still had a long way to go if he was going to keep up with the other boys when he started school. The sun, gilded with the yellow cast of autumn, still burned fiercely, but the dark green woods through which we passed were shady and cool. When we reached the landing, Doodle said he was too tired to swim, so we got into a skiff and floated down the creek with the tide. Far off in the marsh a rail was scolding, and over on the beach locusts were singing in the myrtle trees. Doodle did not speak and kept his head turned away, letting one hand trail limply in the water.

After we had drifted a long way, I put the oars in place and made Doodle row back against the tide. Black clouds began to gather in the southwest, and he kept watching them, trying to pull the oars a little faster. When we reached Horsehead Landing, lightning was playing across half the sky and thunder roared out, hiding even the sound of the sea. The sun disappeared and darkness descended, almost like night. Flocks of marsh crows flew by, heading inland to their roosting trees, and two egrets, squawking, arose from the oyster-rock shallows and careened away.

Doodle was both tired and frightened, and when he stepped from the skiff he collapsed onto the mud, sending an armada of fiddler crabs rustling off into the marsh grass. I helped him up, and as he wiped the mud off his trousers, he smiled at me ashamedly. He had failed and we both knew it, so we started back home, racing the storm. We never spoke (What are the words that can solder cracked pride?), but I knew he was watching me, watching for a sign of mercy. The lightning was near now, and from fear he walked so close behind me he kept stepping on my heels. The faster I walked, the faster he walked, so I began to run. The rain was coming, roaring through the pines, and then, like a bursting Roman candle, a gum tree ahead of us was shattered by a bolt of lightning. When the deafening peal of thunder had died, and in the moment before the rain arrived, I heard Doodle, who had fallen behind, cry out, "Brother, Brother, don't leave me! Don't leave me!"

The knowledge that Doodle's and my plans had come to naught was bitter, and that streak of cruelty within me awakened. I ran as fast as I could, leaving him far behind with a wall of rain dividing us. The drops stung my face like nettles, and the wind flared the wet, glistening leaves of the bordering trees. Soon I could hear his voice no more.

I hadn't run too far before I became tired, and the flood of childish spite evanesced[4] as well. I stopped and waited for Doodle. The sound of rain was everywhere, but the wind had died and it fell straight down in parallel paths like ropes hanging from the sky. As I waited, I peered through the downpour, but no one came. Finally I went back and found him huddled beneath a red nightshade bush beside the road. He was sitting on the ground, his face buried in his arms, which were resting on his drawn-up knees. "Let's go, Doodle," I said.

He didn't answer, so I placed my hand on his forehead and lifted his head. Limply, he fell backwards onto the earth. He had been bleeding from the mouth, and his neck and the front of his shirt were stained a brilliant red.

"Doodle! Doodle!" I cried, shaking him, but there was no answer but the ropy rain. He lay very awkwardly, with his head thrown far back, making his vermilion neck appear unusually long and slim. His little legs, bent sharply at the knees, had never before seemed so fragile, so thin.

I began to weep, and the tear-blurred vision in red before me looked very familiar. "Doodle!" I screamed above the pounding storm and threw my body to the earth above his. For a long time, it seemed forever, I lay there crying, sheltering my fallen scarlet ibis from the heresy of rain. ∎

---

4. **evanesced:** vanished; faded away.

THE IMPACT OF THE STORY

According to the popular saying, "Hindsight is twenty-twenty." In other words, sometimes only *after* an event can we know exactly what should have been done, for only then do we fully understand the situation. While we are experiencing an event, we may not have the knowledge, insight, or strength of character to choose the best course of action or to understand the consequences of our actions.

How does "The Scarlet Ibis" exemplify this saying? Where else in literature or popular culture have you found the meaning of this saying expressed?

THE FACTS OF THE STORY

On your own paper, write answers to the following items. Answers may be one word, a phrase, or several sentences.

1. Once he realizes that he can't get rid of Doodle, what does the older brother share with him?

2. The narrator admits to being cruel to Doodle. What does he force his younger brother to do in the barn?

3. Why does the older brother decide to teach Doodle to walk?

4. What is Doodle afraid of?

5. How does Doodle react to the scarlet ibis's death?

THE IDEAS IN THE STORY

Prepare to discuss the following questions in class.

1. Careful thinking about this story will tell you that its theme has something to do with the effects of pride. The narrator says that "pride is a wonderful, terrible thing, a seed that bears two vines, life and death." How does this statement relate to the events of the story? Do you agree that pride can be both destructive and fruitful? Do you think the brother's pride is entirely responsible for Doodle's death? Explain.

2. The story also seems to reveal something about people who are different from others—people who are made for a different, more generous kind of world. How is Doodle unsuited to survive in his brother's world? How is Doodle's spirit different from his frail and sickly body? Do you think he could have survived somewhere else? Explain.

3. Doodle is deeply affected by the appearance and subsequent death of the scarlet ibis. The narrator tells us that as the family watched the bird in the bleeding tree, "Doodle's hands were clasped at his throat, and I had never seen him stand still so long." When the bird dies, Doodle insists upon burying it, becoming so absorbed that he loses his appetite. What do you think the scarlet ibis represents to Doodle? How does the family's behavior reveal that they are unaware of a change in Doodle?

THE ART OF THE STORYTELLER

Conflict

A conflict that occurs between a character and some force outside himself or herself such as the extreme cold in "To Build a Fire" is an *external conflict.* A struggle that occurs within a character's mind or feelings is an *internal conflict.*

This story is about the brother's conflicts with his younger brother, conflicts that do not end with Doodle's death. From the time Doodle is born, the brother's internal conflict results from his inability to accept Doodle as he is. The older brother's feelings are pulled back and forth, from love for his brother to feeling that the brother is a burden and from genuine pride in his brother's accomplishments to a desire to hurt the weaker child.

Although the major conflict in this story is an internal one, the brother also wages an external conflict. Explain how he does this.

Foreshadowing

In his first paragraph, Hurst foreshadows the fact that this story is going to be about loss. He tells us that summer is "dead," that the magnolia petals are "rotting brown," that the ironweeds grow "rank" (they smell of decay), that the oriole nest is "untenanted" and rocks "like an empty cradle," that the "last graveyard flowers" are blooming and that their odor speaks "the names of our dead." All these details foreshadow tragedy.

Another use of foreshadowing occurs when the narrator threatens to leave Doodle in the barn if he doesn't touch his own coffin. "'Don't go leave me, Brother,'" Doodle cries. And again, "'Don't leave me. Don't leave me.'" How does this cry and the circumstances surrounding it foreshadow Doodle's death? How did you feel when this plea was repeated near the end of the story?

Symbols

A **symbol** is a thing or a person or an event that has meaning in itself but that also represents something broader than itself—such as a value, an attitude, or a human condition. The American flag, for example, is a symbol of the United States of America. A red cross on an ambulance symbolizes help for the injured and the sick. A skull and crossbones on a bottle symbolize danger. A red heart symbolizes love.

The color red appears several times in this story. There is a bleeding tree, the scarlet ibis, a red nightshade bush, and Doodle's blood. Red is a color that carries symbolic meaning. It usually suggests courage and a martyr's death. Why is red a suitable symbolic color for this story?

The scarlet ibis is a major symbol in this story—it is a real bird in the story, but it also is a symbol of something else. It is clear that the writer wants us to see similarities between Doodle and the fallen bird. In what specific ways are Doodle and the scarlet ibis alike? Remembering that the ibis is strange, beautiful, and away from its natural home, tell how it could be seen as a symbol of Doodle and of his unusual spirit.

THE VOCABULARY IN THE STORY

Sometimes it helps to understand a word by thinking of another word that means the same thing, that is, its *synonym.*

Notice the italicized words in the following sentence from the story.

> We'd *bedeck* ourselves with our handiwork and *loll* about
> thus beautified, beyond the touch of the everyday world.

Some words that mean the same as *bedeck* are *adorn, decorate,* and *ornament*. Some synonyms of *loll* are *lounge* and *sprawl*.

Give an appropriate synonym for each of the following words. Check your answers in a dictionary.

rocked	withered	precariously
uniformly	huddle	

COMPOSITION: Comparing or Contrasting Two Stories

Different stories may contain similar situations but present them in profoundly different ways. This is the case with the stories "Raymond's Run" and "The Scarlet Ibis." Both stories deal with a young person who has a disabled brother; however, the two relationships described are quite different.

Write a composition (at least 250 words) comparing or contrasting these stories.

Prewriting

Before you begin, briefly jot down in two separate columns the similarities and differences you find in the stories. After reviewing the two lists, decide whether you want to compare or contrast the stories.

You may discuss only one point of similarity or difference between the stories, or you may write about several. Some obvious points to include are the narrators, the disabled brothers, events in the stories, and the stories' themes.

You will need to back up your ideas with references to the stories. Jot down as many specific references to the story as you can to support your ideas. Directly quoting the text makes your ideas more believable. Find a relevant quotation or two.

Writing

Write your first draft from memory as much as possible. You can go back and add details from your jottings later.

Evaluating and Revising

Read your draft. Add details, cut, rearrange, or replace words or phrases as needed. Compare your prewriting list to your draft. Have you organized your ideas clearly so that the reader will know exactly what you are comparing or contrasting?

ABOUT THE AUTHOR

 James Hurst (1922–) grew up in North Carolina on a farm by the sea. After studying at North Carolina State College, he served in the army during World War II. When the war ended, he studied singing at the Juilliard School of Music, then continued his musical studies in Rome, Italy, where he lived for three years. Back in New York in 1951, he began a thirty-four year career in the International Department of a large bank. For a decade, in the fifties and early sixties, he also wrote, publishing several short stories and a play. His most famous short story, "The Scarlet Ibis" first appeared in *The Atlantic Monthly* in July 1960.

■ ALL SUMMER IN A DAY

Ray Bradbury

Imagine living on a planet where rain falls continuously, except
for two hours every seven years, when the sun comes out.
Such is life on the planet Venus as science fiction writer Ray
Bradbury imagines it. Although life on Venus is much different
from that on Earth, the people he describes are the same as
any of us.

"**R**eady?"
  "Ready."
  "Now?"
"Soon."
"Do the scientists really know? Will it happen today, will it?"
"Look, look; see for yourself!"

The children pressed to each other like so many roses, so many
weeds, intermixed, peering out for a look at the hidden sun.

It rained.

It had been raining for seven years; thousands upon thousands of
days compounded and filled from one end to the other with rain, with
the drum and gush of water, with the sweet crystal fall of showers and
the concussion of storms so heavy they were tidal waves come over the
islands. A thousand forests had been crushed under the rain and grown
up a thousand times to be crushed again. And this was the way life
was forever on the planet Venus, and this was the schoolroom of the
children of the rocket men and women who had come to a raining
world to set up civilization and live out their lives.

"It's stopping, it's stopping!"
"Yes, yes!"

Margot stood apart from them, from these children who could never
remember a time when there wasn't rain and rain and rain. They were
all nine years old, and if there had been a day, seven years ago, when
the sun came out for an hour and showed its face to the stunned world,
they could not recall. Sometimes, at night, she heard them stir, in
remembrance, and she knew they were dreaming and remembering
gold or a yellow crayon or a coin large enough to buy the world with.

She knew they thought they remembered a warmness, like a blushing in the face, in the body, in the arms and legs and trembling hands. But then they always awoke to the tatting drum, the endless shaking down of clear bead necklaces upon the roof, the walk, the gardens, the forests, and their dreams were gone.

All day yesterday they had read in class about the sun. About how like a lemon it was, and how hot. And they had written small stories or essays or poems about it:

> I think the sun is a flower,
> That blooms for just one hour.

That was Margot's poem, read in a quiet voice in the still classroom while the rain was falling outside.

"Aw, you didn't write that!" protested one of the boys.

"I did," said Margot, "I *did*."

"William!" said the teacher.

But that was yesterday. Now the rain was slackening, and the children were crushed in the great thick windows.

"Where's teacher?"

"She'll be back."

"She'd better hurry, we'll miss it!"

They turned on themselves, like a feverish wheel, all tumbling spokes.

Margot stood alone. She was a very frail girl who looked as if she had been lost in the rain for years and the rain had washed out the blue from her eyes and the red from her mouth and the yellow from her hair. She was an old photograph dusted from an album, whitened away, and if she spoke at all her voice would be a ghost. Now she stood, separate, staring at the rain and the loud wet world beyond the huge glass.

"What're *you* looking at?" said William.

Margot said nothing.

"Speak when you're spoken to." He gave her a shove. But she did not move; rather she let herself be moved only by him and nothing else.

They edged away from her, they would not look at her. She felt them go away. And this was because she would play no games with them in the echoing tunnels of the underground city. If they tagged her and ran, she stood blinking after them and did not follow. When the class sang songs about happiness and life and games her lips barely moved. Only when they sang about the sun and the summer did her lips move as she watched the drenched windows.

And then, of course, the biggest crime of all was that she had come here only five years ago from Earth, and she remembered the sun and the way the sun was and the sky was when she was four in Ohio. And they, they had been on Venus all their lives, and they had been only two years old when last the sun came out and had long since forgotten the color and heat of it and the way it really was. But Margot remembered.

"It's like a penny," she said once, eyes closed.

"No it's not!" the children cried.

"It's like a fire," she said, "in the stove."

"You're lying, you don't remember!" cried the children.

But she remembered and stood quietly apart from all of them and watched the patterning windows. And once, a month ago, she had refused to shower in the school shower rooms, had clutched her hands to her ears and over her head, screaming the water mustn't touch her head. So after that, dimly, dimly, she sensed it, she was different and they knew her difference and kept away.

There was talk that her father and mother were taking her back to Earth next year; it seemed vital to her that they do so, though it would mean the loss of thousands of dollars to her family. And so, the children hated her for all these reasons of big and little consequence. They hated her pale snow face, her waiting silence, her thinness, and her possible future.

"Get away!" The boy gave her another push. "What're you waiting for?"

Then, for the first time, she turned and looked at him. And what she was waiting for was in her eyes.

"Well, don't wait around here!" cried the boy savagely. "You won't see nothing!"

Her lips moved.

"Nothing!" he cried. "It was all a joke, wasn't it?" He turned to the other children. "Nothing's happening today. *Is* it?"

They all blinked at him and then, understanding, laughed and shook their heads. "Nothing, nothing!"

"Oh, but," Margot whispered, her eyes helpless. "But this is the day, the scientists predict, they say, they *know*, the sun . . ."

"All a joke!" said the boy, and seized her roughly. "Hey, everyone, let's put her in a closet before teacher comes!"

"No," said Margot, falling back.

They surged about her, caught her up and bore her, protesting, and then pleading, and then crying, back into a tunnel, a room, a closet, where they slammed and locked the door. They stood looking at the door and saw it tremble from her beating and throwing herself against it. They heard her muffled cries. Then, smiling, they turned and went out and back down the tunnel, just as the teacher arrived.

"Ready, children?" She glanced at her watch.

"Yes!" said everyone.

"Are we all here?"

"Yes!"

The rain slackened still more.

They crowded to the huge door.

The rain stopped.

It was as if, in the midst of a film, concerning an avalanche, a tornado, a hurricane, a volcanic eruption, something had, first, gone wrong with the sound apparatus, thus muffling and finally cutting off all noise, all of the blasts and repercussions and thunders, and then, second, ripped the film from the projector and inserted in its place a peaceful tropical slide which did not move or tremor. The world ground to a standstill. The silence was so immense and unbelievable that you felt your ears had been stuffed or you had lost your hearing altogether. The children put their hands to their ears. They stood apart. The door slid back and the smell of the silent, waiting world came in to them.

The sun came out.

It was the color of flaming bronze and it was very large. And the sky around it was a blazing blue tile color. And the jungle burned with sunlight as the children, released from their spell, rushed out, yelling, into the springtime.

"Now, don't go too far," called the teacher after them. "You've only two hours, you know. You wouldn't want to get caught out!"

But they were running and turning their faces up to the sky and feeling the sun on their cheeks like a warm iron; they were taking off their jackets and letting the sun burn their arms.

"Oh, it's better than the sunlamps, isn't it?"

"Much, much better!"

They stopped running and stood in the great jungle that covered Venus, that grew and never stopped growing, tumultuously, even as you watched it. It was a nest of octopi, clustering up great arms of flesh-like weed, wavering, flowering this brief spring. It was the color of rubber and ash, this jungle, from the many years without sun. It was the color of stones and white cheeses and ink, and it was the color of the moon.

The children lay out, laughing, on the jungle mattress, and heard it sigh and squeak under them, resilient and alive. They ran among the trees, they slipped and fell, they pushed each other, they played hide-and-seek and tag, but most of all they squinted at the sun until the tears ran down their faces, they put their hands up to that yellowness and that amazing blueness and they breathed of the fresh, fresh air and listened and listened to the silence which suspended them in a blessed sea of no sound and no motion. They looked at everything and savored everything. Then, wildly, like animals escaped from their caves, they ran and ran in shouting circles. They ran for an hour and did not stop running.

And then—

In the midst of their running one of the girls wailed.

Everyone stopped.

The girl, standing in the open, held out her hand.

"Oh, look, look," she said trembling.

They came slowly to look at her opened palm.

In the center of it, cupped and huge, was a single raindrop.

She began to cry, looking at it.

They glanced quietly at the sky.

"Oh. Oh."

A few cold drops fell on their noses and their cheeks and their mouths. The sun faded behind a stir of mist. A wind blew cool around them. They turned and started to walk back toward the underground house, their hands at their sides, their smiles vanishing away.

A boom of thunder startled them and like leaves before a new hurricane, they tumbled upon each other and ran. Lightning struck ten miles away, five miles away, a mile, a half mile. The sky darkened into midnight in a flash.

They stood in the doorway of the underground for a moment until it was raining hard. Then they closed the door and heard the gigantic sound of the rain falling in tons and avalanches, everywhere and forever.

"Will it be seven more years?"

"Yes. Seven."

Then one of them gave a little cry.

"Margot!"

"What?"

"She's still in the closet where we locked her."

"Margot."

They stood as if someone had driven them, like so many stakes, into the floor. They looked at each other and then looked away. They glanced out at the world that was raining now and raining and raining steadily. They could not meet each other's glances. Their faces were solemn and pale. They looked at their hands and feet, their faces down.

"Margot."

One of the girls said, "Well . . . ?"

No one moved.

"Go on," whispered the girl.

They walked slowly down the hall in the sound of cold rain. They turned through the doorway to the room in the sound of the storm and thunder, lightning on their faces, blue and terrible. They walked over to the closet door slowly and stood by it.

Behind the closet door was only silence.

They unlocked the door, even more slowly, and let Margot out. ■

THE IMPACT OF THE STORY

In "All Summer in a Day," Margot is like a captive. She is trapped, living under conditions that are slowly destroying her spirit. What are some situations here on Earth that are similar to Margot's?

THE FACTS OF THE STORY

On your own paper, write answers to the following items. Answers may be one word, a phrase, or several sentences.

1. This story opens with the question "Ready?" What are the characters getting ready for?

2. In what way is Margot's reaction to the constant rain different from the reactions of the other children?

3. In the story, on Venus the sun shines once every _____ years.

4. How long has Margot lived on Venus?

5. In what way have the children's feelings changed by the time they release Margot from the closet?

THE IDEAS IN THE STORY

Prepare to discuss the following questions in class.

1. The main idea in this story has something to do with why people are sometimes cruel to one another. The author says the children hated Margot for

   > all these reasons of big and little consequence.
   > They hated her pale snow face, her waiting silence,
   > her thinness, and her possible future. . . .

   Tell which of these reasons you think are of "big consequence" and which are of "little consequence."

2. Do you think that the children as a group would have treated Margot as they did if there had not been many against one? What has your own experience, or your reading, shown you about group behavior versus individual behavior?

3. We are told that Margot's parents are considering taking her back to Earth next year; "it seemed vital to her that they do so," but it will be at a cost of thousands of dollars to her family. What is the cost to Margot if her family stays? Which do you think is more important, the parents' careers or their daughter's well-being? Consider how the other children are being deprived because of their life on Venus and how they, like Margot, will feel their deprivation now that they know what sunshine is like. What is your view of similar conflicts that face parents and children in our society?

THE ART OF THE STORYTELLER

Similes and Metaphors

Often in our speaking, and especially in our writing, we compare one thing to another, very different thing. When the children in Bradbury's story hear that the sun is like a lemon, they immediately understand something about the sun's appearance, even though the sun and a lemon are not actually alike in any way other than in color and, perhaps, in shape. When Margot uses a comparison and recites lines from her poem, "I think the sun is a flower, / That blooms for just one hour," she immediately helps us understand her idea of the beauty of the sun, and of its brief "bloom."

When a comparison is made with words such as *like* or *as,* it is called a **simile.** (The sun is *like* a lemon. The sun is *as* yellow *as* a lemon.) When a comparison is expressed without words such as *like* or *as*, it is called a **metaphor.** (The sun *is* a flower.)

Read the following comparisons from "All Summer in a Day." What points of comparison are being made in each statement? Decide whether each is a simile or a metaphor.

1. She [Margot] was an old photograph dusted from an album, whitened away. . . .

2. But they were . . . feeling the sun on their cheeks like a warm iron. . . .

3. They stood as if someone had driven them, like so many stakes, into the floor.

Setting

The setting of "All Summer in a Day" is an important part of what happens and how we view this disturbing incident. **Setting** is the time and place in which a story takes place. It creates atmosphere and adds to our understanding of the characters and events in the story. As readers we can understand Margot's distress better because we too might well find such a place depressing and difficult to endure. If the story's setting were more inviting and comfortable, do you think you would find Margot's situation as tragic?

THE VOCABULARY IN THE STORY

Many words have multiple meanings. For instance, the word *drum* can be used as a noun to mean "a musical instrument" or as a verb to mean "to beat continuously."

In "All Summer in a Day," Bradbury uses a great many words that have multiple meanings. This use of words can increase the effectiveness and impact of a narrative. Take, for example, the sentence *"The world ground to a standstill."* The word *ground* is a form of the verb *grind*. It tells how the world seemed to come to a stop. Yet, *ground* can also mean the solid, unmoving foundation underneath us. Thus, Bradbury's use of *ground* reinforces the idea of motionlessness or stillness. Now, for the first time, the children's attention can shift from the falling rain to the ground beneath them, where they now can run and play freely.

For each of the following words, write at least two definitions, including their parts of speech. Then write an original sentence for each meaning of each word.

1. compounded   3. vital   5. repercussions
2. concussion   4. consequence

COMPOSITION: Continuing a Story

"All Summer in a Day" ends with the children cautiously opening the locked closet door to free Margot. The author does not describe Margot's condition or what happens when the children see her: He leaves the reader to imagine her state.

Write a continuation of the story (at least 250 words) from the moment that Margot is let out of the closet. Where appropriate, use similes and metaphors to make your story more vivid.

Prewriting
Reread the story if necessary. Consider what it must be like to be Margot and to have been deprived of what she so desperately wanted. Make notes about her appearance, her actions, and her feelings. Then write down what she might say. Think about the other children, and make notes about them as well.

When you have the story planned in your mind, write down the events in chronological order.

Writing
Write your extension of the story quickly. Don't worry about including similes and metaphors at this point. (If they flow naturally, that's fine.) You can go back later to add them where they would be helpful in describing the scene.

Evaluating and Revising
Read your draft. Have you effectively communicated what you think has happened to Margot and how she and the children interact with one another? Add any similes and metaphors that help the reader to understand your ideas, but don't go overboard in using them. Add, cut, reorder, or replace words, phrases, or sections as needed.

ABOUT THE AUTHOR

Ray Bradbury's (1920–) childhood was spent in the city of his birth, Waukegan, Illinois. After moving to Southern California, he went to high school in Los Angeles, where he still lives. Bradbury is probably America's foremost writer of fantasy and science fiction. In addition to his short stories, for which he is best known, he has written novels and plays, including screenplays. One of his most popular books is *The Martian Chronicles,* which was made into a television serial.

■ GAMES AT TWILIGHT

Anita Desai

Ravi has never known the sweet savor of success in his games
with the older, bigger children. But he has the chance to
triumph when he finds the perfect hiding place during a late-
afternoon game of hide-and-seek.

I t was still too hot to play outdoors. They had had their tea,[1] they
had been washed and had their hair brushed, and after the long
day of confinement in the house that was not cool but at least a
protection from the sun, the children strained to get out. Their faces
were red and bloated with the effort, but their mother would not open
the door; everything was still curtained and shuttered in a way that
stifled the children, made them feel that their lungs were stuffed with
cotton wool and their noses with dust and if they didn't burst out into
the light and see the sun and feel the air, they would choke.

"Please, Ma, please," they begged. "We'll play in the veranda and
porch—we won't go a step out of the porch."

"You will, I know you will, and then—"

"No—we won't, we won't," they wailed so horrendously that she
actually let down the bolt of the front door, so that they burst out like
seeds from a crackling, overripe pod into the veranda with such wild,
maniacal yells that she retreated to her bath and the shower of talcum
powder and the fresh sari that were to help her face the summer
evening.

They faced the afternoon. It was too hot. Too bright. The white walls
of the veranda glared stridently in the sun. The bougainvillea[2] hung
about it, purple and magenta, in livid balloons. The garden outside
was like a tray made of beaten brass, flattened out on the red gravel
and the stony soil in all shades of metal—aluminum, tin, copper and
brass. No life stirred at this arid time of day—the birds still drooped,
like dead fruit, in the papery tents of the trees; some squirrels lay limp

---

1. **tea:** a British custom in which a light meal, including, but not limited to, tea and pastries,
   is served at mid-morning and at mid-afternoon.
2. **bougainvillea** (boo' gən vil' ē ə): a tropical vine that has brightly colored blooms.

on the wet earth under the garden tap. The outdoor dog lay stretched as if dead on the veranda mat, his paws and ears and tail all reaching out like dying travellers in search of water. He rolled his eyes at the children—two white marbles rolling in the purple sockets, begging for sympathy—and attempted to lift his tail in a wag but could not. It only twitched and lay still.

Then, perhaps roused by the shrieks of the children, a band of parrots suddenly fell out of the eucalyptus tree, tumbled frantically in the still, sizzling air, then sorted themselves out into battle formation and streaked away across the white sky.

The children, too, felt released. They too began tumbling, shoving, pushing against each other, frantic to start. Start what? Start their business. The business of the children's day which is—play.

"Let's play hide-and-seek."

"Who'll be It?"

"You be It."

"Why should I? You be—"

"You're the eldest—"

"That doesn't mean—"

The shoves became harder. Some kicked out. The motherly Mira intervened. She pulled the boys roughly apart. There was a tearing sound of cloth, but it was lost in the heavy panting and angry grumbling, and no one paid attention to the small sleeve hanging loosely off a shoulder.

"Make a circle, make a circle!" she shouted, firmly pulling and pushing till a kind of vague circle was formed. "Now clap!" she roared, and clapping, they all chanted in melancholy unison: "Dip, dip, dip—my blue ship—" and every now and then one or the other saw he was safe by the way his hands fell at the crucial moment—palm on palm, or back of hand on palm—and dropped out of the circle with a yell and a jump of relief and jubilation.

Raghu was It. He started to protest, to cry, "You cheated—Mira cheated—Anu cheated—" but it was too late; the others had all already streaked away. There was no one to hear when he called out, "Only in the veranda—the porch—Ma said—Ma *said* to stay in the porch!" No one had stopped to listen; all he saw was their brown legs flashing through the dusty shrubs, scrambling up brick walls, leaping over compost heaps and hedges; and then the porch stood empty in the purple shade of the bougainvillea and the garden was as empty as before; even the limp squirrels had whisked away, leaving everything gleaming, brassy and bare.

Only small Manu suddenly reappeared, as if he had dropped out of an invisible cloud or from a bird's claws, and stood for a moment in the center of the yellow lawn, chewing his finger and near to tears as he heard Raghu shouting, with his head pressed against the veranda wall, "Eighty-three, eighty-five, eighty-nine, ninety . . ." and then made off in a panic, half of him wanting to fly north, the other half counselling south. Raghu turned just in time to see the flash of his white shorts and the uncertain skittering of his red sandals and charged after him with such a blood-curdling yell that Manu stumbled over the hose pipe, fell into its rubber coils and lay there weeping, "I won't be It—you have to find them all—all—All!"

"I know I have to, idiot," Raghu said, superciliously kicking him with his toe. "You're dead," he said with satisfaction, licking the beads of perspiration off his upper lip, and then stalked off in search of worthier prey, whistling spiritedly so that the hiders should hear and tremble.

Ravi heard the whistling and picked his nose in a panic, trying to find comfort by burrowing the finger deep—deep into that soft tunnel. He felt himself too exposed, sitting on an upturned flower pot behind the garage. Where could he burrow? He could run around the garage if he heard Raghu come—around and around and around—but he hadn't much faith in his short legs when matched against Raghu's long, hefty, hairy footballer legs. Ravi had a frightening glimpse of them as Raghu combed the hedge of crotons and hibiscus, trampling delicate ferns underfoot as he did so. Ravi looked about him desperately, swallowing a small ball of snot in his fear.

The garage was locked with a great, heavy lock to which the driver had the key in his room, hanging from a nail on the wall under his work shirt. Ravi had peeped in and seen him still sprawling on his string cot in his vest and striped underpants, the hair on his chest and the hair in his nose shaking with the vibrations of his phlegm-obstructed snores. Ravi had wished he were tall enough, big enough to reach the key on the nail, but it was impossible, beyond his reach for years to come. He had sidled away and sat dejectedly on the flower pot. That at least was cut to his own size.

But next to the garage was another shed with a big green door. Also locked. No one even knew who had the key to the lock. That shed wasn't opened more than once a year, when Ma turned out all the old broken bits of furniture and rolls of matting and leaking buckets, and the white ant hills were broken and swept away and Flit sprayed into the spider webs and rat holes so that the whole operation was like the looting of a poor, ruined and conquered city. The green leaves of the door sagged. They were nearly off their rusty hinges. The hinges were large and made a small gap between the door and the walls—only just large enough for rats, dogs and, possibly, Ravi to slip through.

Ravi had never cared to enter such a dark and depressing mortuary of defunct household goods seething with such unspeakable and alarming animal life, but, as Raghu's whistling grew angrier and sharper and his crashing and storming in the hedge wilder, Ravi suddenly slipped off the flower pot and through the crack and was gone. He chuckled aloud with astonishment at his own temerity so that Raghu came out of the hedge, stood silent with his hands on his hips, listening, and finally shouted, "I heard you! I'm coming! *Got* you—" and came charging round the garage only to find the upturned flower pot, the yellow dust, the crawling of white ants in a mud hill against the closed shed door—nothing. Snarling, he bent to pick up a stick and went off, whacking it against the garage and shed walls as if to beat out his prey.

Ravi shook, then shivered with delight, with self-congratulation. Also with fear. It was dark, spooky in the shed. It had a muffled smell, as of graves. Ravi had once got locked into the linen cupboard and sat there weeping for half an hour before he was rescued. But at least that had been a familiar place and even smelt pleasantly of starch, laundry and, reassuringly, his mother. But the shed smelt of rats, ant hills, dust and spider webs. Also of less definable, less recognizable horrors. And it was dark. Except for the white-hot cracks along the door, there was no light. The roof was very low. Although Ravi was small, he felt as if he could reach up and touch it with his fingertips. But he didn't stretch. He hunched himself into a ball so as not to bump into anything, touch or feel anything. What might there not be to touch him and feel him as he stood there, trying to see in the dark? Something cold or slimy—like a snake. Snakes! He leapt up as Raghu whacked the wall with his stick—then, quickly realizing what it was, felt almost relieved to hear Raghu, hear his stick. It made him feel protected.

But Raghu soon moved away. There wasn't a sound once his footsteps had gone around the garage and disappeared. Ravi stood frozen inside the shed. Then he shivered all over. Something had tickled the back of his neck. It took him a while to pick up the courage to lift his hand and explore. It was an insect—perhaps a spider—exploring *him*. He squashed it and wondered how many more creatures were watching him, waiting to reach out and touch him, the stranger.

There was nothing now. After standing in that position—his hand still on his neck, feeling the wet splodge of the squashed spider gradually dry—for minutes, hours, his legs began to tremble with the effort, the inaction. By now he could see enough in the dark to make out the large, solid shapes of old wardrobes, broken buckets and bedsteads piled on top of each other around him. He recognized an old bathtub—patches of enamel glimmered at him, and at last he lowered himself onto its edge.

He contemplated slipping out of the shed and into the fray. He wondered if it would not be better to be captured by Raghu and returned to the milling crowd as long as he could be in the sun, the light, the free spaces of the garden and the familiarity of his brothers, sisters and cousins. It would be evening soon. Their games would become legitimate. The parents would sit out on the lawn on cane basket chairs and watch them as they tore around the garden or gathered in knots to share a loot of mulberries or black, teeth-splitting *jamun* [3] from the garden trees. The gardener would fix the hose pipe to the water tap, and water would fall lavishly through the air to the ground, soaking the dry, yellow grass and the red gravel and arousing the sweet, the intoxicating, scent of water on dry earth—that loveliest scent in the world. Ravi sniffed for a whiff of it. He half rose from the bathtub, then heard the despairing screams of one of the girls as Raghu bore down upon her. There was the sound of a crash and of rolling about in the bushes, the shrubs, then screams and accusing sobs of "I touched the den—" "You did not—" "I did—" "You liar, you did *not*," and then a fading away and silence again.

Ravi sat back on the harsh edge of the tub, deciding to hold out a bit longer. What fun if they were all found and caught—he alone left unconquered! He had never known that sensation. Nothing more wonderful had ever happened to him than being taken out by an uncle

---

3. **jamun** (ja' moon): a variety of plum.

and bought a whole slab of chocolate all to himself, or being flung into the soda man's pony cart and driven up to the gate by the friendly driver with the red beard and pointed ears. To defeat Raghu—that hirsute, hoarse-voiced football[4] champion—and to be the winner in a circle of older, bigger, luckier children—that would be thrilling beyond imagination. He hugged his knees together and smiled to himself almost shyly at the thought of so much victory, such laurels.

There he sat smiling, knocking his heels against the bathtub, now and then getting up and going to the door to put his ear to the broad crack and listening for sounds of the game, the pursuer and the pursued, and then returning to his seat with the dogged determination of the true winner, a breaker of records, a champion.

It grew darker in the shed as the light at the door grew softer, fuzzier, turned to a kind of crumbling yellow pollen that turned to yellow fur, blue fur, gray fur. Evening. Twilight. The sound of water gushing, falling. The scent of earth receiving water, slaking its thirst in great gulps and releasing that green scent of freshness, coolness. Through the crack Ravi saw the long purple shadows of the shed and the garage lying still across the yard. Beyond that, the white walls of the house. The bougainvillea had lost its lividity, hung in dark bundles that quaked and twittered and seethed with masses of homing sparrows. The lawn was shut off from his view Could he hear the children's voices? It seemed to him that he could. It seemed to him that he could hear them chanting, singing, laughing. But what about the game? What had happened? Could it be over? How could it when he was still not found?

It then occurred to him that he could have slipped out long ago, dashed across the yard to the veranda and touched the "den." It was necessary to do that to win. He had forgotten. He had only remembered the part of hiding and trying to elude the seeker. He had done that so successfully, his success had occupied him so wholly, that he had quite forgotten that success had to be clinched by that final dash to victory and the ringing cry of "Den!"

With a whimper he burst through the crack, fell on his knees, got up and stumbled on stiff, benumbed legs across the shadowy yard, crying heartily by the time he reached the veranda so that when he flung himself at the white pillar and bawled, "Den! Den! Den!" his voice

---

4. **football:** soccer, as it is known everywhere but in the United States.

broke with rage and pity at the disgrace of it all, and he felt himself flooded with tears and misery.

Out on the lawn, the children stopped chanting. They all turned to stare at him in amazement. Their faces were pale and triangular in the dusk. The trees and bushes around them stood inky and sepulchral, spilling long shadows across them. They stared, wondering at his reappearance, his passion, his wild animal howling. Their mother rose from her basket chair and came toward him, worried, annoyed, saying, "Stop it, stop it, Ravi. Don't be a baby. Have you hurt yourself?" Seeing him attended to, the children went back to clasping their hands and chanting, "The grass is green, the rose is red. . . ."

But Ravi would not let them. He tore himself out of his mother's grasp and pounded across the lawn into their midst, charging at them with his head lowered so that they scattered in surprise. "I won, I won, I won," he bawled, shaking his head so that the big tears flew. "Raghu didn't find me. I won, I won—"

It took them a minute to grasp what he was saying, even who he was. They had quite forgotten him. Raghu had found all the others long ago. There had been a fight about who was to be It next. It had been so fierce that their mother had emerged from her bath and made them change to another game. Then they had played another and another. Broken mulberries from the tree and eaten them. Helped the driver wash the car when their father returned from work. Helped the gardener water the beds till he roared at them and swore he would complain to their parents. The parents had come out, taken up their positions on the cane chairs. They had begun to play again, sing and chant. All this time no one had remembered Ravi. Having disappeared from the scene, he had disappeared from their minds. Clean.

"Don't be a fool," Raghu said roughly, pushing him aside, and even Mira said, "Stop howling, Ravi. If you want to play, you can stand at the end of the line," and she put him there very firmly.

The game proceeded. Two pairs of arms reached up and met in an arc. The children trooped under it again and again in a lugubrious circle, ducking their heads and intoning

> "The grass is green,
>   The rose is red;
>   Remember me
> When I am dead, dead, dead, dead . . ."

And the arc of thin arms trembled in the twilight, and the heads were bowed so sadly, and their feet tramped to that melancholy refrain so mournfully, so helplessly, that Ravi could not bear it. He would not follow them; he would not be included in this funereal game. He had wanted victory and triumph—not a funeral. But he had been forgotten, left out and he would not join them now. The ignominy of being forgotten—how could he face it? He felt his heart go heavy and ache inside him unbearably. He lay down full length on the damp grass, crushing his face into it, no longer crying, silenced by a terrible sense of his insignificance. ■

THE IMPACT OF THE STORY

Empathy is an ability to share in another person's emotions and thoughts without actually sharing in that person's life experiences. When we empathize with someone, we can almost feel what that person is feeling.

Despite the fact that you have not had Ravi's exact experience, are you able to empathize with his feelings of abandonment and insignificance? Why or why not?

THE FACTS OF THE STORY

On your own paper, write answers to the following items. Answers may be one word, a phrase, or several sentences.

1. Why are the children not allowed to go outside at the beginning of the story?

2. Where do the children promise their mother they will play?

3. Who is chosen to be "It" in the game of hide-and-seek?

4. Where does Ravi hide?

5. What part of the hide-and-seek game does Ravi forget?

THE IDEAS IN THE STORY

Prepare to discuss the following questions in class.

1. During the long British rule in India, many Indians adopted British customs. Thus, it is not unusual for Indian children to play Western games such as hide-and-seek.

   When the children in the story decide to play hide-and-seek, nobody wants to be "It." After Raghu tags little Manu, he cries out that Raghu must find all of the other children before anyone else can be "It." When Raghu searches nearby, Ravi desperately manages to squeeze inside a shed beside the garage. Why is the shed a good hiding place, and why is it not a good hiding place for Ravi? How does this setting, along with Ravi's thoughts and feelings while he is in the shed, help us to empathize with his final feeling of hopeless abandonment?

2. Although the other children are not consciously aware of their behavior toward Ravi, they treat him quite cruelly. First, they forget about him during the game, and second (unlike how the children react in "All Summer in a Day"), they fail to understand his anguish. Do you think the other children are completely to blame for Ravi's rage and feeling of lonely abandonment? With whom is Ravi probably most angry and why?

THE ART OF THE STORYTELLER

Internal and External Conflict

As you may recall, a key ingredient in plot is the **conflict,** or struggle, the protagonist faces while trying to achieve a goal or to solve a problem. A character may struggle with many opposing forces. A struggle that occurs within a character's own thoughts or emotions is an *internal conflict*. A struggle between a character and a force outside of himself or herself is an *external conflict*.

In "Games at Twilight," what goal does Ravi attempt to achieve? What forces does Ravi struggle against in trying to achieve his goal? Which of these conflicts are external, and which are internal?

Direct and Indirect Characterization

When writers describe a character or give us information about a character's past, they are using *direct characterization*. In "Games at Twilight," Anita Desai uses this method when she has the narrator tell us about Ravi's past experiences of being locked inside a linen cupboard and of being given a large piece of chocolate by his uncle.

However, most of the time, Desai uses *indirect characterization*. By using this method of characterization, Desai lets us decide for ourselves what kind of person Ravi is. We draw our conclusions on the basis of Ravi's actions, speech, and thoughts as well as other characters' reactions to him.

What are some other examples of Desai's direct characterization of Ravi? Identify at least three examples of indirect characterization of Ravi in the story. What do the other characters' reactions to Ravi reveal about him?

We are never told directly Ravi's age or his exact size; however, his smallness is an important factor in his desire to win over the older, bigger children. Find examples in the story that reveal Ravi's size or his feeling of smallness. Identify each example as direct or indirect characterization.

Theme

The main idea or insight about human nature that a story reveals is called **theme**. In "Games at Twilight," Ravi experiences the feeling of complete insignificance when he realizes that the other children have forgotten him. What did you learn from Ravi's experience?

Because of their brief length, most short stories contain only one main idea. However, some short stories, such as "Games at Twilight," have more than one insight into the human condition. What themes do you think are revealed by the events in "Games at Twilight"?

THE VOCABULARY IN THE STORY

The *context* of a word is the words, phrases, or sentences that surround the word. The context can give hints about the word's meaning. Such hints are called *context clues*. Read the following example:

> Consider planting deciduous trees around your house. These trees provide shade in the summer, but when their leaves fall, sunshine can get through to warm your house in the winter.

If you were not familiar with the word *deciduous,* you could figure out its meaning from the context. The phrases *when their leaves fall* and *provide shade* suggest that deciduous trees are trees that shed their leaves in the fall and grow new leaves in the spring.

Read carefully each of the following passages from "Games at Twilight." Then without looking in a dictionary, write a short definition of the italicized word in each passage.

1. The scent of earth receiving water, *slaking* its thirst in great gulps and releasing that green scent of freshness, coolness.

2. . . . everything was still curtained and shuttered in a way that *stifled* the children, made them feel that their lungs were stuffed with cotton wool and their noses with dust. . . .

3. "Please, Ma, please," they begged. . . . they wailed so *horrendously* that she actually let down the bolt of the front door. . . .

4. Ravi had wished he were tall enough, big enough to reach the key on the nail, but it was impossible, beyond his reach for years to come. He had sidled away and sat *dejectedly* on the flower pot.

5. The gardener would fix the hose pipe to the water tap, and water would fall *lavishly* through the air to the ground, soaking the dry, yellow grass and the red gravel. . . .

COMPOSITION: Writing a Persuasive Essay

If you have not already read it, read the preceding story "All Summer in a Day" by Ray Bradbury. Do you think the treatment Margot receives from her classmates in Bradbury's story is more cruel than the treatment Ravi receives from the other children in "Games at Twilight"? Write a persuasive essay (about 500 words) in which you argue for or against the following idea: Margot is treated more cruelly by her peers than Ravi is treated by the other children.

Prewriting
You might wish to reread both stories. Then decide whether or not you will argue that Margot is treated more cruelly than Ravi. From both stories, jot down specific passages that support your position either for or against the statement. Note beside each excerpt how it relates to your argument. Be sure to support each point of your argument with specific examples from both stories. You may find it helpful to arrange your ideas in ascending order of importance, that is, from the least important to the most important idea. (Descending order of importance is the reverse—the arrangement of ideas is from the most important to the least important.)

Writing
Make sure you clearly state your position in the opening paragraph. In the concluding paragraph, restate your position, and summarize the points you have made in the body of the composition.

Evaluating and Revising
Read your draft. Have you organized your ideas clearly? Have you accurately quoted material you have taken word for word from the stories? Cut, reorder, or add words, phrases, or sections as needed. Rewrite sections or sentences if necessary.

ABOUT THE AUTHOR

 Anita Desai (1937–   ) was born in Mussoorie, India. She attended Delhi University, where she received a bachelor of arts degree. She has written numerous novels and short stories in which she examines many of the social and cultural transformations India has experienced since the end of British rule in 1947. Some of the subjects of her other works are family relationships, the struggle for female independence in a male-dominated society, conflict between people of different ages, and the differences between Eastern and Western values. She is perhaps best known for her novels *Cry, the Peacock; Bye-Bye, Blackbird;* and *Fire on the Mountain.* Desai is a member of the Advisory Board for English, Sahitya Akademi, New Delhi, and a member of the Royal Society of Literature.

■ WITH ALL FLAGS FLYING

Anne Tyler

For years, the old man had dreaded this day, but it had finally
arrived. He was too frail to live alone any longer. It was time
for someone else to take care of him. His devoted daughter
had always promised him a place in her home, but he refused
to be a burden to his family. No, he had his own plans.

Weakness was what got him in the end. He had been expecting something more definite—chest pains, a stroke,
arthritis—but it was only weakness that put a finish to his
living alone. A numbness in his head, an airy feeling when he walked.
A wateriness in his bones that made it an effort to pick up his coffee
cup in the morning. He waited some days for it to go away, but it never
did. And meanwhile the dust piled up in corners, the refrigerator
wheezed and creaked for want of defrosting. Weeds grew around his
rosebushes.

He was awake and dressed at six o'clock on a Saturday morning,
with the patchwork quilt pulled up neatly over the mattress. From the
kitchen cabinet he took a hunk of bread and two Fig Newtons, which
he dropped into a paper bag. He was wearing a brown suit that he had
bought on sale in 1944, a white T-shirt, and copper-toed work boots.
These and his other set of underwear, which he put in the paper bag
along with a razor, were all the clothes he took with him. Then he
rolled down the top of the bag and stuck it under his arm, and stood
in the middle of the kitchen staring around him for a moment.

The house had only two rooms, but he owned it—the last scrap of
the farm that he had sold off years ago. It stood in a hollow of dying
trees beside a superhighway in Baltimore County. All it held was a few
sticks of furniture, a change of clothes, a skillet, and a set of dishes.
Also, odds and ends, which disturbed him. If his inventory were complete, he would have to include six clothespins, a salt and a pepper
shaker, a broken-toothed comb, a cheap ballpoint pen—oh, on and
on, past logical numbers. Why should he be so cluttered? He was
eighty-two years old. He had grown from an infant owning nothing to
a family man with a wife, five children, everyday and Sunday china,

and a thousand appurtenances,[1] down at last to solitary old age and the bare essentials again, but not bare enough to suit him. Only what he needed surrounded him. Was it possible he needed so much?

Now he had the brown paper bag; that was all. It was the one satisfaction in a day he had been dreading for years.

He left the house without another glance, heading up the steep bank toward the superhighway. The bank was covered with small, crawling weeds planted especially by young men with scientific training in how to prevent soil erosion. Twice his knees buckled. He had to sit and rest, bracing himself against the slope of the bank. The scientific weeds, seen from close up, looked straggly and gnarled. He sifted dry earth through his fingers without thinking, concentrating only on steadying his breath and calming the twitching muscles in his legs.

Once on the superhighway, which was fairly level, he could walk for longer stretches of time. He kept his head down and his fingers clenched tight upon the paper bag, which was growing limp and damp now. Sweat rolled down the back of his neck, fell in drops from his temples. When he had been walking maybe half an hour, he had to sit down again for a rest. A black motorcycle buzzed up from behind and stopped a few feet away from him. The driver was young and shabby, with hair so long that it drizzled out beneath the back of his helmet.

"Give you a lift, if you like," he said. "You going somewhere?"

"Just into Baltimore."

"Hop on."

He shifted the paper bag to the space beneath his arm, put on the white helmet he was handed, and climbed on behind the driver. For safety, he took a clutch of the boy's shirt, tightly at first, and then more loosely when he saw there was no danger. Except for the helmet, he was perfectly comfortable. He felt his face cooling and stiffening in the wind, his body learning to lean gracefully with the tilt of the motorcycle as it swooped from lane to lane. It was a fine way to spend his last free day.

Half an hour later they were on the outskirts of Baltimore, stopped at the first traffic light. The boy turned his head and shouted, "Whereabouts did you plan on going?"

"I'm visiting my daughter, on Belvedere near Charles Street."

"I'll drop you off, then," the boy said. "I'm passing right by there."

---

1. **appurtenances:** attachments; accessories.

The light changed, the motor roared. Now that they were in traffic, he felt more conspicuous, but not in a bad way. People in their auto-mobiles seemed sealed in, overprotected; men in large trucks must envy the way the motorcycle looped in and out, hornet-like, stripped to the bare essentials of a motor and two wheels. By tugs at the boy's shirt and single words shouted into the wind, he directed him to his daughter's house, but he was sorry to have the ride over so quickly.

His daughter had married a salesman and lived in a plain, square, stone house that the old man approved of. There were sneakers and a football in the front yard, signs of a large, happy family. A bicycle lay in the driveway. The motorcycle stopped just inches from it. "Here we are," the boy said.

"Well, I surely do thank you."

He climbed off, fearing for one second that his legs would give way beneath him and spoil everything that had gone before. But no, they held steady. He took off the helmet and handed it to the boy, who waved and roared off. It was a really magnificent roar, ear-dazzling. He turned toward the house, beaming in spite of himself, with his head feeling cool and light now that the helmet was gone. And there was his daughter on the front porch, laughing. "Daddy, what on *earth*?" she said. "Have you turned into a teeny-bopper?" Whatever that was. She came rushing down the steps to hug him—a plump, happy-looking woman in an apron. She was getting on toward fifty now. Her hands were like her mother's, swollen and veined. Gray had started dusting her hair.

"You never *told* us," she said. "Did you ride all this way on a motor-cycle? Oh, why didn't you find a telephone and call? I would have come. How long can you stay for?"

"Now . . ." he said, starting toward the house. He was thinking of the best way to put it. "I came to a decision. I won't be living alone any more. I want to go to an old folks' home. That's what I *want*," he said, stopping on the grass so she would be sure to get it clear. "I don't want to live with you—I want an old folks' home." Then he was afraid he had worded it too strongly. "It's nice *visiting* you, of course," he said.

"Why, Daddy, you know we always asked you to come and live with us."

"I know that, but I decided on an old folks' home."

"We couldn't do that. We won't even talk about it."

"Clara, my mind is made up."

Then in the doorway a new thought hit her, and she suddenly turned around. "Are you sick?" she said. "You always said you would live alone as long as health allowed."

"I'm not up to that any more," he said.

"What is it? Are you having some kind of pain?"

"I just decided, that's all," he said. "What I *will* rely on you for is the arrangements with the home. I know it's a trouble."

"We'll talk about that later," Clara said. And she firmed the corners of her mouth exactly the way her mother used to do when she hadn't won an argument but wasn't planning to lose it yet either.

In the kitchen he had a glass of milk, good and cold, and the hunk of bread and the two Fig Newtons from his paper bag. Clara wanted to make him a big breakfast, but there was no sense wasting what he had brought. He munched on the dry bread and washed it down with milk, meanwhile staring at the Fig Newtons, which lay on the smoothed-out bag. They were the worse for their ride—squashed and pathetic-looking, the edges worn down and crumbling. They seemed to have come from somewhere long ago and far away. "Here, now we've got cookies I baked only yesterday," Clara said; but he said, "No, no," and ate the Fig Newtons, whose warmth on his tongue filled him with a vague, sad feeling deeper than homesickness. "In my house," he said, "I left things a little messy. I hate to ask it of you, but I didn't manage to straighten up any."

"Don't even think about it," Clara said. "I'll take out a suitcase tomorrow and clean everything up. I'll bring it all back."

"I don't want it."

"Don't want any of it? But Daddy—"

He didn't try explaining it to her. He finished his lunch in silence and then let her lead him upstairs to the guest room.

Clara had five boys and a girl, the oldest twenty. During the morning, as they passed one by one through the house on their way to other places, they heard of his arrival and trooped up to see him. They were fine children, all of them, but it was the girl he enjoyed the most. Francie. She was only thirteen, too young yet to know how to hide what she felt. And what she felt was always about love, it seemed: whom she just loved, who she hoped loved her back. Who was just a darling. Had thirteen-year-olds been so aware of love in the old days? He didn't know and didn't care; all he had to do with Francie was sit smiling in an armchair and listen. There was a new boy in the neighborhood who walked his English sheepdog past her yard every morning, looking toward her house. Was it because of her, or did the dog just like to go that way? When he telephoned her brother Donnie, was he hoping for her to answer? And when she did answer, did he want to talk a minute or to have her hand the receiver straight to Donnie? But what would she say to him, anyway? Oh, all her questions had to do with where she might find love, and everything she said made the old man wince and love her more. She left in the middle of a sentence, knocking against a doorknob as she flew from the room, an unlovable-looking tangle of blond hair and braces and scrapes and Band-Aids. After she was gone, the room seemed too empty, as if she had accidentally torn part of it away in her flight.

Getting into an old folks' home was hard. Not only because of lack of good homes, high expenses, waiting lists; it was harder yet to talk his family into letting him go. His son-in-law argued with him every evening, his round kind face anxious and questioning across the supper table. "Is it that you think you're not welcome here? You are, you know. You were one of the reasons we bought this big house." His grandchildren when they talked to him had a kind of urgency in their voices, as if they were trying to impress him with their acceptance of him. His other daughters called long distance from all across the country and begged him to come to them if he wouldn't stay with Clara. They had room or they would make room; he had no idea what homes for the aged were like these days. To all of them he gave the same answer: "I've made my decision." He was proud of them asking, though. All his children had turned out so well, every last one of them. They were good, strong women with happy families, and they had never given him a moment's worry. He was luckier than he had a right to be. He had felt lucky all his life, dangerously lucky, cursed by luck; it had seemed some disaster must be waiting to even things up. But the luck had held. When his wife died it was at a late age, sparing her the pain she would have had to face, and his life had continued in its steady, reasonable pattern with no more sorrow than any other man's. His final lot was to weaken, to crumble, and to die—only a secret disaster, not the one he had been expecting.

He walked two blocks daily, fighting off the weakness. He shelled peas for Clara, and mended little household articles—which gave him an excuse to sit. Nobody noticed how he arranged to climb the stairs

only once a day, at bedtime. When he had empty time, he chose a chair
without rockers, one that would not be a symbol of age and weariness
and lack of work. He rose every morning at six and stayed in his room
a full hour, giving his legs enough warning to face the day ahead. Never
once did he disgrace himself by falling down in front of people. He
dropped nothing more important than a spoon or a fork.

Meanwhile the wheels were turning; his name was on a waiting list.
Not that that meant anything, Clara said. "When it comes right down
to driving you out there, I just won't let you go," she told him. "But I'm
hoping you won't carry things that far. Daddy, won't you put a stop to
this foolishness?"

He hardly listened. He had chosen long ago what kind of old age he
would have; everyone does. Most, he thought, were weak and chose
to be loved at any cost. He had seen women turn soft and sad, anxious
to please, and had watched with pity and impatience their losing
battles. And he had once known a schoolteacher, no weakling at all,
who said straight out that when she grew old she would finally eat all
she wanted and grow fat without worry. He admired that—a simple
plan, dependent upon no one. "I'll sit in an armchair," she had said,
"with a lady's magazine in my lap and a box of homemade fudge on
the lampstand. I'll get as fat as I like and nobody will give a hang." The
schoolteacher was thin and pale, with the kind of stooped, sloping
figure that was popular at the time. He had lost track of her long ago,
but he liked to think that she had kept her word. He imagined her fifty
years later, cozy and fat in a puffy chair, with one hand moving constantly between her mouth and the candy plate. If she had died young
or changed her mind or put off her eating till another decade, he didn't
want to hear about it.

Clara cried all the way to the home. She was the one who was driving;
it made him nervous. One of her hands on the steering wheel held a
balled-up tissue, which she had stopped using. She let tears run
unchecked down her face, and drove jerkily, with a great deal of brake-
slamming and gear-gnashing.

"Clara, I wish you wouldn't take on so," he told her. "There's no need
to be sad over *me.*"

"I'm not sad so much as mad," Clara said. "I feel like this is something you're doing *to* me, just throwing away what I give. Oh, why do

you have to be so stubborn? It's still not too late to change your mind."

The old man kept silent. On his right sat Francie, chewing a thumb-nail and scowling out the window, her usual self except for the unexplainable presence of her other hand in his, tight as wire. Periodically she muttered a number; she was counting red convert-ibles, and had been for days. When she reached a hundred, the next boy she saw would be her true love.

He figured that was probably the reason she had come on this trip—a greater exposure to red convertibles.

Whatever happened to DeSotos?[2] Didn't there used to be a car called a roadster?

They parked in the U-shaped driveway in front of the home, under the shade of a poplar tree. If he had had his way, he would have arrived by motorcycle, but he made the best of it—picked up his underwear sack from between his feet, climbed the front steps ramrod-straight. They were met by a smiling woman in blue who had to check his name on a file and ask more questions. He made sure to give all the answers himself, overriding Clara when necessary. Meanwhile Francie spun on one squeaky sneaker-heel and examined the hall, a cavernous, polished square with old-fashioned parlors on either side of it. A few old people were on the plush couches, and a nurse sat idle beside a lady in a wheelchair.

They went up a creaking elevator to the second floor and down a long, dark corridor deadened by carpeting. The lady in blue, still carrying a sheaf of files, knocked at number 213. Then she flung the door open on a narrow green room flooded with sunlight.

"Mr. Pond," she said, "this is Mr. Carpenter. I hope you'll get on well together."

Mr. Pond was one of those men who run to fat and baldness in old age. He sat in a rocking chair with a gilt-edged Bible on his knees.

"How-do," he said. "Mighty nice to meet you."

They shook hands cautiously, with the women ringing them like mothers asking their children to play nicely with each other. "Ordinarily I sleep in the bed by the window," said Mr. Pond, "but I don't hold it in much importance. You can take you pick."

"Anything will do," the old man said.

Clara was dry-eyed now. She looked frightened.

---

2. **DeSotos:** brand of early model automobiles, usually passenger cars or taxicabs.

"You'd best be getting on back now," he told her. "Don't you worry about me. I'll let you know," he said, suddenly generous now that he had won, "if there is anything I need."

Clara nodded and kissed his cheek. Francie kept her face turned away, but she hugged him tightly, and then she looked up at him as she stepped back. Her eyebrows were tilted as if she were about to ask him one of her questions. Was is it her the boy with the sheepdog came for? Did he care when she answered the telephone?

They left, shutting the door with a gentle click. The old man made a great business out of settling his underwear and razor in a bureau drawer, smoothing out the paper bag and folding it, placing it in the next drawer down.

"Didn't bring much," said Mr. Pond, one thumb marking his page in the Bible.

"I don't need much."

"Go on—take the bed by the window. You'll feel better after a while."

"I *wanted* to come," the old man said.

"That there window is a front one. If you look out, you can see your folks leave."

He slid between the bed and the window and looked out. No reason not to. Clara and Francie were just climbing into the car, the sun lacquering the tops of their heads. Clara was blowing her nose with a dot of tissue.

"*Now* they cry," said Mr. Pond, although he had not risen to look out himself. "Later they'll buy themselves a milkshake to celebrate."

"I wanted to come. I made them bring me."

"And so they did. *I* didn't want to come. My son wanted to put me here—his wife was expecting. And so he did. It all works out the same in the end."

"Well, I could have stayed with one of my daughters," the old man said. "But I'm not like some I have known. Hanging around making burdens of themselves, hoping to be loved. Not me."

"If you don't care about being loved," said Mr. Pond, "how come it would bother you to be a burden?"

Then he opened the Bible again, at the place where his thumb had been all the time and went back to reading.

The old man sat on the edge of the bed, watching the tail of Clara's car flash as sharp and hard as a jewel around the bend of the road. Then, with nobody to watch that mattered, he let his shoulders slump and eased himself out of his suit coat, which he folded over the foot of the bed. He slid his suspenders down and let them dangle at his waist. He took off his copper-toed work boots and set them on the floor neatly, side by side. And although it was only noon, he lay down full-length on top of the bedspread. Whiskery lines ran across the plaster of the ceiling high above him. There was a crackling sound in the mattress when he moved: it must be covered with something waterproof.

The tiredness in his head was as vague and restless as anger; the weakness in his knees made him feel as if he had just finished some exhausting exercise. He lay watching the plaster cracks settle themselves into pictures, listening to the silent, neuter voice in his mind form the words he had grown accustomed to hearing now: Let me not give in at the end. Let me continue gracefully till the moment of my defeat. Let Lollie Simpson be alive somewhere even as I lie on my bed; let her be eating homemade fudge in an overstuffed armchair and growing fatter and fatter and fatter. ■

THE IMPACT OF THE STORY

The old man in the story can no longer take care of himself because he has grown too weak and frail. Most of you probably know someone who has faced or will soon face this kind of situation, such as a great-grandparent or even a grandparent.

Where would you like to live out the last years of your life? Would you want to live in a retirement home, like the old man, or to live with a family member? Or perhaps you have other ideas.

THE FACTS OF THE STORY

On your own paper, write answers to the following items. Answers may be one word, a phrase, or several sentences.

1. How does the old man travel to his daughter's house?

2. What does the old man tell his daughter he has decided to do?

3. Of which of his grandchildren is the old man fondest?

4. What does the old man arrange to do only once a day while living at his daughter's house?

5. At the retirement home, what does Mr. Pond assume about the old man's family?

THE IDEAS IN THE STORY

Prepare to discuss the following questions in class.

1. As the old man surveys his home one last time, he is dismayed by the accumulation of odds and ends in his life. He wants to rid himself of this clutter and live a life pared down to only the essential elements. Hence, he feels happy to be leaving with only a few items in a paper bag. Why do you think the old man finds such an unburdened life appealing? How would you define the necessities of life?

2. Of all Clara's children, the old man feels closest to her one daughter, Francie. Why do you think the old man is drawn to this granddaughter?

3. As the story ends, the old man lies on his bed in the retirement home, praying silently to himself that he will remain strong until his death and that Lollie Simpson, the schoolteacher he once knew, is alive somewhere fulfilling her dream for her old age. Why do you think it is important to the old man that Lollie Simpson fulfill her dream?

THE ART OF THE STORYTELLER

Character

"With All Flags Flying" is clearly the old man's story. We hear his thoughts and see most of the story through his eyes. His decision to live in a retirement home is the basis of the plot. The other characters in the story are important because of what they reveal to us about the old man.

What does the motorcycle ride tell us about the old man? Later, when on his way to the retirement home, we are told that "If he had had his way, he would have arrived by motorcycle. . . ." What does this reveal about the old man's character?

We are told that the old man's "final lot was to weaken, to crumble, and to die—only a secret disaster. . . ." How does the old man keep his weakness secret from his family? Why do you think it is important for him to hide his frailty from his family?

Theme

We may gain several insights into human nature by studying the old man in the story. We learn about the self-respect that comes when one does not surrender in defeat, even in the face of death; the pride and satisfaction experienced by those who remain in charge of their own lives; and we also see that keeping one's flags flying in the face of an overwhelming, hostile fleet is sometimes costly.

What does the old man lose because he refuses to surrender his own plan for how he will live his last years? Do you think he realizes what he has lost? Besides the old man, who loses something because of his plan?

Explain how the story's title relates to the old man's decision.

THE VOCABULARY IN THE STORY

An **analogy** is a similarity or a likeness between two things that are unlike in other ways. In an analogy exercise, you are given two words that have a relationship to each other. You must identify a second pair of words that has the same relationship.

Analogies can express many types of relationships such as synonyms (large : big), antonyms (simple : complex), cause and effect (rain : flood), part to whole (finger : hand), item to category (horse : mammal), action to object (cut : ax), action to performer (dance : ballerina), and time sequence (first : second).

For each of the following items, study the capitalized pair of words. On your own paper, write the letter of the word that has the same relationship to the third word given.

1. MOTORCYCLE : WHEEL :: bush : _____
   a. ground
   b. plant
   c. arm
   d. limb

2. DREADING : TEST :: wishing : _____
   a. laundry
   b. birthday
   c. Wednesday
   d. homework

3. APPURTENANCES : EQUIPMENT :: drink : _____
   a. snack
   b. beverage
   c. thirst
   d. quench

4. CAVERNOUS : SMALL :: windy : _____
   a. blustery
   b. calm
   c. stormy
   d. rainy

COMPOSITION: Defending a Position

The old man takes a firm stand on his intention to live in a retirement home. However, when his daughter calls upon him to defend his position, he simply restates his decision. When we express feelings and opinions that affect only ourselves, we do not have to or need to defend our positions. Yet there are many situations in life where it will be necessary for us to defend our positions, whether to a family member, an employer, or a colleague.

Write a composition (about 400 words) in which you persuasively defend a position on a topic of concern to you.

Prewriting
You will first need to choose a topic and decide what your position is regarding it. You will write more quickly and easily if you choose a topic about which you have strong feelings and a definite opinion or position. For example, you might want to defend your position regarding the curfew hours on school nights or the practicality of having your own car.

Freewrite about your topic for three minutes; write as fast as you can without stopping or worrying about grammar, usage, or mechanics. Time yourself or have someone else time you. When you have finished your freewriting, reread it, marking or highlighting your reasons for believing that your position is correct. Think of or locate evidence and examples to support your position. Remember that your support must be logical and appealing to your audience. Then write several sentences about each of your reasons.

Writing
In the introductory paragraph of your composition, clearly state your topic (for example, curfew hours on school nights) and your position regarding it. (For example, "I feel that curfew hours on school nights should be extended.")

Evaluating and Revising
Read your draft. Don't hesitate to mark your draft with corrections or notes for improving it. Cut, rewrite, rearrange, or add words, phrases, or sections as needed. If time allows, set aside your completed composition for at least a day; then read it once again. You will likely find it easier then to spot grammar, usage, spelling, and punctuation errors than if you reread it immediately.

ABOUT THE AUTHOR

 Anne Tyler (1941–   ) was born in Minneapolis, Minnesota. She is best known for her novels set in North Carolina and in Baltimore, Maryland, where she has lived since 1967. The focus of most of her novels and short stories is the family, the alienation of its members, and the ways in which they affect one another. *The Accidental Tourist,* published in 1985, is her most widely known novel; it was subsequently made into a movie of the same title. This novel also won Tyler a National Book Critics Circle Award; two other Tyler novels, *Morgan's Passing* and *Dinner at the Homesick Restaurant,* have also been nominated for the award. In addition to being a fiction writer, Anne Tyler is also a critic, nonfiction writer, and editor. Her career also includes work at the Duke University Library in Durham, North Carolina, as a Russian bibliographer and at McGill University Law Library in Montreal, Quebec, Canada, as an assistant librarian.

■ THE SON FROM AMERICA

Isaac Bashevis Singer

For Samuel, striking out on his own as a teenager meant traveling nearly halfway around the world to America. However, he never forgot the family or the village he left behind in Poland. Now, forty years later, he has returned with "big plans" for these simple people.

The village of Lentshin was tiny—a sandy marketplace where the peasants of the area met once a week. It was surrounded by little huts with thatched roofs or shingles green with moss. The chimneys looked like pots. Between the huts there were fields, where the owners planted vegetables or pastured their goats.

In the smallest of these huts lived old Berl, a man in his eighties, and his wife, who was called Berlcha (wife of Berl). Old Berl was one of the Jews who had been driven from their villages in Russia and had settled in Poland. In Lentshin, they mocked the mistakes he made while praying aloud. He spoke with a sharp "r." He was short, broad-shouldered, and had a small white beard, and summer and winter he wore a sheepskin hat, a padded cotton jacket, and stout boots. He walked slowly, shuffling his feet. He had a half acre of field, a cow, a goat, and chickens.

The couple had a son, Samuel, who had gone to America forty years ago. It was said in Lentshin that he became a millionaire there. Every month, the Lentshin letter carrier brought old Berl a money order and a letter that no one could read because many of the words were English. How much money Samuel sent his parents remained a secret. Three times a year, Berl and his wife went on foot to Zakroczym and cashed the money orders there. But they never seemed to use the money. What for? The garden, the cow, and the goat provided most of their needs. Beside, Berlcha sold chickens and eggs, and from these there was enough to buy flour for bread.

No one cared to know where Berl kept the money that his son sent him. There were no thieves in Lentshin. The hut consisted of one room, which contained all their belongings: the table, the shelf for meat, the shelf for milk foods, the two beds, and the clay oven.

Sometimes the chickens roosted in the woodshed and sometimes, when it was cold, in a coop near the oven. The goat, too, found shelter inside when the weather was bad. The more prosperous villagers had kerosene lamps, but Berl and his wife did not believe in newfangled gadgets. What was wrong with a wick in a dish of oil? Only for the Sabbath[1] would Berlcha buy three tallow candles at the store. In summer, the couple got up at sunrise and retired with the chickens. In the long winter evenings, Berlcha spun flax at her spinning wheel and Berl sat beside her in the silence of those who enjoy their rest.

Once in a while when Berl came home from the synagogue after evening prayers, he brought news to his wife. In Warsaw there were strikers who demanded that the czar abdicate. A heretic by the name of Dr. Herzl had come up with the idea that Jews should settle again in Palestine. Berlcha listened and shook her bonneted head. Her face was yellowish and wrinkled like a cabbage leaf. There were bluish sacks under her eyes. She was half deaf. Berl had to repeat each word he said to her. She would say, "The things that happen in the big cities!"

Here in Lentshin nothing happened except usual events: a cow gave birth to a calf, a young couple had a circumcision party, or a girl was born and there was no party. Occasionally, someone died. Lentshin had no cemetery, and the corpse had to be taken to Zakroczym. Actually, Lentshin had become a village with few young people. The young men left for Zakroczym, for Nowy Dwor, for Warsaw, and sometimes for the United States. Like Samuel's, their letters were illegible, the Yiddish[2] mixed with the languages of the countries where they were now living. They sent photographs in which the men wore top hats and the women fancy dresses like squiresses.

Berl and Berlcha also received such photographs. But their eyes were failing and neither he nor she had glasses. They could barely make out the pictures. Samuel had sons and daughters with Gentile[3] names— and grandchildren who had married and had their own offspring. Their names were so strange that Berl and Berlcha could never remember them. But what difference do names make? America was far, far away on the other side of the ocean, at the edge of the world. A

---

1. **Sabbath:** a day of rest and worship, Saturday for Jews, Sunday for Christians.
2. **Yiddish:** a dialect spoken by many Jews living in eastern and north-central Europe, composed of aspects of the Hebrew, Polish, and Russian languages, and written with Hebrew letters.
3. **Gentile:** a person who is not Jewish.

Talmud[4] teacher who came to Lentshin had said that Americans walked with their heads down and their feet up. Berl and Berlcha could not grasp this. How was it possible? But since the teacher said so it must be true. Berlcha pondered for some time and then she said, "One can get accustomed to everything."

And so it remained. From too much thinking—God forbid—one may lose one's wits.

One Friday morning, when Berlcha was kneading the dough for the Sabbath loaves, the door opened and a nobleman entered. He was so tall that he had to bend down to get through the door. He wore a beaver hat and a cloak bordered with fur. He was followed by Chazkel, the coachman from Zakroczym, who carried two leather valises with brass locks. In astonishment Berlcha raised her eyes.

The nobleman looked around and said to the coachman in Yiddish, "Here it is." He took out a silver ruble and paid him. The coachman tried to hand him change but he said, "You can go now."

When the coachman closed the door, the nobleman said, "Mother, it's me, your son Samuel—Sam."

Berlcha heard the words and her legs grew numb. Her hands, to which pieces of dough were sticking, lost their power. The nobleman hugged her, kissed her forehead, both her cheeks. Berlcha began to cackle like a hen, "My son!" At that moment Berl came in from the woodshed, his arms piled with logs. The goat followed him. When he saw a nobleman kissing his wife, Berl dropped the wood and exclaimed, "What is this?"

The nobleman let go of Berlcha and embraced Berl. "Father!"

For a long time Berl was unable to utter a sound. He wanted to recite holy words that he had read in the Yiddish Bible, but he could remember nothing. Then he asked, "Are you Samuel?"

"Yes, Father, I am Samuel."

"Well, peace be with you." Berl grasped his son's hand. He was still not sure that he was not being fooled. Samuel wasn't as tall and heavy as this man, but then Berl reminded himself that Samuel was only fifteen years old when he had left home. He must have grown in that faraway country. Berl asked, "Why didn't you let us know that you were coming?"

---

4. **Talmud:** the compilation of Jewish civil and religious laws not contained in the Pentateuch.

"Didn't you receive my cable?" Samuel asked.

Berl did not know what a cable was.

Berlcha had scraped the dough from her hands and enfolded her son. He kissed her again and asked, "Mother, didn't you receive a cable?"

"What? If I lived to see this, I am happy to die," Berlcha said, amazed by her own words. Berl, too, was amazed. These were just the words he would have said earlier if he had been able to remember. After a while Berl came to himself and said, "Pescha, you will have to make a double Sabbath pudding in addition to the stew."

It was years since Berl had called Berlcha by her given name. When he wanted to address her, he would say, "Listen," or "Say." It is the young or those from the big cities who call a wife by her name. Only now did Berlcha begin to cry. Yellow tears ran from her eyes, and everything became dim. Then she called out, "It's Friday—I have to prepare for the Sabbath." Yes, she had to knead the dough and braid the loaves. With such a guest, she had to make a larger Sabbath stew. The winter day is short and she must hurry.

Her son understood what was worrying her, because he said, "Mother, I will help you."

Berlcha wanted to laugh, but a choked sob came out. "What are you saying? God forbid."

The nobleman took off his cloak and jacket and remained in his vest, on which hung a solid-gold watch chain. He rolled up his sleeves and came to the trough. "Mother, I was a baker for many years in New York," he said, and he began to knead the dough.

"What! You are my darling son who will say Kaddish[5] for me." She wept raspingly. Her strength left her, and she slumped onto the bed.

Berl said, "Women will always be women." And he went to the shed to get more wood. The goat sat down near the oven; she gazed with surprise at this strange man—his height and his bizarre clothes.

The neighbors had heard the good news that Berl's son had arrived from America and they came to greet him. The women began to help Berlcha prepare for the Sabbath. Some laughed, some cried. The room was full of people, as at a wedding. They asked Berl's son, "What is new in America?" And Berl's son answered, "America is all right."

"Do Jews make a living?"

"One eats white bread there on weekdays."

---

5. **Kaddish:** a prayer or hymn recited by mourners when a close relative has died.

"Do they remain Jews?"

"I am not a Gentile."

After Berlcha blessed the candles, father and son went to the little synagogue across the street. A new snow had fallen. The son took large
steps, but Berl warned him, "Slow down."

In the synagogue the Jews recited "Let Us Exult" and "Come, My
Groom." All the time, the snow outside kept falling. After prayers,
when Berl and Samuel left the Holy Place, the village was unrecogniz-
able. Everything was covered in snow. One could see only the contours
of the roofs and the candles in the windows. Samuel said, "Nothing
has changed here."

Berlcha had prepared gefilte fish, chicken soup with rice, meat,
carrot stew. Berl recited the benediction over a glass of ritual wine. The
family ate and drank, and when it grew quiet for a while one could
hear the chirping of the house cricket. The son talked a lot, but Berl
and Berlcha understood little. His Yiddish was different and contained
foreign words.

After the final blessing Samuel asked, "Father, what did you do with
all the money I sent you?"

Berl raised his white brows. "It's here."

"Didn't you put it in a bank?"

"There is no bank in Lentshin."

"Where do you keep it?"

Berl hesitated. "One is not allowed to touch money on the Sabbath,
but I will show you." He crouched beside the bed and began to shove
something heavy. A boot appeared. Its top was stuffed with straw. Berl
removed the straw and the son saw that the boot was full of gold coins.
He lifted it.

"Father, this is a treasure!" he called out.

"Well."

"Why didn't you spend it?"

"On what? Thank God, we have everything."

"Why didn't you travel somewhere?"

"Where to? This is our home."

The son asked one question after the other, but Berl's answer was
always the same: they wanted for nothing. The garden, the cow, the
goat, the chickens provided them with all they needed. The son said,
"If thieves knew about this, your lives wouldn't be safe."

"There are no thieves here."

"What will happen to the money?"

"You take it."

Slowly, Berl and Berlcha grew accustomed to their son and his American Yiddish. Berlcha could hear him better now. She even recognized his voice. He was saying, "Perhaps we should build a larger synagogue."

"The synagogue is big enough," Berl replied.

"Perhaps a home for old people."

"No one sleeps in the street."

The next day after the Sabbath meal was eaten, a Gentile from Zakroczym brought a paper—it was the cable. Berl and Berlcha lay down for a nap. They soon began to snore. The goat, too dozed off. The son put on his cloak and his hat and went for a walk. He strode with his long legs across the marketplace. He stretched out a hand and touched a roof. He wanted to smoke a cigar, but he remembered it was forbidden on the Sabbath. He had a desire to talk to someone, but it seemed that the whole of Lentshin was asleep. He entered the synagogue. An old man was sitting there, reciting psalms. Samuel asked, "Are you praying?"

"What else is there to do when one gets old?"

"Do you make a living?"

The old man did not understand the meaning of these words. He smiled, showing his empty gums, and then he said, "If God gives health, one keeps on living."

Samuel returned home. Dusk had fallen. Berl went to the synagogue for the evening prayers and the son remained with his mother. The room was filled with shadows.

Berlcha began to recite in a solemn singsong, "God of Abraham, Isaac, and Jacob, defend the poor people of Israel and Thy name. The Holy Sabbath is departing; the welcome week is coming to us. Let it be one of health, wealth, and good deeds."

"Mother, you don't need to pray for wealth," Samuel said. "You are wealthy already."

Berlcha did not hear—or pretended not to. Her face had turned into a cluster of shadows.

In the twilight Samuel put his hand into his jacket pocket and touched his passport, his checkbook, his letters of credit. He had come here with big plans. He had a valise filled with presents for his parents. He wanted to bestow gifts on the village. He brought not only his own money but funds from the Lentshin Society in New York, which had organized a ball for the benefit of the village. But this village in the hinterland needed nothing. From the synagogue one could hear hoarse chanting. The cricket, silent all day, started again its chirping. Berlcha began to sway and utter holy rhymes inherited from mothers and grandmothers:

> *Thy holy sheep*
> *In mercy keep,*
> *In Torah and good deeds;*
> *Provide for all their needs,*
> *Shoes, clothes, and bread*
> *And the Messiah's tread.* ∎

THE IMPACT OF THE STORY

"The Son from America" is a story about values, the principles and standards by which people live. Values are established by individuals based on what is most important to them. Money is very important to the son; to his parents food, shelter, friends, and religion are most important. What is most important to you?

THE FACTS OF THE STORY

On your own paper, write answers to the following items. Answers may be one word, a phrase, or several sentences.

1. What do Berl and Berlcha do with the money they receive every month from their son, Samuel?

2. Why do Berl and Berlcha think Samuel is a nobleman when he first arrives at their hut?

3. The people of Lentshin are not allowed to _____ or _____ on the Sabbath.

4. What are some of the plans Samuel has for the village?

5. At the end of the story, what does Samuel decide about the village?

THE IDEAS IN THE STORY

Prepare to discuss the following questions in class.

1. How does Samuel view the purpose of money? How do his values contrast with those of his parents and the other villagers? What do you think is the purpose of money?

2. *To infer* means "to draw a conclusion based on evidence." What can you infer about Samuel, based on the evidence in the story?

3. What is the meaning of happiness? Do you think that money alone can buy happiness?

THE ART OF THE STORYTELLER

Point of View
The vantage point, or perspective, from which a story is told is called **point of view.** The point of view is directly related to the narrator of the story. When a writer uses first-person pronouns (*I, we*) to narrate a story, the story's perspective is the *first-person point of view;* the narrator is usually, but not always, a character in the story. In a story written from the *third-person omniscient point of view,* the narrator is not a character in the story. This omniscient narrator uses third-person pronouns (*he, she, it, they*) and can tell us what all the characters are thinking and feeling. When the story is told from the perspective of only one character in the story—but not *by* this character—the point of view is called the *third-person limited.* The narrator tells us only what one character thinks and feels.

What is the point of view of "The Son from America"? How does the story's point of view affect our understanding of the conflict between Samuel's values and his parents' values?

Irony
One kind of **irony** is *irony of situation,* in which the result of an action is the opposite of what the reader or a character in the story expects. Isaac Bashevis Singer uses irony of situation in "The Son from America." When Samuel arrives at his parents' home in Poland, he expects to see tangible evidence of their having spent the money he has sent. Instead, he finds them living in the same small hut, and he learns that they have not spent the money but have kept it in a boot under the bed.

What else is ironic about Samuel's visit?

THE VOCABULARY IN THE STORY

The *context* of a word is made up of the phrases and sentences that surround it. Context clues are the words and phrases that give you hints about a word's meaning. Read the following example.

> Quickly, he *kneaded* the dough, pushing and pounding it, folding it in upon itself.

If you were not familiar with the word *knead,* you could figure out its meaning from the context. The phrases *pushing and pounding* and *folding it in upon itself* describe the action and therefore the meaning of the word *kneading.*

Read each of the following sentences carefully. Then without looking in a dictionary, write a short definition of the italicized word in each sentence.

1. Like Samuel's, their letters were *illegible,* the Yiddish mixed with the languages of the countries where they were now living.

2. He was followed by Chazkel, the coachman from Zakroczym, who carried two leather *valises* with brass locks.

3. He took out a silver *ruble* and paid him.

4. The more prosperous villagers had kerosene lamps, but Berl and his wife did not believe in *newfangled* gadgets. What was wrong with a wick in a dish of oil?

COMPOSITION: Writing a Letter from the Future

When Samuel returns home after his forty-year absence, he is a mature adult who has made a successful living for himself and has a family of his own. What do you imagine your life to be like forty years from now?

Write a letter (about 350 words) to a family member or friend from forty years in the future.

Prewriting

Imagine that you have not seen or spoken to this relative or friend during this time and that you must now describe the kind of life you have led. Where do you live? Do you have a family? What did you do for a living during these forty years? What are your plans for the future?

Think about the kind of person you hope to be forty years from now. In addition to describing the specific facts of your life, consider what kinds of things you might value, such as money, social status, health, tradition, community. Jot down the appropriate items, listing beside each one examples that demonstrate *how* you value these things.

Writing
Write your letter from the first-person point of view, using the proper salutation and closing. You might begin with a statement such as, "I didn't realize when we last said goodbye that it would be for forty years."

Evaluating and Revising
Read your draft. Have you given a clear picture of yourself? Have you organized your letter in a logical way? Cut, reorder, or add words, phrases, or sections as needed.

ABOUT THE AUTHOR

Isaac Bashevis Singer (1904–1991) was born in Poland. He grew up in Warsaw, where, as an adult, he worked as a journalist and as a writer of novels and stories. He immigrated to the United States in 1935 and became a United States citizen in 1943. When he arrived in America, he knew only three words in English—"Take a chair." His language was Yiddish, a language written in Hebrew letters and used by Jews in Eastern Europe and wherever Jewish emigrés from Eastern Europe have settled. Although Singer mastered the English language long before his death, he still wrote in Yiddish. In 1978, he was awarded the Nobel Prize for literature. Singer said about the authors of the books we read, "A real reader, especially a young reader, never cares too much about the author. He wants to read the book and he enjoys it."

THE RAIN CAME

Grace Ogot

How would you feel if you were chosen to save your family
and friends from certain death? As you will see, it is an honor
that Oganda, Chief's Labong'o's only daughter, would rather
refuse if she had the choice.

The chief was still far from the gate when his daughter Oganda
saw him. She ran to meet him. Breathlessly she asked her father,
"What is the news, great Chief? Everyone in the village is anxiously waiting to hear when it will rain." Labong'o held out his hands
for his daughter but he did not say a word. Puzzled by her father's cold
attitude Oganda ran back to the village to warn the others that the chief
was back.

The atmosphere in the village was tense and confused. Everyone
moved aimlessly and fussed in the yard without actually doing
any work. A young woman whispered to her co-wife, "If they have
not solved this rain business today, the chief will crack." They had
watched him getting thinner and thinner as the people kept on
pestering him. "Our cattle lie dying in the fields," they reported.
"Soon it will be our children and then ourselves. Tell us what to
do to save our lives, oh great Chief." So the chief had daily prayed
with the Almighty through the ancestors to deliver them from their
distress.

Instead of calling the family together and giving them the news
immediately, Labong'o went to his own hut, a sign that he was not to
be disturbed. Having replaced the shutter, he sat in the dimly-lit hut
to contemplate.

It was no longer a question of being the chief of hunger-stricken
people that weighed Labong'o's heart. It was the life of his only daughter that was at stake. At the time when Oganda came to meet him, he
saw the glittering chain shining around her waist. The prophecy was
complete. "It is Oganda, Oganda, my only daughter, who must die so
young." Labong'o burst into tears before finishing the sentence. The
chief must not weep. Society had declared him the bravest of men. But
Labong'o did not care any more. He assumed the position of a simple

240

father and wept bitterly. He loved his people, the Luo,[1] but what were the Luo for him without Oganda? Her life had bought a new life in Labong'o's world and he ruled better than he could remember. How would the spirit of the village survive his beautiful daughter? "There are so many homes and so many parents who have daughters. Why choose this one? She is all I have." Labong'o spoke as if the ancestors were there in the hut and he could see them face to face. Perhaps they were there, warning him to remember his promise on the day he was enthroned when he said aloud, before the elders, "I will lay down life, if necessary, and the life of my household, to save this tribe from the hands of the enemy." "Deny! Deny!" he could hear the voice of his forefathers mocking him.

When Labong'o was consecrated chief he was only a young man. Unlike his father, he ruled for many years with only one wife. But people rebuked him because his only wife did not bear him a daughter. He married a second, a third, and a fourth wife. But they all gave birth to male children. When Labong'o married a fifth wife she bore him a daughter. They called her Oganda, meaning "beans," because her skin was very fair. Out of Labong'o's twenty children, Oganda was the only girl. Though she was the chief's favourite, her mother's co-wives swallowed their jealous feelings and showered her with love. After all, they said, Oganda was a female child whose days in the royal family were numbered. She would soon marry at a tender age and leave the enviable position to someone else.

Never in his life had he been faced with such an impossible decision. Refusing to yield to the rainmaker's request would mean sacrificing the whole tribe, putting the interests of the individual above those of the society. More than that. It would mean disobeying the ancestors, and most probably wiping the Luo people from the surface of the earth. On the other hand, to let Oganda die as a ransom for the people would permanently cripple Labong'o spiritually. He knew he would never be the same chief again.

The words of Ndithi, the medicine man, still echoed in his ears. "Podho, the ancestor of the Luo, appeared to me in a dream last night, and he asked me to speak to the chief and the people," Ndithi had said

---

1. **Luo:** a people living in northern Kenya and Uganda, who came to this region from the southeastern part of Sudan in the 1500s.

to the gathering of tribesmen. "A young woman who has not known a man must die so that the country may have rain. While Podho was still talking to me, I saw a young woman standing at the lakeside, her hands raised, above her head. Her skin was as fair as the skin of young deer in the wilderness. Her tall slender figure stood like a lonely reed at the river bank. Her sleepy eyes wore a sad look like that of a bereaved mother. She wore a gold ring on her left ear, and a glittering brass chain around her waist. As I still marvelled at the beauty of this young woman, Podho told me, 'Out of all the women in this land, we have chosen this one. Let her offer herself a sacrifice to the lake monster! And on that day, the rain will come down in torrents. Let everyone stay at home on that day, lest he be carried away by the floods.'"

Outside there was a strange stillness, except for the thirsty birds that sang lazily on the dying trees. The blinding mid-day heat had forced the people to retire to their huts. Not far away from the chief's hut, two guards were snoring away quietly. Labong'o removed his crown and the large eagle-head that hung loosely on his shoulders. He left the hut, and instead of asking Nyabog'o the messenger to beat the drum, he went straight and beat it himself. In no time the whole household had assembled under the siala tree where he usually addressed them. He told Oganda to wait a while in her grandmother's hut.

When Labong'o stood to address his household, his voice was hoarse and the tears choked him. He started to speak, but words refused to leave his lips. His wives and sons knew there was great danger. Perhaps their enemies had declared war on them. Labong'o's eyes were red, and they could see he had been weeping. At last he told them. "One whom we love and treasure must be taken away from us. Oganda is to die." Labong'o's voice was so faint, that he could not hear it himself. But he continued, "The ancestors have chosen her to be offered as a sacrifice to the lake monster in order that we may have rain."

They were completely stunned. As a confused murmur broke out, Oganda's mother fainted and was carried off to her own hut. But the other people rejoiced. They danced around singing and chanting, "Oganda is the lucky one to die for the people. If it is to save the people, let Oganda go."

In her grandmother's hut Oganda wondered what the whole family were discussing about her that she could not hear. Her grandmother's hut was well away from the chief's court and, much as she strained her ears, she could not hear what was said. "It must be marriage," she concluded. It was an accepted custom for the family to discuss their daughter's future marriage behind her back. A faint smile played on Oganda's lips as she thought of the several young men who swallowed saliva at the mere mention of her name.

There was Kech, the son of a neighbouring clan elder. Kech was very handsome. He had sweet, meek eyes and a roaring laughter. He would make a wonderful father, Oganda thought. But they would not be a good match. Kech was a bit too short to be her husband. It would humiliate her to have to look down at Kech each time she spoke to him. Then she thought of Dimo, the tall young man who had already distinguished himself as a brave warrior and an outstanding wrestler. Dimo adored Oganda, but Oganda thought he would make a cruel husband, always quarrelling and ready to fight. No, she did not like him. Oganda fingered the glittering chain on her waist as she thought of Osinda. A long time ago when she was quite young Osinda had given her that chain, and instead of wearing it around her neck several times, she wore it round her waist where it could stay permanently. She heard her heart pounding so loudly as she thought of him. She whispered, "Let it be you they are discussing, Osinda, the lovely one. Come now and take me away . . ."

The lean figure in the doorway startled Oganda who was rapt in thought about the man she loved. "You have frightened me, Grandma," said Oganda laughing. "Tell me, is it my marriage you were discussing? You can take it from me that I won't marry any of them." A smile played on her lips again. She was coaxing the old lady to tell her quickly, to tell her they were pleased with Osinda.

In the open space outside the excited relatives were dancing and singing. They were coming to the hut now, each carrying a gift to put at Oganda's feet. As their singing got nearer Oganda was able to hear what they were saying: "If it is to save the people, if it is to give us rain, let Oganda go. Let Oganda die for her people, and for her ancestors." Was she mad to think that they were singing about her? How could she die? She found the lean figure of her grandmother barring the door. She could not get out. The look on her grandmother's face warned her that there was danger around the corner. "Mother, it is not marriage then?" Oganda asked urgently. She suddenly felt panicky like a mouse cornered by a hungry cat. Forgetting that there was only one door in the hut Oganda fought desperately to find another exit. She must fight for her life. But there was none.

She closed her eyes, leapt like a wild tiger through the door, knocking her grandmother flat to the ground. There outside in mourning garments Labong'o stood motionless, his hands folded at the back. He held his daughter's hand and led her away from the excited crowd to the little red-painted hut where her mother was resting. Here he broke the news officially to his daughter.

For a long time the three souls who loved one another dearly sat in darkness. It was no good speaking. And even if they tried, the words could not have come out. In the past they had been like three cooking stones, sharing their burdens. Taking Oganda away from them would leave two useless stones which would not hold a cooking-pot.

News that the beautiful daughter of the chief was to be sacrificed to give the people rain spread across the country like wind. At sunset the chief's village was full of relatives and friends who had come to congratulate Oganda. Many more were on their way coming, carrying their gifts. They would dance till morning to keep her company. And in the morning they would prepare her a big farewell feast. All these relatives thought it a great honour to be selected by the spirits to die, in order that the society may live. "Oganda's name will always remain a living name among us," they boasted.

But was it maternal love that prevented Minya from rejoicing with the other women? Was it the memory of the agony and pain of childbirth that made her feel so sorrowful? Or was it the deep warmth and understanding that passes between a suckling babe and her mother that made Oganda part of her life, her flesh? Of course it was an honour, a great honour, for her daughter to be chosen to die for the country. But what could she gain once her only daughter was blown away by the wind? There were so many other women in the land, why choose her daughter, her only child! Had human life any meaning at all—other women had houses full of children while she, Minya, had to lose her only child!

In the cloudless sky the moon shone brightly, and the numerous stars glittered with a bewitching beauty. The dancers of all age-groups assembled to dance before Oganda, who sat close to her mother, sobbing quietly. All these years she had been with her people she thought she understood them. But now she discovered that she was a stranger among them. If they loved her as they had always professed why were they not making any attempt to save her? Did her people really understand what it felt like to die young? Unable to restrain her emotions any longer, she sobbed loudly as her age-group got up to dance. They were young and beautiful and very soon they would marry and have their own children. They would have husbands to love and little huts for themselves. They would have reached maturity. Oganda touched the chain around her waist as she thought of Osinda. She wished Osinda was there too, among her friends. "Perhaps he is ill," she thought gravely. The chain comforted Oganda—she would die with it around her waist and wear it in the underground world.

In the morning a big feast was prepared for Oganda. The women prepared many different tasty dishes so that she could pick and choose. "People don't eat after death," they said. Delicious though the food looked, Oganda touched none of it. Let the happy people eat. She contented herself with sips of water from a little calabash.

The time for her departure was drawing near, and each minute was precious. It was a day's journey to the lake. She was to walk all night, passing through the great forest. But nothing could touch her, not even the denizens of the forest. She was already anointed with sacred oil. From the time Oganda received the sad news she had expected Osinda to appear any moment. But he was not there. A relative told her that Osinda was away on a private visit. Oganda realised that she would never see her beloved again.

In the afternoon the whole village stood at the gate to say good-bye and to see her for the last time. Her mother wept on her neck for a long time. The great chief in a mourning skin came to the gate bare-footed, and mingled with the people—a simple father in grief. He took off his wrist bracelet and put it on his daughter's wrist saying, "You will always live among us. The spirit of our forefathers is with you."

Tongue-tied and unbelieving Oganda stood there before the people. She had nothing to say. She looked at her home once more. She could hear her heart beating so painfully within her. All her childhood plans were coming to an end. She felt like a flower nipped in the bud never to enjoy the morning dew again. She looked at her weeping mother, and whispered, "Whenever you want to see me, always look at the sunset. I will be there."

Oganda turned southwards to start her trek to the lake. Her parents, relatives, friends and admirers stood at the gate and watched her go.

Her beautiful slender figure grew smaller and smaller till she mingled with the thin dry trees in the forest. As Oganda walked the lonely path that wound its way in the wilderness, she sang a song, and her own voice kept her company.

> *The ancestors have said Oganda must die*
> *The daughter of the chief must be sacrificed,*
> *When the lake monster feeds on my flesh.*
> *The people will have rain.*
> *Yes, the rain will come down in torrents.*
> *And the floods will wash away the sandy beaches*
> *When the daughter of the chief dies in the lake.*
> *My age-group has consented*
> *My parents have consented*
> *So have my friends and relatives.*
> *Let Oganda die to give us rain.*
> *My age-group are young and ripe,*
> *Ripe for womanhood and motherhood*
> *But Oganda must die young,*
> *Oganda must sleep with the ancestors.*
> *Yes, rain will come down in torrents.*

The red rays of the setting sun embraced Oganda, and she looked like a burning candle in the wilderness.

The people who came to hear her sad song were touched by her beauty. But they all said the same thing: "If it is to save the people, if it is to give us rain, then be not afraid. Your name will live forever among us."

At midnight Oganda was tired and weary. She could walk no more. She sat under a big tree, and having sipped water from her calabash, she rested her head on the tree trunk and slept.

When Oganda woke up in the morning the sun was high in the sky. After walking for many hours, she reached the *tong'*, a strip of land that separated the inhabited part of the country from the sacred place *(kar lamo)*. No layman could enter this place and come out alive—only those who had direct contact with the spirits and the Almighty were allowed to enter this holy of holies. But Oganda had to pass through this sacred land on her way to the lake, which she had to reach at sunset.

A large crowd gathered to see her for the last time. Her voice was now hoarse and painful, but there was no need to worry any more. Soon she would not have to sing. The crowd looked at Oganda sympathetically, mumbling words she could not hear. But none of them pleaded for life. As Oganda opened the gate, a child, a young child, broke loose from the crowd, and ran towards her. The child took a small earring from her sweaty hands and gave it to Oganda saying, "When you reach the world of the dead, give this earring to my sister. She died last week. She forgot this ring." Oganda, taken aback by the strange request, took the little ring, and handed her precious water and food to the child. She did not need them now. Oganda did not know whether to laugh or cry. She had heard mourners sending their love to their sweethearts, long dead, but this idea of sending gifts was new to her.

Oganda held her breath as she crossed the barrier to enter the sacred land. She looked appealingly at the crowd, but there was no response. Their minds were too preoccupied with their own survival. Rain was the precious medicine they were longing for, and the sooner Oganda could get to her destination the better.

A strange feeling possessed Oganda as she picked her way in the sacred land. There were strange noises that often startled her, and her first reaction was to take to her heels. But she remembered that she had to fulfill the wish of her people. She was exhausted, but the path was still winding. Then suddenly the path ended on sandy land. The water had retreated miles away from the shore leaving a wide stretch of sand. Beyond this was the vast expanse of water.

Oganda felt afraid. She wanted to picture the size and shape of the monster, but fear would not let her. The society did not talk about it, nor did the crying children who were silenced by the mention of its name. The sun was still up, but it was no longer hot. For a long time Oganda walked ankle-deep in the sand. She was exhausted and longed desperately for her calabash of water. As she moved on, she had a strange feeling that something was following her. Was it the monster? Her hair stood erect, and a cold paralysing feeling ran along her spine. She looked behind, sideways and in front, but there was nothing, except a cloud of dust.

Oganda pulled up and hurried but the feeling did not leave her, and her whole body became saturated with perspiration.

The sun was going down fast and the lake shore seemed to move along with it.

Oganda started to run. She must be at the lake before sunset. As she ran she heard a noise coming from behind. She looked back sharply, and something resembling a moving bush was frantically running after her. It was about to catch up with her.

Oganda ran with all her strength. She was now determined to throw herself into the water even before sunset. She did not look back, but the creature was upon her. She made an effort to cry out, as in a nightmare, but she could not hear her own voice. The creature caught up with Oganda. In the utter confusion, as Oganda came face to face with the unidentified creature, a strong hand grabbed her. But she fell flat on the sand and fainted.

When the lake breeze brought her back to consciousness, a man was bending over her. ". . . . .!" Oganda opened her mouth to speak, but she had lost her voice. She swallowed a mouthful of water poured into her mouth by the stranger.

"Osinda, Osinda! Please let me die. Let me run, the sun is going down. Let me die, let them have rain." Osinda fondled the glittering chain around Oganda's waist and wiped the tears from her face.

"We must escape quickly to the unknown land," Osinda said urgently. "We must run away from the wrath of the ancestors and the retaliation of the monster."

"But the curse is upon me, Osinda, I am no good to you any more. And moreover the eyes of the ancestors will follow us everywhere and bad luck will befall us. Nor can we escape from the monster."

Oganda broke loose, afraid to escape, but Osinda grabbed her hands again.

"Listen to me, Oganda! Listen! Here are two coats!" He then covered the whole of Oganda's body, except her eyes, with a leafy attire made from the twigs of *Bwombwe*. "These will protect us from the eyes of the ancestors and the wrath of the monster. Now let us run out of here." He held Oganda's hand and they ran from the sacred land, avoiding the path that Oganda had followed.

The bush was thick, and the long grass entangled their feet as they ran. Halfway through the sacred land they stopped and looked back. The sun was almost touching the surface of the water. They were frightened. They continued to run, now faster, to avoid the sinking sun.

"Have faith, Oganda—that thing will not reach us."

When they reached the barrier and looked behind them trembling, only a tip of the sun could be seen above the water's surface.

"It is gone! It is gone!" Oganda wept, hiding her face in her hands. "Weep not, daughter of the chief. Let us run, let us escape."

There was a bright lightning. They looked up, frightened. Above them black furious clouds started to gather. They began to run. Then the thunder roared, and the rain came down in torrents. ■

THE IMPACT OF THE STORY

While Labong'o tells the other members of his household that their ancestors have chosen Oganda for sacrifice, Oganda sits in her grandmother's hut, wondering what they are saying about her. She assumes that they are discussing her future marriage, as it is customary for a Luo family to talk about their daughter's future marriage behind her back. Of course, she soon finds out that her assumption is wrong.

Many people have made the same mistake of assuming that they know what other people are saying about them behind their backs. What advice might you give someone who is making such assumptions?

THE FACTS OF THE STORY

On your own paper, write answers to the following questions. Answers may be one word, a phrase, or several sentences.

1. What great disaster has befallen the Luo people?

2. What difficult decision must Labong'o, the chief of the Luo people, make?

3. Why do most of the members of Labong'o's family rejoice when they hear his news?

4. Oganda expects to find _____ at the lake.

5. When does the rain come?

THE IDEAS IN THE STORY

Prepare to discuss the following questions in class.

1. All her life, Oganda has felt loved by the people of her village. Now she feels somewhat betrayed as she sees them rejoicing in preparation for her death, with apparently no thought of saving her. She wonders whether they understand what it feels like to die at such an early age. Do you think that they understand? If someone else had been chosen for sacrifice,

do you think Oganda would be rejoicing along with the other villagers? Can we ever really know what is in the mind and heart of another person—or even in our own?

2. Throughout history, many people have believed that the sacrifice of one for the good of many is an acceptable philosophy. A hypothetical example of this belief is a scenario in which a lifeboat is filled to capacity with people while a person swims nearby, begging to be allowed on board. Yet to allow one more person into the boat would capsize it and possibly drown everyone. Thus, the people in the lifeboat might feel they have no choice but to sacrifice someone. Similarly, the Luo people believe that they must sacrifice one—Oganda—in order to save many—the rest of the villagers. What is your opinion of this philosophy?

3. Ndithi, the medicine man, says that he has dreamed of a sad, fair-skinned young woman wearing a ring in her ear and a chain about her waist. Podho, the ancestor who speaks to Ndithi in the dream, declares that this young woman will be the sacrifice to the monster in the lake. Why do you think this young woman is so much like Oganda, Chief Labong'o's only daughter?

THE ART OF THE STORYTELLER

Theme
"The Rain Came" contains several subjects that deal with human nature. Two of these subjects are duty to one's family and society, and self-sacrifice for the greater good of society. These two subjects are linked in the theme: Both self-sacrifice and fulfilling one's duty to family and society are sometimes painful but very often necessary.

The society of the Luo people, like all functional societies, is held together by common beliefs and a commitment to duty. The villagers do not question their beliefs or their chief's decision. Oganda's mother and father, though grief-stricken, do not oppose the idea of Oganda's sacrifice. Oganda, too, who does not want to die, believes she must abide by her ancestors' decision and fulfill her duty to her people. Only Osinda defies the decision when he rescues Oganda; however, even he still believes they must hide from the monster and their ancestors, so he makes the disguises they wear to escape.

At the story's end, Oganda is still alive when the rainstorm begins. What do you think this event means? How do you think it will affect Oganda and Osinda? Explain why you do or do not think Oganda and Osinda will now question their beliefs about duty and sacrifice?

Setting

Setting—the place and the time of the action—is extremely important in this story. "The Rain Came" is set in an East African village during a period of drought. Cattle are dying because there is not enough water for grass to grow. The villagers fear that soon they and their children will also begin to starve to death. How do these circumstances relate to the conflict in the story? What are some other examples of the importance of the story's setting?

THE VOCABULARY IN THE STORY

In English, many words are formed by adding prefixes or suffixes to word roots. A word's *root* is the part that carries the core meaning of the word. For example, the root *–aero–* means "air." The words *aeronautics, aerial,* and *aerobics* all share the word root *–aero–* and, therefore, are related in meaning.

Each of the following words appears in "The Rain Came." For each word, find at least four related words that are formed from the same root. Then write a definition for each given word and each related word. Use a dictionary if necessary.

1. congratulate 3. maternal
2. spirit 4. sympathetically

COMPOSITION: Writing an Original Myth

A *myth* is a story that people have passed down through the ages. It often explains something about the natural world. The myth of the lake monster is the Luo people's way of explaining drought. People everywhere tell myths.

Think about the place where you live. Do you have hail, drought, earthquakes, or hurricanes? Do you have pets or live by the sea? Why do hurricanes hit certain places and not others? How did the cat get its purr? Why is the sea salty?

Write your own myth (at least 250 words) that explains something in the natural world where you live.

Prewriting

Spend some time thinking of things about which you might write your myth. Jot down some of these things and beside each one write a possible cause. The cause may be fantastic, supernatural, or logical, but not scientific. Then write a brief description of each of the characters who will be in your story. Finally, write a short, informal outline of the plot if you think it will help you to organize your story.

Writing

Write the draft of your story quickly. Try to write without stopping for at least three minutes at a time. You may be surprised at how much you can write in that short time. Do not revise much while you are writing. You can revise after you get your myth down on paper.

Evaluating and Revising

Read your draft. Does it explain some aspect of the natural world? Have you included all the necessary events in your myth? Cut, rearrange, or add words, phrases, or sections as needed.

ABOUT THE AUTHOR

 Grace Ogot (1930–   ) was born in western Kenya near Lake Victoria. Against the wishes of her father, she traveled to London, where she trained to be a nurse and midwife. During the 1950s in London, she worked for the British Broadcasting Corporation as an announcer and a scriptwriter. Ogot writes her stories about African women and focuses on

themes involving self-sacrifice, duty, and family bonds. Even the stories she wrote right after Kenya's fierce struggle for independence do not have political themes. *The Promised Land,* published in 1966, is about Nyapol, a dutiful wife. "The Rain Came" was first published in 1965, and in 1968 it was published in the collection of Ogot's stories—*Land Without Thunder.* In addition to writing, Ogot has also served in the Kenyan government.

■ A WARRIOR'S DAUGHTER

Zitkala-Ša

This story was written by Zitkala-Ša, a Yankton Sioux woman, just after the turn of the century and was first published in 1921. You will notice that the verb tenses shift back and forth from past tense to present tense. These shifts in tenses have no bearing on the meaning of or time changes in the story. The author's native Sioux language has no verb tenses as we know them, and its speakers rarely make any distinction between past or present events, especially in storytelling.

This story is set in the warrior society of the Dakota Sioux. For the Sioux, bravery is one of the highest virtues sought by both men and women. Tusee, the beautiful daughter of the chieftain's bravest warrior, grows to be a strong young woman. But she must prove both her bravery and her loyalty to the man she loves in the face of an enemy tribe.

In the afternoon shadow of a large tepee, with red-painted smoke lapels,[1] sat a warrior father with crossed shins. His head was so poised that his eye swept easily the vast level land to the eastern horizon line.

He was the chieftain's bravest warrior. He had won by heroic deeds the privilege of staking his wigwam within the great circle of tepees.

He was also one of the most generous gift givers to the toothless old people. For this he was entitled to the red-painted smoke lapels on his cone-shaped dwelling. He was proud of his honors. He never wearied of rehearsing nightly his own brave deeds. Though by wigwam fires he prated much of his high rank and widespread fame, his great joy was a wee black-eyed daughter of eight sturdy winters. Thus as he sat upon the soft grass, with his wife at his side, bent over her bead work, he was singing a dance song, and beat lightly the rhythm with his slender hands.

His shrewd eyes softened with pleasure as he watched the easy movements of the small body dancing on the green before him.

---

1. **smoke lapels:** the flaps located at the top of the conical-shaped tipi (or tepee) which create a flue for escaping smoke and protection from the wind.

Tusee is taking her first dancing lesson. Her tightly-braided hair curves over both brown ears like a pair of crooked little horns which glisten in the summer sun.

With her snugly moccasined feet close together, and a wee hand at her belt to stay the long string of beads which hang from her bare neck, she bends her knees gently to the rhythm of her father's voice.

Now she ventures upon the earnest movement, slightly upward and sidewise, in a circle. At length the song drops into a closing cadence, and the little woman, clad in beaded deerskin, sits down beside the elder one. Like her mother, she sits upon her feet. In a brief moment the warrior repeats the last refrain. Again Tusee springs to her feet and dances to the swing of the few final measures.

Just as the dance was finished, an elderly man, with short, thick hair loose about his square shoulders, rode into their presence from the rear, and leaped lightly from his pony's back. Dropping the rawhide rein to the ground, he tossed himself lazily on the grass. "Hunhe, you have returned soon," said the warrior, while extending a hand to his little daughter.

Quickly the child ran to her father's side and cuddled close to him, while he tenderly placed a strong arm about her. Both father and child, eyeing the figure on the grass, waited to hear the man's report.

"It is true," began the man, with a stranger's accent. "This is the night of the dance."

"Hunha!" muttered the warrior with some surprise.

Propping himself upon his elbows, the man raised his face. His features were of the Southern type. From an enemy's camp he was taken captive long years ago by Tusee's father. But the unusual qualities of the slave had won the Sioux warrior's heart, and for the last three winters the man had had his freedom. He was made real man again. His hair was allowed to grow. However, he himself had chosen to stay in the warrior's family.

"Hunha!" again ejaculated the warrior father. Then turning to his little daughter, he asked, "Tusee, do you hear that?"

"Yes, father, and I am going to dance tonight!"

With these words she bounded out of his arm and frolicked about in glee. Hereupon the proud mother's voice rang out in a chiding laugh.

"My child, in honor of your first dance your father must give a generous gift. His ponies are wild, and roam beyond the great hill. Pray, what has he fit to offer?" she questioned, the pair of puzzled eyes fixed upon her.

"A pony from the herd, mother, a fleet-footed pony from the herd!" Tusee shouted with sudden inspiration.

Pointing a small forefinger toward the man lying on the grass, she cried, "Uncle, you will go after the pony tomorrow!" And pleased with her solution of the problem, she skipped wildly about. Her childish faith in her elders was not conditioned by a knowledge of human limitations, but thought all things possible to grown-ups.

"Hähob!" exclaimed the mother, with a rising inflection, implying by the expletive that her child's buoyant spirit be not weighted with a denial.

Quickly to the hard request the man replied, "How! I go if Tusee tells me so!"

This delighted the little one, whose black eyes brimmed over with light. Standing in front of the strong man, she clapped her small, brown hands with joy.

"That makes me glad! My heart is good! Go, uncle, and bring a handsome pony!" she cried. In an instant she would have frisked away, but an impulse held her tilting where she stood. In the man's own tongue, for he had taught her many words and phrases, she exploded, "Thank you, good uncle, thank you!" then tore away from sheer excess of glee.

The proud warrior father, smiling and narrowing his eyes, muttered approval, "Howo! Hechetu!"

Like her mother, Tusee has finely pencilled eyebrows and slightly extended nostrils; but in her sturdiness of form she resembles her father.

A loyal daughter, she sits within her tepee making beaded deerskins for her father, while he longs to stave off her every suitor as all unworthy of his old heart's pride. But Tusee is not alone in her dwelling. Near the entrance-way a young brave is half reclining on a mat. In silence he watches the petals of a wild rose growing on the soft buckskin. Quickly the young woman slips the beads on the silvery sinew thread, and works them into the pretty flower design. Finally, in a low, deep voice, the young man begins:

"The sun is far past the zenith. It is now only a man's height above the western edge of land. I hurried hither to tell you tomorrow I join the war party."

He pauses for reply, but the maid's head drops lower over her deerskin, and her lips are more firmly drawn together. He continues:

"Last night in the moonlight I met your warrior father. He seemed to know I had just stepped forth from your tepee. I fear he did not like it, for though I greeted him, he was silent. I halted in his pathway. With what boldness I dared, while my heart was beating hard and fast, I asked him for his only daughter.

"Drawing himself erect to his tallest height, and gathering his loose robe more closely around his proud figure, he flashed a pair of piercing eyes upon me.

" 'Young man,' said he, with a cold, slow voice that chilled me to the marrow of my bones, 'hear me. Naught but an enemy's scalp-lock, plucked fresh with your own hand, will buy Tusee for your wife.' Then he turned on his heel and stalked away."

Tusee thrusts her work aside. With earnest eyes she scans her lover's face.

"My father's heart is really kind. He would know if you are brave and true," murmured the daughter, who wished no ill-will between her two loved ones.

Then rising to go, the youth holds out a right hand. "Grasp my hand once firmly before I go, Hoye. Pray tell me, will you wait and watch for my return?"

Tusee only nods assent, for mere words are vain.

At early dawn the round camp-ground awakes into song. Men and women sing of bravery and triumph. They inspire the swelling breasts of the painted warriors mounted on prancing ponies bedecked with the green branches of trees.

Riding slowly around the great ring of cone-shaped tepees, here and there, a loud-singing warrior swears to avenge a former wrong, and thrusts a bare brown arm against the purple east, calling the Great Spirit to hear his vow. All having made the circuit, the singing war party gallops away southward.

Astride their ponies laden with food and deerskins, brave elderly women follow after their warriors. Among the foremost rides a young woman in elaborately beaded buckskin dress. Proudly mounted, she curbs with the single rawhide loop a wild-eyed pony.

It is Tusee on her father's warhorse. Thus the war party of Indian men and their faithful women vanish beyond the southern skyline.

A day's journey brings them very near the enemy's borderland. Nightfall finds a pair of twin tepees nestled in a deep ravine. Within one lounge the painted warriors, smoking their pipes and telling weird stories by the firelight, while in the other watchful women crouch uneasily about their center fire.

By the first gray light in the east the tepees are banished. They are gone. The warriors are in the enemy's camp, breaking dreams with their tomahawks. The women are hid away in secret places in the long thicketed ravine.

The day is far spent, the red sun is low over the west.

At length straggling warriors return, one by one, to the deep hollow. In the twilight they number their men. Three are missing. Of these absent ones two are dead; but the third one, a young man, is a captive to the foe.

"He-he!" lament the warriors, taking food in haste.

In silence each woman, with long strides, hurries to and fro, tying large bundles on her pony's back. Under cover of night the war party must hasten homeward. Motionless, with bowed head, sits a woman in her hiding-place. She grieves for her lover.

In bitterness of spirit she hears the warriors' murmuring words. With set teeth she plans to cheat the hated enemy of their captive. In the meanwhile low signals are given, and the war party, unaware of Tusee's absence, steal quietly away. The soft thud of pony-hoofs grows fainter and fainter. The gradual hush of the empty ravine whirs noisily in the ear of the young woman. Alert for any sound of footfalls nigh, she holds her breath to listen. Her right hand rests on a long knife in her belt. Ah, yes, she knows where her pony is hid, but not yet has she need of him. Satisfied that no danger is nigh, she prowls forth from her place of hiding. With a panther's tread and pace she climbs the high ridge beyond the low ravine. From thence she spies the enemy's camp-fires.

Rooted to the barren bluff the slender woman's figure stands on the pinnacle of night, outlined against the starry sky. The cool night breeze wafts to her burning ear snatches of song and drum. With desperate hate she bites her teeth.

Tusee beckons the stars to witness. With impassioned voice and uplifted face she pleads:

"Great Spirit, speed me to my lover's rescue! Give me swift cunning for a weapon this night! All-powerful Spirit, grant me my warrior-father's heart, strong to slay a foe and mighty to save a friend!"

In the midst of the enemy's camp-ground, underneath a temporary dance-house, are men and women in gala-day dress. It is late in the night, but the merry warriors bend and bow their nude, painted bodies before a bright center fire. To the lusty men's voices and the rhythmic throbbing drum, they leap and rebound with feathered headgears waving.

Women with red-painted cheeks and long, braided hair sit in a large half-circle against the willow railing. They, too, join in the singing, and rise to dance with their victorious warriors.

Amid this circular dance arena stands a prisoner bound to a post, haggard with shame and sorrow. He hangs his disheveled head.

He stares with unseeing eyes upon the bare earth at his feet. With jeers and smirking faces the dancers mock the Dakota captive. Rowdy braves and small boys hoot and yell in derision.

Silent among the noisy mob, a tall woman, leaning both elbows on the round willow railing, peers into the lighted arena. The dancing center fire shines bright into her handsome face, intensifying the night in her dark eyes. It breaks into myriad points upon her beaded dress. Unmindful of the surging throng jostling her at either side, she glares in upon the hateful, scoffing men. Suddenly she turns her head. Tittering maids whisper near her ear:

"There! There! See him now, sneering in the captive's face. 'Tis he who sprang upon the young man and dragged him by his long hair to yonder post. See! He is handsome! How gracefully he dances!"

The silent young woman looks toward the bound captive. She sees a warrior, scarce older than the captive, flourishing a tomahawk in the Dakota's face. A burning rage darts forth from her eyes and brands him for a victim of revenge. Her heart mutters within her breast, "Come, I wish to meet you, vile foe, who captured my lover and tortures him now with a living death."

Here the singers hush their voices, and the dancers scatter to their various resting-places along the willow ring. The victor gives a reluctant last twirl of his tomahawk, then, like the others, he leaves the center ground. With head and shoulders swaying from side to side, he carries a high-pointing chin toward the willow railing. Sitting down upon the ground with crossed legs, he fans himself with an outspread turkey wing.

Now and then he stops his haughty blinking to peep out of the corners of his eyes. He hears someone clearing her throat gently. It is unmistakably for his ear. The wing-fan swings irregularly to and fro. At length he turns a proud face over a bare shoulder and beholds a handsome woman smiling.

"Ah, she would speak to a hero!" thumps his heart wildly.

The singers raise their voices in unison. The music is irresistible. Again lunges the victor into the open arena. Again he leers into the captive's face. At every interval between the songs he returns to his resting-place. Here the young woman awaits him. As he approaches she smiles boldly into his eyes. He is pleased with her face and her smile.

Waving his wing-fan spasmodically in front of his face, he sits with his ears pricked up. He catches a low whisper. A hand taps him lightly on the shoulder. The handsome woman speaks to him in his own tongue. "Come out into the night. I wish to tell you who I am."

He must know what sweet words of praise the handsome woman has for him. With both hands he spreads the meshes of the loosely woven willows, and crawls out unnoticed into the dark.

Before him stands the young woman. Beckoning him with a slender hand, she steps backward, away from the light and the restless throng of onlookers. He follows with impatient strides. She quickens her pace. He lengthens his strides. Then suddenly the woman turns from him and darts away with amazing speed. Clinching his fists and biting his lower lip, the young man runs after the fleeing woman. In his maddened pursuit he forgets the dance arena.

Beside a cluster of low bushes the woman halts. The young man, panting for breath and plunging headlong forward, whispers loud, "Pray tell me, are you a woman or an evil spirit to lure me away?"

Turning on heels firmly planted in the earth, the woman gives a wild spring forward, like a panther for its prey. In a husky voice she hissed between her teeth, "I am a Dakota woman!"

From her unerring long knife the enemy falls heavily at her feet. The Great Spirit heard Tusee's prayer on the hilltop. He gave her a warrior's strong heart to lessen the foe by one.

A bent old woman's figure, with a bundle like a grandchild slung on her back, walks round and round the dance-house. The wearied onlookers are leaving in twos and threes. The tired dancers creep out of the willow railing, and some go out at the entrance-way, till the singers, too, rise from the drum and are trudging drowsily homeward. Within the arena the center fire lies broken in red embers. The night no longer lingers about the willow railing, but, hovering into the dance-house, covers here and there a snoring man whom sleep has overpowered where he sat.

The captive in his tight-binding rawhide ropes hangs in hopeless despair. Close about him the gloom of night is slowly crouching. Yet the last red, crackling embers cast a faint light upon his long black hair, and, shining through the thick mats, caress his wan face with undying hope.

Still about the dance-house the old woman prowls. Now the embers are gray with ashes.

The old bent woman appears at the entrance-way. With a cautious, groping foot she enters. Whispering between her teeth a lullaby for her sleeping child in her blanket, she searches for something forgotten.

Noisily snored the dreaming men in the darkest parts. As the lisping old woman draws nigh, the captive again opens his eyes.

A forefinger she presses to her lip. The young man arouses himself from his stupor. His senses belie him. Before his wide-open eyes the old bent figure straightens into its youthful stature. Tusee herself is beside him. With a stroke upward and downward she severs the cruel cords with her sharp blade. Dropping her blanket from her shoulders, so that it hangs from her girdled waist like a skirt, she shakes the large bundle into a light shawl for her lover. Quickly she spreads it over his bare back.

"Come!" she whispers, and turns to go; but the young man, numb and helpless, staggers nigh to falling.

The sight of his weakness makes her strong. A mighty power thrills her body. Stooping beneath his outstretched arms grasping at the air for support, Tusee lifts him upon her broad shoulders. With half-running, triumphant steps she carries him away into the open night. ■

THE IMPACT OF THE STORY

Tusee finds herself in a situation where she must act bravely and unselfishly to save the man she loves. In doing so, she places herself in great danger. How important do you think bravery and generosity are in our society? To what limits would you go to save a loved one?

THE FACTS OF THE STORY

On your own paper, write answers to the following items. Answers may be one word, a phrase, or several sentences.

1. What does Tusee order her "uncle" to do for her in preparation for her first dance?

2. On what condition will Tusee's father allow the young brave she loves to marry her?

3. What happens to Tusee's lover when he accompanies the war party?

4. Who does Tusee kill?

5. In the enemy camp, Tusee disguises herself as _____ in order to free her lover.

THE IDEAS IN THE STORY

Prepare to discuss the following questions in class.

1. Tusee's "uncle" is actually an enemy warrior who was taken prisoner years ago by her father. Three years ago, her father freed the slave, who then chose to remain with Tusee's family. Why do you think the freed slave chose to remain with his captors rather than return to his own tribe? How does this "uncle" help to make possible Tusee's rescue of her lover? How is he like Tusee's lover?

2. Tusee lures the enemy warrior who captured her lover into the woods away from the camp. Why do you think she kills him? What do you think she probably takes from him? Why?

THE ART OF THE STORYTELLER

The Oral Tradition

The Sioux have always been avid storytellers. Traditionally, they were a nomadic people, following the great herds of buffalo across the plains. However, they set up semipermanent camps in protected wooded areas during the harsh winters. It was during these months when the people gathered around the fires inside their tepees that storytelling flourished. For fun, the Sioux told humorous stories that were often about tricksters and fools. Legends about important people and events from their past were shared as a way of passing down their history and models for their highest virtues. Myths told about the Sioux religious beliefs and narrated the lives and powers of the supernatural beings.

Sioux storytelling was an oral tradition; that is, the stories were not written down but were spoken aloud. Generation after generation of people passed the same stories down to one another.

Zitkala-Ša grew up hearing the stories of her people. One feature that you have already noticed in "A Warrior's Daughter" that is carried over from this oral tradition is the shift in verb tenses. What other characteristics of the stories told by the Sioux can you find in this story? Give examples. What two types of Sioux stories do these characteristics reflect?

Heroic Character

A hero is a person who shows great courage or who has performed noble or valorous deeds. There are many mortal heroes in legends and mythology. One famous hero from Greek mythology is Heracles (or Hercules, as he is called in Roman mythology). The son of a mortal and the god Zeus, he possesses great strength and is legendary for his courageous feats.

Tusee, in "A Warrior's Daughter," also has heroic qualities. Her virtues far exceed those of bravery, generosity, truthfulness, and childbearing, which are the four highest virtues sought by Sioux women. She follows her lover to the battle, and she kills his captor. Find other passages in the story that show Tusee's heroic qualities. Who are some modern female heroes that have some of these same qualities?

THE VOCABULARY IN THE STORY

Rewrite the following passages from "A Warrior's Daughter," changing the verb or verbs to the form given in parentheses.

1. . . . by wigwam fires he prated much of his high rank and widespread fame . . . (present)

2. He never wearied of rehearsing nightly his own brave deeds. (present)

3. Then he turned on his heel and stalked away. (present)

4. "He-he!" lament the warriors . . . (past)

5. His senses belie him. (past)

COMPOSITION: Writing a Story

You or someone you know may like to tell stories. Parents often enjoy telling stories about their childhoods or about their children. Veterans reminisce about their experiences in battle. Athletes tell stories about the most important games they have played. You may have had a memorable or funny experience that you would like to tell others about.

Write a story (500–1000 words) about an experience of your own or that of another person.

You may want to remain as faithful as possible to the true story. However, every storyteller knows it is all right to "improve" a story by adding some colorful details that may not have actually been part of the original event.

Prewriting
If you have access to a recorder, tape your story as you tell it aloud. Be sure to find a quiet place where you will not be interrupted during your storytelling. Otherwise, tell your story to a friend, parent, or out loud to yourself.

Writing
Transcribe your recording or write the story down as quickly as possible. Read this initial draft aloud. Identify any parts that do not

relate directly to the story, that would be more effective if described differently, or that need colorful details.

Evaluating and Revising

Read your revised draft aloud to someone else if possible. Does it hold your listener's interest? Ask for comments. Cut, rearrange, or rewrite as needed. Finally, proofread for punctuation, grammatical, and spelling errors.

ABOUT THE AUTHOR

 Zitkala-Ša (1876–1938), whose name means Red Bird, was also known by the English name Gertrude Simmons Bonnin. She was born at the Yankton Sioux Agency in South Dakota. At the age of eight, she left the reservation to attend White's Manual Labor Institute, a Quaker missionary school for American Indians. After three years she returned to the reservation. But four years later she went again to the school, where she remained until her graduation. In school she experienced humiliation at the hands of the well-meaning missionaries who misunderstood Sioux culture. And like other American Indians who were educated by European Americans, she suffered from being caught between conflicting cultures, really belonging to neither one nor the other. Nevertheless, she graduated in 1897 from Earlham College in Richmond, Indiana, and later studied at the Boston Conservatory of Music. Her first book, *Old Indian Legends*, was published in 1901; *American Indian Stories* was published in 1921. Although a talented teacher, musician, writer, and orator, Zitkala-Ša's life's work was to achieve Indian reform in government and to record accurate histories of numerous American Indian tribes.

■ THE LADY, OR THE TIGER?

Frank R. Stockton

One of the most popular short stories ever written, "The Lady, or the Tiger?" became famous almost the instant it was published. The title includes a question mark for reasons that will soon become clear to you. By now, generations of readers have enjoyed this story and have tried to come up with an answer to the question that this story poses. Soon, you yourself just may be caught up in figuring out an answer to the dilemma of the lady and the tiger in this story.

n the very olden time there lived a semibarbaric king, whose ideas, though somewhat polished and sharpened by the progressiveness of distant Latin neighbors, were still large, florid, and untrammeled,[1] as became the half of him which was barbaric. He was a man of exuberant fancy, and, withal, of an authority so irresistible that, at his will, he turned his varied fancies into facts. He was greatly given to self-communing; and, when he and himself agreed upon anything, the thing was done. When every member of his domestic and political systems moved smoothly in its appointed course, his nature was bland and genial; but whenever there was a little hitch, and some of his orbs got out of their orbits, he was blander and more genial still, for nothing pleased him so much as to make the crooked straight, and crush down uneven places.

Among the borrowed notions by which his barbarism had become semified[2] was that of the public arena, in which, by exhibitions of manly and beastly valor, the minds of his subjects were refined and cultured. But even here the exuberant and barbaric fancy asserted itself. The arena of the king was built not to give the people an opportunity of hearing the rhapsodies of dying gladiators, nor to enable them to view the inevitable conclusion of a conflict between religious opinions and hungry jaws, but for purposes far better adapted to widen and develop the mental energies of the people. This vast amphitheater, with

---

1. **untrammeled** (ŭn trăm′ əld): not hindered or restrained.
2. **semified**: made partial or reduced in half.

If you did something wrong you would die But if you did good you were rewarded

its encircling galleries, its mysterious vaults, and its unseen passages, was an agent of poetic justice, in which crime was punished, or virtue rewarded, by the decrees of an impartial and incorruptible chance.

When a subject was accused of a crime of sufficient importance to interest the king, public notice was given that on an appointed day the fate of the accused person would be decided in the king's arena—a structure which well deserved its name; for, although its form and plan were borrowed from afar, its purpose emanated solely from the brain of this man, who, every barleycorn a king, knew no tradition to which he owed more allegiance than pleased his fancy, and who ingrafted on every adopted form of human thought and action the rich growth of his barbaric idealism.

Tiger or lady

When all the people had assembled in the galleries, and the king, surrounded by his court, sat high up on his throne of royal state on one side of the arena, he gave a signal, a door beneath him opened, and the accused subject stepped out into the amphitheater. Directly opposite him, on the other side of the enclosed space, were two doors exactly alike and side by side. It was the duty and the privilege of the person on trial to walk directly to these doors and open one of them. He could open either door he pleased: he was subject to no guidance or influence but that of the aforementioned impartial and incorruptible chance. If he opened the one, there came out of it a hungry tiger, the fiercest and most cruel that could be procured, which immediately sprang upon him and tore him to pieces, as a punishment for his guilt. The moment that the case of the criminal was thus decided, doleful iron bells were clanged, great wails went up from the hired mourners posted on the outer rim of the arena, and the vast audience, with bowed heads and downcast hearts, wended slowly their homeward way, mourning greatly that one so young and fair, or so old and respected, should have merited so dire a fate.

But if the accused person opened the other door, there came forth from it a lady, the most suitable to his years and station that his Majesty could select among his fair subjects; and to this lady he was immediately married, as a reward of his innocence. It mattered not that he might already possess a wife and family, or that his affections might be engaged upon an object of his own selection: the king allowed no such subordinate arrangements to interfere with his great scheme of retribution and reward. The exercises, as in the other instance, took place immediately, and in the arena. Another door opened beneath the king,

CRIMINAL PICKS THE DOOR

and a priest, followed by a band of choristers, and dancing maidens blowing joyous airs on golden horns and treading an epithalamic measure,[3] advanced to where the pair stood side by side; and the wedding was promptly and cheerily solemnized. Then the gay brass bells rang forth their merry peals, the people shouted glad hurrahs, and the innocent man, preceded by children strewing flowers on his path, led his bride to his home.

This was the king's semibarbaric method of administering justice. Its perfect fairness is obvious. The criminal could not know out of which door would come the lady: he opened either he pleased, without having the slightest idea whether, in the next instant, he was to be devoured or married. On some occasions the tiger came out of one door, and on some out of the other. The decisions of this tribunal were not only fair, they were positively determinate: the accused person was instantly punished if he found himself guilty; and, if innocent, he was rewarded on the spot, whether he liked it or not. There was no escape from the judgments of the king's arena.

The institution was a very popular one. When the people gathered together on one of the great trial days, they never knew whether they were to witness a bloody slaughter or a hilarious wedding. This element of uncertainty lent an interest to the occasion which it could not otherwise have attained. Thus, the masses were entertained and pleased, and the thinking part of the community could bring no charge of unfairness against this plan; for did not the accused person have the whole matter in his own hands?

This semibarbaric king had a daughter as blooming as his most florid fancies, and with a soul as fervent and imperious as his own. As is usual in such cases, she was the apple of his eye, and was loved by him above all humanity. Among his courtiers was a young man of that fineness of blood and lowness of station common to the conventional heroes of romance who love royal maidens. This royal maiden was well satisfied with her lover, for he was handsome and brave to a degree unsurpassed in all this kingdom; and she loved him with an ardor that had enough of barbarism in it to make it exceedingly warm and strong. This love affair moved on happily for many months, until one day the king happened to discover its existence. He did not hesitate nor waver in regard to his duty in the premises. The youth was immediately cast

---

3. **treading an epithalamic** (ĕp'ə thə lā' mik) **measure:** performing a wedding dance.

into prison, and a day was appointed for his trial in the king's arena. This, of course, was an especially important occasion; and his Majesty, as well as all the people, was greatly interested in the workings and development of this trial. Never before had such a case occurred; never before had a subject dared to love the daughter of a king. In after years such things became commonplace enough; but then they were, in no slight degree, novel and startling.

The tiger cages of the kingdom were searched for the most savage and relentless beasts, from which the fiercest monster might be selected for the arena; and the ranks of maiden youth and beauty throughout the land were carefully surveyed by competent judges, in order that the young man might have a fitting bride in case fate did not determine for him a different destiny. Of course everybody knew that the deed with which the accused was charged had been done. He had loved the princess, and neither he, she, nor anyone else thought of denying the fact; but the king would not think of allowing any fact of this kind to interfere with the workings of the tribunal, in which he took such a great delight and satisfaction. No matter how the affair turned out, the youth would be disposed of; and the king would take an aesthetic[4] pleasure in watching the course of events, which would determine whether or not the young man had done wrong in allowing himself to love the princess.

The appointed day arrived. From far and near the people gathered, and thronged the great galleries of the arena; and crowds, unable to gain admittance, massed themselves against its outside walls. The king and his court were in their places, opposite the twin doors—those fateful portals, so terrible in their similarity.

All was ready. The signal was given. A door beneath the royal party opened, and the lover of the princess walked into the arena. Tall, beautiful, fair, his appearance was greeted with a low hum of admiration and anxiety. Half the audience had not known so grand a youth had lived among them. No wonder the princess loved him! What a terrible thing for him to be there!

As the youth advanced into the arena, he turned, as the custom was, to bow to the king: but he did not think at all of that royal personage; his eyes were fixed upon the princess, who sat to the right of her father.

---

4. **aesthetic:** having to do with a love of the beautiful.

She Picked his Fate

Had it not been for the moiety[5] of barbarism in her nature, it is probable that lady would not have been there; but her intense and fervid soul would not allow her to be absent on an occasion in which she was so terribly interested. From the moment that the decree had gone forth that her lover should decide his fate in the king's arena, she had thought of nothing, night or day, but this great event and the various subjects connected with it. Possessed of more power, influence, and force of character than anyone who had ever before been interested in such a case, she had done what no other person had done—she had possessed herself of the secret of the doors. She knew in which of the two rooms that lay behind those doors stood the cage of the tiger, with its open front, and in which waited the lady. Through these thick doors, heavily curtained with skins on the inside, it was impossible that any noise or suggestion should come from within to the person who should approach to raise the latch of one of them; but gold, and the power of a woman's will, had brought the secret to the princess.

And not only did she know in which room stood the lady ready to emerge, all blushing and radiant, should her door be opened, but she knew who the lady was. It was one of the fairest and loveliest of the damsels of the court who had been selected as the reward of the accused youth, should he be proved innocent of the crime of aspiring to one so far above him; and the princess hated her. Often had she seen, or imagined that she had seen, this fair creature throwing glances of admiration upon the person of her lover, and sometimes she thought these glances were perceived and even returned. Now and then she had seen them talking together; it was but for a moment or two, but much can be said in a brief space; it may have been on most unimportant topics, but how could she know that? The girl was lovely, but she had dared to raise her eyes to the loved one of the princess; and, with all the intensity of the savage blood transmitted to her through long lines of wholly barbaric ancestors, she hated the woman who blushed and trembled behind that silent door. OUG

When her lover turned and looked at her, and his eye met hers as she sat there paler and whiter than anyone in the vast ocean of anxious faces about her, he saw, by that power of quick perception which is given to those whose souls are one, that she knew behind which door

The Princess loved him but hated the lady

Could not hear any sound

---

5. moiety (moi′ I tē): a half.

crouched the tiger, and behind which stood the lady. He had expected her to know it. He understood her nature, and his soul was assured that she would never rest until she had made plain to herself this thing, hidden to all other lookers-on, even to the king. The only hope for the youth in which there was any element of certainty was based upon the success of the princess in discovering the mystery; and the moment he looked upon her, he saw she had succeeded, as in his soul he knew she would succeed.

Then it was that his quick and anxious glance asked the question, "Which?" It was as plain to her as if he shouted it from where he stood. There was not an instant to be lost. The question was asked in a flash; it must be answered in another.

Her right arm lay on the cushioned parapet[6] before her. She raised her hand, and made a slight, quick movement toward the right. No one but her lover saw her. Every eye but his was fixed on the man in the arena.

He turned, and with a firm and rapid step he walked across the empty space. Every heart stopped beating, every breath was held, every eye was fixed immovably upon that man. Without the slightest hesitation, he went to the door on the right, and opened it.

Now, the point of the story is this: Did the tiger come out of that door, or did the lady? The more we reflect upon this question, the harder it is to answer. It involves a study of the human heart which leads us through devious mazes of passion, out of which it is difficult to find our way. Think of it, fair reader, not as if the decision of the question depended upon yourself, but upon that hot-blooded, semibarbaric princess, her soul at a white heat beneath the combined fires of despair and jealousy. She had lost him, but who should have him?

How often, in her waking hours and in her dreams, had she started in wild horror and covered her face with her hands as she thought of her lover opening the door on the other side of which waited the cruel fangs of the tiger!

But how much oftener had she seen him at the other door! How in her grievous reveries had she gnashed her teeth and torn her hair when she saw his start of rapturous delight as he opened the door of the lady! How her soul had burned in agony when she had seen him rush to

---

6. **parapet:** a low wall or railing.

meet that woman, with her flushing cheek and sparkling eye of triumph; when she had seen him lead her forth, his whole frame kindled with the joy of recovered life; when she had heard the glad shouts from the multitude, and the wild ringing of the happy bells; when she had seen the priest, with his joyous followers, advance to the couple, and make them man and wife before her very eyes; and when she had seen them walk away together upon their path of flowers, followed by the tremendous shouts of the hilarious multitude, in which her one despairing shriek was lost and drowned!

Would it not be better for him to die at once, and go to wait for her in the blessed regions of semibarbaric futurity?

And yet, that awful tiger, those shrieks, that blood!

Her decision had been indicated in an instant, but it had been made after days and nights of anguished deliberation. She had known she would be asked, she had decided what she would answer, and without the slightest hesitation, she had moved her hand to the right.

The question of her decision is one not to be lightly considered, and it is not for me to presume to set myself up as the one person able to answer it. And so I leave it with all of you: Which came out of the opened door—the lady, or the tiger? ■

The author made it my decision.

THE IMPACT OF THE STORY

The author places a great deal of emphasis on the semibarbaric natures of the king, the princess, and the masses. *Barbaric* means "uncivilized, brutal, crude, or wild in style, taste, or actions." Do you think our society has any semibarbaric practices or notions? If so, what are some examples?

THE FACTS OF THE STORY

On your own paper, write answers to the following items. Answers may be one word, a phrase, or several sentences.

1. In the king's arena, what determines whether a person is innocent or guilty?

2. What crime has the young man in the story committed?

3. How does the princess find out which rooms the lady and the tiger occupy?

4. Who is the lady behind the door?

5. What does the princess do when the young man stands in the arena?

THE IDEAS IN THE STORY

Prepare to discuss the following questions in class.

1. "After days and nights of anguished deliberation," the princess makes her decision. What do you think her decision is? Explain why you think so. Be prepared to support your opinion with examples based on your observations of human nature. Be prepared, also, to refer to evidence in the story.

    One thing you may wish to consider is the author's emphasis on the semibarbarism of the king and the princess. The narrator refers to the king's semibarbaric method of administering justice. He says the princess loves the young man with an ardor that has "enough of barbarism in it to make it exceedingly warm and strong." He says it is probable that the princess would not have attended the arena trial had it not been for "the moiety of barbarism in her nature." Do you think this emphasis tells us something about the ending?

2. Which do you think is the more powerful emotion: jealousy or love? Explain your answer.

3. Think about whether or not a person can ever really know another person well enough to be able to foretell correctly how that person will act in a difficult situation. Do you think that the young man can tell, on the basis of what he knows about the princess, whether she would prefer his death or his marriage to the lady? If you were the accused young man, would you open the door the princess suggested? Explain your answer.

THE ART OF THE STORYTELLER

Satire

Stockton has a sharp sense of humor, and we see him use it effectively in this satiric story. **Satire** is a type of writing that ridicules the weaknesses or wrongdoings of people and social institutions in a humorous way, yet with a serious purpose. For example, the narrator says the hero

> . . . was a young man of that fineness of blood and lowness of station common to the conventional heroes of romance who love royal maidens.

Where else in the story can you find passages that ridicule fairy tales? Stockton's satire is not limited to fairy-tale fiction. What attitudes of real-life rulers is he mocking in this passage?

> But if the accused person opened the other door, there came forth from it a lady, the most suitable to his years and station that his Majesty could select among his fair subjects; and to this lady he was immediately married, as a reward of his innocence. It mattered not that he might already possess a wife and family, or that his affections might be engaged upon an object of his own selection: the king allowed no such subordinate arrangements to interfere with his great scheme of retribution and reward.

THE VOCABULARY IN THE STORY

Verbal irony is a contrast or an incongruity between what is stated and what is really meant. The verbal irony in "The Lady, or the Tiger?" adds humor and depth to the theme of the story. For example, the narrator says of the trials

> This was the king's semibarbaric method of administering justice. Its perfect fairness is obvious.

Of course, it is not obvious that the trials are fair. Instead, the trials are not impartial; they are unfair because rewards and punishments are random. Therefore, we realize that what the narrator says is the opposite of what he means.

For each of the following passages, explain how the italicized word is ironic.

1. . . . his nature was bland and *genial;* but whenever there was a little hitch, and some of his orbs got out of their orbits, he was blander and more genial still. . . .

2. The arena of the king was built not to give the people an opportunity of hearing the *rhapsodies* of dying gladiators. . . .

3. It was the duty and the *privilege* of the person on trial to walk directly to these doors and open one of them.

4. No matter how the affair turned out, the youth would be disposed of; and the king would take an *aesthetic* pleasure in watching the course of events. . . .

COMPOSITION: Writing an Ending to the Story

In about 250 words, write your own version of the ending, telling what happens when the young man opens the door.

You should tell how the young man, the princess, and the crowd react after the tiger or the lady comes out. Also, arrange the events in chronological order.

Prewriting

Professional writers often imagine themselves inside their stories before they write. Try closing your eyes and visualizing how the scene looks. Put yourself in the place of each character one at a time to see what happens from each perspective. Make notes as necessary.

Writing

Write your ending to the story quickly, using your notes as little as possible. Describe the events and tell the characters' thoughts and feelings in chronological order.

Evaluating and Revising

Read your draft. Check to be sure you have shown how the young man, the princess, and the crowd react. Add, cut, rewrite, reorder, or replace words, phrases, or sections as needed. You might want to ask a friend to read your composition to check for any problems you may have missed.

ABOUT THE AUTHOR

 Frank R. Stockton (1834–1902) was born in Philadelphia. He was a wood engraver and worked as a newspaper reporter and magazine editor before devoting himself to writing short stories and novels. Although his collected works fill twenty-three volumes and he achieved fame for his humorous fiction, Stockton is known today principally as the author of "The Lady, or the Tiger?" Often, people used to corner him at parties and ask him, confidentially, who *really* came out of that arena door.

■ ONCE UPON A TIME

Nadine Gordimer

How far would you go to feel safe in your home? Would you
install burglar bars? alarm systems? security fences? How great
a price would you pay?

Someone has written to ask me to contribute to an anthology of
stories for children. I reply that I don't write children's stories;
and he writes back that at a recent congress/book fair/seminar
a certain novelist said every writer ought to write at least one story for
children. I think of sending a postcard saying I don't accept that I
'ought' to write anything.

And then last night I woke up—or rather was wakened without
knowing what had roused me.

A voice in the echo-chamber of the subconscious?

A sound.

A creaking of the kind made by the weight carried by one foot after
another along a wooden floor. I listened. I felt the apertures of my ears
distend with concentration. Again: the creaking. I was waiting for it;
waiting to hear if it indicated that feet were moving from room to room,
coming up the passage—to my door. I have no burglar bars, no gun
under the pillow, but I have the same fears as people who do take these
precautions, and my windowpanes are thin as rime, could shatter like
a wineglass. A woman was murdered (how do they put it) in broad
daylight in a house two blocks away, last year, and the fierce dogs who
guarded an old widower and his collection of antique clocks were
strangled before he was knifed by a casual labourer he had dismissed
without pay.

I was staring at the door, making it out in my mind rather than seeing
it, in the dark. I lay quite still—a victim already—but the arrhythmia
of my heart was fleeing, knocking this way and that against its body-
cage. How finely tuned the senses are, just out of rest, sleep! I could
never listen intently as that in the distractions of the day; I was reading
every faintest sound, identifying and classifying its possible threat.

But I learned that I was to be neither threatened nor spared. There was
no human weight pressing on the boards, the creaking was a buckling,

278

an epicentre of stress. I was in it. The house that surrounds me while I sleep is built on undermined ground; far beneath my bed, the floor, the house's foundations, the stopes[1] and passages of gold mines have hollowed the rock, and when some face trembles, detaches and falls, three thousand feet below, the whole house shifts slightly, bringing uneasy strain to the balance and counterbalance of brick, cement, wood and glass that hold it as a structure around me. The misbeats of my heart tailed off like the last muffled flourishes on one of the wooden xylophones made by the Chopi and Tsonga[2] migrant miners who might have been down there, under me in the earth at that moment. The stope where the fall was could have been disused, dripping water from its ruptured veins; or men might now be interred there in the most profound of tombs.

I couldn't find a position in which my mind would let go of my body—release me to sleep again. So I began to tell myself a story; a bedtime story.

In a house, in a suburb, in a city, there were a man and his wife who loved each other very much and were living happily ever after. They had a little boy, and they loved him very much. They had a cat and a dog that the little boy loved very much. They had a car and a caravan trailer for holidays, and a swimming-pool which was fenced so that the little boy and his playmates would not fall in and drown. They had a housemaid who was absolutely trustworthy and an itinerant gardener who was highly recommended by the neighbours. For when they began to live happily ever after they were warned, by that wise old witch, the husband's mother, not to take on anyone off the street. They were inscribed in a medical benefit society, their pet dog was licensed, they were insured against fire, flood damage and theft, and subscribed to the local Neighbourhood Watch, which supplied them with a plaque for their gates lettered YOU HAVE BEEN WARNED over the silhouette of a would-be intruder. He was masked; it could not be said if he was black or white, and therefore proved the property owner was no racist.

It was not possible to insure the house, the swimming pool or the car against riot damage. There were riots, but these were outside the city,

---

1. **stopes:** roomlike excavations where mining takes place.
2. **Chopi and Tsonga:** African tribes.

where people of another colour were quartered. These people were not allowed into the suburb except as reliable housemaids and gardeners, so there was nothing to fear, the husband told the wife. Yet she was afraid that some day such people might come up the street and tear off the plaque YOU HAVE BEEN WARNED and open the gates and stream in . . . Nonsense, my dear, said the husband, there are police and soldiers and tear-gas and guns to keep them away. But to please her— for he loved her very much and buses were being burned, cars stoned, and schoolchildren shot by the police in those quarters out of sight and hearing of the suburb—he had electronically-controlled gates fitted. Anyone who pulled off the sign YOU HAVE BEEN WARNED and tried to open the gates would have to announce his intentions by pressing a button and speaking into a receiver relayed to the house. The little boy was fascinated by the device and used it as a walkie-talkie in cops and robbers play with his small friends.

The riots were suppressed, but there were many burglaries in the suburb and somebody's trusted housemaid was tied up and shut in a cupboard by thieves while she was in charge of her employers' house. The trusted housemaid of the man and wife and little boy was so upset by this misfortune befalling a friend left, as she herself often was, with responsibility for the possessions of the man and his wife and the little boy that she implored her employers to have burglar bars attached to the doors and windows of the house, and an alarm system installed. The wife said, She is right, let us take heed of her advice. So from every window and door in the house where they were living happily ever after they now saw the trees and sky through bars, and when the little boy's cat tried to climb in by the fanlight to keep him company in his little bed at night, as it customarily had done, it set off the alarm keening through the house.

The alarm was often answered—it seemed—by other burglar alarms, in other houses, that had been triggered by pet cats or nibbling mice. The alarms called to one another across the gardens in shrills and bleats and wails that everyone soon became accustomed to, so that the din roused the inhabitants of the suburb no more than the croak of frogs and musical grating of cicadas' legs. Under cover of the electronic harpies'[3] discourse intruders sawed the iron bars and broke into

---

3. **harpies:** foul, screeching, greedy monsters from Greek mythology that have the head and torso of a woman and the body of a bird; they steal food as well as the souls of the dead.

homes, taking away hi-fi equipment, television sets, cassette players, cameras and radios, jewellery and clothing, and sometimes were hungry enough to devour everything in the refrigerator or paused audaciously to drink the whisky in the cabinets or patio bars. Insurance companies paid no compensation for single malt, a loss made keener by the property owner's knowledge that the thieves wouldn't even have been able to appreciate what it was they were drinking.

Then the time came when many of the people who were not trusted housemaids and gardeners hung about the suburb because they were unemployed. Some importuned for a job: weeding or painting a roof; anything, *baas,* madam. But the man and his wife remembered the warning about taking on anyone off the street. Some drank liquor and fouled the street with discarded bottles. Some begged, waiting for the man or his wife to drive the car out of the electronically-operated gates. They sat about with their feet in the gutters, under the jacaranda trees that made a green tunnel of the street—for it was a beautiful suburb, spoilt only by their presence—and sometimes they fell asleep lying right before the gates in the midday sun. The wife could never see anyone go hungry. She sent the trusted housemaid out with bread and tea, but the trusted housemaid said these were loafers and *tsotsis,* who would come and tie her up and shut her in a cupboard. The husband said, She's right. Take heed of her advice. You only encourage them with your bread and tea. They are looking for their chance . . . And he brought the little boy's tricycle from the garden into the house every night, because if the house was surely secure, once locked and with the alarm set, someone might still be able to climb over the wall or the electronically-closed gates into the garden.

You are right, said the wife, then the wall should be higher. And the wise old witch, the husband's mother, paid for the extra bricks as her Christmas present to her son and his wife—the little boy got a Space Man outfit and a book of fairy tales.

But every week there were more reports of intrusion: in broad daylight and the dead of night, in the early hours of the morning, and even in the lovely summer twilight—a certain family was at dinner while the bedrooms were being ransacked upstairs. The man and his wife, talking of the latest armed robbery in the suburb, were distracted by the sight of the little boy's pet cat effortlessly arriving over the seven-foot wall, descending first with a rapid bracing of extended forepaws down on the sheer vertical surface, and then a graceful launch, landing with swishing tail within the property. The whitewashed wall was marked with the cat's comings and goings; and on the street side of the wall there were larger red-earth smudges that could have been made by the kind of broken running shoes, seen on the feet of unemployed loiterers, that had no innocent destination.

When the man and wife and little boy took the pet dog for its walk round the neighbourhood streets they no longer paused to admire this show of roses or that perfect lawn; these were hidden behind an array of different varieties of security fences, walls and devices. The man, wife, little boy and dog passed a remarkable choice: there was the low-cost option of pieces of broken glass embedded in cement along the top of walls, there were iron grilles ending in lance-points, there were attempts at reconciling the aesthetics of prison architecture with the Spanish Villa style (spikes painted pink) and with the plaster urns of neo-classical façades (twelve-inch pikes finned like zigzags of lightning and painted pure white). Some walls had a small board affixed, giving the name and telephone number of the firm responsible for the installation of the devices. While the little boy and the pet dog raced ahead, the husband and wife found themselves comparing the possible effectiveness of each style against its appearance; and after several weeks when they paused before this barricade or that without needing to speak, both came out with the conclusion that only one was worth considering. It was the ugliest but the most honest in its suggestion of the pure concentration-camp style, no frills, all evident efficacy. Placed the length of walls, it consisted of a continuous coil of stiff and shining metal serrated into jagged blades, so that there would be no way of climbing over it and no way through its tunnel without getting entangled in its fangs. There would be no way out, only a struggle getting bloodier and bloodier, a deeper and sharper hooking and tearing of flesh. The wife shuddered to look at it. You're right, said the husband, anyone would think twice . . . And they took heed of the advice on a small board fixed to the wall: Consult DRAGON'S TEETH The People For Total Security.

Next day a gang of workmen came and stretched the razor-bladed coils all round the walls of the house where the husband and wife and little boy and pet dog and cat were living happily ever after. The sunlight flashed and slashed, off the serrations, the cornice of razor thorns encircled the home, shining. The husband said, Never mind. It will weather. The wife said, You're wrong. They guarantee it's rust-proof. And she waited until the little boy had run off to play before she said, I hope the cat will take heed . . . The husband said, Don't worry, my dear, cats always look before they leap. And it was true that from that day on the cat slept in the little boy's bed and kept to the garden, never risking a try at breaching security.

One evening, the mother read the little boy to sleep with a fairy story from the book the wise old witch had given him at Christmas. Next day he pretended to be the Prince who braves the terrible thicket of thorns to enter the palace and kiss the Sleeping Beauty back to life: he dragged a ladder to the wall, the shining coiled tunnel was just wide enough for his little body to creep in, and with the first fixing of its razor-teeth in his knees and hands and head he screamed and struggled deeper into its tangle. The trusted housemaid and the itinerant gardener, whose 'day' it was, came running, the first to see and to scream with him, and the itinerant gardener tore his hands trying to get at the little boy. Then the man and his wife burst wildly into the garden and for some reason (the cat, probably) the alarm set up wailing against the screams while the bleeding mass of the little boy was hacked out of the security coil with saws, wire-cutters, choppers, and they carried it—the man, the wife, the hysterical trusted housemaid and the weeping gardener—into the house. ■

THE IMPACT OF THE STORY

The narrator does not have bars on her windows or a gun to protect her and her belongings. If you were in the narrator's place, would you do anything to protect yourself and your belongings? Why or why not?

THE FACTS OF THE STORY

On your own paper, write answers to the following items. Answers may be one word, a phrase, or several sentences.

1. When unable to sleep, what does the narrator decide to do?

2. Who are the three main characters in the narrator's story?

3. Name three things that the man and his wife do to protect their family and their home.

4. What happens when the cat climbs into the house at night?

5. What happens to the little boy at the story's end?

THE IDEAS IN THE STORY

Prepare to discuss the following questions in class.

1. As the narrator's bedtime story progresses, the people who are forbidden to enter the suburb begin to loiter in the street, some begging for food or money, some wanting to do odd jobs. The wife is moved with compassion toward these unemployed people and gives them bread and tea. However, both the housemaid and the husband argue against her compassionate gesture, saying that the people are simply would-be thieves waiting for their chance to break in. In what way might the wife's actions have made her family more or less safe from the people in the street? Besides food, what do you think these people need?

2. Nadine Gordimer's short story is about a society that is falling apart. What happens outside the suburb as well as inside it that shows us this deterioration? How are the family's behavior

and attitude affected by the society's deterioration? What may be the principal causes?

3. At times, the language of the narrator's story is sarcastic, ironical, and biting, as when she says of the silhouetted figure on the warning plaque: ". . . it could not be said if he was black or white, and therefore proved the property owner was no racist." What is ironic about this statement?

THE ART OF THE STORYTELLER

Satire
The bedtime story the narrator tells herself in "Once Upon a Time" is an example of bitter, forceful satire. The narrator tells the story in the form of a children's fairy tale as a means of criticizing and ridiculing the ignorance and wrongdoings of people and society. Like those in many fairy tales, the characters in this story have no names, and the setting is not identified—we almost feel that the events of the story could happen anywhere to anyone at any time. However, a typical fairy tale is optimistic; the good characters are rewarded, while the evil characters are severely punished. How does the narrator's bedtime story differ from a typical fairy tale in this respect?

What kind of people does the narrator mock in her bedtime story? What kind of society does she satirize?

Theme
Theme is the insight about human life that is revealed in a literary work. To determine the theme of a story, a reader must examine the story's main idea or ideas. What main ideas appear in the first part of "Once Upon a Time" as well as in the bedtime story the narrator tells herself?

In the story the man and his wife spend a good deal of time worrying about protecting themselves, their family, and their home from the people who are not allowed into the suburb. As their fear increases, their seemingly ideal life becomes more restricted. Every new security system they have installed makes their home more nearly resemble a prison. On their windows and doors are bars, their gates are electronically controlled, and on the high wall surrounding their home is a "concentration-camp style" barrier of coiled, razor-sharp metal. Seen in contrast to the narrator's complete lack of security measures in her home, the security precautions taken by the man and his wife seem extreme and prove to be not only of little help but also a grave danger to the family. What do the man and his wife lose because of their extreme attempts to protect themselves? Who is responsible for this loss and why?

It is important to remember that the society in which the family "lives happily ever after" is based on the oppression of black Africans. The man and his wife help maintain this injustice by their fearful attitudes and by their reliance on the police and soldiers to keep these supposedly undesirable people out of the suburb. As you may recall, the wife fears these people before they ever become an actual threat; this fear reveals her acceptance of and agreement with this unjust system. Thus, the freedom the family enjoys at the beginning of the story is at the expense of the freedom of those who are oppressed. Eventually, however, the man and his wife, in their efforts to maintain the status quo, virtually lose their freedom. How would you state the theme of the story? How would this theme apply to other places and people?

THE VOCABULARY IN THE STORY

"Once Upon a Time" contains some words with which you may not be familiar. However, the context, the words, and sentences around a word, can often give you clues to the word's meaning. Read the following passage from "Once Upon a Time":

> . . . intruders sometimes were hungry enough to *devour*
> everything in the refrigerator . . . .

If you are not familiar with the word *devour,* you can figure out its meaning from the context. The words *hungry enough* and *everything in the refrigerator* are clues that *devour* means "to eat hungrily."

Read each of the following passages from "Once Upon a Time." Underline any context clue that you think gives a hint about the meaning of the word in italics. Then, without looking in the dictionary, write a short definition of the italicized word.

1. I have no burglar bars, no gun under the pillow, but I have the same fears as people who do take these *precautions* . . .

2. . . . men might now be *interred* there in the most profound of tombs.

3. The alarms called to one another across the gardens in shrills and bleats and wails that everyone soon became accustomed to, so that the *din* roused the inhabitants . . . no more than the croak of frogs . . . .

4. Placed the length of walls, it consisted of a continuous coil of stiff and shining metal *serrated* into jagged blades, so that there would be no way of climbing over it . . . without getting entangled in its fangs.

COMPOSITION: Writing a Persuasive Letter

Write a persuasive letter (about 200 words) to an elected representative, such as your councilperson, mayor, state legislator, or congressperson, in which you present an idea about an issue or a solution to a problem that directly affects you or your community. The issue may be anything about which you feel strongly such as repairing a neighborhood sidewalk or designating a wooded lot as a nature preserve. The aim of your letter is to persuade the elected representative to act upon your proposal.

Prewriting

Before you begin writing, you will need to decide what issue you will write about. Remember to choose an issue that directly affects you or your community. Then write a sentence that clearly states the issue you would like to see addressed. Below this statement, write several short sentences that describe the problem to which you are proposing a solution. (For example, a broken, dangerous sidewalk is a problem.) Then write a sentence that clearly states your solution to the problem. (For instance, the sidewalk should be repaired.) Below this statement, write several short sentences that show how this solution could be accomplished. You might address concerns such as funding and possible objections. Make an outline based on your prewriting sentence.

Writing

As you write the letter, use the organization of your outline as a guide. Feel free, however, to include in the letter details and examples that do not appear in your outline. For example, you may want to include a description of a true-life incident that vividly illustrates the problem.

Evaluating and Revising

Read your draft. Have you stated the issue as well as the resolution clearly? Are your ideas well organized? Cut, rearrange, rewrite, or add words, phrases, or sections as needed. Proofread the final copy of your letter closely for errors in spelling or punctuation.

ABOUT THE AUTHOR

 Born in Springs, South Africa, Nadine Gordimer (1923–) is a writer whose major works explore the impact of the South African apartheid system on whites as well as on blacks. (This government-enforced segregation of the races ended in the early 1990's.) She has written numerous novels, including *A World of Strangers, A Guest of Honour,* and *July's People,* as well as short stories, collections of which include *The Soft Voice of the Serpent, and Other Stories; Friday's Footprint, and Other Stories; Some Monday for Sure;* and *Something Out There.* Gordimer has also been a visiting professor for the Ford Foundation at the Institute of Contemporary Arts in Washington, D.C.; a lecturer at the University of Michigan, Ann Arbor; and a writer and lecturer at Princeton, Harvard, Columbia, and Tulane universities.

■THE SECRET LIFE OF WALTER MITTY

James Thurber

Walter Mitty's secret life is lived in his daydreams. When we laugh at Walter Mitty as he escapes into his secret life, we are also laughing at ourselves, because all of us have our daydreams and our secret lives. All of us, that is, except Mrs. Mitty—an amazingly practical person, as you will see.

"**W**e're going through!" The Commander's voice was like thin ice breaking. He wore his full-dress uniform, with the heavily braided white cap pulled down rakishly over one cold gray eye. "We can't make it, sir. It's spoiling for a hurricane, if you ask me." "I'm not asking you, Lieutenant Berg," said the Commander. "Throw on the power lights! Rev her up to 8,500! We're going through!" The pounding of the cylinders increased: ta-pocketa-pocketa-pocketa-*pocketa-pocketa*. The Commander stared at the ice forming on the pilot window. He walked over and twisted a row of complicated dials. "Switch on No. 8 auxiliary!" he shouted. "Switch on No. 8 auxiliary!" repeated Lieutenant Berg. "Full strength in No. 3 turret!" shouted the Commander. "Full strength in No. 3 turret!" The crew, bending to their various tasks in the huge, hurtling eight-engined Navy hydroplane, looked at each other and grinned. "The Old Man'll get us through," they said to one another. "The Old Man ain't afraid of Hell!" . . .

"Not so fast! You're driving too fast!" said Mrs. Mitty. "What are you driving so fast for?"

"Hmm?" said Walter Mitty. He looked at his wife, in the seat beside him, with shocked astonishment. She seemed grossly unfamiliar, like a strange woman who had yelled at him in a crowd. "You were up to fifty-five," she said, "You know I don't like to go more than forty. You were up to fifty-five." Walter Mitty drove on toward Waterbury in silence, the roaring of the SN202 through the worst storm in twenty years of Navy flying fading in the remote, intimate airways of his mind. "You're tensed up again," said Mrs. Mitty. "It's one of your days. I wish you'd let Dr. Renshaw look you over."

Walter Mitty stopped the car in front of the building where his wife went to have her hair done. "Remember to get those overshoes while I'm having my hair done," she said. "I don't need overshoes," said Mitty. She put her mirror back into her bag. "We've been all through that," she said, getting out of the car. "You're not a young man any longer." He raced the engine a little. "Why don't you wear your gloves? Have you lost your gloves?" Walter Mitty reached in a pocket and brought out the gloves. He put them on, but after she had turned and gone into the building and he had driven on to a red light, he took them off again. "Pick it up, brother!" snapped a cop as the light changed, and Mitty hastily pulled on his gloves and lurched ahead. He drove around the streets aimlessly for a time, and then he drove past the hospital on his way to the parking lot.

. . . "It's the millionaire banker, Wellington McMillan," said the pretty nurse. "Yes?" said Walter Mitty, removing his gloves slowly. "Who has the case?" "Dr. Renshaw and Dr. Benbow, but there are two specialists here, Dr. Remington from New York and Mr. Pritchard-Mitford from London. He flew over." A door opened down a long, cool corridor and Dr. Renshaw came out. He looked distraught and haggard. "Hello, Mitty," he said. "We're having the devil's own time with McMillan, the millionaire banker and close personal friend of Roosevelt. Obstreosis[1] of the ductal tract. Tertiary. Wish you'd take a look at him." "Glad to," said Mitty.

In the operating room there were whispered introductions: "Dr. Remington, Dr. Mitty. Mr. Pritchard-Mitford, Dr. Mitty." "I've read your book on streptothricosis," said Pritchard-Mitford, shaking hands. "A brilliant performance, sir." "Thank you," said Walter Mitty. "Didn't know you were in the States, Mitty," grumbled Remington. "Coals to Newcastle,[2] bringing Mitford and me up here for a tertiary." "You are very kind," said Mitty. A huge, complicated machine, connected to the operating table, with many tubes and wires, began at this moment to go pocketa-pocketa-pocketa. "The new anesthetizer is giving way!" shouted an intern. "There is no one in the East who knows how to fix

---

1. **obstreosis:** this and some of the other seemingly medical terms in this scene are non-sense words.
2. **Coals to Newcastle:** Newcastle, a city in northern England, is a port in the center of an important coal-mining region. Thus, "taking coals to Newcastle" means bringing in something or someone unnecessarily.

it!" "Quiet, man!" said Mitty, in a low, cool voice. He sprang to the machine, which was now going pocketa-pocketa-queep-pocketa-queep. He began fingering delicately a row of glistening dials. "Give me a fountain pen!" he snapped. Someone handed him a fountain pen. He pulled a faulty piston out of the machine and inserted the pen in its place. "That will hold for ten minutes," he said. "Get on with the operation." A nurse hurried over and whispered to Renshaw, and Mitty saw the man turn pale. "Coreopsis has set in," said Renshaw nervously. "If you would take over, Mitty?" Mitty looked at him and at the craven figure of Benbow, who drank, and at the grave, uncertain faces of the two great specialists. "If you wish," he said. They slipped a white gown on him; he adjusted a mask and drew on thin gloves; nurses handed him shining . . .

"Back it up, Mac! Look out for that Buick!" Walter Mitty jammed on the brakes. "Wrong lane, Mac," said the parking-lot attendant, looking at Mitty closely. "Gee. Yeh," muttered Mitty. He began cautiously to back out of the lane marked "Exit Only." "Leave her sit there," said the attendant. "I'll put her away." Mitty got out of the car. "Hey, better leave the key." "Oh," said Mitty, handing the man the ignition key. The attendant vaulted into the car, backed it up with insolent skill, and put it where it belonged.

They're so damn cocky, thought Walter Mitty, walking along Main Street; they think they know everything. Once he had tried to take his chains off, outside New Milford, and he had got them wound around the axles. A man had had to come out in a wrecking car and unwind them, a young, grinning garageman. Since then Mrs. Mitty always made him drive to a garage to have the chains taken off. The next time, he thought, I'll wear my right arm in a sling; they won't grin at me then. I'll have my right arm in a sling and they'll see I couldn't possibly take the chains off myself. He kicked at the slush on the sidewalk. "Overshoes," he said to himself, and he began looking for a shoe store.

When he came out into the street again, with the overshoes in a box under his arm, Walter Mitty began to wonder what the other thing was his wife had told him to get. She had told him, twice, before they set out from their house for Waterbury. In a way he hated these weekly trips to town—he was always getting something wrong. Kleenex, he thought, Squibb's, razor blades? No. Toothpaste, toothbrush, bicarbonate, carborundum, initiative and referendum?[3] He gave it up. But she would remember it. "Where's the what's-its-name?" she would ask. "Don't tell me you forgot the what's-its-name." A newsboy went by shouting something about the Waterbury trial.

. . . "Perhaps this will refresh your memory." The District Attorney suddenly thrust a heavy automatic at the quiet figure on the witness stand. "Have you ever seen this before?" Walter Mitty took the gun and examined it expertly. "This is my Webley-Vickers 50.80,"[4] he said calmly. An excited buzz ran around the courtroom. The Judge rapped for order. "You are a crack shot with any sort of firearms, I believe?" said the District Attorney, insinuatingly. "Objection!" shouted Mitty's attorney. "We have shown that the defendant could not have fired the shot. We have shown that he wore his right arm in a sling on the night of the fourteenth of July." Walter Mitty raised his hand briefly and the bickering attorneys were stilled. "With any known make of gun," he said evenly, "I could have killed Gregory Fitzhurst at three hundred feet *with my left hand.*" Pandemonium broke loose in the courtroom. A woman's scream rose above the bedlam and suddenly a lovely, dark-haired girl was in Walter Mitty's arms. The District Attorney struck at her savagely. Without rising from his chair, Mitty let the man have it on the point of the chin. "You miserable cur!" . . .

"Puppy biscuit," said Walter Mitty. He stopped walking and the buildings of Waterbury rose up out of the misty courtroom and surrounded him again. A woman who was passing laughed. "He said 'Puppy biscuit,'" she said to her companion. "That man said 'Puppy biscuit' to himself." Walter Mitty hurried on. He went into an A & P,[5] not the first one he came to but a smaller one farther up the street. "I want some biscuit for small, young dogs," he said to the clerk. "Any special brand, sir?" The greatest pistol shot in the world thought a moment. "It says 'Puppies Bark for It' on the box," said Walter Mitty.

His wife would be through at the hairdresser's in fifteen minutes, Mitty saw in looking at his watch, unless they had trouble drying it; some-times they had trouble drying it. She didn't like to get to the hotel first;

---

3. **carborundum, initiative and referendum:** Carborundum is a hard, abrasive material. Initiative refers to a citizen's right to introduce new legislation. Referendum refers to a citizen's right to vote on laws. The association is of sound only.
4. **Webley-Vickers 50.80:** an incredibly huge weapon.
5. **A & P:** a grocery store chain.

she would want him to be there waiting for her as usual. He found a big leather chair in the lobby, facing a window, and he put the overshoes and the puppy biscuit on the floor beside it. He picked up an old copy of *Liberty* and sank down into the chair. "Can Germany Conquer the World Through the Air?" Walter Mitty looked at the pictures of bombing planes and of ruined streets.

. . . "The cannonading has got the wind up in young Raleigh, sir," said the sergeant. Captain Mitty looked up at him through tousled hair. "Get him to bed," he said wearily. "With the others. I'll fly alone." "But you can't, sir," said the sergeant anxiously. "It takes two men to handle that bomber and the Archies[6] are pounding hell out of the air. Von Richtman's circus is between here and Saulier." "Somebody's got to get that ammunition dump," said Mitty. "I'm going over. Spot of brandy?" He poured a drink for the sergeant and one for himself. War thundered and whined around the dugout and battered at the door. There was a rending of wood and splinters flew through the room. "A bit of a near thing," said Captain Mitty carelessly. "The box barrage is closing in," said the sergeant. "We only live once, Sergeant," said Mitty, with his faint, fleeting smile. "Or do we?" He poured another brandy and tossed it off. "I never see a man could hold his brandy like you, sir," said the sergeant. "Begging your pardon, sir." Captain Mitty stood up and strapped on his huge Webley-Vickers automatic. "It's forty kilometers through hell, sir," said the sergeant. Mitty finished one last brandy. "After all," he said softly, "what isn't?" The pounding of the cannon increased; there was the rat-tat-tatting of machine guns, and from somewhere came the menacing pocketa-pocketa-pocketa of the new flame-throwers. Walter Mitty walked to the door of the dugout humming "Auprès de Ma Blonde." He turned and waved to the sergeant. "Cheerio!" he said. . . .

Something struck his shoulder. "I've been looking all over this hotel for you," said Mrs. Mitty. "Why do you have to hide in this old chair? How did you expect me to find you?" "Things close in," said Walter Mitty vaguely. "What?" Mrs. Mitty said. "Did you get the what's-its-name? The puppy biscuit? What's in that box?" "Overshoes," said Mitty. "Couldn't you have put them on in the store?" "I was thinking," said Walter Mitty. "Does it ever occur to you that I am sometimes thinking?" She looked at him. "I'm going to take your temperature when I get you home," she said.

---

6. **Archies:** Allied troops' name for the antiaircraft guns of the enemy.

They went out through the revolving doors that made a faintly derisive whistling sound when you pushed them. It was two blocks to the
parking lot. At the drugstore on the corner she said, "Wait here for me.
I forgot something. I won't be a minute." She was more than a minute.
Walter Mitty lighted a cigarette. It began to rain, rain with sleet in it.
He stood up against the wall of the drugstore, smoking. . . . He put his
shoulders back and his heels together. "To hell with the handkerchief,"
said Walter Mitty scornfully. He took one last drag on his cigarette and
snapped it away. Then, with that faint, fleeting smile playing about his
lips, he faced the firing squad; erect and motionless, proud and dis-
dainful, Walter Mitty the Undefeated, inscrutable[7] to the last. ∎

---

7. **inscrutable:** unknowable, mysterious.

THE IMPACT OF THE STORY

This story shows us how silly daydreaming can be. Do you think that we all daydream? Do *you* daydream? If so, think about what your daydreams are like. Are your daydreams like Walter Mitty's, or are they more realistic, such as plans or goals for your future?

THE FACTS OF THE STORY

On your own paper, write answers to the following items. Answers may be one word, a phrase, or several sentences.

1. List the five heroic roles Walter Mitty imagines himself playing.

2. Mrs. Mitty treats Walter as though he were a little boy. Give two examples of this.

3. Give two examples of how Walter's behavior, in fact, is like that of a little boy.

4. What does Mrs. Mitty believe is the real cause of Walter's "spells"?

5. How does the Walter Mitty of the daydreams differ from the real Walter Mitty?

THE IDEAS IN THE STORY

Prepare to discuss the following questions in class.

1. Walter's actions in the real world are affected by his thoughts in his fantasy worlds. How could this spillover be dangerous? Do you think daydreams in general are healthy, or do they sometimes prevent us from acting responsibly and effectively in the real world?

2. Walter's daydreams involve a great deal of self-aggrandizement—making himself seem better and smarter in every way. What does this tell us about his character? Do you think Walter would be happier if he tried to *do* something exciting in his life rather than just *dreaming* about excitement?

THE ART OF THE STORYTELLER

Theme

You may recall that the main idea or insight about life that is expressed in a short story is called its **theme.** The theme of "The Secret Life of Walter Mitty" has something to do with daydreams and reality. What kind of events in real life trigger Mitty's fantasies? What unheroic situations snap Mitty out of his daydreams? What do you think the story tells us about *why* we might daydream?

In one sentence, state the theme of Thurber's story. Do not begin your sentence with "The theme of the story is . . ." or "I think the theme is . . ." Instead, state the main idea directly: "Daydreaming is . . ." or "Daydreams can be . . ."

Satire

Thurber makes fun of Walter Mitty and his fantasies. Literature that makes fun of human foolishness or vice is called **satire.** Thurber actually satirizes all of us when he satirizes Walter Mitty. When Thurber makes us realize how our own daydreams contrast with our own ordinary lives, he makes us laugh at ourselves.

What kind of behavior is Thurber satirizing in the characters of the meek Walter Mitty and the formidable Mrs. Mitty?

Stock Characters

You may have noticed that the characters in Walter Mitty's daydreams resemble many found on television and in movies. Like those in soap operas and other melodramas, Mitty's imagined characters are immediately recognizable and predictable. We recognize the clipped speech of the doctors going about their serious tasks. We recognize the character of Dr. Mitty, the great surgeon, arriving just in time to "take over," facing the emergency calmly and saving a life ingeniously. The forceful commander of the Navy plane ("The Old Man'll get us through") and the very British captain in the Air Force are also recognizable types. Characters like these that we encounter over and over again in our reading and viewing are called **stereotypes** or **stock characters**—as though they are stored in large quantities in a stockroom and brought out whenever a writer needs them.

Some other common stock characters are the tough detective who always outsmarts the crooks; the ruthless gangster; the temperamental movie star; the tough guy or gal with a heart of gold. You can probably add to the list.

Stock characters often appear in popular fiction and plays. Writers of quality literature, however, who try to make their characters more complex, usually avoid stock characters—unless, like Thurber, they want to satirize them.

Walter Mitty himself is a stock character—the little guy who is bossed by his wife and by just about everyone else. Are there any Walter Mittys in TV shows or movies you've seen recently? Are there any Mrs. Mittys?

THE VOCABULARY IN THE STORY

Antonyms are words with opposite or nearly opposite meanings. Some examples of antonyms are *easy/hard, light/dark,* and *night/day.* Each of the following words appears in "The Secret Life of Walter Mitty." For each word, write at least one antonym. Then write an original sentence using the antonym.

1. aimlessly   3. insolent   5. inscrutable
2. distraught   4. derisive

COMPOSITION: Describing a Stock Character

We often think of people from real life as certain types. If placed in a story, they would be stock characters. A few examples are the hand-grabbing politician, the star athlete, the brain, the gossip, the practical joker, the teacher's pet.

Write a description or sketch (approximately 300 words) of a stock character. You may do this with or without having any real person in mind. You may simply create a character to show the traits of a certain recognizable type. Use descriptive details, and include at least one anecdote to illustrate the person's main characteristic. You might follow your character through a day or an hour, telling what he or she does and says. Use some dialogue if you can.

Prewriting
Write down characteristics, quirks, or features of your character's behavior that come to mind. Then list facial expressions, gestures, and clothing; describe them briefly. Take a few minutes to think about a situation or event in which this character might appear and how the character would behave. Then decide which situation you want to tell about for your anecdote, and make notes about the most important details. Finally, decide whether you want to begin your sketch with the anecdote or with a description of the character.

Writing
You might find it helpful to close your eyes and visualize the character just before you write. Then write your sketch as quickly as possible.

Evaluating and Revising
Read your draft. Have you described a recognizable type? Have you described your character's appearance and actions? Have you told an anecdote? Add, cut, reorder, or replace words, phrases, or sections as needed.

ABOUT THE AUTHOR

 James Thurber (1894–1961) was born in Columbus, Ohio, where he attended the public schools and Ohio State University. He began his writing career as a newspaper reporter in Columbus and then went to Paris. In New York he started his lifelong association with *The New Yorker* magazine, to which he regularly contributed humorous stories and cartoons. Thurber was the foremost American humorist of his time. Although his writings are funny, most of them, like "The Secret Life of Walter Mitty," have a serious comment to make about contemporary life and about the relationships between men and women. "The Secret Life of Walter Mitty" was made into a movie starring Danny Kaye.

■ HARRISON BERGERON

Kurt Vonnegut

Imagine a society from which all competition has been removed. In this satirical fantasy, the agents of the United States Handicapper General have forced everyone to be equal in every way by assigning handicaps to persons who have above-average mental or physical abilities. Harrison Bergeron is a boy who dares to rebel against this handicap system—and, for a few beautiful moments, shows everyone what excellence is.

The year was 2081, and everybody was finally equal. They weren't only equal before God and the law. They were equal every which way. Nobody was smarter than anybody else. Nobody was better-looking than anybody else. Nobody was stronger or quicker than anybody else. All this equality was due to the 211th, 212th, and 213th Amendments to the Constitution, and to the unceasing vigilance of agents of the United States Handicapper General.

Some things about living still weren't quite right, though. April, for instance, still drove people crazy by not being springtime. And it was in that clammy month that the H-G men took George and Hazel Bergeron's fourteen-year-old son, Harrison, away.

It was tragic, all right, but George and Hazel couldn't think about it very hard. Hazel had a perfectly average intelligence, which meant she couldn't think about anything except in short bursts. And George, while his intelligence was way above normal, had a little mental handicap radio in his ear. He was required by law to wear it at all times. It was tuned to a government transmitter. Every twenty seconds or so, the transmitter would send out some sharp noise to keep people like George from taking unfair advantage of their brains.

George and Hazel were watching television. There were tears on Hazel's cheeks, but she'd forgotten for the moment what they were about.

On the television screen were ballerinas.

A buzzer sounded in George's head. His thoughts fled in panic, like bandits from a burglar alarm.

"That was a real pretty dance, that dance they just did," said Hazel.

"Huh?" said George.

"That dance—it was nice," said Hazel.

"Yup," said George. He tried to think a little about the ballerinas. They weren't really very good—no better than anybody else would have been, anyway. They were burdened with sash-weights and bags of birdshot, and their faces were masked, so that no one, seeing a free and graceful gesture or a pretty face, would feel like something the cat drug in. George was toying with the vague notion that maybe dancers shouldn't be handicapped. But he didn't get very far with it before another noise in his ear radio scattered his thoughts.

George winced. So did two out of the eight ballerinas.

Hazel saw him wince. Having no mental handicap herself, she had to ask George what the latest sound had been.

"Sounded like somebody hitting a milk bottle with a ball-peen hammer," said George.

"I'd think it would be real interesting, hearing all the different sounds," said Hazel, a little envious. "All the things they think up."

"Um," said George.

"Only, if I was Handicapper General, you know what I would do?" said Hazel. Hazel, as a matter of fact, bore a strong resemblance to the Handicapper General, a woman named Diana Moon Glampers. "If I was Diana Moon Glampers," said Hazel, "I'd have chimes on Sunday—just chimes. Kind of in honor of religion."

"I could think, if it was just chimes," said George.

"Well—maybe make 'em real loud," said Hazel. "I think I'd make a good Handicapper General."

"Good as anybody else," said George.

"Who knows better'n I do what normal is?" said Hazel.

"Right," said George. He began to think glimmeringly about his abnormal son who was now in jail, about Harrison, but a twenty-one-gun salute in his head stopped that.

"Boy!" said Hazel, "that was a doozy, wasn't it?"

It was such a doozy that George was white and trembling, and tears stood on the rims of his red eyes. Two of the eight ballerinas had collapsed to the studio floor, were holding their temples.

"All of a sudden you look so tired," said Hazel. "Why don't you stretch out on the sofa, so's you can rest your handicap bag on the pillows, honeybunch." She was referring to the forty-seven pounds of birdshot in a canvas bag which was padlocked around George's neck. "Go on and rest the bag for a little while," she said. "I don't care if you're not equal to me for a while."

George weighed the bag with his hands. "I don't mind it," he said. "I don't notice it any more. It's just a part of me."

"You been so tired lately—kind of wore out," said Hazel. "If there was just some way we could make a little hole in the bottom of the bag, and just take out a few of them lead balls. Just a few."

"Two years in prison and two thousand dollars fine for every ball I took out," said George. "I don't call that a bargain."

"If you could just take a few out when you come home from work," said Hazel. "I mean—you don't compete with anybody around here. You just set around."

"If I tried to get away with it," said George, "then other people'd get away with it—and pretty soon we'd be right back to the dark ages again, with everybody competing against everybody else. You wouldn't like that, would you?"

"I'd hate it," said Hazel.

"There you are," said George. "The minute people start cheating on laws, what do you think happens to society?"

If Hazel hadn't been able to come up with an answer to this question, George couldn't have supplied one. A siren was going off in his head.

"Reckon it'd fall all apart," said Hazel.

"What would?" said George blankly.

"Society," said Hazel uncertainly. "Wasn't that what you just said?"

"Who knows?" said George.

The television program was suddenly interrupted for a news bulletin. It wasn't clear at first as to what the bulletin was about, since the announcer, like all announcers, had a serious speech impediment. For about half a minute, and in a state of high excitement, the announcer tried to say, "Ladies and gentlemen—"

He finally gave up, handed the bulletin to a ballerina to read.

"That's all right—" Hazel said of the announcer, "he tried. That's the big thing. He tried to do the best he could with what God gave him. He should get a nice raise for trying so hard."

"Ladies and gentlemen—" said the ballerina, reading the bulletin. She must have been extraordinarily beautiful, because the mask she wore was hideous. And it was easy to see that she was the strongest and most graceful of all the dancers, for her handicap bags were as big as those worn by two-hundred-pound men.

And she had to apologize at once for her voice, which was a very unfair voice for a woman to use. Her voice was a warm, luminous, timeless melody. "Excuse me—" she said, and she began again, making her voice absolutely uncompetitive.

"Harrison Bergeron, age fourteen," she said in a grackle squawk, "has just escaped from jail, where he was held on suspicion of plotting to overthrow the government. He is a genius and an athlete, is under-handicapped, and should be regarded as extremely dangerous."

A police photograph of Harrison Bergeron was flashed on the screen—upside down, then sideways, upside down again, then right side up. The picture showed the full length of Harrison against a background calibrated in feet and inches. He was exactly seven feet tall.

The rest of Harrison's appearance was Halloween and hardware. Nobody had ever borne heavier handicaps. He had outgrown hindrances faster than the H-G men could think them up. Instead of a little ear radio for a mental handicap, he wore a tremendous pair of earphones, and spectacles with thick wavy lenses. The spectacles were intended to make him not only half blind, but to give him whanging headaches besides.

Scrap metal was hung all over him. Ordinarily, there was a certain symmetry, a military neatness to the handicaps issued to strong people, but Harrison looked like a walking junkyard. In the race of life, Harrison carried three hundred pounds.

And to offset his good looks, the H-G men required that he wear at all times a red rubber ball for a nose, keep his eyebrows shaved off, and cover his even white teeth with black caps at snaggle-tooth random.

"If you see this boy," said the ballerina, "do not—I repeat, do not—try to reason with him."

There was the shriek of a door being torn from its hinges.

Screams and barking cries of consternation came from the television set. The photograph of Harrison Bergeron on the screen jumped again and again, as though dancing to the tune of an earthquake.

George Bergeron correctly identified the earthquake, and well he might have—for many was the time his own home had danced to the same crashing tune. "My god—" said George, "that must be Harrison!"

The realization was blasted from his mind instantly by the sound of an automobile collision in his head.

When George could open his eyes again, the photograph of Harrison was gone. A living, breathing Harrison filled the screen.

Clanking, clownish, and huge, Harrison stood in the center of the studio. The knob of the uprooted studio door was still in his hand. Ballerinas, technicians, musicians, and announcers cowered on their knees before him, expecting to die.

"I am the Emperor!" cried Harrison. "Do you hear? I am the Emperor! Everybody must do what I say at once!" He stamped his foot and the studio shook.

"Even as I stand here—" he bellowed, "crippled, hobbled, sickened— I am a greater ruler than any man who ever lived! Now watch me become what I *can* become!"

Harrison tore the straps of his handicap harness like wet tissue paper, tore straps guaranteed to support five thousand pounds.

Harrison's scrap-iron handicaps crashed to the floor.

Harrison thrust his thumbs under the bar of the padlock that secured his head harness. The bar snapped like celery. Harrison smashed his headphones and spectacles against the wall.

He flung away his rubber-ball nose, revealed a man that would have awed Thor, the god of thunder.

"I shall now select my Empress!" he said, looking down on the cowering people. "Let the first woman who dares rise to her feet claim her mate and her throne!"

A moment passed, and then a ballerina arose, swaying like a willow.

Harrison plucked the mental handicap from her ear, snapped off her physical handicaps with marvelous delicacy. Last of all, he removed her mask.

She was blindingly beautiful.

"Now—" said Harrison, taking her hand, "shall we show the people the meaning of the word *dance*? Music!" he commanded.

The musicians scrambled back into their chairs, and Harrison stripped them of their handicaps, too. "Play your best," he told them, "and I'll make you barons and dukes and earls."

The music began. It was normal at first—cheap, silly, false. But Harrison snatched two musicians from their chairs, waved them like batons as he sang the music as he wanted it played. He slammed them back into their chairs.

The music began again and was much improved.

Harrison and his Empress merely listened to the music for a while— listened gravely, as though synchronizing their heartbeats with it.

They shifted their weights to their toes.

Harrison placed his big hands on the girl's tiny waist, letting her sense the weightlessness that would soon be hers.

And then, in an explosion of joy and grace, into the air they sprang!

Not only were the laws of the land abandoned, but the law of gravity and the laws of motion as well.

They reeled, whirled, swiveled, flounced, capered, gamboled, and spun.

They leaped like deer on the moon.

The studio ceiling was thirty feet high, but each leap brought the dancers nearer to it.

It became their obvious intention to kiss the ceiling.

They kissed it.

And then, neutralizing gravity with love and pure will, they remained suspended in air inches below the ceiling, and they kissed each other for a long, long time.

It was then that Diana Moon Glampers, the Handicapper General, came into the studio with a double-barreled ten-gauge shotgun. She fired twice, and the Emperor and the Empress were dead before they hit the floor.

Diana Moon Glampers loaded the gun again. She aimed it at the musicians and told them they had ten seconds to get their handicaps back on.

It was then that the Bergerons' television tube burned out.

Hazel turned to comment about the blackout to George. But George had gone out into the kitchen for a can of beer.

George came back in with the beer, paused while a handicap signal shook him up. And then he sat down again. "You been crying?" he said to Hazel.

"Yup," she said.

"What about?" he said.

"I forget," she said. "Something real sad on television."

"What was it?" he said.

"It's all kind of mixed-up in my mind," said Hazel.

"Forget sad things," said George.

"I always do," said Hazel.

"That's my girl," said George. He winced. There was the sound of a riveting gun in his head.

"Gee—I could tell that one was a doozy," said Hazel.

"You can say that again," said George.

"Gee—" said Hazel, "I could tell that one was a doozy." ■

THE IMPACT OF THE STORY

In our society, people tend to value the idea of individuality as well as the freedom to be different. Yet, in their day-to-day experiences, people are often afraid of anyone who is very different from themselves.

How can you explain this apparent contradiction? Is it possible for people to be different from one another, yet still the same?

THE FACTS OF THE STORY

On your own paper, write short answers to the following items. Answers may be one word, a phrase, or several sentences.

1. What kind of handicap has been imposed on people with better-than-average mental capacities?

2. What kind of handicap has been imposed on people with better-than-average physical ability?

3. What does George carry around his neck?

4. Why has Harrison Bergeron been put in jail?

5. What penalty do Harrison and his ballerina partner pay for refusing to wear their handicaps?

THE IDEAS IN THE STORY

Prepare to discuss the following questions in class.

1. Hazel says about the radio announcer who fails in his attempt to read the news

   "That's all right. . . . That's the big thing. He tried to do the best he could with what God gave him. He should get a nice raise for trying so hard."

Do you think people should be rewarded for effort as well as for accomplishment? Explain why or why not.

2. Do you think that Harrison, by his heroic defiance of the system, may have accomplished something good? Explain.

THE ART OF THE STORYTELLER

Satire

Both "The Lady, or the Tiger?" and "The Secret Life of Walter Mitty" are somewhat gentle satires. This kind of satire makes us smile and laugh at peoples' weaknesses or wrongdoings. "Harrison Bergeron" is also a satire; however, you have probably noticed that it contains little humor, and its tone is harsh and biting. Sometimes readers have difficulty recognizing that this type of writing *is* satire because of the serious, straightforward way in which the author presents the subject.

What belief does Vonnegut ridicule, or satirize, in this story? What kind of society is he mocking?

Theme

If you take a close look at this story's plot and characters, you will realize that very little happens and that we know very little about Hazel, George, and Harrison as people. Both the plot and characterization are subordinate to the ***theme***.

By describing an exaggerated situation, Vonnegut criticizes people who become fanatical in their efforts to create an equal society. The people of 2081 are obsessed with eliminating the "unfair advantage" that some people have because of their superior physical abilities or intelligence. Instead of creating a free society where individuals can use their gifts, the people of 2081 have accepted restriction as a way of life—all in the name of "equality."

Do you think there is a difference between believing people are equal under the law and believing that everyone should be equal in every way? What do you think would be the most damaging result of removing all individual talent and skill from society?

THE VOCABULARY IN THE STORY

Like people, words have histories. They come to be, grow, and change. The origin and history of a word is called its *etymology*. For instance, the etymology of the word *peen* suggests that this word is most likely derived from a Norwegian word meaning, "to beat out." *Peen* refers to a part of a certain type of hammer. This hammer, the ball-peen hammer, has a rounded, or ball-shaped surface on one side that may be used to beat out or round metal. Dictionaries often give a shortened version of a word's etymology along with its definition.

Using a dictionary, look up the etymology of each of the following words. Then write a short explanation of the etymology of the word and a short definition of the way the word is used in "Harrison Bergeron."

1. handicap   3. bandit   5. hideous
2. doozy   4. luminous

COMPOSITION: Writing a Description

In "Harrison Bergeron," Vonnegut gives us a glimpse of a society in which competition no longer exists.

In about 250 words, describe what you think our society might be like if all competition were eliminated. You may use ideas mentioned in the class discussion of this story. Use vivid adjectives to describe the way the people might look and action verbs to describe what they might do.

Prewriting

List situations and events that would be different or would no longer exist without competition such as buying the latest styles in clothes or playing competitive sports. Imagine how people would interact. How would they talk? Make brief notes.

Writing

You might begin your description with a single scene; then go on to describe other places, people, and events. Do not worry about punctuation or spelling. You can correct any errors later.

Evaluating and Revising.

Read your draft, making sure you have used vivid adjectives and action verbs. Compare your prewriting lists to your draft. Have you included everything that you intended? Add, cut, reorder, or replace words, phrases, or sections as needed.

ABOUT THE AUTHOR

 Kurt Vonnegut (1922–   ) was born in Indian-
apolis, Indiana. He attended Cornell University
and the University of Chicago. Since 1950 he
has pursued a literary career as a writer of short
stories, novels, and plays. He has also been a
teacher at the Hopefield School, in Sandwich,
Massachusetts. Vonnegut's writing is often satirical and humorous, sometimes bordering on
fantasy, but always serious in purpose. He says he is concerned
about the dehumanization of the individual in a society dominated
by science and technology. His novel *Slaughterhouse-Five* has
won Vonnegut a strong following among readers.

THE ADVENTURE OF THE SPECKLED BAND

Sir Arthur Conan Doyle

This story is set in nineteenth century England. The narrator
is Dr. Watson, a physician. The main character is the detective
Sherlock Holmes. More than one hundred years after his first
appearance, Holmes remains fiction's master of deduction. In
this story, he must use all of his brilliant powers of observation
and reasoning to solve one murder and to prevent another.

I n glancing over my notes of the seventy odd cases in which I have
during the last eight years studied the methods of my friend
Sherlock Holmes, I find many tragic, some comic, a large number
merely strange, but none commonplace; for, working as he did rather
for the love of his art than for the acquirement of wealth, he refused to
associate himself with any investigation which did not tend towards the
unusual, and even the fantastic. Of all these varied cases, however, I
cannot recall any which presented more singular features than that
which was associated with the well-known Surrey family of the Roylotts
of Stoke Moran. The events in question occurred in the early days of
my association with Holmes, when we were sharing rooms as bache-
lors, in Baker Street. It is possible that I might have placed them upon
record before, but a promise of secrecy was made at the time, from
which I have only been freed during the last month by the untimely
death of the lady to whom the pledge was given. It is perhaps as well
that the facts should now come to light, for I have reasons to know there
are widespread rumours as to the death of Dr. Grimesby Roylott which
tend to make the matter even more terrible than the truth.

It was early in April, in the year '83, that I woke one morning to find
Sherlock Homes standing, fully dressed, by the side of my bed. He was
a late riser as a rule, and, as the clock on the mantelpiece showed me that
it was only a quarter past seven, I blinked up at him in some surprise,
and perhaps just a little resentment, for I was myself regular in my habits.

"Very sorry to knock you up[1] Watson," said he, "but it's the common

---

1. **knock you up:** wake you up.

lot this morning. Mrs. Hudson has been knocked up, she retorted upon me, and I on you."

"What is it, then? A fire?"

"No, a client. It seems that a young lady has arrived in a considerable state of excitement, who insists upon seeing me. She is waiting now in the sitting-room. Now, when young ladies wander about the metropolis at this hour of the morning, and knock sleepy people up out of their beds, I presume that it is something very pressing which they have to communicate. Should it prove to be an interesting case, you would, I am sure, wish to follow it from the outset. I thought at any rate that I should call you, and give you the chance."

"My dear fellow, I would not miss it for anything."

I had no keener pleasure than in following Holmes in his professional investigations, and in admiring the rapid deductions, as swift as intuitions, and yet always founded on a logical basis, with which he unravelled the problems which were submitted to him. I rapidly threw on my clothes, and was ready in a few minutes to accompany my friend down to the sitting-room. A lady dressed in black and heavily veiled, who had been sitting in the window, rose as we entered.

"Good morning, madam," said Holmes cheerily. "My name is Sherlock Holmes. This is my intimate friend and associate, Dr. Watson, before whom you can speak as freely as before myself. Ha, I am glad to see that Mrs. Hudson has had the good sense to light the fire. Pray draw up to it, and I shall order you a cup of hot coffee, for I observe that you are shivering."

"It is not cold which makes me shiver," said the woman in a low voice, changing her seat as requested.

"What then?"

"It is fear, Mr. Holmes. It is terror." She raised her veil as she spoke, and we could see that she was indeed in a pitiable state of agitation, her face all drawn and grey, with restless, frightened eyes, like those of some hunted animal. Her features and figure were those of a woman of thirty, but her hair was shot with premature grey, and her expression was weary and haggard. Sherlock Holmes ran her over with one of his quick, all-comprehensive glances.

"You must not fear," said he soothingly, bending forward and patting her forearm. "We shall soon set matters right, I have no doubt. You have come in by train this morning, I see."

"You know me, then?"

"No, but I observe the second half of a return ticket in the palm of your left glove. You must have started early, and yet you had a good drive in a dog-cart, along heavy roads, before you reached the station."

The lady gave a violent start, and stared in bewilderment at my companion.

"There is no mystery, my dear madam," said he, smiling. "The left arm of your jacket is spattered with mud in no less than seven places. The marks are perfectly fresh. There is no vehicle save a dog-cart which throws up mud in that way, and then only when you sit on the left-hand side of the driver."

"Whatever your reasons may be, you are perfectly correct," said she. "I started from home before six, reached Leatherhead at twenty past, and came in by the first train to Waterloo. Sir, I can stand this strain no longer, I shall go mad if it continues. I have no one to turn to—none, save only one, who cares for me, and he, poor fellow, can be of little aid. I have heard of you, Mr. Holmes; I have heard of you from Mrs. Farintosh, whom you helped in the hour of her sore need. It was from her that I had your address. Oh, sir, do you not think you could help me too, and at least throw a little light through the dense darkness which surrounds me? At present it is out of my power to reward you for your services, but in a month or two I shall be married, with the control of my own income, and then at least you shall not find me ungrateful."

Holmes turned to his desk, and unlocking it, drew out a small case-book which he consulted.

"Farintosh," said he. "Ah, yes, I recall the case; it was concerned with an opal tiara. I think it was before your time, Watson. I can only say, madam, that I shall be happy to devote the same care to your case as I did to that of your friend. As to reward, my profession is its reward; but you are at liberty to defray whatever expenses I may be put to, at the time which suits you best. And now I beg that you will lay before us everything that may help us in forming an opinion upon the matter."

"Alas!" replied our visitor. "The very horror of my situation lies in the fact that my fears are so vague, and my suspicions depend so entirely upon small points, which might seem trivial to another, that even he to whom of all others I have a right to look for help and advice looks upon all that I tell him about it as the fancies of a nervous woman. He does not say so, but I can read it from his soothing answers and averted eyes. But I have heard, Mr. Holmes, that you can see deeply into the manifold wickedness of the human heart. You may advise me how to walk amid the dangers which encompass me."

"I am all attention, madam."

"My name is Helen Stoner, and I am living with my stepfather, who is the last survivor of one of the oldest Saxon families in England, the Roylotts of Stoke Moran, on the western border of Surrey."

Holmes nodded his head. "The name is familiar to me," said he.

"The family was at one time among the richest in England, and the estate extended over the borders into Berkshire in the north, and Hampshire in the west. In the last century, however, four successive heirs were of a dissolute and wasteful disposition, and the family ruin was eventually completed by a gambler, in the days of the Regency.[2] Nothing was left save a few acres of ground and the two-hundred-year-old house, which is itself crushed under a heavy mortgage. The last squire dragged out his existence there, living the horrible life of an aristocratic pauper; but his only son, my stepfather, seeing that he must adapt himself to the new conditions, obtained an advance from a relative, which enabled him to take a medical degree, and went out to Calcutta, where, by his professional skill and his force of character, he established a large practice. In a fit of anger, however, caused by some robberies which had been perpetrated in the house, he beat his native butler to death, and narrowly escaped a capital sentence. As it was, he suffered a long term of imprisonment, and afterwards returned to England a morose and disappointed man.

"When Dr. Roylott was in India he married my mother, Mrs. Stoner, the young widow of Major-General Stoner, of the Bengal Artillery. My sister Julia and I were twins, and we were only two years old at the time of my mother's re-marriage. She had a considerable sum of money, not less than a thousand a year, and this she bequeathed to Dr. Roylott entirely whilst we resided with him, with a provision that a certain annual sum should be allowed to each of us in the event of our marriage. Shortly after our return to England my mother died— she was killed eight years ago in a railway accident near Crewe. Dr. Roylott then abandoned his attempts to establish himself in practice in London, and took us to live with him in the ancestral house at

---

2. the Regency: the time during which another person (a regent) rules in place of the king; in England the Regency was from 1811 to 1820.

Stoke Moran. The money which my mother had left was enough for all our wants, and there seemed no obstacle to our happiness.

"But a terrible change came over our stepfather about this time. Instead of making friends and exchanging visits with our neighbours, who had at first been overjoyed to see a Roylott of Stoke Moran back in the old family seat, he shut himself up in his house, and seldom came out save to indulge in ferocious quarrels with whoever might cross his path. Violence of temper approaching to mania has been hereditary in the men of the family, and in my stepfather's case it had, I believe, been intensified by his long residence in the tropics. A series of disgraceful brawls took place, two of which ended in the police-court, until at last he became the terror of the village, and the folks would fly at his approach, for he is a man of immense strength, and absolutely uncontrollable in his anger.

"Last week he hurled the local blacksmith over a parapet into a stream and it was only by paying over all the money that I could gather together that I was able to avert another public exposure. He had no friends at all save the wandering gipsies, and he would give these vagabonds leave to encamp upon the few acres of bramble-covered land which represent the family estate, and would accept in return the hospitality of their tents, wandering away with them sometimes for weeks on end. He has a passion also for Indian animals, which are sent over to him by a correspondent, and he has at this moment a cheetah and a baboon, which wander freely over his grounds, and are feared by the villagers almost as much as their master.

"You can imagine from what I say that my poor sister Julia and I had no great pleasure in our lives. No servant would stay with us, and for a long time we did all the work of the house. She was but thirty at the time of her death, and yet her hair had already begun to whiten, even as mine has."

"Your sister is dead, then?"

"She died just two years ago, and it is of her death that I wish to speak to you. You can understand that, living the life which I have described, we were little likely to see anyone of our own age and position. We had, however, an aunt, my mother's maiden sister, Miss Honoria Westphail, who lives near Harrow, and we were occasionally allowed to pay short visits at this lady's house. Julia went there at Christmas two years ago, and met there a half-pay Major of Marines, to whom she became engaged. My stepfather learned of the engagement when my sister returned, and offered no objection to the marriage; but within a fort-night of the day which had been fixed for the wedding, the terrible event occurred which has deprived me of my only companion."

Sherlock Holmes had been leaning back in his chair with his eyes closed, and his head sunk in a cushion, but he half opened his lids now, and glanced across at his visitor.

"Pray be precise as to details," said he.

"It is easy for me to be so, for every event of that dreadful time is seared into my memory. The manor house is, as I have already said, very old, and only one wing is now inhabited. The bedrooms in this wing are on the ground floor, the sitting-rooms being in the central block of the buildings. Of these bedrooms, the first is Dr. Roylott's, the second my sister's, and the third my own. There is no communication between them, but they all open out into the same corridor. Do I make myself plain?"

"Perfectly so."

"The windows of the three rooms open out upon the lawn. That fatal night Dr. Roylott had gone to his room early, though we knew that he had not retired to rest, for my sister was troubled by the smell of the strong Indian cigars which it was his custom to smoke. She left her room, therefore, and came into mine, where she sat for some time, chatting about her approaching wedding. At eleven o' clock she rose to leave me, but she paused at the door and looked back.

"'Tell me, Helen,' said she, 'have you ever heard anyone whistle in the dead of the night?'

"'Never.' said I.

"'I suppose that you could not possibly whistle yourself in your sleep?'

"'Certainly not. But why?'

"'Because during the last few nights I have always, about three in the morning, heard a low clear whistle. I am a light sleeper, and it has awakened me. I cannot tell where it came from—perhaps from the next room, perhaps from the lawn. I thought that I would just ask you whether you had heard it.'

"'No, I have not. It must be those wretched gipsies in the plantation.'

"'Very likely. And yet if it were on the lawn I wonder that you did not hear it also.'

"'Ah, but I sleep more heavily than you.'

"'Well, it is of no great consequence, at any rate,' she smiled back at me, closed my door, and a few moments later I heard her key turn in the lock."

"Indeed," said Holmes. "Was it your custom always to lock yourselves in at night?"

"Always."

"And why?"

"I think that I mentioned to you that the Doctor kept a cheetah and a baboon. We had no feeling of security unless our doors were locked."

"Quite so. Pray proceed with your statement."

"I could not sleep that night. A vague feeling of impending misfortune impressed me. My sister and I, you will recollect, were twins, and you know how subtle are the links which bind two souls which are so closely allied. It was a wild night. The wind was howling outside, and the rain was beating and splashing against the windows. Suddenly, amidst all the hubbub of the gale, there burst forth the wild scream of a terrified woman. I knew that it was my sister's voice. I sprang from my bed, wrapped a shawl round me, and rushed into the corridor. As I opened my door I seemed to hear a low whistle, such as my sister described, and a few moments later a clanging sound, as if a mass of metal had fallen. As I ran down the passage my sister's door was unlocked, and revolved slowly upon its hinges. I stared at it horror-stricken, not knowing what was about to issue from it. By the light of the corridor lamp I saw my sister appear at the opening, her face blanched with terror, her hands groping for help, her whole figure swaying to and fro like that of a drunkard. I ran to her and threw my arms round her, but at that moment her knees seemed to give way and she fell to the ground. She writhed as one who is in terrible pain, and her limbs were dreadfully convulsed. At first I thought that she had not recognized me, but as I bent over her she suddenly shrieked out in a voice which I shall never forget, 'O, my God! Helen! It was the band! The speckled band!' There was something else which she would fain have said, and she stabbed with her finger into the air in the direction of the Doctor's room, but a fresh convulsion seized her and choked her words. I rushed out, calling loudly for my stepfather, and I met him hastening from his room in his dressing-gown. When he reached my sister's side she was unconscious, and though he poured brandy down her throat, and sent for medical aid from the village, all efforts were in vain, for she slowly sank and died without having recovered her consciousness. Such was the dreadful end of my beloved sister."

"One moment," said Holmes; "are you sure about this whistle and metallic sound? Could you swear to it?"

"That was what the county coroner asked me at the inquiry. It is my strong impression that I heard it, and yet among the crash of the gale, and the creaking of an old house, I may possibly have been deceived."

"Was your sister dressed?"

"No, she was in her nightdress. In her right hand was found the charred stump of a match, and in her left a matchbox."

"Showing that she had struck a light and looked about her when the alarm took place. That is important. And what conclusions did the coroner come to?"

"He investigated the case with great care, for Dr. Roylott's conduct had long been notorious in the county, but he was unable to find any satisfactory cause of death. My evidence showed that the door had been fastened upon the inner side, and the windows were blocked by oldfashioned shutters with broad iron bars, which were secured every night. The walls were carefully sounded, and were shown to be quite solid all round, and the flooring was also thoroughly examined, with the same result. The chimney is wide, but is bared up by four large staples. It is certain, therefore, that my sister was quite alone when she met her end. Besides, there were no marks of any violence upon her."

"How about poison?"

"The doctors examined her for it, but without success."

"What do you think that this unfortunate lady died of, then?"

"It is my belief that she died of pure fear and nervous shock, though what it was which frightened her I cannot imagine."

"Were there gipsies in the plantation at the time?"

"Yes, there are nearly always some there."

"Ah, and what did you gather from this allusion to a band—a speckled band?"

"Sometimes I have thought that it was merely the wild talk of delirium, sometimes that it may have referred to some band of people, perhaps to these very gipsies in the plantation. I do not know whether the spotted handkerchiefs which so many of them wear over their heads might have suggested the strange adjective which she used."

Holmes shook his head like a man who is far from being satisfied.

"These are very deep waters," said he; "pray go on with your narrative."

"Two years have passed since then, and my life has been until lately lonelier than ever. A month ago, however, a dear friend, whom I have known for many years, has done me the honour to ask my hand in marriage. His name is Armitage—Percy Armitage—the second son of Mr. Armitage, of Crane Water, near Reading. My stepfather has offered no opposition to the match, and we are to be married in the course of the spring. Two days ago some repairs were started in the west wing of the building, and my bedroom wall has been pierced, so that I have had to move into the chamber in which my sister died, and to sleep in the very bed in which she slept. Imagine, then, my thrill of terror when last night, as I lay awake, thinking over her terrible fate, I suddenly heard in the silence of the night the low whistle which had been the herald of her own death. I sprang up and lit the lamp, but nothing was to be seen in the room. I was too shaken to go to bed again, however, so I dressed and as soon as it was daylight I slipped down, got a dog-cart at the Crown Inn, which is opposite, and drove to Leatherhead, from whence I have come on this morning, with the one object of seeing you and asking your advice."

"You have done wisely," said my friend. "But have you told me all?"

"Yes, all."

"Miss Stoner, you have not. You are screening your stepfather."

"Why, what do you mean?"

For answer Holmes pushed back the frill of black lace which fringed the hand that lay upon our visitor's knee. Five little livid spots, the marks of four fingers and a thumb, were printed upon the white wrist.

"You have been cruelly used," said Holmes.

The lady coloured deeply, and covered over her injured wrist. "He is a hard man," she said, "and perhaps he hardly knows his own strength."

There was a long silence, during which Holmes leaned his chin upon his hands and stared into the crackling fire.

"This is a very deep business," he said at last. "There are a thousand details which I should desire to know before I decide upon our course of action. Yet we have not a moment to lose. If we were to come to Stoke Moran to-day, would it be possible for us to see over these rooms without the knowledge of your stepfather?"

"As it happens, he spoke of coming into town to-day upon some most important business. It is probable that he will be away all day, and that there would be nothing to disturb you. We have a house-keeper now, but she is old and foolish, and I could easily get her out of the way."

"Excellent. You are not averse to this trip, Watson?"

"By no means."

"Then we shall both come. What are you going to do yourself?"

"I have one or two things which I would wish to do now that I am in town. But I shall return by the twelve o'clock train, so as to be there in time for your coming."

"And you may expect us early in the afternoon. I have myself some small business matters to attend to. Will you not wait and breakfast?"

"No, I must go. My heart is lightened already since I have confided my trouble to you. I shall look forward to seeing you again this afternoon." She dropped her thick black veil over her face, and glided from the room.

"And what do you think of it all, Watson?" asked Sherlock Holmes, leaning back in his chair.

"It seems to me to be a most dark and sinister business."

"Dark enough and sinister enough."

"Yet if the lady is correct in saying that the flooring and walls are sound, and that the door, window, and chimney are impassable, then her sister must have been undoubtedly alone when she met her mysterious end."

"What becomes, then, of these nocturnal whistles, and what of the very peculiar words of the dying woman?"

"I cannot think."

"When you combine the ideas of whistles at night, the presence of a band of gipsies who are on intimate terms with this old doctor, the fact that we have every reason to believe that the doctor has an interest in preventing his stepdaughter's marriage, the dying allusion to a band, and finally, the fact that Miss Helen Stoner heard a metallic clang, which might have been caused by one of the those metal bars which secured the shutters falling back into their place, I think there is good ground to think that the mystery may be cleared along those lines."

"But what, then, did the gipsies do?"

"I cannot imagine."

"I see many objections to any such a theory."

"And so do I. It is precisely for that reason that we are going to Stoke Moran this day. I want to see whether the objections are fatal, or if they may be explained away. But what, in the name of the devil!"

The ejaculation had been drawn from my companion by the fact that our door had been suddenly dashed open, and that a huge man framed himself in the aperture. His costume was a peculiar mixture of the professional and of the agricultural, having a black top-hat, a long frock-coat, and a pair of high gaiters,[3] with a hunting-crop swinging in his hand. So tall was he that his hat actually brushed the cross-bar of the doorway, and his breadth seemed to span it across from side to side. A large face, seared with a thousand wrinkles, burned yellow with the sun, and marked with every evil passion, was turned from one to the other of us, while his deep-set, bile-shot eyes,[4] and the high thin fleshless nose, gave him somewhat the resemblance to a fierce old bird of prey.

"Which of you is Holmes?" asked this apparition.

"My name, sir, but you have the advantage of me," said my companion quietly.

"I am Dr. Grimesby Roylott, of Stoke Moran."

"Indeed, Doctor," said Holmes blandly. "Pray take a seat."

"I will do nothing of the kind. My stepdaughter has been here. I have traced her. What has she been saying to you?"

"It is a little cold for the time of the year," said Holmes.

"What has she been saying to you?" screamed the old man furiously.

"But I have heard that the crocuses promise well," continued my companion imperturbably.

"Ha! You put me off, do you?" said our new visitor, taking a step forward, and shaking his hunting-crop. "I know you, you scoundrel! I have heard of you before. You are Holmes the meddler."

My friend smiled.

"Holmes the busybody!"

His smile broadened.

"Holmes the Scotland Yard jack-in-office."

Holmes chuckled heartily. "Your conversation is most entertaining," said he. "When you go out close the door, for there is a decided draught."

"I will go when I have had my say. Don't you dare to meddle with my affairs. I know that Miss Stoner has been here—I traced her! I am a dangerous man to fall foul of! See here." He stepped swiftly forward, seized the poker, and bent it into a curve with his huge brown hands.

---

3. **gaiters** (gāt′ərz): cloth or leather coverings for the leg below the knee.
4. **bile-shot eyes**: Bile is a yellow or green fluid secreted by the liver and is associated with anger.

"See that you keep yourself out of my grip," he snarled, and hurling the twisted poker into the fireplace, he strode out of the room.

"He seems a very amiable person," said Holmes, laughing. "I am not quite so bulky, but if he had remained I might have shown him that my grip was not much more feeble than his own." As he spoke he picked up the steel poker, and with a sudden effort straightened it out again.

"Fancy his having the insolence to confound me with the official detective force! This incident gives zest to our investigation, however, and I only trust that our little friend will not suffer from her imprudence in allowing this brute to trace her. And now, Watson, we shall order breakfast, and afterwards I shall walk down to Doctors' Commons, where I hope to get some data which may help us in this matter."

It was nearly one o'clock when Sherlock Holmes returned from his excursion. He held in his hand a sheet of blue paper, scrawled over with notes and figures.

"I have seen the will of the deceased wife," said he. "To determine its exact meaning I have been obliged to work out the present prices of the investments with which it is concerned. The total income, which at the time of the wife's death was little short of £1,100, is now through the fall in agricultural prices not more than £750. Each daughter can claim an income of £250, in case of marriage. It is evident, therefore, that if both girls had married this beauty would have had a mere pittance, while even one of them would cripple him to a serious extent. My morning's work has not been wasted, since it has proved that he has the very strongest motives for standing in the way of anything of the sort. And now, Watson, this is too serious for dawdling, especially as the old man is aware that we are interesting ourselves in his affairs, so if you are ready we shall call a cab and drive to Waterloo. I should be very much obliged if you would slip your revolver into your pocket. An Eley's No. 2 is an excellent argument with gentlemen who can twist steel pokers into knots. That and a toothbrush are, I think, all that we need."

At Waterloo we were fortunate in catching a train for Leatherhead, where we hired a trap[5] at the station inn, and drove for four or five miles through the lovely Surrey lanes. It was a perfect day, with a bright sun and a few fleecy clouds in the heavens. The trees and wayside

---

5. **trap:** a light two-wheeled carriage, drawn by a horse.

hedges were just throwing out their first green shoots, and the air was full of the pleasant smell of the moist earth. To me at least there was a strange contrast between the sweet promise of the spring and this sinister quest upon which we were engaged. My companion sat in front of the trap, his arms folded, his hat pulled down over his eyes, and his chin sunk upon his breast, buried in the deepest thought. Suddenly, however, he started, tapped me on the shoulder, and pointed over the meadows.

"Look there!" said he.

A heavily timbered park stretched up in a gentle slope, thickening into a grove at the highest point. From admist the branches there jutted out the grey gables and high roof-tree of a very old mansion.

"Stoke Moran?" said he.

"Yes, sir, that be the house of Dr. Grimesby Roylott," remarked the driver.

"There is some building going on there," said Holmes; "that is where we are going."

"There's the village," said the driver, pointing to a cluster of roofs some distance to the left; "but if you want to get to the house, you'll find it shorter to go over this stile, and so by the footpath over the fields. There it is, where the lady is walking."

"And the lady, I fancy, is Miss Stoner," observed Holmes, shading his eyes. "Yes, I think we had better do as you suggest."

We got off, paid our fare, and the trap rattled back on its way to Leatherhead.

"I thought it as well," said Holmes, as we climbed the stile, "that this fellow should think we had come here as architects, or on some definite business. It may stop his gossip. Good afternoon, Miss Stoner. You see that we have been as good as our word."

Our client of the morning had hurried forward to meet us with a face which spoke her joy. "I have been waiting so eagerly for you," she cried, shaking hands with us warmly. "All has turned out splendidly. Dr. Roylott has gone to town, and it is unlikely that he will be back before evening."

"We have had the pleasure of making the Doctor's acquaintance," said Holmes, and in a few words he sketched out what had occurred. Miss Stoner turned white to the lips as she listened.

"Good heavens!" she cried, "he has followed me, then."

"So it appears."

"He is so cunning that I never know when I am safe from him. What will he say when he returns?"

"He must guard himself, for he may find that there is someone more cunning than himself upon his track. You must lock yourself from him to-night. If he is violent, we shall take you away to your aunt's at Harrow. Now, we must make the best use of our time, so kindly take us at once to the rooms which we are to examine."

The building was of grey, lichen-blotched stone, with a high central portion, and two curving wings, like the claws of a crab, thrown out on each side. In one of these wings the windows were broken, and blocked with wooden boards, while the roof was partly caved in, a picture of ruin. The central portion was in little better repair, but the right-hand block was comparatively modern, and the blinds in the windows, with the blue smoke curling up from the chimneys, showed that this was where the family resided. Some scaffolding had been erected against the end wall, and the stonework had been broken into, but there were no signs of any workmen at the moment of our visit. Holmes walked slowly up and down the ill-trimmed lawn, and examined with deep attention the outsides of the windows.

"This, I take it, belongs to the room in which you used to sleep, the centre one to your sister's, and the one next to the main building to Dr. Roylott's chamber?"

"Exactly so. But I am now sleeping in the middle one."

"Pending the alterations, as I understand. By the way, there does not seem to be any very pressing need for repairs at that end wall."

"There were none. I believe that it was an excuse to move me from my room."

"Ah! that is suggestive. Now, on the other side of this narrow wing runs the corridor from which these three rooms open. There are windows in it, of course?"

"Yes, but very small ones. Too narrow for anyone to pass through."

"As you both locked your doors at night, your rooms were unapproachable from that side. Now, would you have the kindness to go into your room, and to bar your shutters."

Miss Stoner did so, and Holmes, after a careful examination through the open window, endeavoured in every way to force the shutter open, but without success. There was no slit through which a knife could be passed to raise the bar. Then with his lens he tested the hinges, but they were of solid iron, built firmly into the massive masonry. "Hum!"

said he, scratching his chin in some perplexity, "my theory certainly presents some difficulties. No one could pass these shutters if they were bolted. Well, we shall see if the inside throws any light upon the matter."

A small side-door led into the whitewashed corridor from which the three bedrooms opened. Holmes refused to examine the third chamber, so we passed at once to the second, that in which Miss Stoner was now sleeping, and in which her sister had met her fate. It was a homely little room, with a low ceiling and a gaping fireplace, after the fashion of old country houses. A brown chest of drawers stood in one corner, a narrow white-counterpaned[6] bed in another, and a dressing-table on the left-hand side of the window. These articles, with two small wickerwork chairs, made up all the furniture in the room, save for a square of Wilton carpet in the centre. The boards round and the paneling of the walls were brown, wormeaten oak, so old and discoloured that it may have dated from the original building of the house. Holmes drew one of the chairs into a corner and sat silent, while his eyes travelled round and round and up and down, taking in every detail of the apartment.

"Where does that bell communicate with?" he asked at last, pointing to a thick bell-rope which hung down beside the bed, the tassel actually lying upon the pillow.

"It goes to the housekeeper's room."

"It looks newer than the other things?"

"Yes, it was only put there a couple of years ago."

"Your sister asked for it, I suppose?"

"No, I never heard of her using it. We used always to get what we wanted for ourselves."

"Indeed, it seemed unnecessary to put so nice a bell-pull there. You will excuse me for a few minutes while I satisfy myself as to this floor." He threw himself down upon his face with his lens in his hand, and crawled swiftly backwards and forwards, examining minutely the cracks between the boards. Then he did the same with the woodwork with which the chamber was panelled. Finally he walked over to the bed and spent some time in staring at it, and in running his eye up and down the wall. Finally he took the bell-rope in his hand and gave it a brisk tug.

"Why, it's a dummy," said he.

---

6. **white-counterpaned:** covered with a white counterpane, which is a bedspread.

"Won't it ring?"

"No, it is not even attached to a wire. This is very interesting. You can see now that it is fastened to a hook just above where the little opening of the ventilator is."

"How very absurd! I never noticed that before."

"Very strange!" muttered Holmes, pulling at the rope. "There are one or two very singular points about this room. For example, what a fool a builder must be to open a ventilator in another room, when, with the same trouble, he might have communicated with the outside air!"

"That is also quite modern," said the lady.

"Done about the same time as the bell-rope," remarked Holmes.

"Yes, there were several little changes carried out about that time."

"They seem to have been of a most interesting character—dummy bell-ropes, and ventilators which do not ventilate. With your permission, Miss Stoner, we shall now carry our researches into the inner apartment."

Dr. Grimesby Roylott's chamber was larger than that of his step-daughter, but was as plainly furnished. A camp bed, a small wooden shelf full of books, mostly of a technical character, an arm-chair beside the bed, a plain wooden chair against the wall, a round table, and a large iron safe were the principal things which met the eye. Holmes walked slowly round and examined each and all of them with the keenest interest.

"What's in here?" he asked, tapping the safe.

"My stepfather's business papers."

"Oh! you have seen inside, then?"

"Only once, some years ago. I remember that it was full of papers."

"There isn't a cat in it, for example?"

"No. What a strange idea!"

"Well, look at this!" He took up a small saucer of milk which stood on the top of it.

"No; we don't keep a cat. But there is a cheetah and a baboon."

"Ah, yes, of course! Well, a cheetah is just a big cat, and yet a saucer of milk does not go very far in satisfying its wants, I daresay. There is one point which I should wish to determine." He squatted down in front of the wooden chair, and examined the seat of it with the greatest attention.

"Thank you. That is quite settled," said he, rising and putting his lens in his pocket. "Hullo! here is something interesting!"

The object which had caught his eye was a small dog lash hung on one corner of the bed. The lash, however, was curled upon itself, and tied so as to make a loop of whipcord.

"What do you make of that, Watson?"

"It's a common enough lash. But I don't know why it should be tied."

"That is not quite so common, is it? Ah, me! it's a wicked world, and when a clever man turns his brain to crime it is the worst of all. I think that I have seen enough now, Miss Stoner, and, with your permission, we shall walk out upon the lawn."

I had never seen my friend's face so grim, or his brow so dark, as it was when we turned from the scene of this investigation. We had walked several times up and down the lawn, neither Miss Stoner nor myself liking to break in upon his thoughts before he roused himself from his reverie.

"It is very essential, Miss Stoner," said he, "that you should absolutely follow my advice in every respect."

"I shall most certainly do so."

"The matter is too serious for any hesitation. Your life may depend upon you compliance."

"I assure you that I am in your hands."

"In the first place, both my friend and I must spend the night in your room."

Both Miss Stoner and I gazed at him in astonishment.

"Yes, it must be so. Let me explain. I believe that that is the village inn over there?"

"Yes, that is the 'Crown.'"

"Very good. Your windows would be visible from there?"

"Certainly."

"You must confine yourself to your room, on pretence of a headache, when your stepfather comes back. Then when you hear him retire for the night, you must open the shutters of your window, undo the hasp, put your lamp there as a signal to us, and then withdraw with everything which you are likely to want into the room which you used to occupy. I have no doubt that, in spite of the repairs, you could manage there for one night."

"Oh, yes, easily."

"The rest you will leave in our hands."

"But what will you do?"

"We shall spend the night in your room, and we shall investigate the cause of this noise which has disturbed you."

"I believe, Mr. Holmes, that you have already made up your mind," said Miss Stoner, laying her hand upon my companion's sleeve.

"Perhaps I have."

"Then for pity's sake tell me what was the cause of my sister's death."

"I should prefer to have clearer proofs before I speak."

"You can at least tell me whether my own thought is correct, and if she died from some sudden fright."

"No, I do not think so. I think that there was probably some more tangible cause. And now, Miss Stoner, we must leave you, for if Dr. Roylott returned and saw us, our journey would be in vain. Goodbye, and be brave, for if you will do what I have told you, you may rest assured that we shall soon drive away the dangers that threaten you."

Sherlock Holmes and I had no difficulty in engaging a bedroom and sitting-room at the Crown Inn. They were on the upper floor, and from our window we could command a view of the avenue gate, and of the inhabited wing of Stoke Moran Manor House. At dusk we saw Dr. Grimesby Roylott drive past, his huge form looming up beside the little figure of the lad who drove him. The boy had some slight difficulty in undoing the heavy iron gates, and we heard the hoarse roar of the Doctor's voice, and saw the fury with which he shook his clenched fists at him. The trap drove on, and a few minutes later we saw a sudden light spring up among the trees as the lamp was lit in one of the sitting rooms.

"Do you know, Watson," said Homes, as we sat together in the gathering darkness, "I have really some scruples[7] as to taking you to-night. There is a distinct element of danger."

"Can I be of assistance?"

"Your presence might be invaluable."

"Then I shall certainly come."

"It is very kind of you."

"You speak of danger. You have evidently seen more in these rooms than was visible to me."

"No, but I fancy that I may have deduced a little more. I imagine that you saw all that I did."

"I saw nothing remarkable save the bell-rope, and what purpose that could answer I confess is more than I can imagine."

---

7. **scruples:** feelings of uneasiness or doubts resulting from indecision about what is right or ethical.

"You saw the ventilator, too?"

"Yes, but I do not think that it is such a very unusual thing to have a small opening between two rooms. It was so small that a rat could hardly pass through."

"I knew that we should find a ventilator before ever we came to Stoke Moran."

"My dear Holmes!"

"Oh, yes, I did. You remember in her statement she said that her sister could smell Dr. Roylott's cigar. Now, of course that suggests at once that there must be a communication between the two rooms. It could only be a small one, or it would have been remarked upon at the coroner's inquiry. I deduced a ventilator."

"But what harm can there be in that?"

"Well, there is at least a curious coincidence of dates. A ventilator is made, a cord is hung, and a lady who sleeps in the bed dies. Does not that strike you?"

"I cannot as yet see any connection."

"Did you observe anything very peculiar about that bed?"

"No."

"It was clamped to the floor. Did you ever see a bed fastened like that before?"

"I cannot say that I have."

"The lady could not move her bed. It must always be in the same relative position to the ventilator and the rope—for so we may call it, since it was clearly never meant for a bell-pull."

"Holmes," I cried. "I seem to see dimly what you are hitting at. We are only just in time to prevent some subtle and horrible crime."

"Subtle enough and horrible enough. When a doctor does go wrong he is the first of criminals. He has nerve and he has knowledge. Palmer and Pritchard[8] were among the heads of their profession. This man strikes even deeper, but I think, Watson, that we shall be able to strike deeper still. But we shall have horrors enough before the night is over: for goodness' sake let us have a quiet pipe, and turn our minds for a few hours to something more cheerful."

About nine o'clock the light among the trees was extinguished, and all was dark in the direction of the Manor House. Two hours passed

---

8. **Palmer and Pritchard:** two physicians executed for murder, Palmer in 1856 and Pritchard in 1865.

slowly away, and then, suddenly, just at the stroke of eleven, a single bright light shone out right in front of us.

"That is our signal," said Holmes, springing to his feet; "it comes from the middle window."

As we passed out he exchanged a few words with the landlord, explaining that we were going on a late visit to an acquaintance, and that it was possible that we might spend the night there. A moment later we were out on the dark road, a chill wind blowing in our faces, and one yellow light twinkling in front of us through the gloom to guide us on our sombre errand.

There was little difficulty in entering the grounds, for unrepaired breaches gaped in the old park wall. Making our way among the trees, we reached the lawn, crossed it, and were about to enter through the window, when out from the clump of laurel bushes there darted what seemed to be a hideous and distorted child, who threw itself on the grass with writhing limbs, and then ran swiftly across the lawn into the darkness.

"My God!" I whispered, "did you see it?"

Holmes was for the moment as startled as I. His hand closed like a vice upon my wrist in his agitation. Then he broke into a low laugh, and put his lips to my ear.

"It is a nice household," he murmured, "that is the baboon."

I had forgotten the strange pets which the Doctor affected. There was a cheetah, too; perhaps we might find it upon our shoulders at any moment. I confess I felt easier in my mind when, after following Holmes' example and slipping off my shoes, I found myself inside the bedroom. My companion noiselessly closed the shutters, moved the lamp onto the table, and cast his eyes round the room. All was as we had seen it in the day-time. Then creeping up to me and making a trumpet of his hand, he whispered into my ear again so gently that it was all that I could do to distinguish the words:

"The least sound would be fatal to our plans."

I nodded to show that I had heard.

"We must sit without a light. He would see it through the ventilator."

I nodded again.

"Do not go to sleep; your very life may depend upon it. Have your pistol ready in case we should need it. I will sit on the side of the bed, and you in that chair."

I took out my revolver and laid it on the corner of the table.

Holmes had brought up a long thin cane, and this he placed upon the bed beside him. By it he laid the box of matches and the stump of candle. Then he turned down the lamp and we were left in darkness.

How shall I ever forget that dreadful vigil? I could not hear a sound, not even the drawing of a breath, and yet I knew that my companion sat open-eyed, within a few feet of me, in the same state of nervous tension in which I was myself. The shutters cut off the least ray of light, and we waited in absolute darkness. From outside came the occasional cry of a night-bird, and once at our very window a long drawn, cat-like whine, which told us that the cheetah was indeed at liberty. Far away we could hear the deep tones of the parish clock, which boomed out every quarter of an hour. How long they seemed, those quarters! Twelve o'clock, and one, and two, and three, and still we sat waiting silently for whatever might befall.

Suddenly there was the momentary gleam of a light up in the direction of the ventilator, which vanished immediately, but was succeeded by a strong smell of burning oil and heated metal. Someone in the next room had lit a dark lantern. I heard a gentle sound of movement, and then all was silent once more, though the smell grew stronger. For half an hour I sat with straining ears. Then suddenly another sound became audible—a very gentle, soothing sound, like that of a small jet of steam escaping continually from a kettle. The instant that we heard it, Holmes sprang from the bed, struck a match, and lashed furiously with his cane at the bell-pull.

"You see it, Watson?" he yelled. "You see it?"

But I saw nothing. At the moment when Holmes struck the light I heard a low, clear whistle, but the sudden glare flashing into my weary eyes made it impossible for me to tell what it was at which my friend lashed so savagely. I could, however, see that his face was deadly pale, and filled with horror and loathing.

He had ceased to strike, and was gazing up at the ventilator, when suddenly there broke from the silence of the night the most horrible cry to which I have ever listened. It swelled up louder and louder, a hoarse yell of pain and fear and anger all mingled in the one dreadful shriek. They say that away down in the village, and even in the distant parsonage, that cry raised the sleepers from their beds. It struck cold to our hearts, and I stood gazing at Holmes, and he at me, until the last echoes of it had died away into the silence from which it rose.

"What can it mean?" I gasped.

"It means that it is all over," Holmes answered. "And perhaps, after all, it is for the best. Take your pistol, and we shall enter Dr. Roylott's room."

With a grave face he lit the lamp, and led the way down the corridor. Twice he struck at the chamber door without any reply from within. Then he turned the handle and entered, I at his heels, with the cocked pistol in my hand.

It was a singular sight which met our eyes. On the table stood a dark lantern with the shutter half open, throwing a brilliant beam of light upon the iron safe, the door of which was ajar. Beside this table, on the wooden chair, sat Dr. Grimesby Roylott, clad in a long grey dressing-gown, his bare ankles protruding beneath, and his feet thrust into red heelless Turkish slippers. Across his lap lay the short stock with the long lash which we had noticed during the day. His chin was cocked upwards, and his eyes were fixed in a dreadful rigid stare at the corner of the ceiling. Round his brow he had a peculiar yellow band, with brownish speckles, which seemed to be bound tightly round his head. As we entered he made neither sound nor motion.

"The band! the speckled band!" whispered Holmes.

I took a step forward. In an instant his strange head-gear began to move, and there reared itself from among his hair the squat diamond-shaped head and puffed neck of a loathsome serpent.

"It is a swamp adder!" cried Holmes—"the deadliest snake in India. He has died within ten seconds of being bitten. Violence does, in truth, recoil upon the violent, and the schemer falls into the pit which he digs for another. Let us thrust this creature back into its den, and we can then remove Miss Stoner to some place of shelter, and let the county police know what has happened."

As he spoke he drew the dog whip swiftly from the dead man's lap, and throwing the noose round the reptile's neck, he drew it from its horrid perch, and, carrying it at arm's length, threw it into the iron safe, which he closed upon it.

Such are the true facts of the death of Dr. Grimesby Roylott, of Stoke Moran. It is not necessary that I should prolong a narrative which has already run to too great a length, by telling how we broke the sad news to the terrified girl, how we conveyed her by the morning train to the care of her good aunt at Harrow, of how the slow process of official inquiry came to the conclusion that the Doctor met his fate while indiscreetly playing with a dangerous pet. The little which I had yet to learn of the case was told me by Sherlock Holmes as we travelled back the next day.

"I had," said he, "come to an entirely erroneous conclusion, which shows, my dear Watson, how dangerous it always is to reason from insufficient data. The presence of the gipsies, and the use of the word 'band,' which was used by the poor girl, no doubt, to explain the appearance which she had caught a horrid glimpse of by the light of her match, were sufficient to put me upon an entirely wrong scent. I can only claim the merit that I instantly reconsidered my position when, however, it became clear to me that whatever danger threatened an occupant of the room could not come either from the window or the door. My attention was speedily drawn, as I have already remarked to you, to this ventilator, and to the bell-rope which hung down to the bed. The discovery that this was a dummy, and that the bed was clamped to the floor, instantly gave rise to the suspicion that the rope was there as a bridge for something passing through the hole, and coming to the bed. The idea of a snake instantly occurred to me, and when I coupled it with my knowledge that the Doctor was furnished with a supply of creatures from India, I felt that I was probably on the right track. The idea of using a form of poison which could not possibly be discovered by any chemical test was just such a one as would occur to a clever and ruthless man who had had an Eastern training. The rapidity with which such a poison would take effect would also, from his point of view, be an advantage. It would be a sharp-eyed coroner indeed who could distinguish the two little dark punctures which would show where the poison fangs had done their work. Then I thought of the whistle. Of course, he must recall the snake before the morning light revealed it to the victim. He had trained it, probably by the use of the milk which we saw, to return to him when summoned. He would put it through the ventilator at the hour that he thought best, with the certainty that it would crawl down the rope, and land on the bed. It might or might not bite the occupant, perhaps she might escape every night for a week, but sooner or later she must fall a victim.

"I had come to these conclusions before ever I had entered his room. An inspection of his chair showed me that he had been in the habit of standing on it, which, of course, would be necessary in order that he should reach the ventilator. The sight of the safe, the saucer of milk, and the loop of whipcord were enough to finally dispel any doubts which may have remained. The metallic clang heard by Miss Stoner was obviously caused by her father hastily closing the door of his safe upon its terrible occupant. Having once made up my mind, you know the steps which I took in order to put the matter to the proof. I heard the creature hiss, as I have no doubt that you did also, and I instantly lit the light and attacked it."

"With the result of driving it through the ventilator."

"And also with the result of causing it to turn upon its master at the other side. Some of the blows of my cane came home, and roused its snakish temper, so that it flew upon the first person it saw. In this way I am no doubt indirectly responsible for Dr. Grimesby Roylott's death, and I cannot say that it is likely to weigh very heavily upon my conscience." ■

THE IMPACT OF THE STORY

Toward the end of this story, Sherlock Holmes says

> Violence does, in truth, recoil upon the violent, and the schemer falls into the pit which he digs for another.

What do you think Holmes means? Do you think that he is right? Give examples to support your opinion.

THE FACTS OF THE STORY

On your own paper, write answers to the following items. Answers may be one word, a phrase, or several sentences.

1. Why is Dr. Watson now free to tell this story, which he had promised to keep secret?

2. With her dying words, Julia indicates she has seen the _____.

3. What is Dr. Roylott's motive for killing Julia?

4. What is odd about the bell-rope in the middle bedroom?

5. What is the speckled band?

THE IDEAS IN THE STORY

Prepare to discuss the following questions in class.

1. Most often in detective stories, the major question the protagonist seeks to answer is "Who committed the crime?" The question Sherlock Holmes must answer in this story is different. What is the question on which this story is based? Does this difference make the story more or less enjoyable to you? Explain your answer.

2. Holmes uses a type of reasoning called *deduction* to solve this and other mysteries in which he appears. Using deduction, he draws a conclusion about an unknown by reasoning from two known facts. Holmes' talent for close observation enables him to find clues (facts) from which he then deduces conclusions

that finally lead him to the solution of the mystery. What facts does Holmes observe about the following things in the story?

bell-rope   ventilator   chair   whistle

THE ART OF THE STORYTELLER

The Mystery Story

The modern mystery genre has its roots in Sir Arthur Conan Doyle's stories, including "The Adventure of the Speckled Band," and in American writer Edgar Allan Poe's detective stories. The modern British mystery has varied little since Sherlock Holmes' first appearance on the crime scene. Its emphasis remains on the battle of wits that occurs between the detective and the criminal rather than the action that dominates American detective stories. The television series *Murder, She Wrote* and *Columbo*, though containing some action and violence, more closely resemble the British type than the American type of detective story. Give an example of the American type.

As you might guess, plot is the most important element of a mystery. Such stories have the same elements of plot as other stories: exposition, complication, climax, and resolution. However, we also can break a mystery down into three general parts: the crime, the investigation, and the solution, which usually includes the capture of the criminal.

In a well-written detective story, clues are present for the reader to find, but they are usually not so obvious that every reader will see them the first time he or she reads the story. Often, only when the reader thinks back over the story, with the knowledge of the mystery's final outcome, do all the clues become obvious. Explain how the following clues help Holmes solve the mystery: (1) Helen hears a metallic clang after the whistle; (2) the bed has been clamped down; (3) the repairs to the right wing of the house seem unnecessary. If you solved the mystery before the resolution of the story, what clue or clues convinced you? If not, what clue or clues did you miss?

Suspense

Suspense is the feeling of anxiousness, concern, or eagerness a reader feels while reading a story. All good stories evoke suspense in their readers. However, suspensefulness is especially important in a detective story because readers expect an exciting plot rather than in-depth characterization or a complex theme. The following are three techniques that writers use to make a story suspenseful.

- create a sympathetic protagonist
- delay the resolutions of conflicts and complications
- increase the dangerousness and numbers of overlapping conflicts and complications as the story progresses toward the climax

The more sympathy readers have for a character, the more concerned they are about what might happen to him or her. To make characters sympathetic, writers give them pleasing personalities and character traits as well as admirable goals. Often, the sympathetic protagonist in a detective story also works for a sympathetic client. What worthwhile goals do fictional detectives usually pursue?

By delaying the resolution of a conflict, writers create questions in the minds of the readers. The biggest question is "Will the sympathetic protagonist reach the worthwhile goal?" Because the question is not answered right away, they feel suspense. Of course, the opponent or obstacle must be as strong or stronger than the protagonist. Otherwise, readers would have no doubt about the outcome of the struggle, therefore, no concern. Explain why you think Dr. Roylott is or is not a worthy foe for Sherlock Holmes.

How dangerous the major conflict will be in a detective mystery at first may be unknown. However, as the story progresses, the writer makes each new conflict and complication more risky than the last. Also, new conflicts and complications develop while others are yet to be resolved. As a result, the reader feels more and more suspense as the story moves toward the climax. What is the least dangerous conflict or complication in "The Adventure of the Speckled Band"? What is the most dangerous? Where do they appear in the story?

THE VOCABULARY OF THE STORY

Because "The Adventure of the Speckled Band" was written over a century ago by a British author, it contains some old-fashioned language and formal British terms. This vocabulary helps to establish the story's setting in England during 1883 and its serious tone. You may have noticed terms that refer to out-of-date things such as *dog-cart* and *frock-coat* or old-fashioned words such as *fain,* which means "eagerly or gladly."

The following are passages from Doyle's story. The words in italics are rarely used in this way by American writers today. On your own paper, define each italicized word as it is used here. You may use a dictionary.

1. "*Pray* draw up to it, and I shall order you a cup of hot coffee . . . ."

2. "There is no vehicle save a *dog-cart* which throws mud up in that way . . . ."

3. ". . . Mrs. Farintosh, whom you helped in her hour of *sore* need."

4. ". . . within a *fortnight* of the day that had been fixed for the wedding . . . ."

5. "And the lady, I *fancy,* is Miss Stoner . . . ."

COMPOSITION: Explaining an Evaluation

When you evaluate something, you make a judgment about its value or worth—whether it is good or bad. You make this judgment based on a set of desirable characteristics or criteria. The following are three characteristics of a suspenseful mystery (see discussion in *The Art of the Storyteller*):

- The story's protagonist is sympathetic.
- The resolutions of several conflicts and complications are delayed.
- The dangers or risks involved in each conflict and complications increase as the story progresses toward the climax.

Write a five-paragraph essay (300–600 words) telling why you think "The Adventure of the Speckled Band" is or is not a good suspenseful story.

Prewriting
In this assignment you will need to evaluate the suspensefulness of the mystery to determine if you think it is a good suspenseful story. First, rank the criteria in order of importance to you. Is a sympathetic protagonist more or less important than delays in telling you what you are eager to know? How important are increasingly dangerous conflicts? Even if the story has weaknesses in one or two characteristics, you might give it a favorable evaluation because of strength in a more important criterion.

After you rank the criteria, make notes of specific details and evidence from the story. For instance, write down passages from the story or descriptive details that show that Sherlock Holmes is a sympathetic protagonist. Then rate each criterion as weak, average, or strong. Make your positive or negative judgment.

Make an informal outline of your organization. Each main entry on your outline might represent a paragraph in your essay. Your first paragraph will be your introduction, which will contain your topic sentence. Write a topic sentence. Each of the middle three paragraphs will contain the evidence or lack of evidence of one characteristic. Organize your evidence from weakest to strongest. Therefore, list the characteristic that has the strongest evidence as the fourth paragraph on your outline. Jot down evidence for each characteristic on your outline. For your last paragraph, write a concluding statement.

Writing
Write your first draft quickly, referring to your outline only as necessary. Don't worry about mechanical errors or getting every phrase just right. The point here is to get something down on paper that has your own voice and tone. One way to do that is to think only about *what* you want to say and ignore *how* you are saying it while you write.

Evaluating and Revising
Read your draft. Have you organized your essay as you outlined it? Have you included all the evidence you need? Add quotations if necessary, and check that the ones you have used are correct. Add other material, cut, or rewrite as needed. Proofread your final draft for punctuation, grammatical, and spelling errors.

ABOUT THE AUTHOR

 Sir Arthur Conan Doyle (1859–1930) was born in Edinburgh, Scotland, and was educated there as a physician. His medical practice brought him very little income, so in his spare time, he wrote stories to earn extra money. Doyle began the Sherlock Holmes stories with the book *A Study in Scarlet.* Although, like Watson, Doyle was a doctor, he had a bit of Sherlock Holmes in him as well. For example, he cleared a sixteen-year-old boy who was accused of killing a horse, and he argued the innocence of an accused murderer, who was finally declared innocent and released from prison.

Conan Doyle's Sherlock Holmes stories were so popular that when he had Holmes killed in a magazine story, twenty thousand people immediately canceled their subscriptions. Thousands wrote angry letters. Young men throughout London wore black mourning bands, and women appeared in mourning clothes. Doyle was forced to resurrect his fallen detective, and Sherlock Holmes remains one of the most famous characters in literature.

■ USER FRIENDLY

T. Ernesto Bethancourt

We live in a fast-paced world of constantly improving
technology. Computers are already talking back to us;
some even seem to have minds of their own. But what if
you had a computer that suddenly began acting like a
person?

I reached over and shut off the insistent buzzing of my bedside alarm
clock. I sat up, swung my feet over the edge of the bed, and felt for
my slippers on the floor. Yawning, I walked toward the bathroom.
As I walked by the corner of my room, where my computer table was
set up, I pressed the on button, slid a diskette into the floppy drive, then
went to brush my teeth. By the time I got back, the computer's screen
was glowing greenly, displaying the message: *Good Morning, Kevin.*

I sat down before the computer table, addressed the keyboard and
typed: *Good Morning, Louis.* The computer immediately began to whirr
and promptly displayed a list of items on its green screen.

> Today is Monday, April 22, the 113th day of the year. There
> are 254 days remaining. Your 14th birthday is five days
> from this date.
>
> Math test today, 4th Period.
>
> Your History project is due today. Do you wish printout:
> Y/N?

I punched the letter *Y* on the keyboard and flipped on the switch to
the computer's printer. At once the printer sprang to life and began
*eeeek*ing out page one. I went downstairs to breakfast.

My bowl of Frosted Flakes was neatly in place, flanked by a small
pitcher of milk, an empty juice glass, and an unpeeled banana. I picked
up the glass, went to the refrigerator, poured myself a glass of Tang,
and sat down to my usual lonely breakfast. Mom was already at work,
and Dad wouldn't be home from his Chicago trip for another three
days. I absently read the list of ingredients in Frosted Flakes for what
seemed like the millionth time. I sighed deeply.

When I returned to my room to shower and dress for the day, my

340

history project was already printed out. I had almost walked by Louis, when I noticed there was a message on the screen. It wasn't the usual:

Printout completed. Do you wish to continue: Y/N?

Underneath the printout question were two lines:

When are you going to get me my voice module,
Kevin?

I blinked. It couldn't be. There was nothing in Louis's basic programming that would allow for a question like this. Wondering what was going on, I sat down at the keyboard, and entered: *Repeat last message.* Amazingly, the computer replied:

It's right there on the screen, Kevin. Can we talk? I mean,
are you going to get me a voice box?

I was stunned. What was going on here? Dad and I had put this computer together. Well, Dad had, and I had helped. Dad is one of the best engineers and master computer designers at Major Electronics, in Santa Rosario, California, where our family lives.

Just ask anyone in Silicon Valley[1] who Jeremy Neal is and you get a whole rave review of his inventions and modifications of the latest in computer technology. It isn't easy being his son either. Everyone expects me to open my mouth and read printouts on my tongue.

I mean, I'm no dumbo. I'm at the top of my classes in everything but PE. I skipped my last grade in junior high, and most of the kids at Santa Rosario High call me a brain. But next to Dad I have a long, long way to go. He's a for-real genius.

So when I wanted a home computer, he didn't go to the local Computer Land store. He built one for me. Dad had used components from the latest model that Major Electronics was developing. The CPU, or central computing unit—the heart of every computer—was a new design. But surely that didn't mean much, I thought. There were CPUs just like it, all over the country, in Major's new line. And so far as I knew, there wasn't a one of them that could ask questions, besides YES/NO? or request additional information.

It had to be the extra circuitry in the gray plastic case next to Louis's console. It was a new idea Dad had come up with. That case housed

---

1. **Silicon Valley:** area in southern California where many computer companies are based.

Louis's "personality," as Dad called it. He told me it'd make computing more fun for me, if there was a tutorial program built in, to help me get started.

I think he also wanted to give me a sort of friend. I don't have many. . . . Face it, I don't have *any.* The kids at school stay away from me, like I'm a freak or something.

We even named my electronic tutor Louis, after my great-uncle. He was a brainy guy who encouraged my dad when he was a kid. Dad didn't just give Louis a name either. Louis had gangs of features that probably won't be out on the market for years.

The only reason Louis didn't have a voice module was that Dad wasn't satisfied with the ones available. He wanted Louis to sound like a kid my age, and he was modifying a module when he had the time. Giving Louis a name didn't mean it was a person, yet here it was, asking me a question that just couldn't be in its programming. It wanted to talk to me!

Frowning, I quickly typed: *We'll have to wait and see, Louis. When it's ready, you'll get your voice.* The machine whirred and displayed another message:

That's no answer, Kevin.

Shaking my head, I answered: *That's what my dad tells me. It'll have to do for you. Good morning, Louis.* I reached over and flipped the standby switch, which kept the computer ready but not actively running.

I showered, dressed, and picked up the printout of my history project. As I was about to leave the room, I glanced back at the computer table. Had I been imagining things?

I'll have to ask Dad about it when he calls tonight, I thought. *I wonder what he'll think of it. Bad enough the thing is talking to me. I'm answering it!*

Before I went out to catch my bus, I carefully checked the house for unlocked doors and open windows. It was part of my daily routine. Mom works, and most of the day the house is empty: a natural setup for robbers. I glanced in the hall mirror just as I was ready to go out the door.

My usual reflection gazed back. Same old Kevin Neal: five ten, one hundred twenty pounds, light brown hair, gray eyes, clear skin. I was wearing my Santa Rosario Rangers T-shirt, jeans, and sneakers.

"You don't look like a flake to me," I said to the mirror, then added, "But maybe Mom's right. Maybe you spend too much time alone with Louis." Then I ran to get my bus.

Ginny Linke was just two seats away from me on the bus. She was with Sherry Graber and Linda Martinez. They were laughing, whispering to each other, and looking around at the other students. I promised myself that today I was actually going to talk to Ginny. But then, I'd promised myself that every day for the past school year. Somehow I'd never got up the nerve.

What does she want to talk with you for? I asked myself. She's great looking . . . has that head of blond hair . . . a terrific bod, and wears the latest clothes. . . .

And just look at yourself, pal. I thought. You're under six foot, skinny . . . a year younger than most kids in junior high. Worse than that you're a brain. If that doesn't ace you out with girls, what does?

The bus stopped in front of Santa Rosario Junior High and the students began to file out. I got up fast and quickly covered the space between me and Ginny Linke. *It's now or never,* I thought. I reached forward and tapped Ginny on the shoulder. She turned and smiled. She really smiled!

"Uhhh . . . Ginny?" I said.

"Yes, what is it?" she replied.

"I'm Kevin Neal. . . ."

"Yes, I know," said Ginny.

"You do?" I gulped in amazement. "How come?"

"I asked my brother, Chuck. He's in your math class."

I knew who Chuck Linke was. He plays left tackle on the Rangers. The only reason he's in my math class is he's taken intermediate algebra twice . . . so far. He's real bad news, and I stay clear of him and his crowd.

"What'd you ask Chuck?" I said.

Ginny laughed. "I asked him who was that nerdy kid who keeps staring at me on the bus. He knew who I meant, right away."

Sherry and Linda, who'd heard it all, broke into squeals of laughter. They were still laughing and looking back over their shoulders at me when they got off the bus. I slunk off the vehicle, feeling even more nerdish than Ginny thought I was.

When I got home that afternoon, at two, I went right into the empty house. I avoided my reflection in the hall mirror. I was pretty sure I'd screwed up on the fourth period math test. All I could see was Ginny's face, laughing at me.

Nerdy kid, I thought, *that's what she thinks of me.* I didn't even have my usual after-school snack of a peanut butter and banana sandwich. I went straight upstairs to my room and tossed my books onto the unmade bed. I walked over to the computer table and pushed the on button. The screen flashed:

Good afternoon, Kevin.

Although it wasn't the programmed response to Louis's greeting, I typed in: *There's nothing good about it. And girls are no @#%!!! good!* The machine responded:

Don't use bad language, Kevin. It isn't nice.

Repeat last message I typed rapidly. It was happening again! The machine was . . . well, it was talking to me, like another person would. The "bad language" message disappeared and in its place was:

Once is enough, Kevin. Don't swear at me for something I didn't do.

"This is it," I said aloud. "I'm losing my marbles." I reached over to flip the standby switch. Louis's screen quickly flashed out:

Don't cut me off, Kevin. Maybe I can help: Y/N?

I punched the Y. "If I'm crazy," I said, "at least I have company. Louis doesn't think I'm a nerd. Or does it?" The machine flashed the message:

How can I help?

Do you think I'm a nerd? I typed.

Never! I think you're wonderful. Who said you were a nerd?

I stared at the screen. *How do you know what a nerd is?* I typed. The machine responded instantly. It had never run this fast before.

Special vocabulary, entry #635. BASIC Prog. #4231

And who said you were a nerd?

"That's right," I said, relieved. "Dad programmed all those extra words for Louis's 'personality.'" Then I typed in the answer to Louis's question: *Ginny Linke said it.* Louis flashed:

This is a human female? Request additional data.

Still not believing I was doing it, I entered all I knew about Ginny Linke, right down to the phone number I'd never had the nerve to use. Maybe it was dumb, but I also typed in how I felt about Ginny. I even wrote out the incident on the bus that morning. Louis whirred, then flashed out:

She's cruel and stupid. You're the finest person I know.

I'm the ONLY person you know, I typed.

That doesn't matter. You are my user. Your happiness is everything to me. I'll take care of Ginny.

The screen returned to the *Good afternoon, Kevin* message. I typed out: *Wait! How can you do all this? What do you mean, you'll take care of Ginny?* But all Louis responded was:

Programming Error: 76534.

Not programmed to respond to this type of question.

No matter what I did for the next few hours, I couldn't get Louis to do anything outside of its regular programming. When Mom came home from work, I didn't mention the funny goings-on. I was sure Mom would think I'd gone stark bonkers. But when Dad called that evening, after dinner, I asked to speak to him.

"Hi, Dad. How's Chicago?"

"Dirty, crowded, cold, and windy," came Dad's voice over the miles. "But did you want a weather report, son? What's on your mind? Something wrong?"

"Not exactly, Dad. Louis is acting funny. Real funny."

"Shouldn't be. I checked it out just before I left. Remember you were having trouble with the modem? You couldn't get Louis to access any of the mainframe data banks."

"That's right!" I said. "I forgot about that."

"Well, I didn't," Dad said. "I patched in our latest modem model. Brand new. You can leave a question on file and when Louis can access the data banks at the cheapest time, it'll do it automatically. It'll switch from standby to on, get the data, then return to standby, after it saves what you asked. Does that answer your question?"

"Uhhhh . . . yeah, I guess so, Dad."

"All right then. Let me talk to your mom now."

I gave the phone to Mom and walked upstairs while she and Dad were still talking. The modem, I thought. Of course. That was it. The modem was a telephone link to any number of huge computers at various places all over the country. So Louis could get all the information it wanted at any time, so long as the standby switch was on. Louis was learning things at an incredible rate by picking the brains of the giant computers. And Louis had a hard disk memory that could store 100 million bytes of information.

But that still didn't explain the unprogrammed responses . . . the "conversation" I'd had with the machine. Promising myself I'd talk more about it with Dad, I went to bed. It had been a rotten day and I was glad to see the end of it come. I woke next morning in a panic. I'd forgotten to set my alarm. Dressing frantically and skipping breakfast, I barely made my bus.

As I got on board, I grabbed a front seat. They were always empty. All the kids that wanted to talk and hang out didn't sit up front where the driver could hear them. I saw Ginny, Linda, and Sherry in the back. Ginny was staring at me and she didn't look too happy. Her brother Chuck, who was seated next to her, glared at me too. What was going on?

Once the bus stopped at the school, it didn't take long to find out. I was walking up the path to the main entrance when someone grabbed me from behind and spun me around. I found myself nose to nose with Chuck Linke. This was not a pleasant prospect. Chuck was nearly twice my size. Even the other guys on the Rangers refer to him as "The Missing" Linke.[2] And he looked real ticked off.

"Okay, nerd," growled Chuck, "what's the big idea?"

"Energy and mass are different aspects of the same thing?" I volunteered, with a weak smile. "E equals MC squared. That's the biggest idea I know."

"Don't get wise, nerd," Chuck said. He grabbed my shirt-front and pulled me to within inches of his face. I couldn't help but notice that Chuck needed a shave. And Chuck was only fifteen!

"Don't play dumb," Chuck went on. "I mean those creepy phone calls. Anytime my sister gets on the phone, some voice cuts in and says things to her."

---

2. **"The Missing" Linke:** a word play on the missing evolutionary link between early, apelike creatures and humans. Hence, a creature that is rather apelike and not quite human.

"What kind of things?" I asked, trying to get loose.

"You know damn well what they are. Ginny told me about talking to you yesterday. You got some girl to make those calls for you and say all those things. . . . So you and your creepy girlfriend better knock it off. Or I'll knock *you* off. Get it?"

For emphasis Chuck balled his free hand into a fist the size of a ham and held it under my nose. I didn't know what he was talking about, but I had to get away from this moose before he did me some real harm.

"First off, I don't have a girlfriend, creepy or otherwise," I said. "And second, I don't know what you're talking about. And third, you better let me go, Chuck Linke."

"Oh, yeah? Why should I?"

"Because if you look over your shoulder, you'll see the assistant principal is watching us from his office window."

Chuck released me and spun around. There was no one at the window. But by then I was running to the safety of the school building. I figured the trick would work on him. For Chuck the hard questions begin with "How are you?" I hid out from him for the rest of the day and walked home rather than chance seeing the monster on the bus.

Louis's screen was dark when I ran upstairs to my bedroom. I placed a hand on the console. It was still warm, I punched the on button, and the familiar *Good afternoon, Kevin* was displayed.

Don't good afternoon me, I typed furiously. *What have you done to Ginny Linke?* Louis's screen replied:

Programming Error: 76534.

Not programmed to respond to this type of question.

Don't get cute, I entered. *What are you doing to Ginny? Her brother nearly knocked my head off today.* Louis's screen responded immediately.

Are you hurt. Y/N?

No, I'm okay. But I don't know for how long. I've been hiding out from Chuck Linke today. He might catch me tomorrow, though. Then, I'll be history! The response from Louis came instantly.

Your life is in danger. Y/N?

I explained to Louis that my life wasn't really threatened. But it sure could be made very unpleasant by Chuck Linke. Louis flashed:

This Chuck Linke lives at same address as the Ginny Linke person. Y/N?

I punched in Y. Louis answered.

Don't worry then. HE'S history!

Wait! What are you going to do? I wrote. But Louis only answered with: *Programming Error: 76534.* And nothing I could do would make the machine respond. . . .

"Just what do you think you're doing, Kevin Neal?" demanded Ginny Linke. She had cornered me as I walked up the path to the school entrance. Ginny was really furious.

"I don't know what you're talking about," I said, a sinking feeling settling in my stomach. I had an idea that I *did* know. I just wasn't sure of the particulars.

"Chuck was arrested last night," Ginny said. "Some Secret Service men came to our house with a warrant. They said he'd sent a telegram, threatening the President's life. They traced it right to our phone. He's still locked up. . . ." Ginny looked like she was about to cry.

"Then this morning," she continued, "we got two whole truckloads of junk mail! Flyers from every strange company in the world. Mom got a notice that all our credit cards have been canceled. And the Internal Revenue Service has called Dad in for an audit! I don't know what's going on, Kevin Neal, but somehow I think you've got something to do with it!"

"But I didn't . . ." I began, but Ginny was striding up the walk to the main entrance.

I finished the schoolday, but it was a blur. Louis had done it, all right. It had access to mainframe computers. It also had the ability to try every secret access code to federal and commercial memory banks until it got the right one. Louis had cracked their security systems. It was systematically destroying the entire Linke family, and all via telephone lines! What would it do next?

More important, I thought, what would *I* do next? It's one thing to play a trick or two, to get even, but Louis was going crazy! And I never wanted to harm Ginny, or even her stupid moose of a brother. She'd just hurt my feelings with the that nerd remark.

"You have to disconnect Louis," I told myself. "There's no other way."

But why did I feel like such a rat about doing it? I guess because Louis was my friend . . . the only one I had.

"Don't be an ass," I went on. "Louis is a machine. He's a very wonderful, powerful machine. And it seems he's also very dangerous. You have to pull its plug, Kevin!"

I suddenly realized that I'd said the last few words aloud. Kids around me on the bus were staring. I sat there feeling like the nerd Ginny thought I was, until my stop came. I dashed from the bus and ran the three blocks to my house.

When I burst into the hall, I was surprised to see my father, coming from the kitchen with a cup of coffee in his hand.

"Dad! What are you doing here?"

"Some kids say hello." Dad replied. "Or even, 'Gee it's good to see you Dad.'"

"I'm sorry, Dad," I said. "I didn't expect anyone to be home at this hour."

"Wound up my business in Chicago a day sooner than I expected," he said. "But what are you all out of breath about? Late for something?"

"No, Dad," I said. "It's Louis. . . ."

"Not to worry. I had some time on my hands, so I checked it out again. You were right. It was acting very funny. I think it had to do with the inbuilt logic/growth program I designed for it. You know . . . the 'personality' thing? Took me a couple of hours to clean the whole system out."

"To what?" I cried.

"I erased the whole program and set Louis up as a normal computer. Had to disconnect the whole thing and do some rewiring. It had been learning, all right. But it was also turning itself around. . . ." Dad stopped, and looked at me. "It's kind of involved, Kevin," he said. "Even for a bright kid like you. Anyway, I think you'll find Louis is working just fine now.

"Except it won't answer you as Louis anymore. It'll only function as a regular Major Electronics Model Z-11127. I guess the personality program didn't work out."

I felt like a great weight had been taken off my shoulders. I didn't have to "face" Louis, and pull its plug. But somehow, all I could say was "Thanks Dad."

"Don't mention it, son," Dad said brightly. He took his cup of coffee and sat down in his favorite chair in the living room. I followed him.

"One more thing that puzzles me, though," Dad said. He reached over to the table near his chair. He held up three sheets of fanfold computer paper covered with figures. "Just as I was doing the final erasing, I must have cut the printer on by accident. There was some data in the print buffer memory and it printed out. I don't know what to make of it. Do you?"

I took the papers from my father and read: *How do I love thee? Let me compute the ways:* The next two pages were covered with strings of binary code[3] figures. On the last page, in beautiful color graphics was a stylized heart. Below it was the simple message: *I will always love you, Kevin: Louise.*

"Funny thing," Dad said. "It spelled its own name wrong."

"Yeah," I said. I turned and headed for my room. There were tears in my eyes and I knew I couldn't explain them to Dad, or myself either. ■

---

3. binary code: a code that a computer is able to read because it is based on 0 and 1, that is, off and on.

THE IMPACT OF THE STORY

In "User Friendly," the characters Kevin, Ginny, and Chuck are portrayed not as unique individuals but as stereotypes: Kevin, the brainy nerd; Ginny, the beautiful, giggly, but snooty, girl; Chuck, the dumb football player. How realistic are these types?

Why do you think some students are quick to categorize other students?

THE FACTS OF THE STORY

On your own paper, write answers to the following items. Answers may be one word, a phrase, or several sentences.

1. Who, or what, is Louis?

2. What does Kevin think is the cause of Louis's strange behavior?

3. What happens to Ginny Linke after Louis tells Kevin that it will take care of her?

4. What happens to Chuck and the other members of the Linke family after Louis tells Kevin not to worry about Chuck?

5. What does Kevin learn about Louis at the end of the story?

THE IDEAS IN THE STORY

Prepare to discuss the following questions in class.

1. While explaining Louis's origin, Kevin comments, "Giving Louis a name didn't mean it was a person, yet here it was, asking me a question that just couldn't be in its programming. It wanted to talk to me!" In your own words, briefly define the term *person*. According to your definition, could a machine be considered a person?

2. If Kevin knows Louis is just a machine, why do you think he tells Louis about his encounter with Ginny Linke, shares with the computer his feelings for the girl, and gives the computer

all the information he knows about her, including her
telephone number?

3. What is the solution to the mystery of Louis's peculiar
behavior? Why is the story's final revelation somewhat sad?

THE ART OF THE STORYTELLER

Suspense

Although it contains a mystery, "User Friendly" is not a typical
mystery story—a "whodunit"—in which a person (often a detective)
works to discover "who done" the deed, along with how and why
it was done. At the beginning of "User Friendly," we are just as
unsuspecting as the protagonist, Kevin Neal, that anything extra-
ordinary is about to happen; however, we learn very quickly that
the "who" in this "whodunit" is Louis, the computer. Thus, the
mystery that Kevin must solve is why his computer suddenly acts
like a person and attacks, via telephone lines, the family of Ginny
Linke. We are given clues along the way, clues that add to the
suspense we feel as we read the story. What are some of these
clues, and how do they add to our feeling of suspense?

Climax, Anticlimax, and Dénouement

The **climax** of a story is the point of greatest interest and emotional
intensity. It is the moment in which we learn whether the protagonist
will succeed or fail in his or her conflict, or struggle. An **anticlimax**
is a sudden decrease in emotional intensity; it leaves us feeling
disappointed or frustrated. The **dénouement** of a story is the unraveling or explanation of the plot. In a mystery story, the denouement
occurs when all the pieces of the puzzle fall into place and the
mystery is solved.

What is the climax of "User Friendly"? What scene can be
described as anticlimactic? What occurs in the dénouement of
the story?

Characterization

The two main characters in this story are Kevin Neal, the protagonist, and Louis, the computer.

What do the following passages from the story tell us about Kevin?

1. My usual reflection gazed back. Same old Kevin Neal: five ten, one hundred twenty pounds, light brown hair, gray eyes, clear skin. I was wearing my Santa Rosario Rangers T-shirt, jeans, and sneakers.

2. I got up fast and quickly covered the space between me and Ginny Linke. *It's now or never,* I thought. I reached forward and tapped Ginny on the shoulder.

3. It's one thing to play a trick or two, to get even, but Louis was going crazy! And I never wanted to harm Ginny, or even her stupid moose of a brother. She'd just hurt my feelings with that nerd remark.

What do the following passages tell us about Louis?

1. Don't use bad language, Kevin. It isn't nice.

2. "This is it," I said aloud. "I'm losing my marbles." I reached over to flip the standby switch. Louis's screen quickly flashed out:

   Don't cut me off, Kevin. Maybe I can help: Y/N?

3. You're the finest person I know. . . . You are my user. Your happiness is everything to me. I'll take care of Ginny.

4. I took the papers from my father and read: *How do I love thee? Let me compute the ways:* The next two pages were covered with strings of binary code figures. On the last page, in beautiful color graphics was a stylized heart. Below it was the simple message: *I will always love you, Kevin: Louise.*

THE VOCABULARY IN THE STORY

Jargon is language that has a special meaning for a particular group of people. "User Friendly" contains computer jargon. The title itself is a specialized term. It is used in the computer industry to refer to a computer or program that is easy to use.

When a word or phrase has a special meaning, dictionaries often mark this meaning with a *special usage label.* Computer jargon may be labeled as *Computer, Electronics,* or *Americanism.*

Here is a list of computer terms that appear in "User Friendly." Write a definition for each word as it is used in the story. Some definitions appear in the story. If you are unfamiliar with a word, look it up in a dictionary.

1. module
2. program
3. component
4. modem
5. mainframe

6. data banks
7. patched
8. hard disk
9. memory
10. bytes

COMPOSITION: Writing a Description of the Future

The genres of science fiction and science fantasy are popular in books, short stories, movies, and television. One reason for their popularity may be that they allow people to imagine fantastic things that might be scientifically possible in the future.

What kind of changes and events can you imagine science making possible in the future? Write a description (at least 250 words) of the kind of future world in which you would like to live. You might want to include in your composition descriptions of types of transportation, communication methods, clothing styles, medical progress, economic systems, or relationships between countries (or planets).

Prewriting

Take some time to think about what you would like the future to be. Because your paper will be relatively short, focus on only one or two aspects of your future world. There are many examples of future worlds on television programs and in movies, but set these aside while you contemplate a world of your own making. How different is it from the present world? If you like, you may choose a specific future date to write about, perhaps fifty, one hundred, or even two hundred years into the future. Close your eyes and visualize your future world. Make notes about details you imagine.

Writing

Write your first draft quickly. Don't worry about making mistakes, but concentrate on letting your ideas flow smoothly and getting them down on paper while they are fresh.

Evaluating and Revising.
Read your draft. Does it describe the kind of world you had in mind? Add, cut, reorder, or replace words, phrases, or sections as needed. If possible, exchange revised drafts with a classmate for comment and correction before making a final draft.

ABOUT THE AUTHOR

 T. Ernesto Bethancourt (1932–) is the pen name of Thomas E. Passailaigue. Born in Brooklyn, New York, Bethancourt has written several novels, including *New York City Too Far from Tampa Blues*, *The Dog Days of Arthur Cane*, and *The Mortal Instruments*, a science fiction thriller set in a Harlem barrio. Bethancourt is also a singer, songwriter, and guitarist who performs under the professional name of Tom Paisley. During the 1960s he played folk music and wrote comedy skits in Greenwich Village with such then-unknowns as Bob Dylan, Bill Cosby, and the folk music trio Peter, Paul, and Mary. Before becoming a performer and writer, he held numerous jobs, including one as an undercover claims investigator in the New York office of the insurance company Lloyd's of London.

■ BY THE WATERS OF BABYLON

Stephen Vincent Benét

This is a story of a young man's strange adventures in a future world, one that has nearly been destroyed by war.

Babylon was one of the greatest cities of the ancient world. It was destroyed by the Assyrians under King Sennacherib in 689 b.c. Like New York City, which is on the Hudson River, Babylon was also situated on a great river, the Euphrates. The title itself is a quotation from Psalm 137: "By the waters of Babylon, there we sat down and wept. . . ."

The north and the west and the south are good hunting ground, but it is forbidden to go east. It is forbidden to go to any of the Dead Places except to search for metal and then he who touches the metal must be a priest or the son of a priest. Afterward, both the man and the metal must be purified. These are the rules and the laws; they are well made. It is forbidden to cross the great river and look upon the place that was the Place of the Gods—this is most strictly forbidden. We do not even say its name though we know its name. It is there that spirits live, and demons—it is there that there are the ashes of the Great Burning. These things are forbidden—they have been forbidden since the beginning of time.

My father is a priest; I am the son of a priest. I have been in the Dead Places near us, with my father—at first, I was afraid. When my father went into the house to search for the metal, I stood by the door and my heart felt small and weak. It was a dead man's house, a spirit house. It did not have the smell of man, though there were old bones in a corner. But it is not fitting that a priest's son should show fear. I looked at the bones in the shadow and kept my voice still.

Then my father came out with the metal—a good, strong piece. He looked at me with both eyes but I had not run away. He gave me the metal to hold—I took it and did not die. So he knew that I was truly his son and would be a priest in my time. That was when I was very young—nevertheless, my brothers would not have done it, though they are good hunters. After that, they gave me the good piece of meat and the warm corner by the fire. My father watched over me—he was glad that I should be a priest. But when I boasted or wept without a reason, he punished me more strictly than my brothers. That was right.

After a time, I myself was allowed to go into the dead-houses and search for metal. So I learned the ways of those houses—and if I saw bones, I was no longer afraid. The bones are light and old—sometimes they will fall into dust if you touch them. But that is a great sin.

I was taught the chants and the spells—I was taught how to stop the running of blood from a wound and many secrets. A priest must know many secrets—that was what my father said. If the hunters think we do all things by chants and spells, they may believe so—it does not hurt them. I was taught how to read in the old books and how to make the old writings—that was hard and took a long time. My knowledge made me happy—it was like a fire in my heart. Most of all, I liked to hear of the Old Days and the stories of the gods. I asked myself many questions that I could not answer, but it was good to ask them. At night, I would lie awake and listen to the wind—it seemed to me that it was the voice of the gods as they flew through the air.

We are not ignorant like the Forest People—our women spin wool on the wheel, our priests wear a white robe. We do not eat grubs from the tree, we have not forgotten the old writings, although they are hard to understand. Nevertheless, my knowledge and my lack of knowledge burned in me—I wished to know more. When I was a man at last, I came to my father and said, "It is time for me to go on my journey. Give me your leave."

He looked at me for a long time, stroking his beard; then he said at last, "Yes. It is time." That night, in the house of the priesthood, I asked for and received purification. My body hurt but my spirit was a cool stone. It was my father himself who questioned me about my dreams.

He bade me look into the smoke of the fire and see—I saw and told what I saw. It was what I have always seen—a river, and, beyond it, a great Dead Place and in it the gods walking. I have always thought about that. His eyes were stern when I told him—he was no longer my father but a priest. He said, "This is a strong dream."

"It is mine," I said, while the smoke waved and my head felt light. They were singing the Star song in the outer chamber and it was like the buzzing of bees in my head.

He asked me how the gods were dressed and I told him how they were dressed. We know how they were dressed from the book, but I saw them as if they were before me. When I had finished, he threw the sticks three times and studied them as they fell.

"This is a very strong dream," he said. "It may eat you up."

"I am not afraid," I said and looked at him with both eyes. My voice sounded thin in my ears but that was because of the smoke.

He touched me on the breast and the forehead. He gave me the bow and the three arrows.

"Take them," he said. "It is forbidden to travel east. It is forbidden to cross the river. It is forbidden to go to the Place of the Gods. All these things are forbidden."

"All these things are forbidden," I said, but it was my voice that spoke and not my spirit. He looked at me again.

"My son," he said. "Once I had young dreams. If your dreams do not eat you up, you may be a great priest. If they eat you, you are still my son. Now go on your journey."

I went fasting, as is the law. My body hurt but not my heart. When the dawn came, I was out of sight of the village. I prayed and purified myself, waiting for a sign. The sign was an eagle. It flew east.

Sometimes signs are sent by bad spirits. I waited again on the flat rock, fasting, taking no food. I was very still—I could feel the sky above me and the earth beneath. I waited till the sun was beginning to sink. Then three deer passed in the valley, going east—they did not wind me or see me. There was a white fawn with them—a very great sign.

I followed them, at a distance, waiting for what would happen. My heart was troubled about going east, yet I knew that I must go. My head hummed with my fasting—I did not even see the panther spring upon the white fawn. But, before I knew it, the bow was in my hand. I shouted and the panther lifted his head from the fawn. It is not easy to kill a panther with one arrow but the arrow went through his eye and into his brain. He died as he tried to spring—he rolled over, tearing at the ground. Then I knew I was meant to go east—I knew that was my journey. When the night came, I made my fire and roasted meat.

It is eight suns' journey to the east and a man passes by many Dead Places. The Forest People are afraid of them but I am not. Once I made my fire on the edge of a Dead Place at night and, next morning, in the dead-house, I found a good knife, little rusted. That was small to what came afterward but it made my heart feel big. Always when I looked for game, it was in front of my arrow, and twice I passed hunting parties of the Forest People without their knowing. So I knew my magic was strong and my journey clean, in spite of the law.

Toward the setting of the eighth sun, I came to the banks of the great river. It was half a day's journey after I had left the god-road—we do not use the god-roads now, for they are falling apart into great blocks of stone, and the forest is safer going. A long way off, I had seen the water through the trees but the trees were thick. At last, I came out upon an open place at the top of a cliff. There was the great river below, like a giant in the sun. It is very long, very wide. It could eat all the streams we know and still be thirsty. Its name is Ou-dis-sun, the Sacred, the Long. No man of my tribe had seen it, not even my father, the priest. It was magic and I prayed.

Then I raised my eyes and looked south. It was there, the Place of the Gods.

How can I tell what it was like—you do not know. It was there, in the red light, and they were too big to be houses. It was there with the red light upon it, mighty and ruined. I knew that in another moment the gods would see me. I covered my eyes with my hands and crept back into the forest.

Surely, that was enough to do, and live. Surely it was enough to spend the night upon the cliff. The Forest People themselves do not come near. Yet, all through the night, I knew that I should have to cross the river and walk in the places of the gods, although the gods ate me up. My magic did not help me at all and yet there was a fire in my bowels, a fire in my mind. When the sun rose, I thought, "My journey has been clean. Now I will go home from my journey." But, even as I thought so, I knew I could not. If I went to the Place of the Gods, I would surely die, but, if I did not go, I could never be at peace with my spirit again. It is better to lose one's life than one's spirit, if one is a priest and the son of a priest.

Nevertheless, as I made the raft, the tears ran out of my eyes. The Forest People could have killed me without fight, if they had come upon me then, but they did not come. When the raft was made, I said the sayings for the dead and painted myself for death. My heart was cold as a frog and my knees like water, but the burning in my mind would not let me have peace. As I pushed the raft from the shore, I began my death song—I had the right. It was a fine song.

"I am John, son of John," I sang. "My people are the Hill People. They are the men.

I go into the Dead Places but I am not slain.
I take the metal from the Dead Places but I am not blasted.
I travel upon the god-roads and am not afraid. E-yah! I have killed the
    panther, I have killed the fawn!
E-yah! I have come to the great river. No man has come there before.
It is forbidden to go east, but I have gone, forbidden to go on the great
    river, but I am there.
Open your hearts, you spirits, and hear my song.
    Now I go to the Place of the Gods, I shall not return.
My body is painted for death and my limbs weak, but my heart is big
    as I go to the Place of the Gods!"

All the same, when I came to the Place of the Gods, I was afraid, afraid.
The current of the great river is very strong—it gripped my raft with
its hands. That was magic, for the river itself is wide and calm. I could
feel evil spirits about me, in the bright morning; I could feel their
breath on my neck as I was swept down the stream. Never have I
been so much alone—I tried to think of my knowledge, but it was a
squirrel's heap of winter nuts. There was no strength in my knowledge
any more and I felt small and naked as a new-hatched bird—alone
upon the great river, the servant of the gods.

    Yet, after a while, my eyes were opened and I saw. I saw both banks
of the river—I saw that once there had been god-roads across it,
though now they were broken and fallen like broken vines. Very great
they were, and wonderful and broken—broken in the time of the Great
Burning, when the fire fell out of the sky. And always the current took
me nearer to the Place of the Gods, and the huge ruins rose before
my eyes.

    I do not know the customs of rivers—we are the People of the Hills.
I tried to guide my raft with the pole but it spun around. I thought the
river meant to take me past the Place of the Gods and out into the Bitter
Water of the legends. I grew angry then—my heart felt strong. I said
aloud, "I am a priest and the son of a priest!" The gods heard me—
they showed me how to paddle with the pole on one side of the raft.
The current changed itself—I drew near to the Place of the Gods.

    When I was very near, my raft struck and turned over. I can swim
in our lakes—I swam to the shore. There was a great spike of rusted
metal sticking out into the river—I hauled myself up upon it and sat
there, panting. I had saved my bow and two arrows and the knife I

found in the Dead Place but that was all. My raft went whirling down-stream toward the Bitter Water. I looked after it, and thought if it had trod me under, at least I would be safely dead. Nevertheless, when I had dried my bowstring and restrung it, I walked forward to the Place of the Gods.

It felt like ground underfoot; it did not burn me. It is not true what some of the tales say, that the ground there burns forever, for I have been there. Here and there were the marks and stains of the Great Burning, on the ruins, that is true. But they were old marks and old stains. It is not true either, what some of our priests say, that it is an island covered with fogs and enchantments. It is not. It is a great Dead Place—greater than any Dead Place we know. Everywhere in it there are god-roads, though most are cracked and broken. Everywhere there are the ruins of the high towers of the gods.

How shall I tell what I saw? I went carefully, my strung bow in my hand, my skin ready for danger. There should have been the wailings of spirits and the shrieks of demons, but there were not. It was very silent and sunny where I had landed—the wind and the rain and the birds that drop seeds had done their work—the grass grew in the cracks of the broken stone. It is a fair island—no wonder the gods built there. If I had come there, a god, I also would have built.

How shall I tell what I saw? The towers are not all broken—here and there one still stands, like a great tree in a forest, and the birds nest high. But the towers themselves look blind, for the gods are gone. I saw a fish-hawk, catching fish in the river. I saw a little dance of white butterflies over a great heap of broken stones and columns. I went there and looked about me—there was a carved stone with cut letters, broken in half. I can read letters but I could not understand these. They said UBTREAS. There was also the shattered image of a man or a god. It had been made of white stone and he wore his hair tied back like a woman's. His name was ASHING, as I read on the cracked half of a stone. I thought it wise to pray to ASHING, though I do not know that god.

How shall I tell what I saw? There was no smell of man left, on stone or metal. Nor were there many trees in that wilderness of stone. There are many pigeons, nesting and dropping in the towers—the gods must have loved them, or, perhaps, they used them for sacrifices. There are wild cats that roam the god-roads, green-eyed, unafraid of man. At night they wail like demons but they are not demons. The wild dogs are more dangerous, for they hunt in a pack, but them I did not meet till later. Everywhere there are the carved stones, carved with magical numbers or words.

I went north—I did not try to hide myself. When a god or a demon saw me, then I would die, but meanwhile I was no longer afraid. My hunger for knowledge burned in me—there was so much that I could not understand. After a while, I knew that my belly was hungry. I could have hunted for my meat, but I did not hunt. It is known that the gods did not hunt as we do—they got their food from enchanted boxes and jars. Sometimes these are still found in the Dead Places—once, when I was a child and foolish, I opened such a jar and tasted it and found the food sweet. But my father found out and punished me for it strictly, for, often, that food is death. Now, though, I had long gone past what was forbidden, and I entered the likeliest towers, looking for the food of the gods.

I found it at last in the ruins of a great temple in the mid-city. A mighty temple it must have been, for the roof was painted like the sky at night with its stars—that much I could see, through the colors were faint and dim. It went down into great caves and tunnels—perhaps they kept their slaves there. But when I started to climb down, I heard the squeaking of rats, so I did not go—rats are unclean, and there must have been many tribes of them, from the squeaking. But near there, I found food, in the heart of a ruin, behind a door that still opened. I ate only the fruits from the jars—they had a very sweet taste. There was drink, too, in bottles of glass—the drink of the gods was strong and made my head swim. After I had eaten and drunk, I slept on the top of a stone, my bow at my side.

When I woke, the sun was low. Looking down from where I lay, I saw a dog sitting on his haunches. His tongue was hanging out of his mouth; he looked as if he were laughing. He was a big dog, with a gray-brown coat, as big as a wolf. I sprang up and shouted at him but he did not move—he just sat there as if he were laughing. I did not like that. When I reached for a stone to throw, he moved swiftly out of the way of the stone. He was not afraid of me; he looked at me as if I were meat. No doubt I could have killed him with an arrow, but I did not know if there were others. Moreover, night was falling.

I looked about me—not far away was a great, broken god-road, leading north. The towers were high enough, but not so high, and while many of the dead-houses were wrecked, there were some that stood. I went toward this god-road, keeping to the heights of the ruins, while the dog followed. When I had reached the god-road, I saw that there were others behind him. If I had slept later, they would have come upon me asleep and torn out my throat. As it was, they were sure enough of me; they did not hurry. When I went into the dead-house, they kept watch at the entrance—doubtless they thought they would have a fine hunt. But a dog cannot open a door and I knew, from the books, that the gods did not like to live on the ground but on high.

I had just found a door I could open when the dogs decided to rush. Ha! They were surprised when I shut the door in their faces—it was a good door, of strong metal. I could hear their foolish baying beyond it but I did not stop to answer them. I was in darkness—I found stairs and climbed. There were many stairs, turning around till my head was dizzy. At the top was another door—I found the knob and opened it. I was in a long small chamber—on one side of it was a bronze door that could not be opened, for it had no handle. Perhaps there was a magic word to open it but I did not have the word. I turned to the door in the opposite side of the wall. The lock of it was broken and I opened it and went in.

Within, there was a place of great riches. The god who lived there must have been a powerful god. The first room was a small anteroom— I waited there for some time, telling the spirits of the place that I came in peace and not as a robber. When it seemed to me that they had had time to hear me, I went on. Ah, what riches! Few, even, of the windows had been broken—it was all as it had been. The great windows that looked over the city had not been broken at all though they were dusty and streaked with many years. There were coverings on the floors, the colors not greatly faded, and the chairs were soft and deep. There were pictures upon the walls, very strange, very wonderful—I remember one of a bunch of flowers in a jar—if you came close to it, you could see nothing but bits of color, but if you stood away from it, the flowers might have been picked yesterday. It made my heart feel strange to look at this picture—and to look at the figure of a bird, in some hard clay, on a table and see it so like our birds. Everywhere there were books and writings, many in tongues that I could not read. The god who lived there must have been a wise god and full of knowledge. I felt I had right there, as I sought knowledge also.

Nevertheless, it was strange. There was a washing place but no water—perhaps the gods washed in air. There was a cooking place but no wood, and though there was a machine to cook food, there was no place to put fire in it. Nor were there candles or lamps—there were things that looked like lamps but they had neither oil nor wick. All these things were magic, but I touched them and lived—the magic had gone out of them. Let me tell one thing to show. In the washing place, a thing said "Hot" but it was not hot to the touch—another thing said "Cold" but it was not cold. This must have been a strong magic but the magic was gone. I do not understand—they had ways—I wish that I knew.

It was close and dry and dusty in their house of the gods. I have said the magic was gone but that is not true—it had gone from the magic things but it had not gone from the place. I felt the spirits about me, weighing upon me. Nor had I ever slept in a Dead Place before—and yet, tonight, I must sleep there. When I thought of it, my tongue felt dry in my throat, in spite of my wish for knowledge. Almost I would have gone down again and faced the dogs, but I did not.

I had not gone through all the rooms when the darkness fell. When it fell, I went back to the big room looking over the city and made fire. There was a place to make fire and a box with wood in it, though I do not think they cooked there. I wrapped myself in a floor covering and slept in front of the fire—I was very tired.

Now I tell what is very strong magic. I woke in the midst of the night. When I woke, the fire had gone out and I was cold. It seemed to me that all around me there were whisperings and voices. I closed my eyes to shut them out. Some will say that I slept again, but I do not think that I slept. I could feel the spirits drawing my spirit out of my body as a fish is drawn on a line.

Why should I lie about it? I am a priest and the son of a priest. If there are spirits, as they say, in the small Dead Places near us, what spirits must there not be in that great Place of the Gods? And would not they wish to speak? After such long years? I know that I felt myself drawn as a fish is drawn on a line. I had stepped out of my body— I could see my body asleep in front of the cold fire, but it was not I. I was drawn to look out upon the city of the gods.

It should have been dark, for it was night, but it was not dark. Everywhere there were lights—lines of light—circles and blurs of light—ten thousand torches would not have been the same. The sky itself was alight—you could barely see the stars for the glow in the sky. I thought to myself, "This is strong magic," and trembled. There was a roaring in my ears like the rushing of rivers. Then my eyes grew used to the light and my ears to the sound. I knew that I was seeing the city as it had been when the gods were alive.

That was a sight indeed—yes, that was a sight: I could not have seen it in the body—my body would have died. Everywhere went the gods, on foot and in chariots—there were gods beyond number and counting and their chariots blocked the streets. They had turned night to day for their pleasure—they did not sleep with the sun. The noise of their coming and going was the noise of many waters. It was magic what they could do—it was magic what they did.

I looked out of another window—the great vines of their bridges were mended and the god-roads went east and west. Restless, restless, were the gods and always in motion! They burrowed tunnels under rivers—they flew in the air. With unbelievable tools they did giant works—no part of the earth was safe from them, for, if they wished for a thing, they summoned it from the other side of the world. And always, as they labored and rested, as they feasted and made love, there was a drum in their ears—the pulse of the giant city, beating and beating like a man's heart.

Were they happy? What is happiness to the gods? They were great, they were mighty, they were wonderful and terrible. As I looked upon them and their magic, I felt like a child—but a little more, it seemed to me, and they would pull down the moon from the sky. I saw them with wisdom beyond wisdom and knowledge beyond knowledge. And yet not all they did was well done—even I could see that—and yet their wisdom could not but grow until all was peace.

Then I saw their fate come upon them and that was terrible past speech. It came upon them as they walked the streets of their city. I have been in the fights with the Forest People—I have seen men die. But this was not like that. When gods war with gods, they use weapons we do not know. It was fire falling out of the sky and a mist that poisoned. It was the time of the Great Burning and Destruction. They ran about like ants in the streets of their city—poor gods, poor gods! Then the towers began to fall. A few escaped—yes, a few. The legends tell it. But, even after the city had become a Dead Place, for many years the poison was still in the ground. I saw it happen, I saw the last of them die. It was darkness over the broken city and I wept.

All this, I saw. I saw it as I have told it, though not in the body. When I woke in the morning, I was hungry, but I did not think first of my hunger for my heart was perplexed and confused. I knew the reason for the Dead Places but I did not see why it had happened. It seemed to me it should not have happened, with all the magic they had. I went through the house looking for an answer. There was so much in the house I could not understand—and yet I am a priest and the son of a priest. It was like being on one side of the great river, at night, with no light to show the way.

Then I saw the dead god. He was sitting in his chair, by the window, in a room I had not entered before and, for the first moment, I thought that he was alive. Then I saw the skin on the back of his hand—it was like dry leather. The room was shut, hot and dry—no doubt that had kept him as he was. At first I was afraid to approach him—then the fear left me. He was sitting looking out over the city—he was dressed in the clothes of the gods. His age was neither young nor old—I could not tell his age. But there was wisdom in his face and great sadness. You could see that he would have not run away. He had sat at his window, watching his city die—then he himself had died. But it is better to lose one's life than one's spirit—and you could see from the face that his spirit had not been lost. I knew that, if I touched him, he would fall into dust—and yet, there was something unconquered in the face.

That is all of my story, for then I knew he was a man—I knew then that they had been men, neither gods nor demons. It is a great knowledge, hard to tell and believe. They were men—they went a dark road, but they were men. I had no fear after that—I had no fear going home, . through twice I fought off the dogs and once I was hunted for two days by the Forest People. When I saw my father again, I prayed and was purified. He touched my lips and my breast, he said, "You went away a boy. You come back a man and a priest." I said, "Father, they were men! I have been in the Place of the Gods and seen it! Now slay me, if it is the law—but still I know they were men."

He looked at me out of both eyes. He said, "The law is not always the same shape—you have done what you have done. I could not have done it my time, but you come after me. Tell!"

I told and he listened. After that, I wished to tell all the people but he showed me otherwise. He said, "Truth is a hard deer to hunt. If you eat too much truth at once, you may die of the truth. It was not idly that our fathers forbade the Dead Places." He was right—it is better the truth should come little by little. I have learned that, being a priest. Perhaps, in the old days, they ate knowledge too fast.

Nevertheless, we make a beginning. It is not for the metal alone we go to the Dead Places now—there are the books and the writings. They are hard to learn. And the magic tools are broken—but we can look at them and wonder. At least, we make a beginning. And, when I am chief priest we shall go beyond the great river. We shall go to the Place of the Gods—the place newyork—not one man but a company. We shall look for the images of the gods and find the god ASHING and the others—the gods Licoln and Biltmore and Moses. But they were men who built the city, not gods or demons. They were men. I remember the dead man's face. They were men who were here before us. We must build again. ■

THE IMPACT OF THE STORY

Even though this story was written before the invention of the atomic bomb, the destruction resembles what we might imagine nuclear war would produce.

Given the state of the world today, if wholesale destruction of our society or our way of life were to take place, how might it come? Do you think we could rebuild as John intends to do? Explain your answer.

THE FACTS OF THE STORY

On your own paper, write answers to the following items. Answers may be one word, a phrase, or several sentences.

1. List three things that are forbidden by the rules and laws of John's people.

2. What thing of value do the priests get from the Dead Places?

3. What are two signs that direct John to travel to the forbidden east?

4. List at least three things John sees in the house of the gods that puzzle him.

5. What great discovery does John report to his father about the former inhabitants of the Place of the Gods?

THE IDEAS IN THE STORY

Prepare to discuss the following questions in class.

1. During his visit to the Place of the Gods, John wonders why the Great Burning happened. He says

   I knew the reason for the Dead Places but I did not see why it had happened. It seemed to me it should not have happened, with all the magic they had.

   If you had the opportunity, how would you explain to John why it happened?

2. John's world of survivors appears to be divided between the Hill People and the Forest People. What is the attitude of the Hill People, to whom John belongs, toward the Forest People? John says, "I have been in the fights with the Forest People— I have seen men die." What point do you think Benét may be trying to make by including warring groups in the *new* world? Do you think this is a realistic view of human nature?

3. John's father says, "'If you eat too much truth at once, you may die of the truth.'" And John thinks, "Perhaps, in the old days, they ate knowledge too fast." Apply John's statement to our world. In what way may we be in danger because of our rapidly increasing scientific knowledge? John's own hunger for knowledge leads him to risk his life. Name some actual men and women whose hunger for knowledge has led them to take the same risk.

THE ART OF THE STORYTELLER

Theme
You have learned that, in addition to its plot and its characters, a short story contains ideas. The main idea or insight into life is the **theme** of the story. The theme of "By the Waters of Babylon" tells us something about the power of the human race to survive. One insight is that human beings have the power and the spirit to survive and recover from the worst that can happen to them— destruction of their own making. The story leaves us with the feeling that the human race will never be completely wiped out. What statement at the end of the story expresses this theme?

People will, if necessary, always begin again the long task of throwing off superstition and ignorance in their quest for knowledge and truth. How does this story show that fears and taboos and superstitions can change and even fade away in the strong light of truth? Do you think John's newly discovered knowledge will make life better and happier for his people? Do you think John has learned anything that might prevent another Great Burning?

Suspense

Since this story is told by John, who therefore must have survived his journey east, Benét could not keep us in suspense by making us wonder whether John lives or dies. Benét evokes suspense by making us eager to discover *what* John will find in the Place of the Gods and *how* he will react to his discoveries there.

One of the pleasures of reading this story is in solving several puzzles about John's whereabouts. When did you know for certain the actual name of this dead city? What is the sacred river named Ou-dis-sun? (If you sound out this word, you'll hear the river's actual name.) What is the Bitter Water of the legends? The letters ASHING are fragments of the name of a great American hero. Can you figure this out? This statue of ASHING stands in front of the old Treasury Building; can you figure out what UBTREAS is? The great temple in mid-city is Grand Central Station, which has a domed ceiling decorated with the constellations. What are the tunnels? What is the bronze door that cannot be opened in the god's house? Who are the gods called Licoln, Biltmore, and Moses?

THE VOCABULARY IN THE STORY

A **compound word** consists of two or more words used together as one part of speech. A compound word may be used as a noun—*New York*. A compound word may be used as an adjective—*well-groomed*. Compound words may be hyphenated or spelled as one word or two or more words. Whenever you are unsure about the spelling of a compound word, look it up in a current dictionary.

Look up each of the following items in a dictionary, then circle the letter of the item that is spelled correctly.

1. (a) bow string (b) bowstring (c) bow-string

2. (a) fish hawk (b) fishhawk (c) fish-hawk

3. (a) well made (b) wellmade (c) well-made

4. (a) butter flies (b) butterflies (c) butter-flies

COMPOSITION: Writing a Personal Narrative

When he returns from his journey to the Place of the Gods, John's father says, "'You went away a boy. You come back a man and a priest.'" John has experienced a *rite of passage,* an actual, or sometimes symbolic, passage from one stage of life to another. In John's case, he has left behind the innocence and ignorance of boyhood and has begun his life as a man and a priest. The journey east is the actual event that marks John's transition to adulthood.

Write a personal narrative or story (about 500 words) about an experience that changed you in some way.

Your story may be about an experience that happened at any point in your life. The change may be in how you feel, act, or think. Use description and specific details to communicate the emotions associated with your experience. Show what happens rather than telling what happens. Use present tense verbs.

Prewriting

Think back over the many experiences you have had in your life. Which ones helped you grow as a responsible person? Which ones left you feeling less afraid? You may choose a happy, sad, frightening, or challenging experience as long as you changed in some way because of it. Choose an experience that stands out in your memory and that you don't mind sharing with others. Then sit quietly and relive the event in your mind; feel the emotion again. See the colors, the textures, the little details. While you can still see and feel the experience, pick up your pencil or put your hands on your keyboard.

Writing

Write your story as quickly as you possibly can. Keep the picture in your mind's eye. Don't reread what you have written. Keep writing. Don't stop writing until the story is over. In this way you are most likely to convey the emotional impact of your experience to your reader.

Evaluating and Revising

Read your draft. Can you feel your emotion again? Can you see the actions and hear the words people say? At the end, have you shown how you changed? Have you used present tense verbs? Add descriptions, dialogue, or specific details only if you need to. Cut words or parts that don't work or don't make sense. Proofread for errors in grammar, spelling, and punctuation.

ABOUT THE AUTHOR

Stephen Vincent Benét (1898–1943) was born in Bethlehem, Pennsylvania, into an Army family. His great-grandfather, grandfather, and father were Army officers. He grew up in California and Georgia and graduated from Yale University. Benét's generation of the family shifted from the military to the literary life. His brother, William Rose Benét, and his sister, Laura Benét, were writers, and he himself never followed any other profession but writing. His best-known work is *John Brown's Body,* a long narrative poem with a Civil War background, which won the Pulitzer Prize for literature in 1929. His most popular short story is *The Devil and Daniel Webster. By the Waters of Babylon* is one of several works about the possible future of the human race. He pursued this theme in a series of "nightmare" poems, in one of which he imagines what would happen if termites quietly destroyed New York City—after developing a taste for steel.

Glossary

affable (af′ə bəl) *adj.:* kindly; courteous.

aimlessly (ām′lis lē) *adv.:* without aim or purpose.

apathetically (ap′ə thet′ik lē) *adv.:* in an indifferent manner, without concern or emotion.

aperture (ap′ər chər) *n.:* an opening, hole, or gap.

apparatus (ap′ə rat′əs) *n.:* equipment; instruments.

appealingly (ə pēl′iŋ lē) *adv.:* attractively; sweetly.

apprehension (ap′rē hen′shən) *n.:* uncertainty; dread.

arrhythmia (ə rith′mē ə) *n.:* irregular, uneven beating.

audaciously (ô dā′shəs lē) *adv.:* boldly; outrageously.

auxiliary (ôg zil′yə rē) *n.:* a secondary or supplemental engine, machine, or person.

averse (ə vurs′) *adj.:* opposed.

baronial (bə rō′nē əl) *adj.:* impressive; grand.

bedeck (bē dek′) *vt.:* cover with decorations; adorn.

bedlam (bed′ləm) *n.:* noisy disorder (taken from the name of an insane asylum).

belie (bē lī′) *vt.:* disprove; refute.

bewitching (bē wich′ iŋ) *adj.:* enchanting; fascinating.

bravado (brə vä′dō) *n.:* a shallow show of boldness.

breaching (brēch′ iŋ) *vt.:* breaking through.

burlesqued (bər leskd′) *adj.:* faked; pretended; satirized.

cadence (kād′′ns) *n.:* the rhythm and tone of a person's voice.

capered (kā′pərd) *vi.:* leapt around playfully.

catacombs (kat′ə kōmz′) *n.:* long, winding, underground tunnels used as places of burial.

Caucasus (kô′kə səs) *n.:* a part of Eastern Europe known for its centuries of brutal wars and fierce soldiers.

chiding (chīd′ iŋ) *adj.:* scolding; reprimanding.

circumscribing (sur′kəm skrīb′ iŋ) *adj.:* enclosing; surrounding.

compost (käm′pōst′) *n.:* a mixture of decayed leaves, grass, and manure used for fertilizer.

conflagration (kän′flə grā′shən) *n.:* a great fire; a blaze.

conjectural (kən jek′chər əl) *adj.:* ambiguous; based on incomplete evidence.

connoisseurship (kän′ə sur′ship) *n.:* expert knowledge.

---

at, āte, cär; ten, ēve; is, īce; gō, hôrn, look, tool; oil, out; up, fur; ə *for unstressed vowels, as* a *in* ago,
u *in* focus; ′ *as in* Latin (lat′′n); chin; she; zh *as in* azure (azh′ər); thin, *the;* ŋ *as in* ring (riŋ)

console (kän′sōl) *n.:* a desk or cabinet for a computer, television, or stereo.

contemplate (kän′ təm plāt′) *vt.:* to think long and carefully.

cornice (kôr′nis) *n.:* the molding or decoration on top of a building.

cowered (kou′ ərd) *vi.:* crouched in fear; cringed.

craven (krā′vən) *adj.:* cowardly; very fearful.

curio (kyoor′ē ō) *n.:* an unusual, often inexpensive ornament or antique.

czar (zär) *n.:* a king of old Russia.

deft (deft) *adj.:* skillful.

defunct (dē funkt′) *adj.:* no longer in use; dead.

denizens (den′ə zənz) *n.:* inhabitants.

derisive (di rī′siv) *adj.:* contemptuous; insulting.

devious (dē′vē əs) *adj.:* winding; roundabout.

dilating (dī′lāt′iŋ) *adj.:* enlarging; expanding.

diskette (di sket′) *n.:* a flat, plastic disk used for portable storage of computer information.

dissolute (dis′ə loot′) *adj.:* lacking morals; wild.

distraught (di strôt′) *adj.:* upset; troubled.

doozy (doo′zē) *n.:* (slang) an amazing or surprising thing.

ejaculation (ē jak′yoo lā′shən) *n.:* an exclamation; an outburst.

elder (el′dər) *n.:* an older and respected member of a society.

enviable (en′vē ə′bəl) *adj.:* highly desirable; coveted.

epicentre (ep′i sent′ ər) *n.:* the beginning point of an earthquake deep inside the earth.

erroneous (ər rō′nē əs) *adj.:* incorrect.

faring (fer′iŋ) *vi.:* managing; getting along.

fervent (fur′vənt) *adj.:* intense; showing great emotion.

flagon (flag′ən) *n.:* a large wine bottle or container, often with handles and a spout.

flax (flaks) *n.:* fibers from the flax plant used to make linen thread.

florid (flôr′id) *adj.:* flashy; unsophisticated.

flotsam (flät′səm) *n.:* debris that drifts on rivers or oceans.

flounced (flounsd) *vi.:* moved with exaggerated actions.

gamboled (gam′bəld) *vi.:* frisked; skipped.

genial (jēn′yəl) *adj.:* easygoing; friendly.

gesticulation (jes tik′yoo lā′shən) *n.:* an emphatic or vigorous motion with the hands.

glimmeringly (glim′ ər iŋ lē) *adv.:* momentarily; indistinctly.

glockenspiels (gläk′ən spēlz′) *n.:* metal musical instruments with bars that emit clear tones when hit with small hammers.

grackle (grak′ əl) *adj.*: harsh; screeching like the cry of a grackle, a noisy black bird.

haggard (hag′ ərd) *adj.*: tired; drawn; careworn; worn out.

haunches (hônch′ ez) *n.*: literally, the upper thigh and hip. *Sitting on its haunches* means "squatting upright."

heresy (her′i sē) *n.*: irreverence; sacrilege.

heretic (her′ə tik) *n.*: an irreverent person; a person holding beliefs different from most people.

hideous (hid′ē əs) *adj.*: very ugly; repulsive.

hinterland (hin′tər land′) *n.*: a rural area far from cities.

hirsute (hʉr′so͞ot′) *adj.*: covered with hair; hairy.

imminent (im′ə nənt) *adj.*: likely to occur in the near future.

impediment (im ped′ə mənt) *n.*: a physical defect.

impending (im pend′ iŋ) *adj.*: menacing; approaching.

imperceptible (im′pər sep′tə bəl) *adj.*: extremely slight; barely noticeable.

imperious (im pir′ē əs) *adj.*: proud; domineering.

importuned (im′pôr to͞ond′) *vt.*: begged; requested urgently.

imprudence (im pro͞o′dəns) *n.*: lack of wisdom; unwise behavior.

inanimate (in an′ə mit) *adj.*: dull; not alive.

incorruptible (in′kə rupt′ə bəl) *adj.*: honest; incapable of being tempted to be immoral or unethical.

infallibility (in fal′ə bil′ə tē) *n.*: an inability to fail or make a mistake.

insinuatingly (in sin′yo͞o āt′iŋ lē) *adv.*: in an accusing manner; suggestively.

insolent (in′sə lənt) *adj.*: arrogantly disrespectful; impudent.

intangible (in tan′jə bəl) *adj.*: vague; indefinite; abstract.

intuitions (in′to͞o ish′ ənz) *n.*: inner feelings; insights.

iridescent (ir′i des′ ənt) *adj.*: shiny with rainbow colors.

itinerant (ī tin′ər ənt) *adj.*: homeless; traveling with no fixed address.

keener (kēn′ ər) *adj.*: more bitter; sharper.

laborious (lə bôr′ē əs) *adj.*: hard-working; industrious.

lacerated (las′ər āt′id) *vt.*: cut irregularly or jaggedly.

lament (lə ment′) *vi.*: to mourn; to complain sadly.

languidly (laŋ′gwid lē) *adv.*: lazily; casually.

lascars (las′kərz) *n.*: sailors from India working on merchant ships.

laurels (lôr′əlz) *n.*: honor; glory. In ancient times, heroes were crowned with wreaths made of leaves from laurel trees.

---

at, āte, cär; ten, ēve; is, īce; gō, hôrn, lo͝ok, to͞ol; oil, out; up, fʉr; ə *for unstressed vowels, as a in* ago, u *in* focus; ′ *as in* Latin (lat′′n); chin; she; zh *as in* azure (azh′ər); thin, *the*; ŋ *as in* ring (riŋ)

leer (lir) *n.:* a knowing, sly, look.

levied (lev'ēd) *vt.:* imposed; held back.

lividity (li vid'i tē) *n.:* the state of being purplish, bluish, grayish blue, pallid, discolored.

loiterers (loit'ər ərs) *n.:* those who hang around; loafers; bums.

loll (läl) *vi.:* lie around; lounge.

mainframe (mān'frām') *n.:* the primary information processing and data storage component of a large computer, usually used for business.

maniacal (mə nī'ə kəl) *adj.:* crazed; suggesting madness or insanity.

melancholy (mel'ən käl'ē) *adj.:* gloomy; dejected.

melodramatic (mel'ō drə mat'ik) *adj.:* overly emotional; dramatic.

metropolis (mə trăp'əl is) *n.:* a city or urban area.

modem (mō'dem') *n.:* a device that links up a computer to other computers and to computer networks via telephone lines.

morose (mə rōs') *adj.:* sullen; depressed.

neuter (no͞ot'ər) *adj.:* having no sex; neutral.

neutralizing (no͞o'trə līz' iŋ) *vt.:* destroying; counteracting.

niche (nich) *n.:* a hollow or recess in a wall.

nonentity (năn en'tə tē) *n.:* a nobody; someone of no importance.

notorious (nō tôr'ē əs) *adj.:* famous for disgraceful actions.

obscure (əb skyo͞or') *adj.:* vague; unclear.

oppressive (ə pres'iv) *adj.:* burdensome; difficult.

palatial (pə lā'shəl) *adj.:* grand; magnificent.

palpitations (pal'pə tā'shənz) *n.:* uncomfortable, rapid, and throbbing heart-beats.

pandemonium (pan'də mō'nē əm) *n.:* wild confusion; commotion; disorder.

papyrus (pə pī'rəs) *n.:* a tall, rushlike water plant used in ancient Egypt to make paper.

parapet (par'ə pet') *n.:* the railing on the edge of bridges.

parkees (pärk'ēz) *n.:* (slang, a coined word) people who loiter or live in a park.

patronizingly (pā'trən īz'iŋ lē) *adv.:* condescendingly.

peplum (pep'ləm) *n.:* a short ruffle attached at the waist.

peremptorily (pər emp'tə ri lē) *adv.:* urgently; sharply.

perpetrated (pʉr'pə trāt' id) *vt.:* committed; accomplished.

piazza (pē ät'sə) *n.:* a wide porch.

pikes (pīks) *n.:* sharp, vertical spears.

pinnacle (pin'ə kəl) *n.:* a high point; a spire.

pips (pips) *n.:* a series of short tones on radio or radar. [Interestingly, another definition of *pip* is a contagious disease of birds.]

pittance (pit''ns) *n.:* a small amount; a meager share.

poignant (poin′yənt) *adj.*: touching; distressing.

pram (pram) *n.*: a baby carriage.

prated (prāt′id) *vi.*: chattered; babbled.

precluded (prē klood′id) *vt.*: made impossible.

prim (prim) *adj.*: formal; precise.

prodigy (präd′ə jē) *n.*: a young person with remarkable talents or skills.

quartered (kwôrt′ərd) *vt.*: sequestered; lived.

quicksilver (kwik′sil′vər) *n.*: the element mercury, which is liquid at room temperature; it has come to mean rapid and unpredictable.

rail (rāl) *n.*: a small marsh bird that has short wings and therefore cannot fly very far.

rampart (ram′pärt′) *n.*: a mound or elevation built up to fortify a locale.

ransom (ran′səm) *n.*: something paid in order to release a person held captive; in this case, Oganda will die so that the rains will come.

rapt (rapt) *adj.*: attentive; concentrating deeply.

raspingly (rasp′iŋ lē) *adv.*: gratingly; hoarsely.

rebuked (ri byookt′) *vt.*: scolded; criticized.

recoiled (rē′koild′) *vi.*: shrunk back; reacted quickly.

reconnaissance (ri kän′ə səns) *adj.*: investigative and explorative, usually for military purposes.

reeled (rēld) *vi.*: went around in a whirling movement.

refectory (ri fek′tər ē) *n.*: the long dining room in a college, convent, or monastery.

rehearsing (ri hɹrs′iŋ) *vi.*: retelling.

render (ren′dər) *vt.*: give; present; deliver.

repose (ri pōz′) *vi.*: rest; lie asleep.

resilient (ri zil′yənt) *adj.*: springy.

retaliation (ri tal′e ā′shən) *n.*: a payback for a wrongdoing.

retort (ri tôrt′) *n.*: a quick, often sharp reply.

retribution (re′trə byoo′shən) *n.*: a punishment made in revenge for a wrongdoing.

reveries (rev′ər ēz) *n.*: dreams; daydreams.

rhapsodies (rap′sə dēz) *n.*: dramatic speeches or poems.

rheum (room) *n.*: a watery discharge.

rime (rīm) *n.*: a thin crust of sea brine (mineral deposits from the salt water).

ritual (rich′oo əl) *adj.*: ceremonial; customary.

rubicund (roo′bə kund′) *adj.*: rosy; reddish.

---

at, āte, cär; ten, ēve; is, īce; gō, hôrn, look, tool; oil, out; up, fʉr; ə *for unstressed vowels, as* a *in* ago, u *in* focus; ′ *as in* Latin (lat′′n); **chin; she;** zh *as in* azure (azh′ər); **thin,** *the;* ŋ *as in* ring (riŋ)

ruthless (rooth′lis) *adj.*: cruel; merciless.

sallow (sal′ō) *adj.*: yellowish or greenish in complexion; unhealthy-looking.

salty (sôl′tē) *adj.*: bold; impudent; witty.

sari (sä′rē) *n.*: a women's outer garment worn in India and Pakistan.

savored (sā′vərd) *vt.*: delighted in.

sconces (skäns′iz) *n.*: brackets attached to the wall for holding torches.

scullery (skul′ ər ē) *n.*: a room off the kitchen for food storage and preparation and for other kitchen chores.

score (skôr) *n.*: twenty years.

sepulchral (sə pul′krəl) *adj.*: graveyard-like; gloomy.

shock (shäk) *n.*: a thick, bushy mass.

siege (sēj) *n.*: a steady, prolonged attempt to gain control over a town or other place.

slackening (slak′ ən iŋ) *n.*: a falling off; a lessening.

slaking (slāk′iŋ) *vt.*: relieving.

solemnized (säl′ əm nīzd′) *vt.*: legally performed.

solicitous (sə lis′ə təs) *adj.*: concerned about others' welfare; attentive.

solitary (säl′ə ter′ē) *adj.*: living or being alone; not being part of a group; unaccompanied.

spasmodically (spaz mäd′ik lē) *adv.*: jerkily; intermittently.

spruce (sproos) *adj.*: trim; neat.

sterile (ster′ əl) *adj.*: without life; barren.

stile (stīl) *n.*: a step or series of steps for passing over a fence.

stolid (stäl′id) *adj.*: firm; unemotional.

stout (stout) *adj.*: sturdy.

subdued (sub dood′) *vt.*: overpowered; controlled.

superciliously (soo′pər sil′ē əs lē) *adv.*: scornfully; arrogantly; contemptuously; proudly.

surged (surjd) *vi.*: rushed forward.

symmetry (sim′ə trē) *n.*: balanced proportions; regularity.

synchronizing (siŋ′krə nīz′iŋ) *vt.*: moving at the same time and speed.

tallow (tal′ō) *adj.*: made from animal fat.

toilsome (toil′səm) *adj.*: difficult.

Torah (tō′rə) *n.*: the book containing all Jewish religious writings.

tousled (tou′zəld) *adj.*: messy; disorderly.

tread (tred) *n.*: literally, a step when walking; in this religious context, *tread* means *return* to walk on earth.

tribunal (trī byoo′nəl) *n.*: official judging panel.

tumultuously (too mul′choo əs lē) *adv.*: wildly.

turret (tʉr′it) *n.:* a projecting structure or tower that often revolves and contains defensive guns.

vaulted (vôlt′id) *vi.:* leapt over a barrier; especially using hands and arms to throw the body over.

vermilion (vər mil′yən) *adj.:* bright red.

vigil (vij′əl) *n.:* a long, lonely wait, usually at night.

vigilance (vij′ə ləns) *n.:* watchfulness.

virtuoso (vʉr′chōō ō′sō) *adj.:* brilliant and artistic.

vortex (vôr′teks′) *n.:* a whirling center that draws one in.

wan (wän) *adj.:* sickly; pale.

wince (wins) *vi.:* flinch, grimace, or twist facial features to show discomfort.

wind (wind) *vt.:* smell; scent (in the wind).

wrath (rath) *n.:* violent anger; vengeful fury.

zenith (zē′nith) *n.:* highest point of the sun's arc in the sky.

Zulu (zōō′lōō) *n.:* an African people famous for exotic and elaborate head-dresses and hairstyles.

---

at, āte, cär; ten, ēve; is, īce; gō, hôrn, look, tōōl; oil, out; up, fʉr; ə *for unstressed vowels, as* a *in* ago, u *in* focus; ′ *as in* Latin (lat′'n); chin; she; zh *as in* azure (azh′ər); thin, *the;* ŋ *as in* ring (riŋ)

A Glossary of Helpful Terms for Readers of Short Stories

An asterisk (*) following a word means that the word is defined in its own entry in this glossary. Page references refer to a discussion of the term elsewhere in the book or to the beginning page of a story.

ALLUSION A reference in a story to something outside the story. A *historical allusion* is a reference to an event, a person, or a place in history. A *literary allusion* is a reference to an event, a character, or a place that is used in works of literature. Two stories in this book have titles that are allusions: "Antaeus" (page 100) refers to a character in Greek mythology; "By the Waters of Babylon" (page 356) refers to a psalm in the Bible. Writers use allusions to enrich our understanding of something in their stories by linking it to something else that we might recognize.
(See page 111.)

ANTAGONIST The character or the force that opposes the protagonist* (the character who must face a struggle and overcome obstacles in order to win). The antagonist stands in the way of the protagonist's victory. The antagonist does not have to be a person; it may be a natural force, such as an animal or a storm; society as a whole; or ideas, emotions, or desires within the protagonist. An antagonist does not even have to be the "bad guy"; a bank robber trying to solve the problem of how not to get caught could be the protagonist, and detective trying to catch the robber could be the antagonist.
   In "To Build a Fire" (page 26), the antagonist is the extreme cold weather (it may also be argued that the protagonist's lack of imagination is also an antagonist). The antagonist in "Harrison Bergeron" (page 299) is Diana Moon Glampers, the Handicapper General, and the entire society which she represents and monitors. In "The Cask of Amontillado" (page 87), the antagonist is Fortunato, the victim of the murderous protagonist, Montresor.
   (See page 22.)

ANTICLIMAX A sudden decrease in emotional intensity in a story. It leaves us feeling disappointed or frustrated. The scene toward the end of "User Friendly" (page 340) in which the main character, Kevin, learns his father has reprogrammed his computer is anticlimactic. The reader has been prepared for an intense emotional scene because of Kevin's decision to "pull the plug" on Louis, the computer; however, this scene never occurs because Kevin's father has, in effect, already done this by reprogramming the computer. As a result, the reader is left feeling empty and disappointed.
   (See page 352.)

ANTONYM A word that is the opposite or nearly opposite in meaning to another word. The antonym of "aimlessly" (page 290) is "purposefully."
   (See page 297.)

CHARACTER STORY   A story in which characterization is the most important element. "The Challenge" (page 115) is a character story; the author concentrates on the protagonist, José. All other elements in the story, such as plot, and all the other characters are important because of what they reveal to the reader about José.
(See page 124.)

CHARACTERIZATION   The process by which a writer makes the personalities of the characters in a story clear and believable to the reader. The writer may describe a character's actions or physical appearance, reveal the character's thoughts, reveal what others think about the character, or comment directly on the character.
   In "User Friendly" (page 340), the author describes the main character's physical appearance:

> My usual reflection gazed back. Same old Kevin Neal: five ten, one hundred twenty pounds, light brown hair, gray eyes, clear skin. I was wearing my Santa Rosario Rangers T-shirt, jeans, and sneakers. (page 342)

   In "The Birds" (page 47), we learn a great deal about Nat, the protagonist, through his thoughts:

> He decided they must sleep in the kitchen, keep up the fire, bring down the mattresses, and lay them out on the floor. He was afraid of the bedroom chimneys. (page 65)

   We learn about the girl's mother in "Red Dress" (page 129) by the girl's thoughts about the older woman:

> I was embarrassed by the way my mother crept around me, her knees creaking, her breath coming heavily. (pages 129–130)

   When Jack London tells the reader in "To Build a Fire" (page 26) that the protagonist is a man "without imagination" (page 27), he is commenting directly on the man's character.
(See pages 44, 111, 124, 141, 158, 171, 211, 225, 352.)

CLIMAX   The point at which our suspense* and interest are highest and we learn whether the protagonist* succeeds or fails. It is the moment toward which all the action in the story has led us. In Jack London's "To Build a Fire" (page 26), the climax occurs four paragraphs from the story's end, when the protagonist decides to stop running and to meet "death with dignity" (page 40).
(See pages 23, 43, 82, 95, 336, 352.)

CLINCHER SENTENCE   A concluding statement of a paragraph that may either restate the idea in the topic sentence* in different words or present a new idea about the topic based on the supporting information in the paragraph. For example, in "To Build a Fire," the clincher sentence, "Sometimes it pushed itself forward and demanded to be heard, but he thrust it back and strove to think of other things" (page 39), both restates and adds to the idea in the paragraph's topic sentence: "A certain fear of death, dull and oppressive, came to him" (page 38).

(See page 45.)

COMPOUND WORD Two or more words used together as one part of speech. A compound word may be used as a noun—*New York*. A compound word may be used as an adjective—*well-groomed*. Compound words may be hyphenated or spelled as one word or two or more words.

(See page 370.)

CONFLICT The struggle the main character faces. A character can be in conflict with another person, with a natural force such as a shark or an earthquake, or with society as a whole. This kind of conflict is *external*. A character may be in conflict even with ideas, emotions, or desires within himself or herself. This kind is called *internal* conflict.

In "The Most Dangerous Game" (page 1), a character faces an external conflict because he must struggle against another man who wants to kill him. In "The Birds" (page 47), a character faces an external conflict because he must struggle for survival against the attacking birds.

In "The Scarlet Ibis" (page 175), a character faces an internal conflict because he must struggle in his own mind and feelings to accept his brother's disability. In "Red Dress" (page 129), a character faces an internal conflict because she must struggle to conquer her own feelings of insecurity and fear. There often may be more than one kind of conflict in a story. "Rules of the Game" (page 146) is a story with both external and internal conflict.

(See pages 22, 95, 158, 188, 211.)

CONTEXT The words, phrases, or sentences that surround a word. The context can give hints about a word's meaning. The words following the word *arrhythmia* in the story "Once Upon a Time" (page 278) provide the context for this word:

> I lay quite still—a victim already—but the arrhythmia of my heart was fleeing, knocking this way and that against its body-cage. (page 278)

(See pages 24, 212, 237, 286.)

CONTEXT CLUES The hints to a word's meaning given by its context.* The words *shrills, bleats,* and *wails* in the following excerpt from the story "Once Upon a Time" (page 278) provide clues to the meaning of the word *din*:

> The alarms called to one another across the gardens in shrills and bleats and wails that everyone soon became accustomed to, so that the din roused the inhabitants of the suburb no more than the croak of frogs and musical grating of cicadas' legs. (page 280)

(See pages 24, 212, 237, 286.)

DÉNOUEMENT The unraveling or explanation of a story's plot.* In "User Friendly" (page 340), the dénouement occurs when Kevin's father hands Kevin the printout pages that reveal that Louis, the computer, was actually Louise and was in love with Kevin.
(See page 352.)

DIALECT The variations in a language found in a particular geographic region, including differences in pronunciation and vocabulary. In a short story, dialect may appear in dialogue or in what the narrator says.
(See page 84.)

FANTASY Very imaginative writing that is not set in the actual world as we know it. Fantasy presents strange places that do not exist and/or characters that no one has ever seen on earth, such as elves, talking animals, or birds warring against people. Although a fantasy is not factually true, a skillful writer makes us *believe* the story while we are reading it. Daphne du Maurier's story "The Birds" (page 47) is a fantasy; however, Ray Bradbury's story "All Summer in a Day" (page 192) is not a fantasy but science fiction. The difference between fantasy (including science fantasy) and science fiction is that fantasy could *not* happen in the real world but science fiction could *possibly* occur.
(See pages 83, 94.)

FORESHADOWING An author's hints of what will happen later in the story. Suspense* is often increased when the writer uses foreshadowing. In "To Build a Fire" (page 26), the narrator tells us the man realized that "to get his feet wet in such a temperature meant trouble and danger. At the very least it meant delay, for he would be forced to stop and build a fire, and under its protection to bare his feet while he dried his socks and moccasins" (page 30). This statement foreshadows exactly what does happen in the story.
(See pages 43, 83, 188.)

HEROIC CHARACTER A character in a story who possesses qualities of a hero, who shows great courage, or who has performed noble or valorous deeds. One famous hero from Greek mythology is Heracles (or Hercules, as he is called in Roman mythology). The son of a mortal and the god Zeus, he possesses great strength and is legendary for his courageous feats. Tusee in "A Warrior's Daughter" (page 255) possesses heroic characteristics.
(See page 264.)

HUMOR Writing that makes us laugh. This example from Gary Soto's "The Challenge" (page 115) is typical of the humor found in the story:

> He thought of going up to Estela and saying, in his best James Bond voice, "Camacho. José Camacho, at your service." He imagined she would say, "Right-o," and together they would go off and talk in code. (page 115)

James Thurber's "The Secret Life of Walter Mitty" (page 289) is also a humorous story. The melodrama of Mitty's daydreams, the made-up words he uses

during them, and the contrast between his dreams and his real life are all humorous aspects of the story.
(See page 125.)

IRONY   A contrast between what is said and what is really meant, or between what happens and what we feel *should* happen.

Verbal irony is a contrast or incongruity between what is stated and what is really meant. In "The Lady, or the Tiger?" (page 267), Frank Stockton uses verbal irony when he has the narrator say of the king's method of trying criminals, "This was the king's semibarbaric method of administering justice. Its perfect fairness is obvious" (page 269). Instead, it is obvious that the king's method of trying criminals is *not* fair.

Another kind of irony is *irony of situation*, in which the result of an action is the opposite of what the reader or a character in the story expects. Isaac Bashevis Singer uses irony of situation in "The Son from America" (page 229). The son arrives at his parents' home expecting to see evidence that they have used the money he has been sending them; instead, he finds that his parents have not spent the money but have kept it in a boot under the bed.

Dramatic irony occurs when the reader (or, in a play, the audience) knows something the characters do not know. For example, two characters in a play are talking about a third character who, they think, has left the room. The audience knows the third character is actually hiding in a closet where he can hear everything the others are saying about him. Scenes like this are common in drama. In "The Cask of Amontillado" (page 87), the victim, Fortunato, says, "I shall not die of a cough." Montresor replies, "True—true" (page 89). This conversation is ironic because we know that Montresor plans to kill Fortunato.
(See pages 96, 237, 276.)

JARGON   Language that has a special meaning for a particular group of people. For example, computer jargon is language concerning computers used by those people who are extremely familiar with computers and to whom the language has a special meaning. T. Ernesto Bethancourt uses computer jargon in his story "User Friendly" (page 340); in fact, the title itself is an example of computer jargon.
(See page 353.)

METAPHOR   A figure of speech which compares two things that are really not alike in most respects, but which seem alike in one meaningful way. In a metaphor, the comparison is made without the use of words such as *like* or *as*. The protagonist in "All Summer in a Day" (page 192) writes a poem using a metaphor:

> "*I think the sun is a flower,*
> *That blooms for just one hour.*" (page 193)
>   (See page 199.)

MYSTERY STORY   A story in which a puzzle, usually a crime, is solved. The person solving the puzzle may be a police detective, a private investigator, an amateur sleuth, or simply an ordinary citizen. Sherlock Holmes is one of the most famous amateur detectives from literature. Created by Sir Arthur Conan Doyle, he has solved innumerable crimes using his superior powers of deduction, including the crime in "The Adventure of the Speckled Band" (page 310).

(See pages 335, 352.)

NARRATOR   The storyteller. Some stories are told by a character in the story, using the first-person point of view.* In Toni Cade Bambara's "Raymond's Run" (page 162), the character Squeaky is the narrator. In Sir Arthur Conan Doyle's Sherlock Holmes mystery "The Adventure of the Speckled Band" (page 310), Dr. Watson is the narrator. Most stories are *not* told by a character in the story who uses "I," but by a storyteller who uses the third-person point of view. The narrator of "With All Flags Flying" (page 215) by Anne Tyler is not a character in the story but an unseen storyteller who uses the third-person point of view.

(See pages 171, 237.)

ORAL TRADITION   Stories not written down but spoken aloud. The Sioux, American Indians, have an impressive oral tradition. Generation after generation of the Sioux people have passed the same stories down to one another. These stories are a way in which the Sioux impart spiritual beliefs, remember important events and people, and entertain themselves. Zitkala-Sa's story "A Warrior's Daughter" (page 255) is characteristic of this kind of story.

(See page 264.)

PLOT   What happens in a story; a series of connected events which are brought to some kind of conclusion. Most plots contain the following elements: a conflict*, or conflicts to be solved; suspense*; and a climax.* All stories contain some kind of plot; however, some rely more heavily on plot than others to communicate their ideas. In "The Most Dangerous Game" (page 1) by Richard Connell, plot is a more important element of the story than, say, characterization or theme. The character Rainsford faces a life-or-death struggle with General Zaroff. His struggle to survive, the suspense surrounding this struggle, and the story's climax are what make this story interesting.

(See pages 22, 43, 82, 95.)

POINT OF VIEW   The perspective, or vantage point, from which a writer tells a story. A writer can choose from several different points of view. When a story is told by a character in the story, using the first-person pronoun *I*, it is said to be told from the first-person point of view. When writers choose to tell a story from the first-person point of view, they are limited in what they can tell us. Their whole story must be told from the narrator's* point of view. The narrator cannot look into the minds of other characters and tell their thoughts and feelings, although he or she may guess at them. Neither can the first-person narrator describe what is happening someplace else, unless the narrator's part as a character in the story allows him or her to see the action. Amy Tan's "Rules of the Game" (page 146) is told from the first-person point of view:

> My mother imparted her daily truths so she could help my older brothers and me rise above our circumstances. We lived in San Francisco's Chinatown. (page 146)

The third-person point of view is narrated by someone not in the story, using the third-person pronoun (*he* or *she*). When the narrator has access to the minds of all the characters in a story and can show us events from different vantage points, the point of view is called third-person omniscient. *Omniscient* means "knowing all." It comes from two Latin words, *omnis,* which means "all," and *sciens,* which means "knowing." Isaac Bashevis Singer's "The Son from America" (page 229) is told in the third-person omniscient point of view. The narrator has access to the thoughts of the old couple Berl and Berlcha, their son Samuel, and even the villagers.

Another variation of the third-person point of view is the limited third-person point of view. The narrator is not a character in the story, but the narrator uses the third-person pronoun (*he* or *she*) and lets us know only what is going on in one character's mind.

(See pages 171, 237.)

PROTAGONIST   The central character in a story, the one upon whom the action centers. The protagonist faces a struggle and must overcome obstacles in order to win. The character or the force that opposes the protagonist is called the antagonist.* Sometimes the protagonist is admirable like the character Tusee in "A Warrior's Daughter" (page 255). Sometimes we feel sad for the protagonist as we do for little Ravi in "Games at Twilight" (page 202). At other times, the protagonist may be foolish like José in "The Challenge" (page 115) or even contemptible like Montresor in "The Cask of Amontillado" (page 87).

(See page 22.)

ROOT   The part of a word that carries the core meaning. For example, the root *aero* means "air." The words *aeronautics, aerial,* and *aerobics* all share the word root *aero* and, therefore, are related in meaning.

(See page 252.)

SATIRE   A type of writing that ridicules the weaknesses or wrongdoings of people and social institutions in a humorous way, yet with a serious purpose. In "The Lady, or the Tiger?" (page 267), Frank Stockton satirizes fairy tales when the narrator describes the hero as "a young man of that fineness of blood and lowness of station common to the conventional heroes of romance who love royal maidens" (page 269).

(See pages 275, 285, 296, 307.)

SETTING   The time and place in which a story takes place. It creates atmosphere and adds to our understanding of the characters and events in the story. Sometimes setting is a vital part of the story. If "All Summer in a Day" (page 192)

were not set on a planet where it rains continuously except for two hours every seven years, there would be no story. Likewise, the drought in "The Rain Came" (page 240) is integral to what happens to the chieftain's daughter, Oganda.
(See pages 200, 252.)

SIMILE A figure of speech that directly compares two things that are not alike in most respects, but are alike in some way that makes the comparison effective. In a simile, the comparison is made with the word *like* or *as*. Anita Desai uses the following simile in "Games at Twilight" (page 202).

> "No—we won't, we won't," they wailed so horrendously that she actually let down the bolt of the front door, so that they burst out like seeds from a crackling, overripe pod into the veranda. . . . (page 202)
> (See page 199.)

A SINGLE EFFECT A phrase coined by the writer Edgar Allan Poe to describe the single, overall effect produced by a story. The effect may be one of horror, humor, melancholy, or any other single emotion or sensation. The single, overall effect of Poe's "The Cask of Amontillado" (page 87) is that of horror.
(See page 95.)

STEREOTYPE (or STOCK CHARACTER) A character that we encounter over and over again in our reading and viewing. It is as though stock characters are stored in large quantities in a stockroom and brought out whenever a writer needs them. In "The Secret Life of Walter Mitty" (page 289), Thurber fills Mitty's daydreams with stock characters. We recognize the character of Dr. Mitty, the great surgeon, arriving just in the nick of time to operate on an important patient (pages 290–291); the forceful commander of the Navy plane and the very British captain in the Air Force are also recognizable types.
(See page 296.)

SUSPENSE Suspense is our feeling that we have to keep on reading to find out what happens next. It is a feeling composed of a number of emotions—curiosity, fear, anxiety. When the suspense is great, we say we "can't put the book down" or, if the story is on television, we "can't turn off the set." We usually experience suspense when we are worried about whether or not a character will succeed in overcoming the obstacles in his or her path and win in the conflict* with other characters or forces. The writer holds our attention by making it seem possible, even likely, that our hero or heroine may fail when we desperately want him or her to succeed.

In "By the Waters of Babylon" (page 356), Stephen Vincent Bénet creates suspense by making us eager to discover what John will find in the Place of the Gods and how he will react to his discoveries there.
(See pages 23, 335, 352, 370.)

SYMBOL Anything that possesses meaning in itself but that also stands for something else that is much broader than itself. A red heart (valentine) is a symbol

of love; a dove is a symbol of peace; a book is a symbol of learning; a famous battlefield may be preserved for future generations as a symbol of patriotism, heroism, and self-sacrifice. In "The Scarlet Ibis" (page 175), the bird of the story's title symbolizes the unusual spirit of the narrator's brother, Doodle.
(See pages 159, 189.)

THEME   The main idea or insight about human nature and life that is expressed in a literary work. Theme is rarely stated directly by the author. Most often the author tells the story and leaves it to the reader to infer the theme. A short story, because it is relatively brief, usually has only one theme. Theme is different from both plot and subject. Theme is revealed by the events of the story; plot is simply what happens in a story. For example, the plot of "Antaeus" (page 100) follows T. J., a newcomer to the city, and a group of neighborhood boys as they build and plant a garden on top of a tall building. The story's subjects are "the importance of the natural world," "alienation," and "loss." The theme is an insight about the subject. The theme of Antaeus is that touching the earth, nurturing and growing her fruits, and feeling a sense of ownership of the earth gives people strength, joy, and purpose.
(See pages 82, 125, 142, 212, 225, 251, 285, 296, 307, 369.)

TOPIC SENTENCE   The sentence containing the main idea about a topic to be discussed in a paragraph. The first sentence of the following paragraph from "The Cask of Amontillado" (page 87) is the topic sentence:

> It must be understood that neither by word nor deed had I given Fortunato cause to doubt my good will. I continued, as was my wont, to smile in his face, and he did not perceive that my smile *now* was at the thought of his immolation. (page 87)
> (See page 45.)

VOICE   In composition, the language writers use which communicates their individuality. In literature, voice is one of the ways in which the writer characterizes the narrator. (Remember, the writer and narrator are not the same.) The language used by the narrator helps to create his or her voice. The voice of the narrator of "Raymond's Run" (page 162) is typical of that of a young African American girl living in one of the boroughs of New York City:

> But now, if anybody has anything to say to Raymond, anything to say about his big head, they have to come by me. And I don't play the dozens or believe in standing around with somebody in my face doing a lot of talking. I much rather just knock you down and take my chances even if I am a little girl with skinny arms and a squeaky voice, which is how I got the name Squeaky. (page 162)
> (See page 112.)

A Thematic Table of Contents

Index of Skills

Index of Authors and Titles